A DROWNING ON NANTUCKET

A Novel

by Garth Jeffries

ISBN-13: 978-0-9999067-9-8

Dedicated to the amazing women in my life

To JCT, for making it all possible

To K for her 40 years of love, support and encouragement

And to Mads for just being the best

CHAPTER ONE

Last Summer

The unconscious body of Charles Post hit the water at just over twenty knots. The shock of the impact and the cool water temperature rousted him back to awareness. Instinctively, being a man who had spent much of his time on the ocean, he began to tread water.

What the hell had just happened?

The seas surrounding the northeast coast of Nantucket, an area known as Great Point, was in a state of constant motion as the tides ebbed and flowed, following their lunar god as she made her way around the globe. Despite the turmoil of the waters below, it was a stunning evening. To the west, a brilliant sunset filled the sky with deep reds and oranges, the lower edges of clouds hinting at purple. To the east, a nearly full pale yellow moon had just broken the surface of the water. The Corn Moon, as native Americans called the first in September, was living up to its name. Above, the sky had darkened just enough to see the first bright stars emerge.

Where was he?

His body ached from the impact, and the back of his head pounded. He rubbed the top of his skull, his hand coming back bloodied. He massaged the area slowly, trying to soothe the pain. Confusion slowly gave way to recognition.

The droning of an engine stirred a memory. He turned to his right and could just see the white transom of a sports fishing boat. Then it clicked. Minutes before, he had been on that boat. He had spent the day fishing with his business partners. He called out futilely and waved his arms in the hope of securing their attention. But they were motoring away from him at nearly full speed.

Did they not see me fall off the boat?

And why didn't my life preserver inflate?

The first dash of panic spread through him, the adrenaline coursing through his blood, warming him in an unpleasant way. Charles knew the sea and knew his survival was dependent on his life preserver. He pulled at the manual inflation tab by his lower waist, but nothing happened. He tried again, with greater force. Nothing.

Despite his age, he was in good physical shape but knew it was only a matter of time before he would tire. A man, regardless of age and condition, could only survive so long in the open water without a flotation device, especially in the middle of the Great Point rip at the height of a tidal change.

He fumbled with the preserver, trying to locate the oral inflation tube. Memories of a flight attendant demonstrating its usage flashed through his head. He found the yellow tube and angled it towards his mouth just as a breaking wave swamped him, filling his mouth with warm salt water. He gagged and spit out the water, coughing hard. He tried again to bring the inflation tube to his mouth and successfully blew in his first breath, only to see it bubbling from a split at the base of the tube. Somehow, it had been damaged, probably from the force of impact. Another burst of adrenaline as he realized he would have no help keeping his head above water.

A few hundred yards to his left, he could see the Great Point Lighthouse. Its familiar black lantern room capped the brick body that gracefully flared down to the sand. All white, it was missing the red band of its big brother, Sankaty Head Light, just eight miles to the south. The small shed-like appendage with its red roof was just visible behind it.

Great Point. This bony stretch of sand had been a central part of his being for most of his life. He had fished there, boated there, and made love there. He had also proposed to his wife there, kneeling in the sand, extending his arm with the ring box opened for her to see. They had spent the afternoon fishing and grilling their catch. She enjoyed the outdoors as much as he did, and he knew their partnership would be one of joy. That had been nearly forty years ago, and not a day had gone by that he was thankful that she had said yes.

He realized with a stab to his heart that he might never see her again - those blue eyes, that easy smile, that beautiful face that had burned in his brain since the first time he had laid eyes on her.

What am I doing here?

The current was picking up as the high tide started to recede, and Charles was beginning to struggle. His legs kicked harder as he worked to keep his head above the sea. Despite his efforts, he was still overwashed by the foaming breakers every few waves, causing him to sputter and the salt to sting his eyes.

Snippets of memories coursed through his mind. His daughter, just weeks old, giggling at him when he changed her diaper... the pride on his young son's face when he caught his first bluefish... the look in Ann's eyes when she said 'I Do'.

To save energy, he tried to float on his back and use his arms to keep him atop the water, but the breaking waves overwhelmed him. He pivoted his body upright and fought to get his head clear as he coughed out another mouthful of salt water.

Could he make it to shore?

He eyed the lighthouse again and was shocked to see how quickly the current had pulled him away from it. He had to be at least a half mile away, if not more. There was no way he could swim against that - the rip was just too strong. It would probably be easier to turn north and try to swim to the Cape, but Monomoy Point was over nine miles away.

Slowly, he realized that this was it. For much of his life, he had wondered, as most men do, how the end would finally come. Now that it was here, he felt terribly and utterly sad. His life had been so good to him; a wonderful marriage, two great and happy children, a prosperous business, and a supportive community had made his years complete.

Why the hell aren't they turning around? How could they just leave me out here to die?

Sadness turned to anger at the thought of his partners cruising away from him, safe, warm and comfortable in the boat and likely looking forward to a good meal and rest.

How could they be so oblivious to what had happened?

His anger subsided as he realized he must have been at fault. Somehow, he had fallen off the boat, maybe hitting his head on the gunwale or transom. His life preserver must have been damaged then. Or maybe it got caught on something as he fell and damaged the arming device?

The salt he tasted was not from the ocean but from his tears.

He wished he could ask Ann to marry him again.

He sobbed at the thought of what he would be missing. What was going to be taken away. With a shock, he realized that the birth of their first grandchild, just a month away, would happen without him. He and Ann had had such fun discussing plans to decorate one of the bedrooms for the occasion. And he had been looking forward to introducing the child to his love of Nantucket, of sailing, fishing, and the natural beauty of the island. His grandchild would grow up knowing him only through stories, pictures, and mementos.

His legs were tiring. He felt the burning of the muscles in his arms, calves, and chest. He wasn't sure how much longer he could do this.

The waves were picking up. His leg pumping slowed. His arms tired. It was time.

Charles Post, sixty-four years of age, husband of thirty-nine years, father of two, and expectant grandparent, beloved by family, friends, and community alike, took his last breath and slipped silently under the water just a few thousand yards from the land he loved so much. The smiling, beautiful face of his wife was the last thing he saw before his world went black.

CHAPTER TWO

It was a cool, damp early September Saturday morning off the northeast tip of Nantucket island. The sun was still an hour from crossing the perfect line of the horizon where the sky met the water. The air was heavy with fog, and a light breeze swayed the beach grass. Great Point, the thin, bony forearm of the island, was a favorite fishing spot for locals and tourists alike. Its briny Atlantic water filled with bluefish, striped bass, and the rare and elusive Spanish Mackerel. And it was that elusive mackerel that Tommy Jersig was hoping to catch this morning.

His wife, a local artist with a well-deserved reputation, was having a gallery event that evening, displaying a new series of plein air works completed on the south shore. The series featured the same landscape but varied the time of day, weather, and season of the year. It was expected to be very well received, with pieces commanding well into five figures. To help facilitate the anticipated transfer of wealth, Tommy thought some fresh mackerel sushi might help to loosen the wallets of those in attendance. Properly prepared, its taste and texture resembled that of freshly churned butter. It would be a rare treat for the patrons.

It was getting late in the year for mackerel. But Tommy had had luck at the Point before, and he felt it again this morning. And even if he was skunked on the mackerel, he could be almost guaranteed to land a number of bluefish and stripers, though his menu would require adjustment. Sushi would not be an option with these fish, but fresh smoked bluefish pate and grilled striper would be very well received by tonight's patrons, especially when paired with some of the local brewery's finest.

Tommy had left his house in Tom Nevers just after 4:00 a.m., hoping to catch the changing tides at the Point as the sun broke the surface of the water. In early September, the sky starts to lighten around five, with sunrise just after six. Having spent the better part of his life on the island, Tommy had made these "dawn raids" hundreds of times. His father had first taken him to fish the Point at sunrise when he was just five years old. Now closer to sixty, the allure and magic of these trips remained just as special and awe-inspiring as when he was a small boy.

Sadly for him, what had changed since those earlier days was the growing population of harbor and gray seals. These seals, once a rare occurrence on the island, had seen their populations dramatically increase, almost to the point of surplus. In addition to attracting great white sharks, it also led to the closure of the tip of Great Point. This magical spot where the waters of Nantucket Sound and the Atlantic met formed a tremendous rip and, with it, some of the best fishing on the East Coast.

However, because of the exploding seal population, it had been closed permanently to people, regardless of whether they were fishing or just walking. Reluctantly, Tommy parked his white Ford F-150 a few hundred yards to the south and got out of the truck. He looked westward over Nantucket Sound and felt the breeze wash over him. Small waves curled and broke just feet from shore, the sound of the water settling on him like a warm memory. Gulls, squawking and curious as to his intent, settled a few yards away, hoping for breakfast. Dew settled on his beard from the fog.

He dropped the tailgate and pulled a fishing rod from the rack attached to the side of the bed. He rummaged through the tackle box to find just the right lure. Spanish Mackerels were picky and wouldn't hit just anything. He rummaged through his tackle box and settled on a tried and true Deadly Dick, a three-inch sliver of metal that sliced just below the surface and did a perfect mimicry of small baitfish swimming aggressively - as if trying to escape a predator. They were irresistible to his target fish, and he hoped that they would work their magic today.

Securing the lure, Tommy adjusted the drag on the reel and walked to the edge of the surf. The water washed over his feet, and he could feel the sand filter through his toes as the wave receded. Despite the lightening sky, he could still make out dozens of constellations and planets. The Big Dipper to the north, Orion to the south, and even the Little Dipper to the northeast. He looked to the west and could see Saturn just above the horizon as it prepared to set. Above him, Mars and Jupiter burned brightly. He sighed, happy. *Does it get any better than this?*

He flipped the bail, secured the line with his finger, and cast the lure out into the water. The sea was calm, and with his eyes adjusted to the dim light, he could just make out where his fishing line intersected the surface. He reeled the lure in quickly, and in no time, it arose out of the water in front of him, dripping. He removed a small bit of seaweed from the treble hook, flipped the bail, and cast again, repeating this motion every minute or so. As he fished, he walked slowly down the deserted beach. By mid-afternoon, he knew this spot would be cheek to jowl with Jeeps, pickups, and SUVs all enjoying a beautiful summer day. But now, with the sun still a few minutes from peeking out of the water, he was alone. And he relished the time.

Fifteen minutes went by without even a strike, and his hope of catching a mackerel started to fade. He thought briefly about changing the lure. Maybe the fish would prefer a surface popper or a rubber squid? Tommy even thought of breaking out his fly fishing gear when he suddenly felt a heavy load on the line.

At first, he suspected he had hooked a massive striper. Mackerel were aggressive fighters, and one would know immediately when they took the lure. They would usually run hard and jump, trying to free the hook. Bluefish, too, were strong fighters. But stripers could go either way. Sometimes, they took the lure and ran. Other times - especially with bigger fish - it felt like you hooked into a clump of seaweed. Hoping he had hooked a large and lazy striper, Tommy slowly started cranking the reel. He didn't feel any fight from this fish; it just stayed on his line like a lead weight. Perhaps he had foul-hooked some driftwood or even a sunfish, the weird-looking behemoths that he would occasionally see swimming slowly along the shore, paralleling the surf, a lone fin popping out of the water like a shark. Or, for that matter, it could have been a shark, maybe a dogfish, or even something bigger. Great Whites were much more common now with the increase in the seal populations, but Tommy felt quite certain that was not the case. He likely would have lost all of his line - and perhaps even his rod and reel - had he hooked a large shark like that.

Curious, he continued to reel in the catch slowly. The tide and slight wind were both in his favor, helping to push his catch toward the beach. After a few minutes, he gave a final tug on the rod, and he could just make out what looked like a large white fish breaking the surface of the water. Its stillness and lack of fighting suggested it was probably dead. The meat would be of no value to Tommy, but he wanted his lure back. They were not inexpensive, and Tommy took pride in his frugality.

He paused to grab his fishing gloves and pliers from his back pocket. Putting on the gloves, he curled the line around his fingers and pulled. He backed slowly from the water, careful not to put too much strain on the fifteen-pound monofilament. As the sun broke the surface of the water behind him, the catch rode a breaking wave onto the beach. Gathering his line as he walked toward it, Tommy was shocked to look down on the semi-nude body of a man.

He was older, probably around Tommy's age, and had clearly not been in the water too long. The skin was white and wrinkled, but there was no outward evidence of sea life causing any damage. As a doctor, Tommy had seen many a dead body, but the shock of reeling one in caused him to sit down heavily in the sand. The body rolled lazily in the light surf, its vacant eyes staring at Tommy as if pleading for answers to what had happened to him.

Gathering his senses, Tommy stood and walked back to the truck. He reached through the windows and grabbed his phone off the front seat. He called 911 and reported the find to the operator. Ending the call, he sat back and waited for the authorities to come. Given his location and the challenges of getting there, he knew he would have at least an hour alone with the body. And with the incoming tide, he knew he needed to secure the scene.

Still wearing his gloves, he grabbed both hands of the man and dragged him up the beach and out of the surf, trying to do as little damage as possible to any possible latent evidence. Fortunately, he was still alone on the beach, so he didn't have to deal with anyone crowding in trying to get a picture or video to enhance their social media followings. Instead, Tommy sat quietly and stared intently at the man without recognition. He was a white male, sixty to seventy years of age, thinning gray hair and no noticeable scars, birthmarks, piercings, or tattoos. He was naked save a pair of Nantucket red Bermuda-style swimming trunks, a yellow deflated flotation device, and a gold wedding band. His face was not familiar.

Had he been swimming somewhere on the island and drowned? Had he fallen from a boat? How had he ended up being hooked by an early morning fisherman just south of Great Point? Tommy pondered those questions as the first sound of sirens disturbed the air. He looked out to see a Coast Guard inflatable rapidly approaching from the direction of Nantucket Harbor. To the south, a white Ford Explorer approached rapidly over the sand, its rooftop bar ablaze with blue and red flashing lights. Soon the scene was covered from land and sea.

The authorities questioned Tommy intently, but it soon became apparent he had nothing to do with the victim other than having the bad luck of catching him. Released from their investigation, Tommy made his way back to his truck and headed home. There would be no Spanish Mackerel sushi, smoked bluefish pate, or grilled striper from him tonight. A change of menu would be in order.

CHAPTER THREE

Friday Afternoon

Off Georges Bank, 70 miles east of Nantucket

Between a vibrant, cloudless blue sky above grayish-green water below, the forty-six sport fisherman *Hedged* swayed gently in a calm sea. This area, south of Nova Scotia and east of Nantucket, was known for fishing, particularly big game fish such as tuna and swordfish. The three men had had success here before and were hoping to repeat those prior conquests.

Charles Post was sitting in the fighting chair, his turn to monitor the two rods they had off the back. They were trolling with a squid rig, and Charles was watching the tips intently, looking for the telltale subtle taps of a swordfish biting at the bait. He had a seltzer in the cup holder to his right and was munching on a bag of pretzels.

Sean Axmacher, at the wheel above, was scanning the surface for any signs of the big fish. The third man, Cormac Walsh, emerged from the cabin and stood at the mezzanine, looking down at Charles in the cockpit. He popped a beer and took a long drink.

"Can I get you anything Charles?" he yelled down. "A beer, perhaps?"

Charles squinted, looked at Cormac, and took a drink of his seltzer. "No, I'm good."

Cormac nodded and joined him next to the chair. "See anything?"

"No. Just a lot of bird activity. We had a couple of whales breach off the stern a few hundred yards out, but other than that, things have been pretty quiet."

The three were the founders and sole partners at Miacomet Capital, a small hedge fund run by the men from offices on Nantucket Island. They had started the firm over thirty years prior and had managed to build a successful business over that time. Together, they had secured investors, generated substantial returns for those investors, bought homes, raised families, and enjoyed the trappings of their success. If one were to be asked, he would no doubt state that they were more of a family than a business, each of the partners like a brother to the others.

Sean climbed down from the flybridge. "I've got the autopilot set to maintain this course and a speed of four knots. Should be the right speed given the current and the rigging." He looked at his watch. "We can give this another couple of hours, but then we will need to head back. I'd like to be in port by nine at the latest. The weather radio predicts increasing winds after sunset, and we will be running through the Great Point rip right after high tide. It is going to get a little bumpy."

Charles looked back at Sean. "I have full confidence in you and your piloting skills. I know Cormac and I are in good hands."

"Thanks, buddy," said Sean. "And really, no strikes? I thought for sure, given the conditions, we would at least have some success."

"Me too. I guess it's just not meant to be today. Cormac. I think you are up." He unbuckled himself from the reel, lifted the base of the rod from the fighting chair, and handed it to Cormac. The bulky Irishman sat heavily into the fighting chair, slid the base of the rod into the holder between his legs, and attached his fighting belt to the reel. He planted his feet on the big teak footrest, tugged gently on the rod, and leaned back into the chair. Squinting at the piercing blue sky, he turned to his partners and said, "Aye. It's a good day to be on the water, isn't it, guys?"

Sean smiled and nodded.

Charles walked behind the fighting chair and placed his hand on Cormac's shoulder. "Any day on the water is better than a day in the office," he said and laughed.

Cormac turned and looked up at his partner. "That sounds like some feckin' bumper sticker saying."

Charles chuckled. "Yes, yes, it does. Anyway, I hope you have better luck than I did."

"So, any plans for the weekend, big guy?" asked Sean. Charles was the oldest of the three by a few months and the tallest by an inch over Sean.

"Ann wants to start working on the nursery for Scott and Lizzie's baby."

Sean smiled. "A nursery? That baby's going to spend what, at most, a week or two a year here?"

"I know. Scott and Lizzie seem quite content in Denver. You know we'd love for them to move closer, Boston or New York, but that's not going to happen. What can we expect when he goes off and marries a West Coast girl."

"So true. What about you, Cormac? Who's the lucky lady this weekend?"

As the only lifelong bachelor in the group, his frequent girlfriends were often the topic of discussion. Although he was far from what anyone would describe as a handsome man, his wealth and his accent proved popular with the women, in particular, forty and fifty-year-old recent divorcees.

Cormac smiled and fidgeted in the fighting chair. "I'm not going to kiss and tell."

Sean snickered and glanced slyly at Charles. "I think that's code that he's going to be alone this weekend."

"Piss off, you," said Cormac, playfully punching Sean on the shoulder.

Charles looked at his two partners and smiled. They had been through a lot during their years together. They suffered a number of crises, both driven by external factors out of their control and the occasional misstep in their investment strategy. He felt proud of what the three of them had accomplished. Despite his misgivings about the firm's recent performance, he knew they would manage through the latest challenges. He pushed the negative thoughts from his mind and went into the cabin to grab another seltzer.

CHAPTER FOUR

Boston

Rick Caton piloted his FBI-issued Dodge Charger through the narrow streets of Boston, heading to the field office in Chelsea. Contrary to popular belief, agents didn't always drive black SUVs but rather a relatively ordinary assortment of civilian vehicles, all the better to blend into the general population. And this car was no exception. It blended well with other hurried Boston commuters, and had numerous war scars on its exterior from many battles with the infamous Boston traffic. Even though it had only thirty thousand on the odometer, the car seemed much older than it was, which is probably why Rick felt a certain kinship to it.

He had left his apartment on Berkshire Street in Cambridge early, trying to beat the brutal traffic that infected the streets of this Massachusetts town. But it didn't seem to matter what time of day it was; the traffic was always the same. Given that the city had been laid out hundreds of years before when horses and buggies were the key transportation modes, it was understandable why the traffic was the way it was. It was simply a collision of 21st-century mobility technology with 17th-century urban design. He had briefly entertained the idea of taking the subway, but that meant connecting through the Red Line, the epitome of poor city management and lack of long-term planning. A common game played by many that relied on this unreliable branch of the "T" was to see if they could outrun or outwalk the Red Line train between stations. Not surprisingly, the runners or walkers usually won.

That is why, at 7:15 a.m. on an unusually cold Monday morning in early September, Rick was sitting stationary on the Tobin bridge, breathing diesel fumes from the MBTA bus in front of him. An accident at the Chestnut Street exit had backed things up several miles, leaving Rick free to think about the meeting ahead of him with his boss. He expected it to go well.

At thirty-three, he had joined the FBI fairly late in his career, sneaking in under their mandatory age restriction with a few years to spare. Born and raised on Nantucket, the small but exclusive island a hundred miles to the south, he had spent most of the summers as a Community Service Officer for the Nantucket Police Department. His responsibilities were focused on maintaining quality of life for the locals and visitors alike, including directing traffic, managing parking issues, and assisting with major events. It was his first taste of law enforcement, and he loved it despite having to deal with a lot of entitled college kids who thought they had the right to park wherever they wanted just because of their family name. He had heard "Do you know who my family is?" too many times to count.

After graduating from the local high school, he enrolled at UMass Lowell, where he earned his degree in criminal justice. Returning to the island, he joined the Nantucket Police Department as a recruit. He was sent off for intensive training at the police academy in Plymouth. Following graduation, he returned to the NPD and started his career as a police officer with a plan to build his skills and become a detective. He had hoped to spend his entire career there, perhaps one day even assuming the role of chief of police.

But it didn't work out as he had planned. After being fired from the NPD, Rick left the island and bounced around from job to job, not really sure what he wanted to do. Adjusting to the very different way of life on the mainland didn't help much. Gone was the sense of community, of knowing most everyone - at least the year-rounders - and the sheer natural beauty. He had tried real estate, selling insurance, and even had a short stint as a car salesman. But he missed law enforcement. He missed making a difference. So, a couple of years after leaving the Nantucket force, he applied to join the FBI. At first, he thought his termination would count him out, but with excellent performance in his interviews, his strong educational record, and outstanding physical fitness, he was accepted. After a grueling 20 weeks of training at Quantico, he successfully lobbied to be placed in New England as a special agent out of the Boston Field Office. That had been eight years ago, and he had blossomed in his role within the Financial Crimes department, focusing on embezzlement and white-collar crimes.

Thankfully, the FBI had taken a chance on him despite the incident with the NPD, and he had worked twice as hard to prove his worth and validate their choice. The FBI had recognized his hard work and promoted him rapidly through the ranks. With the closing of this most recent case, Rick was hoping that he could secure a promotion to supervisory special agent and lead his own team within the department. Anxious not to get too far ahead of himself, Rick thought about his upcoming meeting with the Assistant Agent in Charge, Hanna Fines.

ASAC Fines had been his direct supervisor for just over three years. Despite a rocky start—Fines wasn't sure the FBI should have selected him and made sure he knew it—his hard work and successful prosecutions had gradually won her over. His performance on this most recent case should further solidify that reputation.

The case he had just closed was a co-conspiracy to embezzle funds through vendor fraud. A product development executive at Sharefield Biotech, a Cambridge pharmaceutical company, and her fiance had managed to extract nearly three million dollars from the firm. The fiancé, who didn't work for Sharefield, had set up a shell consulting company called FDA FastTrax, complete with a phony website and supporting testimonials from other pharma businesses. Their pitch claimed that their proprietary process could cut FDA drug registration time in half, meaning new drugs could get to market faster and start generating sales and profits sooner. However, the only thing their process turned out was phony invoices billing the firm for services that were never rendered.

Sharefield had called the FBI when they discovered anomalies in the accounts payable system. A preliminary internal investigation suggested some sort of fraudulent activity was occurring, and as a publicly traded company, they had called in the FBI to take over the investigation. For Rick, the case had been pretty cut and dry. He had spent several weeks undercover at the company as a new employee in the finance department. Working closely with the Chief Financial Officer and her team, it didn't take him long to pinpoint the source of the fraud and where the fraud prevention techniques had broken down. The rest of his time had been spent documenting the steps taken by the executive and her fiance and securing the necessary evidence to ensure a conviction.

In addition, he had to document where the funds had gone once they had hit the perpetrators' bank accounts. Thinking about it made him chuckle out loud and again wonder about the sheer stupidity of some criminals. Rather than keep a low profile or move the money offshore, the duo had instead spent it on their upcoming life together. A hundred thousand had gone to a local venue for their forthcoming wedding, fifty thousand for an engagement ring, nearly two hundred thousand went to a high-end Mercedes sedan, and two million went for a downpayment on a luxury condominium in Boston's Seaport district. In the end, the couple had spent nearly all of the money they had stolen. How did they not know that they should save for the future?

The traffic finally started moving, and a horn blared behind him. Rick flipped a finger to the following car and deftly fended off the beat-to-hell minivan that tried to cut in front of him. On a trip to visit the New England Aquarium when he was young, his dad had taught him how to drive in Boston. "Always look ahead. Never to the left. Never to the right. Show no weakness." Surprisingly, the tactic still worked thirty years later. He just hoped he would never meet another driver who followed the same strategy.

Rick drove the final few miles to the office and parked in the gated lot just past 8:00. He made his way through the front door, scanned his badge at security, and made his way to Fines' office on the sixth floor. He saw her door was open and tapped lightly on the frame.

"Hanna?"

She looked up from her computer and smiled. "Rick. Come in."

He approached her desk, shook her hand, and settled into one of the two overstuffed leather chairs facing her desk.

"How are you doing this morning?" She said, while she shuffled some papers on her desk and then settled in, looking at him in the intent way she always did.

Rick rolled his eyes and smiled at her. "Traffic was light today. Only took an hour to get here from Cambridge," he remarked dryly.

Fines smiled knowingly. "Have you thought of maybe moving closer to the office?"

Rick shook his head. "You know I love Cambridge. It's expensive, yes. And parking a car is a major pain in the ass. But it's a great neighborhood. It would be tough to leave."

Pleasantries out of the way, Hines nodded and changed the subject. "Great job on the Sharefield case."

"Thanks. To be honest, it really couldn't have been any easier. Some criminals just really aren't that smart. Even those that work for a major biotech firm." He folded his hands in his lap, trying not to betray his excitement at the success.

Hanna chuckled. "So true. Reading your report, I just couldn't get over how they spent all that money."

"I just don't know what they were thinking. Talk about calling attention to yourself. And a four-million-dollar condo in Seaport? Even with a two million dollar downpayment, the monthlies would be at least twenty thousand. Clearly, they must have had plans to keep their little enterprise going."

"Well, thanks to you, they'll be spending the next ten years at FMC Devens. And given the stature of Sharefield Biotech and the way you handled the case, the FBI has gotten some great PR out of it, too." She smiled at him, and he warmed, knowing how scarce her praise was.

"Thanks." He relaxed his shoulders a bit. "So what's next?"

"Glad you brought that up. I want to send you back to Quantico for some additional training." She slid a navy folder over to him with the FBI seal on the front.

"Really?" He asked, shock evident in his voice. Internally, he wondered what was lacking in his current skill set. He picked up the folder and leafed through the pages.

She nodded. "Well, it's more of a workshop than training. The FBI is leading an inter-agency project to improve communication and collaboration and streamline complex multi-agency investigations. Given your competency in managing white-collar and financial crimes, I thought you could best represent the Boston office. There will be participants from other field offices, as well as the SEC, Postal Service, IRS, and Treasury."

"Sounds fascinating," said Rick sarcastically. "When does it start?"

She chuckled, having received the exact response she expected. "Monday, oh eight hundred hours, so you'll need to fly on Sunday. You'll be there for two weeks so you should plan accordingly. Any details to finalize with the DA on the Sharefield case?"

Rick nodded. "I'll make sure the Suffolk DA office has everything they need."

"Anything else?" She raised an eyebrow.

Rick thought for a minute. "The only other case needing immediate attention is Crosby. But Nia's been involved in the investigation, if only tangentially. I'm sure she wouldn't mind making the final arrest once the warrants come through.

"Great." She nodded, and turned back to her computer, clearly dismissing him.

Rick got up to leave, pushing his chair in.

She turned back to him briefly. "And Rick?"

He paused and looked at her.

"Good luck at Quantico," she said, sending him a cheeky wink.

Rick smiled ruefully. "Thanks," and left her office.

CHAPTER FIVE

Nantucket

Detective Tina Fisch, known to her friends and colleagues as Tuna, knocked on the door at Miacomet Capital Partners. She had been handed what she expected would be an open-and-shut investigation into the accidental drowning of a local resident. Given the circumstances involved and what she knew to date, she expected little more than a mountain of paperwork to be her biggest challenge—lots of boxes to check, T's to cross, and I's to dot.

She was an attractive woman in her mid-forties, and she sported curly, shoulder-length brown hair. She had been with the Nantucket police for her entire career, save for a few years when she lived in New York City. She had acquired the nickname Tuna in third grade at the Nantucket Intermediate School, and it had followed her like a lost stray ever since. At first, she bristled at the moniker, but eventually, she came to embrace it as her own. She had even gotten a small tattoo of a bluefin tuna to seal the deal, but only her wife of over fifteen years would ever see it.

She had gotten the call about the discovery earlier in the day from the Nantucket County Sheriff, Fred Boston. The victim, Charles Post, had been found by a local fisherman early that morning at Great Point. The first responders from the Coast Guard, sheriff's office, and Nantucket Police had processed the scene and recovered the body. The initial consensus from the group believed it had been an accidental drowning. The body showed no evidence of trauma or foul play. Post had been wearing nothing more than a bathing suit and a deflated life preserver and lacked any formal identification. He had been reported missing in the vicinity the night before in a panicked 911 call by one of his business partners, and it wasn't often that sixty-year-old men washed up on shore.

Tuna had met with the dispatcher earlier in the day and listened to the recording of the call. It had come in just after 9:00 p.m. the night before from an adult male who announced himself as Cormac Walsh. Given his Irish accent and the panic in his voice, Tuna struggled to make out the details. According to the dispatcher who took the call, she believed that Charles Post had been out on a fishing trip with Walsh and another man aboard the forty-two-foot vessel *Hedged*. The boat was returning from an all-day offshore fishing trip. Cormac claimed Post had fallen off the stern of the boat while trying to relieve himself just as the boat was passing through the Great Point rip. The sea had been far from calm with four to six foot swells and an active rip current. Failing light and emerging fog meant they had been unable to locate him in the water despite searching desperately for an hour.

It was unknown why the life preserver had failed to inflate. Tuna made a note to have that checked.

The Coast Guard immediately dispatched their forty-seven-foot lifeboat from the Nantucket station to the scene along with a Jayhawk helicopter from Air Station Cape Cod. Despite their efforts, given the fog, darkness, and the target's lack of a flotation device, they called off the search at midnight. It was barely six hours later that the body of Charles Post was discovered.

A quick call to the medical examiner confirmed to Tuna the identification and the likelihood she was looking at an accidental drowning. The ME had promised her he would issue an official cause of death within the week once tox screens and an autopsy had been completed.

Prior to her visit, Tuna had done some background research on the business and learned that Post had been a partner in a hedge fund with the two other men on the boat, both roughly the same age as the victim. While she did not know much about the world of business and high finance, what she did understand was that this trio of men appeared to run a very successful and profitable enterprise. She had reached out to them and agreed to meet at their office. Both partners would be present.

Tuna knocked again. Miacomet Capital Partners sat in a small, single-story, gray-shingled building off Water Street. It sat just feet from a busy intersection, and the constant parade of vehicles moving provided a hushed background of white noise. As Nantucket properties go, home of multi-million dollar compounds and historic mansions, it was drab and forgettable. The shingles were split and curling and looked in desperate need of replacement. The trim, a rather drab olive green, was dull and flaking. Bare wood was visible in some spots. Tuna stood on a brick walkway that was full of weeds. The door in front of her was a chalky, faded red with a tarnished brass knocker set in the center of the door. Above her, a sign creaked on rusty hinges. It showed a golf flag overlaid on an outline of Nantucket. Below, it is stated that the firm was founded in 1990. The building was more representative of a failing medical office than the global headquarters of a highly successful hedge fund.

She heard steps approaching, and the door swung open, revealing a middle-aged man with broad shoulders, a slight belly, and a full head of graying, ginger hair. He was shaped like a fireplug and not much taller than her, maybe five foot ten. He looked to be built for rugby, not business, and clearly hadn't had a shave in a few days. His skin had a ruddy complexion as if he had spent years on the sea, and his eyes were red rimmed.

"Good morning, I'm Detective Tina Fisch," she said and extended her hand.

The man shook it firmly. "Ah, detective. I'm Cormac Walsh," he said in a strong Irish accent. He stepped back to allow her into the foyer. "We are so glad you are here. Please come in."

"Thanks so much for seeing me on such short notice." She stepped into the building, wrinkling her nose at the musty odor that accompanies many older buildings by the sea.

"Of course. To be honest, we are still in shock. I just can't believe it. Charles gone." Walsh shook his head and looked like he might start crying again.

Tuna reached out and touched his arm. "I am so sorry for your loss. I will make this as quick as possible. I just need to confirm a few details."

Cormac nodded and sniffed. "Let's go down to the conference room. Sean's waiting for us, and we will have a little more room. Please follow me."

The interior of the building was in better shape but still nothing fancy. Tuna trailed Cormac down a short hall lined with antique furniture and large paintings of ships at sea. She passed several empty offices with the lights off before reaching a conference room where the maritime theme continued. A dark plank table was surrounded by half a dozen captain's chairs. One of them was occupied, and as she entered the room, he stood.

He was tall and thin, the opposite of Walsh, and completely bald. He had very fair skin, and his face showed signs of acne scarring when he was much younger. He was wearing Bermuda shorts with a navy cable knit sweater. His eyes, too, were red, as if he'd been crying.

Cormac turned to him. "Sean, this is Detective Tina Fisch."

"Detective. I'm Sean Axmacher." His voice was nasally, and he reached his hand out halfheartedly.

They shook hands, Tuna noting that his handshake was limp and lifeless. Not typical of the many businessmen she had met over the years. "Thank you for taking the time to meet with me. Both of you."

Cormac motioned to the chair at the head of the table. "Please have a seat. Can I get you anything? Water, coffee?"

"Thank you, no. This shouldn't take long. I just wanted to get a little more detail about what happened." She settled into the rather uncomfortable chair and shifted, trying to adjust.

"Of course," said Walsh.

The Irishman sat across from her to the right. Sean sat on her other side, to the left. If this hadn't been an interview about the death of their colleague, she might have made the joke 'You must be wondering why I brought you here today.' Instead, she pulled out her notebook and set it on the table.

"Can you tell me a little bit about your relationship with Mr. Post?"

Cormac let out a long sigh and glanced at Sean, who had his head bowed. "Well, we've known each other for what seems like forever. The three of us met back in the summer of 1980 when we were working jobs during our break from Uni. Charles was working for a local contractor as a general laborer, Sean was doing landscaping, and I was bussing tables at the Rose & Crown."

Tuna nodded, her head in her notebook, writing quickly. "And how did you meet?"

"Golf." Cormac laughed quietly to himself, shaking his head softly.

"Golf?" She stopped writing and looked up at them.

Cormac smiled sadly. "Yes, golf. We all enjoy the game. One afternoon, by accident, the three of us were paired up at the local course, Miacomet. And that was that. From then on, we have been fast friends."

Sean also smiled sadly, reliving the memory.

"And how did that lead to this?" Tuna motioned around the room with her pen.

Cormac took the lead again. Tuna made a mental note that he seemed to be the authority in the room. "Charles and Sean here graduated a year before me and took jobs on Wall Street. Finance. I joined them in New York the following year. We all worked in different firms and despite our success, we just weren't happy. We were working crazy hours and felt like the only people really making money were our bosses. So, in 1990, we quit our jobs and started Miacomet Capital. The name being a nod to where we had all met the decade before."

Sean abruptly stood. "Excuse me for a moment."

Tuna followed him with her eyes as he left the room.

"Please forgive him. He is just so upset and really struggling. The three of us were like brothers."

Sean returned with a box of tissues and sat down. "My apologies," he said, rubbing his nose. He held the box out to Cormac, who subtly shook his head.

"And what is it you do here?" asked Tuna.

Cormac replied, "Miacomet Capital is a hedge fund. We pool investor money and then use those assets to make strategic investments. And I'm proud to say we have an excellent record of returns. Since our founding, we've only had three years of sub-double-digit performance. The dot com bubble, the 2008 financial crisis, and of course, Covid."

She nodded, knowing how hard the financial sector had been hit during each of these periods. "And who are your investors?"

She looked up just in time to see Cormac and Sean exchange a loaded glance.

"I'm sorry, but we are really not at liberty to discuss specific organizations or individuals."

"I understand. And what was Charles' role here?"

Sean jumped in. "He managed our clients."

Tuna turned to him. "How so?"

"Charles was an extrovert and comfortable in just about any setting or with anyone. As the saying goes, he never met a stranger. Over the years, he had built a sizable network of successful people, so we had no shortage of investors who were anxious to join one of our funds. All thanks to Charles." Sean was now shredding the tissue in his hands.

She opened the question to both of them. "And what about you? What are your roles?"

Cormac responded. "I'm the CFO, essentially the head accountant. Sean here is our CIO or Chief Investment Officer. In addition to being very close, we also had skills that complemented each other nicely. I think that was one of the key reasons for our success."

"And any other employees?"

Cormac responded again. "Well, we have support staff, of course. Administration, technology, the usual. We also have three interns, one working for each of us."

"And were they with you on the boat?"

"No. Our summer internships officially ended the first of September, and the 'three amigos,' as they called themselves, had gone out together to celebrate and vent a little steam. Our internships are pretty intense, so once they start to wrap up, it tends to be a relief to the participants. We're scheduled to have a formal celebration as an organization next week. Charles had been planning it." He looked like he might start crying again. Sean wordlessly passed him the tissue box.

"Thank you for sharing that. Can you tell me what happened last night?" She carefully studied the body language of both men.

Sean sniffled, his eyes watering up. Cormac looked at him empathetically and then turned to Tuna. "It was just a fishing trip like we have done dozens of times before. Only this time," his voice trailed off.

"This time?" Tuna asked gently.

"This time, we lost Charles," said Cormac quietly. He reached for the tissues.

"Again, I am so sorry for your loss. Can you tell me how Charles fell off the boat?"

Cormac took a few moments to compose himself. "We spent the day fishing offshore, trolling for bigeye tuna and swordfish. We didn't catch anything, unfortunately, but we did have a fair amount to drink. Just beer, mind you, but a fair quantity of it."

Tuna looked up at him accusingly. "And who was driving the boat when all this beer was being consumed?"

Sean answered testily, "It was not like that at all! I am the captain of the boat and take that role very seriously. I had only one beer. At lunch. Otherwise, it was just seltzer for me."

Tuna's pen moved furiously in her notebook. She looked at Cormac. "And you?"

"I had a few. Quite a few to be honest. It was a gorgeous day; the sea was calm, and the weather was perfect."

Tuna noted that his Irish accent was more pronounced when he was defending himself. "And Charles?" she asked.

Sean answered. "Charles isn't much of a drinker. Never had been. He will enjoy the occasional glass of wine or fine bourbon. He was not a man's man in that respect."

"Was he drinking on the boat?"

Cormac and Sean exchanged another glance. Cormac responded. "That was the thing. He actually was drinking—a lot. At first, I thought he was letting loose a bit, something he rarely did. But as it continued, I thought maybe something else was bothering him."

"But," interrupted Sean.

"But what?" asked Tuna.

"I personally didn't really see him drinking that much. I guess I wasn't paying attention." Sean shrugged, looking confused.

Tuna made some additional notes.

"Any idea why he was drinking? Could it have been something with the business? Or maybe at home?" asked Tuna.

Sean shook his head. "The business is doing well; there are no concerns there. And I know Charles was very happy at home. He's been married nearly forty years, and he and his wife, Ann, were expecting their first grandchild. By all accounts, Charles was a very happy man."

Tuna wrote for a minute and looked at Cormac. "So why the drinking then?"

"I wish I knew." Sean hit the table with his fist. "Dammit! I should have intervened. I should have said something. Maybe Charles would still be with us if I did!"

Tuna sat quietly for a moment, letting the emotions settle in the room. "So what happened on the trip back?"

"As we said, the weather was perfect, and the sea was smooth when we left Georges. I had put the boat on autopilot, and we were cruising nicely. But as we approached Great Point, things got a little hairy," Sean responded.

"Hairy? In what way?" asked Tuna.

"The wind had picked up considerably and had shifted to the northeast. It was also the height of the tidal change, so the rip was extremely active. Waves were probably five feet or so and breaking. *Hedged* is a hell of a boat, though, and she handled it easily," Sean said. Cormac nodded in agreement.

"Were you all wearing life preservers?" She looked at both of them, knowing it was not uncommon for men, especially on a bigger boat, to feel like there was no need to wear one, as if it were a sign of weakness.

Sean nodded emphatically. "Yes. I insisted we put them on when we left the fishing grounds. I knew the weather was changing, and the ride was probably going to get rough."

She looked at Sean. "Do you have those serviced regularly?"

"Of course!" said Sean defensively. "I have eight of the best PFDs available on the boat, and they are checked at the start of every season."

"Any thoughts as to why the one Charles was wearing didn't inflate?" she said, keeping her tone even so it didn't sound like she was being accusatory.

"None. It should have inflated as soon as it hit the water. And Charles also could have inflated it manually. There's a little handle down by the waist that you can pull to activate. Somehow, the arming mechanism must have malfunctioned."

Tuna nodded. "And what was Charles doing when things got hairy?"

Cormac spoke. "He was sitting on the transom, apparently lost in thought. Then he stood up and climbed on the transom as if he was going to pee off the back of the boat."

Tuna looked at Sean. "This is a forty foot boat, no?"

"Actually, forty-two."

"Do you not have a bathroom, er, I mean, a head on board?"

Sean nodded. "We have two staterooms below, each with their own bathroom. Charles could have used either one. I'm not sure why he decided to relieve himself off the back of the boat."

"And would you say this is typical behavior for Charles? To take such a risk?"

"Absolutely not!" said Sean. "I wouldn't say he was a prude, but he was still fairly conservative as far as risk-taking went."

Tuna looked at Sean and then slowly turned to Cormac. "So why this time? What was different? Why would he be drinking much more than normal? And taking such a crazy risk to pee?"

"I wish we knew." Cormac sighed, and put his head in his hands.

"Did you not try and stop him? Or try to pull him off the transom?" asked Tuna.

Cormac looked at her, his eyes heavy. "I was sitting in the fighting chair and, to be honest, had nodded off, probably from all the beer. I opened my eyes just in time to see him fall off. At first, I thought it was just a weird dream, almost a vision. But then I realized what had happened and yelled to Sean."

She turned her gaze at Sean "And did you see anything?"

"No. I was focused on the compass and double-checking our plot through the rip. When I heard Cormac yell, I turned and could just see Charles's head in the wake off the back."

Tuna nodded. "So after he fell, what did you do?"

Sean responded quickly. "I throttled back and turned the boat around. I also grabbed the life ring and threw it in the water. I wanted to make sure we noted the location and drift. I also thought Charles might be able to swim to it and put it on."

Cormac interrupted. "And I called nine one one. Asking for immediate help."

Tuna turned a few pages of her notebook. "And that was, um, let's see, eight-twelve p.m.?"

"That sounds about right, yes." Cormac nodded.

"So let's see if I have this right," said Tuna. She looked down at her notes. Both Sean and Cormac looked at her intensely.

She continued, "You spent the day off-shore. You," she pointed with her pen at Cormac, "were drinking beer pretty heavily. As was Charles. You caught nothing. Oh, wait. What time did you pack up the fishing and decide to head back?"

Sean looked at the ceiling. "Um, I would have to check the autopilot to be sure, but it was probably close to six. We were trying to make port by nine."

Tuna added to her notes. "So you left the fishing grounds at roughly six o'clock, were cruising at thirty knots, and you crossed the Great Point rip at, let's say, close to eight. Then Charles, for some reason unknown, jumped up on a swaying transom and decided to pee off the back of a boat going thirty knots. Sound about right?"

Both Sean and Cormac looked down like two toddlers being scolded for not sharing toys. Finally, Cormac broke the silence. "Yes, that sounds about right."

Tuna sat quietly, gathering her thoughts. "One last question, then. Was Charles seeing anyone, like a therapist? Was he experiencing any sort of mental health issues?"

Cormac shook his head. "No. Charles was by all accounts very happy and sharp as a tack. None of this behavior makes any sense."

Tuna closed her notebook and stood up. "Thank you again for your time. Both of you." She pulled out a couple of business cards and handed one to each of them. "And if you can think of anything, even if it seems like nothing, please don't hesitate to reach out."

"Thank you, detective," said Cormac. "Let me walk you to the door."

Sean watched as Cormac escorted Tuna down the hall. He heard a few mumbled words and then the closing of the door. Footsteps approached, and Cormac reappeared in the room.

Sean looked at him anxiously. "I can't believe this. You don't think they are going to find out about, you know, our friends?"

"Absolutely not, Sean. Please don't worry. This will all blow over." Cormac laid a hand on Sean's shoulder, gripping it tightly.

"I hope you're right, Cormac. I don't like this attention one bit." He looked back down at his hands, the shredded tissues weirdly reminding him of the white caps from the night before.

"Nor do I, lad. Nor do I."

CHAPTER SIX

It was late Sunday afternoon, and Ann Post was sitting in an oversized armchair in the family room of her Nantucket home, quietly weeping. Behind her, generous windows opened up to an expansive green lawn that led down to Nantucket Harbor, where the sun crafted diamonds on the rippling water.

"I'm so sorry for your loss," said Detective Tina Fisch.

"Thank you," sniffed Ann. She wiped her nose with a tissue and adjusted herself on the chair. "And you are absolutely sure it is Charles?"

Tuna nodded slowly. "Yes. The medical examiner confirmed the identity this morning. Again, I'm so sorry. And both of his partners confirmed the events of the day."

"I just don't understand," exclaimed Ann. "Charles has been on the water his entire life. He's what other mariners call salty. There is just no way he would have done the things they are claiming! He doesn't drink, at least very often, and there's no way he would have stood on the back of the boat to go to the bathroom. It's like they are talking about a stranger!"

"The partners agreed. They said it was very odd behavior for Charles. Could he maybe have taken something?"

"Taken something? Like what?"

"Any kind of recreational drugs?"

Ann looked at Tuna with red, water-filled eyes. "Not possible. Charles would never do drugs. He didn't even take any prescriptions. Oh, wait, there was one for his cholesterol."

Tuna nodded. "So, no recreational drug use? Ever?"

"Never!"Ann responded adamantly.

Tuna noted a comment. "What have your observations been of Charles lately? Have you noticed any unusual behavior recently? Anything at all out of the ordinary?"

Ann wiped her nose again, thinking. "If I'm being honest with myself, then I have to say yes. I mean, nothing weird or unusual. He just didn't seem like himself the last few months. Distracted."

"Can you be a little more specific?" asked Tuna.

Ann turned and looked out the window. "Things between us were good. Our marriage has always been strong, and we have always been close. And that hasn't changed. But I could tell that something was on his mind. He just seemed, I don't know, preoccupied?"

"Any thoughts as to what it might have been? Was his health okay? Financial problems?"

Ann shook her head. "His health was great. He just had his annual physical, and the doctor was very pleased. I mean, he got the usual advice to exercise some more and cut down on red meat - his cholesterol has always been stubbornly high - but aside from that, it was a clean bill of health."

"Any family issues?"

Ann shook her head slowly. "Quite the opposite. We have two children, and both are healthy and successful. Our daughter, Felicity, is thirty-one and works in a non-profit in Providence. Our son, Scott, is thirty-four and lives in Denver. He's in banking. Scott and his wife are expecting their first child next month. Charles was so excited at the thought of being a grandfather."

Tuna made a notation. "Could it be money then?"

Again, Ann shook her head. "No. Financially, we are very secure. And I'm not just parroting what Charles tells me. I've always been the one to manage our household finances, and I can assure you there are no issues there. We have more than enough, and in fact, we are, er, were, working to establish a foundation that would give a lot of it back." Her eyes welled back up.

Tuna handed her a fresh tissue. "I have to say I was a bit taken aback by the state of the offices for Miacomet Capital. Is it possible that there might have been some problem there? Were they having any financial issues?"

"No, things there were good as well. They just reported their second-quarter results, which were quite impressive - just over twelve percent on an annualized basis. Charles didn't go into the details with me but he did share that it was one of their best quarters ever. But now that I'm thinking about it..." She got quiet, contemplating something.

"What is it?" asked Tuna, her curiosity piqued.

"Miacomet Capital has been in business for over thirty years, and Charles and I have been through the best and worst of all those years. We enjoyed the booms as well as the busts and, honestly, had a few scary times when we weren't sure we were going to make it," Ann reflected, still staring through the window at the water.

"And?" Tuna prompted.

"If the second quarter results were as good as Charles said, I would have thought he would have been happier. More pleased - especially as he was the face of the firm." Ann nodded to herself. "He was the one who had to field the calls from upset investors when they didn't perform. So I would have thought he'd been tickled."

"And he didn't seem pleased?" Tuna made a note.

"No. It's not that he was sad per se. It was more of a disappointment like he thought that maybe they should have done better. I don't know. He was just subdued."

Tuna continued taking notes, her pen scratching rapidly on the paper. "Can I ask you why the offices were pretty much a dump? Especially if the firm is doing so well?"

Ann smiled sadly. "I know. That was always a bit of a sticking point with Charles. He wanted to spend a little money to fix up their offices - get them back in shape. He thought it reflected badly on the firm."

"And they didn't because?"

"Cormac always took pride in keeping their management fees as low as possible. He felt it was one of the things that made Miacomet Capital so unique. He also made the point - correctly - that clients very rarely visit the offices, so why spend the money? He thought working in such a run-down space would make clients think they spent the money where it counts. Total virtue signaling, right?" Ann rolled her eyes. "In the big scheme of things the money needed to fix the offices up was pennies to the three of them. But Cormac wanted to keep up those appearances." She finished, shrugging.

Tuna nodded. "I guess that makes sense."

Ann looked back out over the lawn to the harbor. She could just make out their small dock and Charles' pride and joy, a Herreshoff 25. It was a classic design that he had enjoyed sailing and racing at every opportunity. She was a frequent passenger but didn't have the same love for the wind as him. Now, what was she going to do with the boat? She started crying again. This was just unbelievable.

"Mrs. Post?" Tuna said gently.

She snapped out of her thoughts. "Sorry."

"It's okay. Is there anything I can do for you? Is there anyone that you would like me to call?"

Ann sniffled and wiped her eyes. "No, but thank you. I've talked to our daughter, Felicity. She's on her way over and should be here in a few hours. Scott is in Asia on business, and with the time difference, it's the middle of the night there. I'll try him again shortly. Not a call I really want to make." She sniffled and wiped her nose with a tissue. "And I think Cormac is working to put out a statement from the firm about Charles'..." Her voice trailed off.

Tuna reached out and grabbed her hand. "Can I make a suggestion?'

"Sure."

"My partner, Ellen, is a grief counselor for the hospital. Given my profession, I have referred quite a few patients her way and have seen impressive results. I'm sure she would be happy to talk with you." Tuna squeezed Ann's hand briefly before releasing it.

"Thank you, detective. I'll take that under consideration." She wiped her nose again, sat up in the chair, and looked intently at Tuna. "What is next in your investigation?"

"We have a few more items to address, namely the final report from the medical examiner. We are also waiting on the analysis of the life preserver, which we assume is defective. Then, well, we will consider the case closed. Of course, you may want to consider legal action against the manufacturer of that life preserver."

Ann sat up straight, staring at Tuna in disbelief. "Detective, there is something not right here. There is no way this happened the way you are saying," she said, upset. "I want a more detailed investigation to discover what really happened! And why didn't his life preserver inflate?" She shook her head quickly, before standing up and pacing in front of the fireplace.

Tuna also stood, and said calmly, "Mrs. Post. I know that this is a huge shock, and I understand your grief. But I've been a detective for a long time. Everything points to the same conclusion."

"But that's not Charles!" Ann exclaimed, turning back to look beseechingly at Tuna.

Tuna replied her voice firm but assuring. "I understand your frustration. But one thing that I have learned in this business is that sometimes people behave differently than expected."

Ann snorted. "So you're saying Charles really did these things? That he acted in a way that was so out of character for him?"

"I'm just saying that sometimes there are things we don't know about the people we love."

Ann walked to the door, standing stiffly. "I think it would be better if you leave now."

"Mrs. Post. I didn't mean to insinuate anything." Tuna knew that the conversation was over. If her job had taught her anything, it was that everyone grieves differently. Ann shook her head silently, clearly done with answering questions.

Tuna walked to the door and said, "Please don't hesitate to reach out if you have any questions or concerns." This pat response made Tuna feel about a foot tall. She stepped out onto the driveway.

"Thank you, detective. Good day," said Ann. She turned and shut the door behind Tuna.

Tuna sighed and walked back to her cruiser. Was she missing something? She didn't know Charles Post personally, so she couldn't assess his character or judgment from experience. But clearly, his wife believed that his death was not so cut and dry. For now, though, everything pointed to the same conclusion, and nothing she had discovered during her investigation suggested otherwise. Charles Post, sixty-four years old and an expectant grandfather, had died from accidental drowning during a fishing trip with his partners.

She got in her car and headed back to the office, ready to finalize the mountain of paperwork sitting on the corner of her desk.

CHAPTER SEVEN

Boston

Rick Caton was sitting at his desk at the Boston field office for the FBI. His office was smaller than Hanna's, but still enjoyed pleasant views through the floor-to-ceiling windows. He looked out at a dreary sky laden with low-hanging gray clouds. It was going to rain. He turned his attention back to his desk, and the dozen manila files organized alphabetically on top. With his upcoming inter-agency cluster workshop, he was making sure his active cases would be managed while he was gone. Most were still in the very early stages, but one, another corporate embezzlement case, would need more active babysitting. He had just filed the papers to secure the arrest warrant and was worried that the target might catch wind of the upcoming detention and flee.

Unlike the Sharefield Bio case, this was a classic scheme of banking fraud. A branch manager of a Boston-based community bank had managed to direct nearly half a million dollars of customer deposits into his accounts. Using his executive position, he had crafted emails, internal memos, and other official documents to hide his activities and was careful to take relatively small amounts from accounts with significant deposits so as not to garner attention. What he didn't take count on was a sprightly octogenarian named Judy Cramer. Her account held in excess of two million dollars, and she was extremely diligent in balancing her ledger every month. Noting the discrepancies and their clockwork appearance, she brought it to the attention of her grandson, a sergeant in the Boston Police Department.

The case had worked its way through the bureaucratic red tape of the BPD, and given that the accounts involved included branches in Massachusetts, New Hampshire, and Rhode Island, it had been turned over to the FBI. With his expertise in financial crimes, it didn't take long to find its way to Rick's desk.

He picked up the folder and made his way down the hall. He stopped outside an office much like his own and knocked on the door frame. A trim Black woman looked up from behind her desk and smiled broadly.

"Rick!"

"Hey, Nia. How goes the battle?"

She leaned back in her chair and laced her fingers behind her neck. "It's going. Please come in. Sit down. What's going on with you?"

Rick stood by the government-issued chairs that faced her desk. Nia had added a bit of a personal touch to hers with two small pillows that gave them a strong, feminine touch. One pillow read *If I'm Too Much, Go Find Less*, the other *My Guns Are Closer Than They Appear*. Rick sat in the chair with the latter and looked across the desk at his colleague.

"You're looking good."

"Same could be said of you, RC."

Their frequent banter and flirtation had never led to anything, and they both planned on keeping it that way, especially since Nia's husband was currently an active-duty Marine stationed with a Raider Regiment. He was six feet of nearly zero body fat and hardcore muscle who could break Rick in half over his knee if he wanted to. But given that he was also one of Rick's best friends, it was unlikely to ever come to that.

"How's Jon handling the transition?"

"He's good. Just waiting on his next deployment orders. We are hoping he stays in the States, but the Middle East is a strong possibility."

"I'm sorry. Fingers crossed, he stays here. I'd miss the old guy."

"Thanks. Me too. But whatever happens, we'll get through it. We've had to manage this since we met." She said, making it clear she didn't want to think about it anymore.

Rick nodded and changed the subject. "Can I ask a favor?"

She laughed, "I am not going to feed your cat!"

Rick smiled at the old joke. "I don't have a cat."

Nia laughed and winked. "I know. Just love giving you crap." She leaned forward and put her elbows on the desk. "Sure, what can I do for you?"

Rick handed her the manila folder. "This is the Crosby case file."

"The bank manager with the sticky fingers?" She opened it, glancing down at the papers in the file.

"Yes. Hanna just informed me that I'm heading to Quantico Monday for an inter-agency workshop and I'll be gone a couple of weeks. The arrest warrants on Crosby are due in the next few days, and I certainly don't want to wait until I get back before executing them." He folded his hands in his lap.

"So, you want me to holster my Glocks and take this bastard down?"

Rick laughed. "Larry Crosby is about as dangerous as a high school math teacher. He won't put up any fight. I just don't want him to catch wind of things and make a run for it. He has plenty of resources at his disposal and enough smarts to probably get to a country without an extradition agreement."

Nia paged through the folder. "Sure, RC. I'm happy to take this over. And take the credit, too," she smiled.

"Credit is all yours. Just get this bastard. There are a number of senior citizens wanting to get their money back." He clapped his hands together and stood back up.

"Done. Anything else?"

He shook his head. "Just wish me luck. Any time the term 'workshop' enters the discussion, it is sure to be as boring as hell and a complete and total waste of my time."

She looked at him apologetically. "Can't you just tell Hanna no?"

Rick laughed. "I wish. But this is all about improving coordination among agencies on large-scale financial crimes. It's kind of in my wheelhouse, so I need to go, as painful as it's going to be."

She shrugged, then grinned. "Look on the bright side, RC."

"And what's that, beautiful?"

"You get to spend two weeks with your cohorts across the various federal agencies. Maybe one of them will be a beautiful woman who shares your passion for bank fraud." Nia giggled.

"Lovely," said Rick sarcastically. "Call me if you have any questions on that," he said, pointing at the file.

"Will do, RC. Cheers."

"Later."

Rick made his way back to the office and had just started sorting the remaining files when his phone rang. He pulled it out of his pocket and looked at the screen. Area code and prefix were from Nantucket. He hadn't talked to anyone on the island in three years and that had been when his parents had retired and moved to Florida. They were asking him to come back to the island and go through the house to claim anything he wanted to keep. He had politely refused.

He tapped on the screen. "Rick Caton," he said cautiously.

"Rick?" said a familiar voice on the other end. "This is Ann Post."

Rick stopped sorting, surprised. "Mrs. Post. How are you? How long has it been?"

Her tone was serious. "I was thinking about that earlier. We last talked before you moved off island after that nasty business. Never thought they were very fair to you."

"Thanks, Mrs. P. How's Scott?" Rick had been her son's babysitter throughout high school, but had lost touch with him after he was fired from NPD.

"Please call me Ann, Rick." She said, and then remarked, "He's good. Living in Denver. Married. Getting ready to have a baby."

Rick detected an almost wistful note in her voice. He sat back in his chair. "Wow. Having a baby? Doesn't seem that long ago when I babysat him, and he wanted to ride on my back like a horse. He wanted me to buck him off. Sometimes, he laughed so hard." Rick smiled at the memory. "And to think he will soon be a father. Scary how fast time goes by."

"It is," she agreed, sounding sad.

Glancing down at his watch, Rick changed the subject. "Well, it's good to hear from you. To what do I owe the pleasure?"

She paused, then said, "It's about my husband."

"Mr. P?" said Rick excitedly. "How is he?"

This time, the pause was longer. Finally, she said quietly, "He passed away three days ago."

Rick felt his shoulders slump. "Oh, Mrs. P, I am so sorry. What happened?"

She sighed, "That's why I'm calling, Rick. The official findings are listing accidental drowning as the cause of death."

Rick's eyes widened. "Drowning? Really? That man loved the water. He was a great swimmer, sailor, you name it. I think he had salt water in his veins."

"Which is why this is so disturbing. And why I don't believe his drowning was accidental," she said, getting choked up.

Rick looked out at the approaching storm. Raindrops had started hitting the window, and the swaying trees outside showed that the winds were picking up. "Not accidental? Was there another cause of death, maybe medical? Heart attack or a stroke?"

"No," Ann replied. "He just had his annual physical and was in perfect health. The medical examiner even said so. He's the one that listed accidental drowning as the official cause."

"But you don't agree?"

"I don't," she responded with conviction. "I know my Charles, and what they are saying he did that led to the drowning just doesn't make any sense. The man they are talking about is not my husband."

"I'm so sorry, Mrs., er, um, Ann. Is there anything I can do?"

"Yes, please. I don't know where else to turn."

"Of course. What is it you need?"

"I need someone I trust to look into this in more detail. Find out what really happened to Charles. I need someone to get to the truth. I need you," she pleaded.

Rick was taken aback. "Well, sure, Ann. I understand. But I'm not sure I'll be able to investigate this. I've got my own cases. What about someone at NPD?"

Ann's tone took on a defeated note. "I tried. But they won't listen. I even reached out to the new chief. She was kind and courteous but stood by the conclusion of her department. Didn't want to hear another word about it even with Charles' position in the community."

"Hmm," said Rick. "They must be very confident in their findings."

"Their findings are wrong!" said Ann forcefully. "I know it. Please, as a favor to me and my family, help us get to the truth."

Rick leaned back in his chair, looked up at the ceiling, and let out a long sigh. "I'll tell you what. Let me make a few phone calls. I still know a few people with the Nantucket police and the sheriff's office. Let me see if I can get a better handle on what is going on."

Rick heard her sigh with relief. "That would be great. Thank you."

"Of course, I owe a lot to you and Mr. Post. I'm happy to help. I just don't know how much more I'll be able to do."

"This is a start. And knowing you, you'll get to the bottom of it quickly."

"I appreciate the confidence. But if the NPD and the medical examiner are claiming accidental drowning, surely they have the evidence to support it. Not sure anything I can do will change that."

"I understand. But just knowing you are looking into it is a relief."

"Just give me some time. Let me make those calls and see what I can find out. I'll call you back in a day or two."

"Perfect. Thanks, Rick. Talk soon." The call disconnected.

Rick put his phone on the desk, screen down. Despite what Ann had said, accidental drowning can happen to anybody. But most of the most common causes - alcohol, drugs, poor swimming skills - didn't apply to Mr. Post. The man lived on the water and knew all of the necessary survival skills from his boating experience. No, if it were accidental, there would be another factor involved, most likely medical: heart attack, stroke, aneurysm, seizure. Surely, the ME must have missed something.

He cracked open his laptop and opened his browser. Navigating to the Town of Nantucket's official webpage, he followed the link to the NPD and clicked on the *Contact Us* button. He found the number he was looking for, picked up his phone, and dialed.

CHAPTER EIGHT

Rick listened as the call connected. It was dead air for a few seconds before he finally heard the ringing. A confident voice answered on the third.

"This is Detective Fisch." A straightforward tone echoed down the line.

"Hi, Tuna. It's Rick Caton," he said, bracing himself for her response.

"Rick! Oh my god, you are a bolt from the blue. How long's it been? Eight years?" asked Tuna.

"Ten if you can believe it," replied Rick.

"Wow. Doesn't seem possible. How have you been? You're FBI now, right?"

"I am. Assigned out of the Boston Field Office working on financial and white-collar crimes. How are things with you? How's Ellen?" At one point, he had been rather close with Tuna's wife, often meeting her to shop the fresh produce at Bartlett's Farm after discovering their mutual love of cooking.

"We are good. Really no complaints except that the island seems to get more and more crowded every year. But my caseload stays pretty consistent. The usual: illegal drugs, B and E's, and the occasional car theft," Tuna said, trying her best not to sound bored.

Rick picked up the dryness in her tone. "No murders or interesting cases in the last few years?"

She hummed to herself, debating on whether or not to share with Rick."Well, I did work a suspicious disappearance last year. You remember Jack Reiner? The super-wealthy guy that lived out on Polpis Road?"

Rick snorted, reflecting on the few memorable moments he had of Jack. "I think so. Wasn't he a major asshole? Thought he owned the island?" One time, Rick's lawn guy complained to him that Jack had called him out to his house, at eleven p.m. on the Saturday of Memorial Day Weekend, over a 'landscaping emergency.'

"That's him. His second wife vanished a few years back. The thinking then was that she was mentally unstable and had likely run away." Tuna paused.

"Did something change?"

"Yeah," snorted Tuna. "I guess you could say that. But I'd rather tell you in person, maybe over a drink or lunch some time, if you ever come back to the island."

"That sounds interesting," said Rick. "I'll look forward to hearing how you worked it all out." He paused, unsure of where to start.

Tuna picked up on his hesitation. "What do I owe the pleasure, Rick? Is there a financial crime you are working on that involves Nantucket?"

Rick sighed. "No. I am just following up on a case you're working on for an old friend."

"Really?" exclaimed Tuna, suddenly feeling caught off guard. "Which case would that be?"

"Charles Post."

Tuna relaxed back in her chair. "Ah, okay. Were the Posts friends of your family?"

"Not really friends. They lived in a far different world than we did. But I babysat their son, Scott, and occasionally their daughter and got to know the family pretty well. They were always kind to me. For a few summers, I would crew for Mr. Post on his

Herreshoff. In fact, I was crew when he won the Opera House Cup in 2001."

"That's the annual regatta for wooden boats, isn't it?" asked Tuna. "I don't get out on the water much, I'm afraid."

"It is. And it's a big deal with the local sailors on the island. Mr. Post had a well-deserved reputation for being a great helmsman and racer. And he was also just a really nice guy, which you don't always get with someone with that wealth and status."

"Very true. I can think of several wealthy people right now who definitely don't fit that description," said Tuna, chuckling softly.

Rick smiled. "I remember dealing with them as a Community Service Officer. They always acted like they could do whatever they wanted. But Mr. Post wasn't that way. At all."

"I wish I had had a chance to meet him."

"You would have liked him."

"I'm sure. So what do you want to know about the case?" Tuna had to admit to herself she wasn't surprised that Ann had reached out to Rick given how upset she had been during their conversation.

"First, please understand that I am not questioning your skills or conclusions in any way. I'm just trying to do a favor for a sweet lady."

Tina nodded, "I understand. And no concerns here. What do you want to know?"

"From what I know of the case, it's been ruled accidental?"

"Yes. Mr. Post was fishing with his business partners. According to their statements, Mr. Post fell off the boat while urinating off the transom."

There was a brief silence on the other end of the line before Rick asked, "Was this a small boat?"

"No. It was a forty-two-foot sport fisherman."

Rick said surprised, "Were the heads not functioning?"

"No. They were. According to the owner, Sean Axmacher, the boat had two staterooms, each with a working bathroom."

"Hmm," said Rick. "That doesn't make any sense."

"Does that surprise you?"

Rick took in a breath. "Well, yes. That is so out of character for the man. I mean, he wasn't what I would call a prude, but he was a gentleman. He would have used one of the heads to relieve himself. What about his PFD? Did that not activate?"

"No. Apparently not. When he was found, the PFD was uninflated. Apparently the arming mechanism failed to trigger when he hit the water."

"So it never inflated? At all?"

"That's what we are thinking. We've sent it to a local shop for evaluation. Should know something within the next few days."

"And they are saying that he climbed on the transom to urinate? Where were they when this happened?" Rick exclaimed.

"Returning from Georges Bank. They had just entered the Great Point Rip."

What?" exclaimed Rick. "No way. I mean, I could potentially see him taking a pee off the boat if seas were calm and they were trolling or stationary. But coming through the rip? Uh uh. He knew better."

Tuna paused, thinking. "Can you think of any reason why he would have urinated then? In the rip?"

"No. No way. Whoever said that is either mistaken or lying," Rick said with conviction.

"Could it have been a mental break? Or maybe early signs of dementia? I know Mr. Post was just in his sixties, but..."

"I'd be surprised. Mrs. Post said her husband had just had his annual physical and gotten a clean bill of health from his doctor. I would have thought that if any signs of dementia or mental disease would have come up."

"His partner, Cormac, also stated he was drinking pretty heavily."

"Mr. Post? I never saw him have more than an occasional beer. Of course, that was years ago, so maybe that's changed. Did the tox confirm that?"

"Preliminary screen was positive for alcohol, but the full toxicology won't be available for a few more days."

Rick thought to himself. "Hmm. Did you think of doing an ethyl glucuronide test?"

"No reason to. I mean, all signs pointed to accidental drowning, including two eyewitness statements. The autopsy was pretty straightforward and did confirm drowning as the cause of death. His lungs were full of water. The only finding of note was a contusion on the back of his head. The ME believes it was caused when he fell off the boat - maybe his head hitting the edge of the transom. There was no evidence of anything suspicious."

"Did the ME take x-rays or any other post-mortem imaging?"

"Again, no reason to. You know how tight budgets are. We were lucky to get what we did as quickly as we did. Usually, autopsies can take several days."

Rick sighed. "I just don't know. This just doesn't feel right to me."

"Rick?"

"Yeah?"

"How long has it been since you've seen or talked to Mr. Post?" Tuna asked, feeling a little tired of getting the third degree from everyone.

"It was before I left the island after, you know, I got fired."

"So, ten years? More?" asked Tuna.

"What's your point?"

"People change. Especially as they grow older. I've seen it before. They start to have a sense of their own mortality and maybe want to change things up. Take more risks. Drink more beer. Chase young women."

"That is not the Charles Post I know!" Rick said adamantly.

Tuna's voice was calm and reassuring. "I know. But I think you need to accept that the man likely has changed since you last saw him. And I'm sure his wife, Mrs. Post, either didn't see that side of him or refused to accept it. The human mind can play terrible tricks on us, especially as we get older."

Rick sighed. "I'm sure you are right. It's just not easy to accept. Mr. Post was such a presence growing up. To me, he was a force of nature. And now I need to accept that he died taking a piss off the back of a boat? It just seems so sad. So wrong."

"I understand your feelings, Rick. I really do."

"Thanks, Tuna. I appreciate your time and candor. I'll need to call Mrs. Post. Would you be okay with me sharing our conversation with her?"

"Of course! And please pass along my thoughts as well. I don't think she likes me very much, and the findings of the investigation have been very difficult for her to hear."

"I will. And thanks, again."

"My pleasure. It was great hearing from you. Let's stay in touch, okay? I don't want it to be another ten years and another death until we talk again."

Rick smiled wanly. "Will do. Take care of yourself and say hi to Ellen for me."

"Sure thing."

Rick placed the phone on his desk. He was dreading the call to Mrs. Post. He had hoped to have something that might bring solace to her, but the discussion with Tuna negated that possibility. No matter how he framed it, it was going to be received as bad news.

Maybe this would be better to handle in person. The thought excited him but also stirred up emotions he thought he had buried for good.

He pulled up his calendar and scanned the commitments for the week. Given the upcoming trip to Quantico he had already started clearing appointments. He hadn't been back on the island in years, and the thought of returning made him excited and nervous at the same time. He had tried to banish Nantucket from his thoughts: the fond memories of growing up, the natural beauty, the lovely homes, the friends, lovers, and acquaintances, the incident, the firing, the embarrassment. He had left the island with his tail between his legs and hadn't looked back. But for the first time since that shameful day, he wanted to see the island again. Maybe it was finally time to go.

He launched his browser and looked up the island ferry schedule for Tuesday to confirm that the 6:00 a.m. high speed was still an option. Informally, it was known as the "Contractors Express," as it was usually filled with carpenters, plumbers, electricians, and other tradespeople heading to the island for a day of work. That would put him on the island by seven-thirty, leaving nearly the entire day to visit Mrs. Post and do a little sightseeing. Booking the return trip on the 6:00 p.m. boat should have him back in Cambridge by nine if traffic and weather cooperated.

His trip confirmed; he now just had to clear things with his boss. He got up from his desk and walked down the hall. Hanna was staring intently at her screen and didn't hear his approach. He tapped softly on the frame.

"Hanna?"

She looked up from her screen. "Please don't tell me that you have found some reason not to go next week."

Rick smiled. "No. I'm full steam ahead with those plans. But I do have a favor."

"Sure. What's up?" She looked at him expectantly.

"I know it's a bit last minute, but can I take the day tomorrow?"

"Okay," she said, drawing out the word into three syllables. "Why?"

"I've got to handle something on Nantucket. For an old friend."

She sat up. "Why the hell would you want to go back there after the way you were treated?"

Rick stood in front of her desk, his hands clenched in front of him. For some reason, he was nervous, like he was a child asking a difficult parent for permission to go play at a friend's house.

"A lot of time has passed. Hell, my ex-wife doesn't even live there anymore. She moved off island a few years ago."

Hanna paused, contemplating her words. "I know, but has anything changed at the NPD?"

He looked down at his feet, trying to understand the nerves he was feeling. Was he really that worried about what Hanna would say? Or was he simply worried about returning to Nantucket and confronting the ghosts of his past? Or was it something else, something in between?

He looked up at his boss. "Actually, there is new leadership in the department. I don't know her, but maybe she will change that culture. Anyway, I think it's time to go back. I grew up there, after all, and I can't let one isolated event dictate my life like it has."

Hanna smiled softly. "I totally understand. I'm not going to go all therapist on you, but please take care of yourself. Listen to that inner voice. If you feel like things are going off the rails then please evac the scene as quickly as possible."

Rick returned the smile. "I will. Promise. And I'll be back here on Wednesday to finish wrapping things up before I head to Quantico."

She nodded, trusting him. "I'll see you then."

He turned to leave the office and paused. He looked back at Hanna. "Thanks, boss. I really appreciate this."

Hanna nodded and returned her eyes to the monitor on her desk.

CHAPTER NINE

Friday Afternoon

Off Georges Bank, 70 miles east of Nantucket

Cormac slipped his sunglasses down over his eyes and scanned the rod tips. Still, nothing was happening. They were floating atop one of the greatest concentrations of marine life on the planet, and not one damn fish had any interest in their bait. He sighed.

Charles returned from the cabin with a seltzer. He popped the top and took a long drink. "Do you guys mind if we talk shop? I know we usually try to keep these trips free of business, but given there are no fish…"

"Sure," said Sean. "What's on your mind?"

"I've gotten calls from a few of the investors following our third quarter results. They are pretty happy with their statements, as you can imagine."

Sean smiled. "I'm so glad. Clearly, it's confirmation of the new strategies we implemented last year. If this continues, then we'll have our best year ever."

Charles did not share Sean's excitement. "Yes. But given the current economic conditions and the downturn for the markets in general, how are we delivering the returns we are?"

Sean looked at him curiously. "As I said, Charles, it's confirmation of the new investing strategy we agreed to last year. If you recall, we decided to focus investments in two new key areas. High-quality commercial; think high-tech warehouses and fulfillment in the Southeast. And alternative investments, namely private lending within the technology space. Both have done exceedingly well, thank you very much."

Charles played with the pop tab on his seltzer. "I'm glad the new strategy is working out. But it really doesn't fully explain our returns, does it?"

Cormac sighed, took his eyes off the rod tips and turned in the fighting chair to look at Charles. "Why the concern, Charles? Aren't your clients happy with how we are managing their money?"

Charles forced a smile. "Of course they are. Most of them are ecstatic. But a few are understandably curious. They are asking me how we are doing it. How are we bucking the trend when other firms are barely treading water? I'd like to be able to answer their questions."

Cormac looked at Sean and then turned back to Charles. "I would simply say that we have our own secret weapon in this guy right here," he motioned to Sean. "His strategy has been nothing short of brilliant."

Charles looked down and continued playing with the top of the seltzer can. "Can you assure me that everything we are doing is one hundred percent above board?"

Cormac looked shocked. "What the hell are you asking Charles?"

He stopped fingering the top of his seltzer but didn't look up. He said softly, "What is Eel Point Amusements?"

Cormac stiffened and stole a glance at Sean, who looked as if he had just seen a ghost.

"What?" asked Cormac, acting surprised.

"Eel Point Amusements. I found a spreadsheet on the server with that name but didn't see them listed in any of our funds.

Based on the results in that spreadsheet, they appear to be the one investment we are managing that is doing exceptionally well." Charles finally looked up and glanced at both of them. "All the others? From what I can see, they are either losing money or barely breaking even. What the hell is going on?"

Cormac could tell Charles was getting more upset. In a calm voice, he said, "Why does it matter, Charles? Overall, we are delivering great returns for our investors. And thanks to Sean's strategy, we have some funds that do well when others don't."

"Bullshit." Charles finally made eye contact with Cormac, determined to get an actual answer.

"Bullshit?" asked Cormac, getting angry.

Sean stood quietly, pale, watching the discussion between his two friends and partners.

"Yes, bullshit," said Charles. "From what I can see, there is something not right about Eel Point. It's not in 'quality commercial' or 'alternative' investments." Charles used air quotes to highlight his comment. "What is it?"

Cormac looked at Charles condescendingly. "Why don't you leave the financials and reporting to me and the investment strategy to Sean? Focus on the investors. Relish in the fact that we are delivering great results and making them a lot of money."

Charles let out a long sigh. "So what you are telling me is to ignore my gut, swallow my concerns, and go slap backs and press the flesh as if everything is great?"

"In short, yes. Because it is. Great, I mean," said Cormac, ready to be done with the conversation.

Charles shook his head, glancing back down. "I'm sorry. I don't believe you, Cormac. How long have I known you and Sean? Forty-four years? I can tell when you are lying to me. You have that same little twitch in your cheek as you did when we played liar's poker on Wall Street. So tell me," he said, turning to Sean. "Or you tell me. What the hell is going on?"

Cormac looked at Sean, concerned. Sean gave a subtle nod and a shrug of his shoulders. Cormac got up out of the chair and sat on the transom facing Charles. "We wanted to keep you out of it."

"Out of what?" said Charles concerned, his voice rising. He hadn't missed the silent exchange between his partners and felt his gut clench, knowing he was on a precipice of something he couldn't go back on.

Sean sighed and joined Cormac on the transom. "It was my strategy, really, that started it all."

"What are you saying?" Charles looked at both of them.

Sean continued, "The new strategy we aligned on last year turned out to be a loser. The one component I hadn't planned on was the rapid increase in rates from the Fed. As a result, a lot of our bets on commercial property went south." He sighed, looking at Cormac. "We were holding paper with a two or three percent rate while paying seven. To make matters worse, several of our alternative investments didn't pan out."

"Didn't pan out?" asked Charles, getting angry learning that his lifelong friends had clearly been lying to him. And for a while.

Cormac backed up Sean. "This wasn't the fault of any one person or strategy. We are just victims of really bad timing."

Charles huffed and threw his arms out. "Bad timing? Really? Okay, I get that. We've had bad years before and managed our way through them. But now we are reporting double-digit gains, some of our highest returns ever. If things truly went south with the new strategy, then how in hell are we doing that?"

"That's the beauty of Eel Point," said Cormac.

CHAPTER TEN

Rick's phone blared a quacking duck to wake him at 4:00 a.m. He quickly shut off the annoying alarm and rolled out of bed. He sat on the edge, rubbing his eyes and preparing for the long day ahead. Was this really a good idea? He briefly entertained the thought of slipping back under the covers and going back to sleep. With the day off, he could enjoy a nice, lazy day. Grab some breakfast at Mamela's, maybe lunch at Cambridge Brewing Company, a nice nap and then finish with dinner at Plank. It sounded wonderful and certainly more enjoyable than confirming Mrs. Post's worst fears about her husband and sharing what little he had found.

The responsible side of him gradually beat back the devil on his shoulder, and he made his way into the bathroom to get ready. Showered and shaved, he had retrieved his car from the nearby garage and was heading southbound on I-93 by 4:30. Opposing traffic was already building even with the early hour, but fortunately, he was going against rush hour and expected to have it relatively easy for the 75 mile drive down to Hyannis. He set the cruise at 80.

Hyannis was little changed even though he hadn't been there in years. He navigated his way to the parking lot on Main Street and pulled the Charger into the first spot he found. It was a ten-minute walk to the Hy-Line terminal, and by 6:15, he was already boarding the ferry in line with dozens of contractors, many of them carrying canvas sacks of tools. With the recent Labor Day weekend, he was not surprised to see how few tourists were on his boat. Few vacationers would want to be on the water so early in the morning.

The air was cool, with an early hint of fall as the mooring lines were released, and the captain slowly backed the vessel out of the berth. He deftly pivoted the boat around and pointed the bow towards the main channel. Rick, preferring the fresh air, had found a spot outside on the top level. From his vantage point, he could see the busy harbor spread out in front of him. Several fishing boats were preparing to set out, and the crews at the Steamship Authority were loading the early car ferry. Still in the height of the summer season - at least for another week - the marina was full of personal boats ranging from small daysailers to a few mega yachts.

Rick took a deep breath of the salt-tinged air and sighed. Once again, his anxiety crept in, and he fought hard to push it down. Forcing some positive self-talk, Rick gained control of his nerves and tried to relax and enjoy the hour-long trip to Nantucket. Born and raised on a small island thirty miles to sea, he was instilled with a love of the water and the sheer beauty of marine nature.

The vessel cleared the jetties at Kalmas Park, and the captain opened the throttles. Rick was always amazed at how quickly a large boat could reach its 35 MPH cruising speed. The ocean was calm with a gentle swell. Despite his anxiety about the day ahead, the early morning start, the bright sun on his face, and the gentle rocking of the boat conspired to put Rick to sleep.

He awoke with a start as the boat rapidly decelerated as it entered Nantucket Harbor a little under an hour later. Rick stood, yawned, stretched, and made his way to the rail. Nantucket had most definitely changed since he had last been here over a decade before. There were more houses, more boats and certainly many more people than when he lived and worked here full time. But the sheer natural beauty remained. The sun glinted off the water as they rounded Brant Point and Rick could see the historic downtown, the twin steeples at the United Methodist and Unitarian churches, and make out the wind turbine at the high school. He was home. And his belly started to gnaw with dread.

The boat made its way to the wharf and eased up the dock. The crew quickly tied the mooring lines and rolled in the catwalk to disembark passengers. Just a few minutes after rounding Brant Point, the doors opened, and the vessel disgorged people at an alarming rate, like a drunk vomiting up his breakfast after an all-night bender. In no rush to start his day, Rick stood by the rail and watched as the town absorbed the people. A gull cried out above him as a uniformed crewman started sweeping the upper deck and preparing the ship for the return voyage. Rick nodded to the young man and made his way down the stairs and off the boat.

A jolt of electricity spiked through his body as his feet touched Nantucket for the first time in years. Looking around he saw how truly little things had changed in his time gone. There were a couple of new stores but most of the old stalwarts were still there, their doors not yet open with the early hour. In the harbor he saw the same charter fishing boats that ran when he was younger. And, of course, the friendship sloop *Endeavor* was ready to take him on a sunset cruise just as it had fifteen years ago when he had asked his then-girlfriend to marry him. Looking back, that had been the start of the end of his life on Nantucket.

Pushing those black memories aside, he made his way down Straight Wharf to Main Street. As always, a line of cabs was sitting just outside the Club Car. He went to the first in the line and hopped in.

"Where to my friend?" asked a young man with a Jamaican accent.

"Downy Flake restaurant, please," responded Rick. He thought it best to start his day with a good breakfast, and this, by far, was the best he remembered on the island. The driver made his way over the cobblestones paving Main Street, the suspension of the old minivan creaking and groaning all the way. It seemed like an hour before he reached Orange Street, just a block away. Finally clear of the cobbles and crowds, the driver made quick work of the remaining trip and dropped him off at the restaurant just a few minutes later.

After a breakfast of eggs and bacon, toast made with the local Portuguese bread, and one of the restaurant's name-sake doughnuts, Rick could delay his day no longer. He pulled out his phone and mapped the route to the Post's house. He knew the way by heart. The Posts lived in a beautiful 19th-century whaling captain's home on Monomoy Road but wanted to confirm the distance. At just under 2 miles, he felt it would be the perfect light exercise to complement his morning.

A vivid blue sky above him and temperatures in the sixties proved perfect walking weather. Rick kept up a quick pace and, dodging lots of traffic on Monomoy, arrived at the Post driveway thirty minutes later. The home, known as Sea View, was set back from the street and protected by tall, manicured privet hedges bisected only by an opening for the gravel drive. The stones crunching under his feet, Rick made his way past the carriage house, the small gardening shed, and up to the front door. It was painted a deep crimson red and sported a brass knocker in the shape of a whale fluke. Nervously, Rick pulled the whale's tail back and let the hammer strike home.

As he waited, he thought maybe he should have called ahead to let Mrs. Post know that he was on his way. But he also knew that if he had, he probably would have shared his findings—or lack of them—and chickened out of the whole plan to come to the island.

He was about to knock again when he heard footsteps echoing through the hall. The big door swung open, and a beautiful, vaguely familiar woman, her eyes red and swollen, appeared at the door.

"Felicity?" asked Rick, surprised. The last time he had seen the Post's daughter was before she had gone off to college. She was three years younger than her brother and, at the time, was invisible to Rick.

"Yes," she said, warily. She sniffled and looked at Rick suspiciously.

He smiled and held out his hand. "Rick. Rick Caton. Don't you remember me? I used to babysit you and your brother Scott."

Her face relaxed in remembrance, and she shook his hand. Rick noted how soft her hand felt. "I'm sorry. I didn't recognize you."

He smiled softly again. "It's okay. I was so sorry to hear about your dad. He was such a good guy. Always so nice to me."

"Thank you," she said and sniffled. She raised a tissue and wiped her nose.

"Is your mom here? She asked me to look into some things about your dad, and I wanted to update her." Rick looked around, noting how empty the house felt from the one he had been in as a teenager.

Felicity burst out in fresh tears and sobbed uncontrollably.

Rick reached out to touch her shoulder. Felicity stepped forward and put her head on Rick's chest. Instinctively, Rick put his arms around her and felt her body shake from the sobs. After a minute, Felicity pulled back and wiped her eyes.

Haltingly, she said, "My mom. She's dead."

"What?" he exclaimed, feeling his heart sink.

"She died in a car accident last night," Felicity said, struggling to compose herself.

"Oh my god, Felicity. What happened?" He rubbed her arms, noting that she was clearly in shock. Walking her over to the couch, he grabbed a blanket and wrapped it around her shoulders before sitting down in the armchair next to her

She sniffled and wiped her nose. "She was coming back from a friend's in Quidnet. The police said that a deer must have jumped out in front of her, she veered, and then…," her voice trailed off, replaced by crying.

Rick was stunned. First, Mr. Post, and now Mrs. Post? What are the odds that a married couple would suffer fatal accidents independently of each other in just a matter of days?

"I am so sorry, Felicity. I really am. Is there anything I can do?"

Felicity shook her head. "No," she said. "Oh, I don't know." She looked out the window towards the harbor.

Giving her a moment to compose herself, he looked down the hall, past the central staircase, through the expansive windows of the family room to the green yard and harbor out beyond. He remembered the amazing views from his days of babysitting.

He sighed and turned back to her. "I am so shocked to hear about your mom. I had just talked to her yesterday."

Felicity nodded. "Me too. I guess I should be thankful that I was able to spend a couple of days with her. She called me Saturday afternoon to tell me about Dad. I live in Providence now, so it was easy for me to get over here quickly." She paused, lost in thought.

"I'm glad for that. I'm sure she appreciated having you home."

"We had just started to go through Dad's things yesterday. I mean the paperwork, you know. The will. Last wishes. She didn't want to do it on her own."

Rick winced, unable to truly understand how difficult this must be for her. Both of his parents were happy and healthy living in Florida and having the time of their lives in retirement. "Can't say that I blame her. Did you find anything unexpected?"

"My dad was very much a perfectionist. Everything was in the safe, nicely organized. He even left a letter for my mom with instructions on what to do, who to call. That sort of thing. So no, we found nothing out of the ordinary."

Shuffling forward to put his hand on her knee comfortingly, he asked. "Have you told Scott? About your mom?" he asked.

She nodded as her tears welled up. She played with the tissue in her hands. "Finally. He's been in Asia on a business trip and has been trying to get back since he got the news about Dad. I caught him in San Francisco this morning. He took a red-eye from Tokyo and was waiting for a midday flight to Denver," she said and started crying again. Rick reached out and placed his arm around her.

"Thank you," she said.

Rick glanced down at the time on his phone. "When do you think he'll get here?"

She shrugged. "With luck, maybe late tonight. Worst case tomorrow."

Rick paused, not wanting to overwhelm her with questions but still wanting to help. "What about the services for Mr. Post? Will he be here in time?" he asked cautiously.

She laughed through her tears. "You know how Dad was - he made it pretty clear that he did not want a funeral. His letter to Mom stated that we wanted to be cremated and his ashes spread over Nantucket harbor. He didn't even want a memorial service."

"That sounds like him. Can I make you some coffee? Or maybe some breakfast?"

She smiled sadly. "Thanks. But I'm not hungry. Maybe some coffee though."

"Of course." He nodded and squeezed her knee before standing.

Rick made his way to the kitchen and saw that little had changed since he was last in the house. He was able to find the coffee quickly and had the machine brewing in minutes. He opened a cabinet and pulled out a couple of mugs. Both of them featured the flag of the Wharf Rat Club, a blue and white triangular pennant with a well-dressed rat holding a cane and smoking a pipe. He had no idea that Mr. Post had been a member of the eclectic club. Rick grabbed some creamer from the refrigerator and poured two cups.

Felicity had taken a seat at the long trestle table in the breakfast room, and Rick joined her. The table was set in a bay of windows on the north side of the house. Sea View sat on the edge of the marsh that bordered the harbor and, as its name implies, featured wonderful views of the harbor and, farther out, Nantucket Sound. Rick had a clear view of Brant Point, the car ferry rounding the small lighthouse making its return trip to Hyannis. Closer to him, a small fleet of sailing dinghies were racing, the canvas of each sporting a different color of the rainbow. He couldn't see their faces, but given the gorgeous day, he imagined the sailors were having a wonderful time.

The beauty of the view was in sharp contrast to the pain in the house.

Felicity took a sip of her coffee and let out a sigh. "So what were you going to share with her?"

"I'm sorry. What?"

"You said you had come here to update my mom on something."

Felicity had turned to look at him, and he briefly paused, not remembering how striking her eyes had been. "Oh, right. Sorry." Rick put his coffee down. "She asked me to look into your father's drowning. She didn't believe it could have happened the way it has been described."

"She's right," said Felicity. "No way Dad would do anything like that. My mom and I both think something is not right with this." She shook her head and repeated. "There is no way Dad would do that."

He nodded. "I know. I sailed with him for a few summers. But things happen. People change. They get older. Forgetful. Less risk averse."

"No way. Not with Dad. Something is not right about his death," she said, as adamant as her mother had been.

Rick reached over and placed his hand on hers. He said gently, "I know this must be so hard, especially with your mom. But I've looked at the case; I talked with the lead detective. It all points to the same conclusion: that it was an accident."

"Respectfully Rick, I knew him better than you. Dad would not behave like they say he did. I just don't believe it, and neither did my mom. He hasn't changed. I had dinner with him last month when he was over for a meeting. He is the same man he has always been." She looked at him.

"I know, but it could have been a combination of things that led to that behavior. He had been drinking a bit, according to the tox reports. And maybe he had a medical issue, a stroke or aneurysm, that impacted his behavior. I've seen it before." He tried to squeeze her hand, but she took it away and shook her head.

She looked at him skeptically through tear filled eyes.

He sat back and paused before continuing. "It was an accident. Plain and simple. We'll never know what caused him to do what he did. But I truly believe it was accidental."

She nodded slowly. "I'm sure you're right. I hadn't thought of what a stroke might have done to him. I just wish..." She looked out towards the harbor, fighting back the tears.

Rick stood. "I'm just so sorry for your losses. I have such fond memories of your mom and dad. They were great people who always treated me as family. I never forgot that."

She tried to smile at him. "They thought highly of you as well. I know my mom was especially pleased when she heard you had joined the FBI. Especially after all that nasty business."

"You know about that," Rick asked hesitantly.

She shrugged. "Just what my mom told me. Sounded like you weren't treated very fairly. Of course, I really had no idea who she was talking about. I have only very vague memories of you when I was young."

Rick smiled. "I remember you in pigtails with a big gap in your smile when you lost your two front teeth."

Felicity smiled at the memory. "I just remember being very jealous that Scott would get horsey rides on your back. You thought I was too young."

They were both quiet as each recollected those times so many years before. It was Rick that broke the silence. "I think I should be going." Opening his wallet, he pulled out a business card and handed it to Felicity. "Please call me if you or Scott need anything. I'm heading back to Boston tonight but can easily come back if you guys need me."

Felicity took the card. "Thank you." She stood up and embraced him. "I appreciate your concern and will certainly let you know if you can help in any way."

She led him down the hall, where she opened the front door. He paused and turned. "Despite the circumstances, it was good to see you." He leaned over and pecked her cheek. Smiling softly, he walked out the door, his feet crunching in the gravel.

"Rick?" She asked from behind him. He turned, seeing her framed in the doorway, the light behind her catching her hair. "Call me Fel. Felicity makes me feel like I'm getting caught sneaking out to a beach party by my parents." She smiled bittersweetly at the memory.

"Sure. It was great seeing you again, Fel."

She closed the door softly, leaned against the frame, and wept.

CHAPTER ELEVEN

Rick walked down the driveway, still feeling shocked upon hearing about Ann's death. Even with all of his years in law enforcement, he never was able to adjust to the sudden disappearance of someone around him through death. One minute, he is talking to Ann and hearing her concerns about her husband's drowning. The next day, she is gone, and Rick will never be able to report back to her what he had found out.

He continued down Monomoy dodging traffic along the narrow road. There wasn't a sidewalk or bike path so he was walking against traffic with eyes up and looking for drivers texting on their phones or simply not paying attention. He quickly made it to Milestone Road and a few hundred yards later discovered a new park just off the rotary. Curious, he followed the road into the parking lot and came upon an expansive, rolling space with a couple of paths meandering through the grass. He followed one of the paths and soon found himself in an open space with a number of picnic tables and a commanding view of Nantucket Harbor.

Rick eased his leg over the bench and sat down at one of the tables. Looking out over the harbor, he could make out a number of megayachts, some even bigger than the ferry he had come in on a few hours earlier. One even looked like it had a helicopter sitting on the top deck. Yes, Nantucket had certainly changed. He remembered a number of big boats growing up, but they seemed built with purpose - like sailing or sports fishing. These boats? They just seemed like flagrant displays of ridiculous money. How the hell did people even afford these?

His phone dinged. He pulled it from his pants pocket and looked at the screen. It was a text from his boss, Hanna, checking in to see how he was doing.

How's ACK? You doing ok?

Smiling, Rick tapped out a quick reply.

Yep. All good here. :-)

He watched bubbles on the screen followed by another ding.

He thought of Hanna and was grateful to have her as his boss. She was known throughout the office as a tough-as-nails agent with a well-deserved reputation for taking down hardened criminals. Those who didn't know her suspected she was a cold and demanding boss. Rick had been working with Hanna for several years now, and yes, she was tough, but she also cared deeply for her people. He had only wished she - or someone like her - had been her superior at NPD. Maybe his life would be different now.

Thinking of the NPD, he pulled up the recent calls on his phone and tapped. The recipient picked up almost immediately.

"What, has it been ten years already?" joked Tuna. "And please tell me it's not another body."

Rick found it hard to laugh. "Morning, Tuna. Sorry to say it is. About another body I mean."

She sobered immediately. "I'm sorry, Rick. Just trying to be funny. What happened?"

"Mrs. Post. Charles' wife, Ann. Apparently she died in a car accident last night."

"That was her?" exclaimed Tuna. "I had heard there was a fatal accident on Polpis Road but thought it was probably just one of the rollover crashes we seem to get every summer."

"That was her. I talked to her daughter this morning. Apparently, she was coming back from a friend's at Quidnet. Swerved to miss a deer. Went into a tree." Rick watched as a small fleet of sailboats, each sporting a different color sail, crossed the harbor in front of him.

"That's not unheard of - especially given all the deer we have on the island now. I am so sorry to hear that. She seemed like a nice lady," Tuna remarked, still surprised.

"She was. I know she was really upset about her husband's death. Maybe that distracted her."

"Possible. But still awful. First Mr. Post and now his wife? Must be hell for the kids. There are two, right?"

"Yes, Scott and a daughter, Fel. Felicity." Rick felt tense, not quite understanding how the day had led to so much emotion and stress.

Tuna let out a deep sigh, all too familiar with breaking bad news to family. She knew it never got easier. "Well, please pass along my condolences if you talk to them."

"I will," Rick paused. "I do have a favor to ask."

"Sure," Tuna said, hesitantly.

"Would you mind confirming the details of the accident for me? Maybe talk with the investigating officer and get the final report? I'd do it, but as you remember, the NPD and I aren't on the best of terms."

"Happy to. Do you suspect something?" Tuna asked curiously.

"No. It just seems weird to me. First Charles drowns pissing off the back of a boat, something his family - and me as well - swear up and down that he would never do. Then a few days later his wife dies in a car accident. Two unrelated accidental deaths of a happy and prosperous couple just days apart. It's probably a coincidence but I don't believe in coincidences."

Tuna laughed softly, knowing how those in law enforcement felt about coincidences. "I'm happy to get the details. It's definitely unusual but I'm sure it's nothing. If it was anywhere else, maybe, but nothing like this ever happens on Nantucket."

"Thanks, Tuna. I appreciate it. You have plans this afternoon?" Rick stood up, stretching.

"No, my calendar is pretty open at the moment."

"Do you want to meet for an early dinner? I'm on the six o'clock Hy-Line back to Hyannis but would love to meet up beforehand."

"What? You're on the island? Why the hell didn't you tell me?" she replied, shocked.

"It was a last minute thing. I was going to call Mrs. Post with my findings about her husband and thought it would be better to do it face-to-face. That's when I found out she had died as well, from her daughter, Felicity."

Tuna understood. "I would love to meet. Shall we say four at the the Brotherhood? They have a nice patio where we can sit. It will also be a bit more private."

"Perfect. I'll see you then."

"Look forward to it," said Tuna and ended the call.

Rick pocketed his phone and looked out over the harbor. The sheer amount of wealth floating on the water amazed him. Where did all the money come from? He thought about the couple he had caught defrauding Sharefield Biotech and wondered if their aspirations included a large boat to go along with their multi-million dollar condo. He smiled at the thought.

His stomach rumbled. Rick glanced at his watch and realized it was already past noon. He was close to one of his favorite sandwich shops, which he frequented as a cop, and was hopeful it was still in business. He stood, walked back down the path, and followed Orange Street down to Henry J's. He was happy to see it seemed to be doing well and walked up to the window to place his order, an Italian grinder, no olives with plenty of oil and vinegar. He paired that with some sea salt and vinegar kettle chips and a water. He slid over a twenty and placed the change in the tip jar.

He stood back to wait for the order when he heard a voice behind him.

"Rick Caton? Is that really you?" said in a deep baritone.

He turned and stared at a tall, trim, Black man. "Noah?"

Noah smiled broadly and extended his hand. Rick grasped it and was immediately pulled into a warm embrace. Noah Coffin had been a classmate at Nantucket High School and in the same rookie class with him at the police department.

"Man it is good to see you. It has been ages," said Noah, stepping back and looking at Rick.

"And you as well." Nodding at the uniform and the three chevron patch on his upper arm. "I see you are still with NPD. Sergeant?"

"Yes sir. I made sergeant two years ago."

"Sergeant Noah Coffin? That has a nice ring to it. Glad that you are doing well."

Noah's tone shifted. "Thanks. But Honestly it should be you with this patch. You were such a good cop. They really did you dirty."

"I won't argue that but it is all water under the bridge. I'm in Boston now, with the Feds." Rick felt a sense of pride that he hadn't let what had happened deter him from a good future.

"FBI?" Noah said, clearly impressed.

Rick nodded. "Yes. I focus mainly on white collar crime. Fraud, extortion, that kind of thing."

"You were always good with numbers," said Noah. He lightly punched Rick's arm and grinned. "Man, it is good to see you. So what are you doing here? Thinking of returning to our lovely community?"

Rick smiled. "No. Just here for the day. I was looking into the Charles Post drowning for the family. I was pretty close to them. His wife asked that I review the findings and give her my thoughts."

"I heard about that. Something going down?" Noah raised an eyebrow at him.

"No, not at all. Everything points to it being accidental. But then I get here and find out Mrs. Post was killed in a car accident."

Noah's eyes widened in recognition. "That was her? The fatality on Polpis last night?" He grimaced.

"Sadly, yes. It's been a real shock to the family. And to me as well. I spent a lot of time with the Posts growing up."

"I'm sorry to hear that." His eyes darted to the window, realizing it was his turn. "Hang on, let me get my order in."

"Sure." Rick stepped back and let Noah approach the window. He ordered a roast beef and cheddar grinder, a bag of nachos, and a diet soda.

"Some things never change," said Rick, fondly.

Noah smiled. "I am most certainly a man who likes routine. So are you going to be around for a while? I'd love to have you over for dinner. And I know Jess would love to see you." Jess had been the dispatch supervisor at the NPD during Rick's time and had also been a good friend.

"I wish. But heading back to Boston tonight."

"Rick?" a young voice called out. An arm extended from the window holding a small white bag and a bottle of water. He slipped by Noah to grab his order.

"Any plans on another trip?" asked Noah hopefully.

"No, no reason to. To be honest I wasn't even planning on being here today. Brings back some bad memories." Rick shifted, uncomfortable.

"Yeah, I understand that. Where are you gonna' eat that?" Noah said, pointing at Rick's lunch.

"Actually I discovered this new park just down the street by the rotary. Has some amazing views of the harbor."

"You mean Creeks Preserve," Noah said purposefully.

"Is that the name? It is beautiful."

"It is. And we are so thankful for the families that made it happen selling the acreage to the Land Bank for a fraction of what they could have gotten for it on the open market. I know many developers were chomping at the bit to get a hold of it, but now it is protected and open to everyone. It really is a little jewel."

"Nice to see that the community spirit is alive and well," said Rick. "Looking at those boats in the harbor and all of the huge houses, you'd think that we'd have lost that."

"Thankfully, no. There is still a large percentage of people here who love Nantucket for its beauty, isolation, and community."

"Noah!" His order was ready.

Noah grabbed his food and looked at Rick. "How about we go grab a seat at one of the picnic tables at Creeks Preserve and have lunch together?"

"That sounds great, Noah. I'd love to get caught up."

They made their way back to the park and found one of the picnic tables free. They took opposing sides, opened their bags and started eating.

Through a half chewed bite, Rick asked, "How is the department these days?"

Noah replied through a small puff of crumbs. "It's good. I don't think you'd recognize it. The leadership from your time? All gone. We have a new Chief now. She's a good cop and a great leader."

"That's good to hear."

"I think they would welcome you back if you were interested," said Noah. "They know you were not treated fairly. And that you were a good cop."

Rick looked out over the harbor. "You know, five years ago I might have considered it. But now? I'm really happy with my career. I enjoy the work and have a great team around me."

"I'm happy to hear that. Disappointed, but happy."

Noah's radio crackled. He pulled it from his belt and listened for a few moments. "Ten four. On my way."

"Gotta' go?"

"Yeah. Looks like we have a wealthy seasonal resident who is upset about being pulled over for speeding in a school zone. They are demanding to talk to the boss," said Noah, using air quotes.

Rick chuckled. "I see that hasn't changed. Rich people behaving badly and then complaining when they get caught."

Noah smiled. "It was really good to see you, RC."

"You too, Noah, " he said, pulling out his wallet. "Here's my card. Give me a call. Drop me an email. Or pop by next time you are on the mainland."

"Sounds good. Safe travels," said Noah. He turned and hustled quickly down the pathway.

Rick watched him go and then turned his attention to the harbor. With all of the money on display, he wondered if it was all earned legitimately.

Might be kind of fun to investigate some of these people.

CHAPTER TWELVE

He killed the next few hours walking through town. From his years as a Community Service Officer he got to know a lot of the downtown shops and store owners and was pleasantly surprised to see that not too much had changed. There were a few new restaurants, and one of the two pharmacies on Main Street was now a jewelry store, but the overall space was little different than when he was last here ten years ago.

He stopped by the Hub for an iced coffee and then settled in on one of the green benches that lined Main Street. He always enjoyed people-watching, and this vantage point provided an excellent opportunity to see a wide variety of subjects. Visiting day trippers over from the Cape stood out in their t-shirts and sandals. Rick chuckled to watch a trio of overdressed young women pulling their luggage while they tried to navigate the brick sidewalk and cobblestones in high-heeled shoes more appropriate for a night in New York City. He recognized a few locals and even had a couple of head nods directed his way.

Glancing at his watch, Rick was surprised to see it was nearly time to meet Tuna. He finished his coffee in one long swallow, stood and stretched, and threw his empty cup into the recycling bin. He took a long look down Main Street, thinking it might be the last time he would ever see it. Then, he turned and walked down Federal Street toward the Brotherhood.

The familiar sign still hung above the door, slowly swinging back and forth, creaking in a light breeze. A hostess at a lectern directed him down the side of the building to the partially covered patio area. He saw Tuna already seated at a corner table and walked quickly toward her. Seeing him, she stood, smiled broadly, and gave him a big hug.

"It is so good to see you."

"And you, Tuna," he said, noting the crows feet and laugh lines that hadn't been there ten years ago.

Rick looked around. "This is really interesting. What I remember about the Brotherhood was that it was situated below grade, almost a basement. And dark. Kind of felt like you were in the hold of a whaling ship. It was such a cool vibe."

"That's still there, of course," said Tuna, pointing to the old colonial structure next to them. "But they really needed to expand. This opened not long after you left."

"Nice."

A server approached their table and poured a couple of waters. After ordering their drinks, Rick picked up the menu and perused the options. "A lot more choices today than I remember. I'm hoping they still have their famous burger."

"Absolutely," said Tuna. "Best on the island."

"Sold," said Rick and put his menu down.

Tuna did the same and looked intently at him. "So tell me what you've been up to. How are you doing?"

"I'm doing well. Those first few years were tough, you know, after, but joining the FBI was the best decision I could have made."

She smiled encouragingly. "I'm so glad for you. You're in the Boston office? And I think I remember you said you were in financial crimes?"

"Yes. Living in Cambridge. Traffic is a major pain, but it's such a great town. And the work is interesting."

"I bet." She smiled slyly. "Have you settled down at all?"

"No. I've dated a bit, but to be honest, I'm still a bit gun shy."

"Can't say I blame you there," said Tuna. "After what you went through."

They both sat quietly, lost in memories for a moment. The server arrived, disrupting the reflection. "Are we ready to order?"

Tuna looked at Rick, who nodded. She turned to the waitress. "I'll just have the Cobb salad with the ranch dressing," she paused and smiled, "and some extra dressing on the side, please?"

The waitress grinned and jotted on her order pad. "And you, sir?"

"Brotherhood burger, please. Medium with the curly fries."

She grabbed the menus. "I'll get that right in."

Rick watched her leave and turned to Tuna. "Enough about me. How are things with you?"

Tuna took a drink of water. "Honestly, I can't complain. We are very lucky. Ellen is doing well and is still working at Cottage Hospital as a grief counselor. My career is stable and interesting."

"Kids?"

Tuna smiled sadly. "No. We decided not to adopt. But we do have two dogs, both rescues. Blue is a lab mix, and Striper is a Jack Russell."

"Love the names! I guess you two are still fishing a lot?"

"A couple of times a week, if not more."

Rick toyed with his glass. "I would love a dog, but realistically, I'm not sure it would work."

Tuna nodded. "So how has it been to be back on the island?"

"Aside from the awful news about Mrs. Post, things have been okay. Better than I expected, really. I ran into Noah Coffin at

Henry J's. It was good to see him and hear that the NPD has changed."

"The department is in good hands. I don't think you'd recognize it."

"That's what Noah said. He also thought they would take me back if I were interested," Rick said, hesitant to even bring the idea up but curious to the answer.

"And are you?" asked Tuna hopefully.

He paused, reflecting. "No, I don't think so. It's a nice thought, and that does help bring some level of comfort to the past ten years. But I'm really happy now at the FBI. I enjoy the work, there are good career opportunities and I'm lucky to be part of a great team."

"Good. That's all that matters."

Their conversation was interrupted by the arrival of their food. Both of them began eating, Rick had forgotten how much the sea air made him ravenous.

Through his first bite, he said, "Speaking of Mrs. Post, were you able to talk to the investigating officer?"

Tuna leaned down into a small brown satchel bag and pulled out the report. She handed it to Rick. "That's a full copy of Officer Downs' report. He was the investigating officer on scene."

Rick wiped his fingers on a napkin and then scanned the document. "Anything unusual or unexpected?"

"No, nothing unusual. It appears to be exactly what was first suspected. She was traveling around forty and made a sudden avoidance maneuver, lost control, and veered off the road straight into a tree."

Tuna paused to spread some extra dressing across her salad. Rick munched on a few fries while he continued to review the report.

"Was she wearing her seatbelt?" he asked.

"Yes. Airbags also deployed. Unfortunately, a tree limb came through the windshield and struck Mrs. Post in the head. If it wasn't for that, she might have walked away with little more than a few bruises from the airbag."

"Do you know what she was doing out there? To be honest, given her husband's death, I'm surprised that she would want to be anywhere but home."

"She was returning from a visit with one of her husband's partners, the Axmacher's. They have a home off Quidnet. Apparently, she had arrived unannounced. According to Clair Axmacher, Mrs. Post was angry and frustrated. She wanted to know what had really happened on that boat."

Rick shook his head. "She just refused to believe it was an accident. Can't say that I blame her, but not sure what answers she was hoping to get from the Axmacher's. I mean, what could they say that would possibly change her mind?"

"Are you accepting then that Mr. Post's death was accidental?"

"Honestly, it still doesn't sit well with me. It just doesn't sound like the behavior of the man I knew. But what other options do I have? Some sort of murder conspiracy?" he scoffed.

Tuna nodded. "And I think Mrs. Post was also coming to that conclusion, albeit slowly Claire Axmacher said that she had calmed down quite a bit after they talked. Even had a glass of wine during which she reminisced about their past times together. She stayed a couple of hours and left the house a little before nine, which fits the timeline."

"Thanks for this," said Rick, nodding to the report. "Is it ok to share with Scott and Felicity?"

"Sure. However, you may want to leave out the details about the tree limb. Officer Downs said it wasn't a pretty sight," she said wincing.

"Of course," Rick said and sighed. Mr. and Mrs. Charles Post, two of the nicest people from his childhood, were dead. "Thanks for all your help, Tuna. I appreciate it."

"It was nothing. Just glad I was able to see you in person. It's been too long."

"Agreed." Rick glanced at his phone. "I still have some time before my boat. How about telling me more about that missing person case you were working on?"

"Ah, you mean Jack Reiner and the runaway wife?" said Tuna, chuckling. "Sure." She took another bite of salad. "It all started when this aspiring writer from St. Louis rented a cottage out in Sconset. Things got a bit spooky and strange from there."

"Because nothing strange or spooky ever happens on Nantucket?" said Rick, sarcastically.

"I know. But it gets weirder."

Rick listened, fascinated, as Tuna recounted the story from when she was called in by the Sheriff, Fred Boston, to the final, fateful evening. Rick was entranced. Fifteen minutes later, Tuna finished.

"So, that's my ghost story."

"Wow. Unbelievable. So much more interesting than corporate embezzlement or bank fraud. Thanks so much for sharing." He smiled.

"Of course." She picked up her fork, ready to continue with her salad.

Rick's phone rang. It was not a number he recognized. He picked it up and tapped the screen. "Rick Caton."

"Rick, it's Fel." Her voice sounded concerned.

"Hi, Fel, what's up?" asked Rick, holding up his finger to Tuna.

"Is there any chance you could come back to the house? I was going through my dad's office and found his latest journal. I think there's some information in there you might want to see."

Rick shook his head. "I'm sorry. I'm booked on the six o'clock ferry. In fact, I was just getting ready to walk over to Straight Wharf to get ready to board."

"Any chance you could delay that? Maybe take a later ferry?"

"Hang on a second." He put his hand over the phone and looked at Tuna. "Is there still the nine o'clock Hy-Line to Hyannis?"

"I believe so, why?" she responded curiously

"The daughter, Fel, found Mr. Posts' journal. She thinks there is something I should see."

Tuna raised her eyebrows.

He lifted the phone back to his ear. "Fel? Yeah, there's a nine o'clock boat I could take. I'll grab a taxi and be there shortly."

"Thanks so much. I really appreciate it," said Felicity.

Rick disconnected the call. "Sorry, I better go."

Tuna looked at him seriously. "Do you really think she's found something?"

He shook his head. "No. It's probably some note or mention that she has now construed into something meaningful. Honestly, can't say that I blame her. She's lost both parents in two different incidents over the course of a long weekend. She's just trying to find some reason behind it."

"I feel bad for her and her brother. It certainly can't be easy dealing with either death. But both? Brutal." Tuna shook her head sadly.

Rick nodded, pulled out his wallet, and motioned to the waiter.

Tuna put her hand on Rick's. "This one's on me."

"Are you sure?"

"Yes. It was just great to see you. Now go. And please let me know if there is anything I can do."

They stood and hugged.

"Thanks, Tuna. I appreciate it."

"Take care of yourself."

"You too."

CHAPTER THIRTEEN

Rick hustled down to Lower Main Street to grab a taxi. He supposed that rideshare services were available on the island, but the thought of using them didn't occur to him. In his mind, Nantucket was much more of an analog place where things were done a little differently, more old school. He found the line of cabs waiting as usual and jumped into another well-used minivan. The driver, an older lady this time, turned and smiled as he got in.

"Where to son?"

"Three twenty Monomoy Pond Road, please."

The driver turned, put the car in drive, and eased over the cobblestones. "Where are you in from?"

"Um, Boston."

"Nice town. Is this your first time here?"

Rick chuckled softly. "No. Actually, I was born and raised here. I moved off island about ten years ago."

"Really? Well, welcome back."

"Thanks. What about you?"

"My husband and I came here for years. From Philly. We always rented the same cottage in Madaket in July for a couple of weeks."

"Busy time."

She laughed. "Busy *and* expensive. But our kids loved it. We always had a wonderful time."

"Did you guys move here permanently?"

The driver turned to look at Rick. "No. My husband passed away six years ago."

"I'm sorry."

"Thank you," she said and paused. "I just couldn't adjust to the life we had lived in Philadelphia, so I took a gamble and decided to move here full-time. That was almost five years ago."

"How's it been?"

"You know, it was really difficult at first. I mean, I knew the island, right? But I didn't know many people. And I had always been here when it was busy. Adjusting to those long, dark, and quiet winter days was a bit of a challenge." She paused. "But it's all worked out. I'm lucky to have found a nice place to live that I can afford. And I drive the cab a few days a week to keep me out of trouble," she laughed. "And I get to meet interesting people like you."

Rick smiled. "I'm glad to hear it."

The minivan pulled into the Posts' driveway. The driver hit a button on the dash, and the long door slid open next to Rick. He handed her the fare and a generous trip.

"That is way too much, sir," said the driver and tried to hand it back.

Rick held up his hand. "Please. Consider it a little extra for great service."

The driver smiled. "Thank you."

Rick smiled, nodded, and turned towards the house. Felicity was waiting for him at the front door and motioned for him to come in. The sad young lady with the red and swollen eyes he had seen that morning had been replaced by a determined woman looking for answers. Her auburn hair was fixed in a short bun, and her green eyes blazed with energy. The ten-year-old he had known with the pigtails and toothless smile had grown up into a beautiful woman. Rick was almost too shocked to speak.

"Are you okay?" asked Felicity.

He took a moment to gather his senses. "Of course. I'm fine. Just a little surprised to be back here so soon."

"I'm sorry," said Felicity. "I know it's a lot to ask, but I really wanted to share something I found in my dad's journals with you."

"It's okay, Fel. You know I'm happy to help."

"Thanks. Let's go to his office."

They walked down the main hall to a small study opposite the kitchen. Like the kitchen, it featured large windows with amazing views of the harbor. An expansive green lawn, freshly striped from a recent cut, extended down to the water, where it connected to a large wooden deck. From the deck, a slender dock extended into the harbor where Rick could see Mr. Posts' beloved Herreshoff. Seeing the boat brought back a flood of memories.

Felicity's voice broke his reverie. "Rick?"

He turned to her. "Sorry. Just enjoying the view. And remembering some fun races with your Dad on his boat," he said and motioned toward the Herreshoff.

Her eyes followed. "He did love that boat." Her voice dropped. "And now I guess I'll have to figure out what to do with it."

"One step at a time," said Rick. "So, tell me what you found."

She walked over to a dark brown antique desk with a glass top. It was set in the middle of the room, facing the windows. Surrounding the windows were built-in bookcases full of novels, collections, and reference books. A section below the window held dozens and dozens of nearly identical leather-bound books. Some looked new, while others had the telltale patina of a well-used tome. The overall feel of the study reminded Rick of an old English library.

Felicity motioned to the bookshelf under the window. "My dad has always kept a journal. He said it started in college as a way to capture his thoughts and ambitions, and it became an important part of his life. My mom used to joke that it was his confessional, but I know it was really a way for him to document his life. He would often refer back to his journals to help him remember certain events or things."

"Impressive," said Rick, staring at the line of journals. "There must be a hundred there."

"Eighty-nine to be exact. They are arranged chronologically - as I said, my dad was a perfectionist - starting with the first one he began in college in 1981," she brushed her hand down the rows of journals, "all the way to this year. Each journal has about seven to nine months of entries."

"Amazing," said Rick. "My mom always encouraged me to keep a journal, but I never did. Too lazy, I think. But not your dad."

"No. He didn't write every day but rarely let more than a few days pass before making an entry."

"Did he allow you to read them?"

She smiled at the thought. "He did. His journals were never off limits. In fact, he encouraged both Scott and me to peruse them. Said not only would we get to know him better but we would probably learn a few things as well." She reached out and grabbed the last journal off the shelf. She lay the book on the desk and cracked it open. "But, I use the term 'read' generously," she said and turned the pages to Rick.

He glanced down and saw nothing but geometric gibberish. In neat blue ink, a series of orderly lines, vees, and dots proceeded across the page.

Confused, he looked at Felicity. "I don't understand. What is this?"

Felicity laughed. "Yes, my dad's journals were open to all. But you had to know the code to understand what he had written."

"The code?"

She smiled. "Yes, the code. Many people keep their journals in some sort of code so even if they are discovered, they won't reveal their secrets, or at least not without a bit of work."

"Was your dad hiding something?" asked Rick cautiously.

This brought a hearty laugh from Felicity. "Oh dear god, no. My dad was most certainly a rule follower and definitely not trying to hide anything. Quite the contrary. But he enjoyed the process and said that he found it easier to write in code than it was in longhand."

"Do you know the code? I mean, did you break it?"

Felicity laughed again. "Nothing to break. Dad was always very open about the code and actually taught me how to write and read in it."

"Really? What is it?"

"It's often referred to as the Pigpen or the Freemason code. The funny thing is it's not really a code but a simple geometric substitution."

"How so?"

"Traditionally, a code uses a key that is needed to decipher the message. For example, the Roman emperor Julius Caesar wrote a very straightforward code known as a shift or mono-alphabetic rotation cipher. With it, you replace one letter with another, which is a set number of steps down the alphabet. To break the code, you need to know how many steps down it was, say thirteen. Then, to decode the message, you would shift thirteen spots down the alphabet. So if the cipher had the letter G, then the actual letter would be T, thirteen spots down the alphabet, and so on. But even with this simple cipher, it would take a lot of work to understand what was being said. And the shift could change on a frequent basis."

Rick looked at her with admiration. "How did you learn all this?"

She smiled. "My dad. He was a military history buff, especially World War Two ciphers and the role they played in the war. He'd tell me stories about the codebreakers, the Enigma machine, and even how the U.S. broke the Japanese code to confirm they were going to attack Midway. In fact, did you know the U.S. used Native Americans from the Navajo tribe to communicate? I always found it fascinating."

He nodded. "So what about this?" said Rick, pointing to the journal.

"This," said Felicity, "is a simple geometric substitution. I think a better way to put it is that it is just a different way to write an alphabet. Here, let me show you." She grabbed a yellow legal pad from the top drawer and a pen from the holder on the corner of the desk. "The Pigpen cipher replaces letters with fragments of a grid." She drew out what looked like the game board for Tic Tac Toe and then put the letters A through I in each cell. She drew another grid next to it and then placed the letters J through R in each cell, but this time with a dot. Next, she drew an X shape and placed the letters S through V, starting at the top. She then repeated this for the letters W, X, Y & Z, except these each got a dot.

"Okay, this is the grid system you use to write in cipher. So an A would look like this." On the pad, she drew a _|. " The letter B looks like this." On the pad, she drew a |_|. "And a C looks like this," she said, drawing |_ "But here's the thing, those symbols never change. What looks like this A is always an A. So if you memorize each of the geometric shapes and understand which letter they represent, then you can read and write the Pigpen cipher fluently."

"Fascinating," said Rick. "So you can write in this, er, code?"

She nodded.

"Okay. What would 'I'm happy to be on Nantucket' look like?"

Felicity smiled and turned the pad back toward her. After a quick flurry of strokes, she rotated the pad back to Rick.

He glanced down at a geometric scribble.

⌐˙⌐ ⊓⅃⅂⅂< >⊏ ⊔⊓ ⊏⊡ ⊡⅃⊡><⊔⊔⊓>

"That's really what I said?" asked Rick, surprised. She was impressive.

"It is," said Felicity.

For a moment, they just smiled at each other. Rick felt something tug in his gut.

They heard the front door open. And a voice rang out, "Hello?"

"Oh my god, it's Scott!" Felicity ran out of the study and down the hall. Shaking the moment off, Rick followed and found Felicity hugging a tired-looking man. Rick gave the siblings a few moments. When they finally parted, the man looked over at Rick, a bit confused.

"Hi, Scott," said Rick, taken aback by how much Scott resembled Charles. His white blond hair of childhood had faded to a dirty blond, but a few freckles still stood out on his face. He was handsome, only the purple bags beneath his eyes betrayed the chaos of the past few days.

"Rick, is that really you? My god, it's been ages," said Scott, extending his hand. Rick grabbed his hand and pulled him into a hug.

"I am so sorry for your loss, Scott. Your mom and dad were such good people. It was so awful to hear about them." Rick stepped back.

"Thank you. It is an awful reason to see you again. How long has it been?" Scott smiled sadly, trying to make any part of the situation as normal as he could.

"A while. I think the last time was the summer before your junior year at Dartmouth."

"That's right. That was the summer I interned at Dad's firm."

Felicity broke in, clearly impatient with the small talk. "Rick is helping me look into Dad's death."

"What?" said Scott, confused. "I thought it was accidental. Are you saying…"

Rick cut him off. "It *was* accidental." He glanced at Felicity. "We are just trying to understand better how that could have happened."

Scott nodded. "I see. So sorry it took me so long. As much as I love Nantucket, it's not the easiest place to get to, especially from Asia."

"Were you there on business?" asked Rick.

"Yeah. I run a small hedge fund in Denver. One of our largest investments is an electric vehicle start-up in Taiwan. It was our annual review of their performance and expected returns. Always need to keep the investors happy, right?" he said and smiled sadly.

"Like father, like son, eh? That's pretty awesome, Scott."

"Thanks," replied Scott softly. "Do you have any food? I'm starving. I haven't had a thing to eat since this morning."

"Sure," said Felicity. "Put those bags down. I can whip something up." She turned and walked down the hall to the kitchen. Rick and Scott followed.

"So, Scott, I hear you are expecting," said Rick. "That is so exciting."

"It is. I had wanted my wife, Lizzie, to join me here, but the doctor nixed that. She's due in a few weeks."

Felicity was standing at the refrigerator with the door open. "What sounds good? How about a ham and cheese sandwich?"

"That would be perfect, thanks," said Scott, turning to Rick. "How long are you in town for?"

Rick glanced at his phone. "Oh, about another hour or so. I'm on the nine-o'clock boat to Hyannis. It's a school night for me."

Felicity whirled around and cut him off. "You absolutely cannot leave! We haven't had a chance to review what I found in Dad's journals."

Rick opened his mouth to respond but Scott cut in. "You've been going through Dad's journals?" he said accusingly. "Aren't they private?"

Felicity looked at her brother. "I know you were never interested in them, but Dad always said there was nothing to hide. We were welcome to read them."

"I could never figure out that damn code he wrote in," said Scott.

"Well, I did," said Felicity proudly. "And I think I may have found a few things in his latest journal that we should explore in a little more detail."

"Like what?" asked Scott, frustrated. "What did you find in that journal? And is it going to explain how the hell he fell off that damn boat?" His eyes filled with tears.

Felicity's face crumpled and she started to cry. "I'm only trying to understand how such a thing could have happened. I'm sorry, I didn't mean to upset you."

Scott held out his arms. Felicity slid in, and they hugged. After a few moments, she stepped back, sniffling. "Let me finish your sandwich," she said.

Rick felt uncomfortable. "I think it's best I go," he said. "I'm not sure there is much I can do here anyway."

"Please stay," pleaded Felicity. We haven't had a chance to look at Dad's journals, and I just want someone with your experience to determine if there's anything there."

Rick sighed, torn. "I've got to work tomorrow. Besides, where would I stay?"

"Right here!" exclaimed Felicity. "We have several guest bedrooms. And as for clothes, you and my dad were close in size; I'm sure you could find some things that would fit."

"I don't know," said Rick. "I should leave you and Scott to your grief."

"Please stay," said Scott. We can catch up. It'll help keep our minds off things."

Rick mulled it over. He pulled out his phone. "Let me see what the boss says." He quickly texted Hanna.

Ok to take an extra day? Back in the office Thursday?

He watched bubbles for a few moments before his phone dinged.

Everything ok? Is it good to stay?

He typed back.

Yes. All good. Just met up with some old friends.

Bubbles, then a ding.

I'll see you Thursday.

He tapbacked that he liked her message and looked up at Scott and Felicity. "Okay. You have me for another twenty-four hours."

"Yay!" exclaimed Fel. She ran over to Rick and hugged him. "Thanks so much for staying."

Rick smiled, embarrassed at the attention.

Scott stood, having finished his sandwich. "I'm going to run up and wash this travel off of me. I haven't showered since ten time zones ago. Rick, why don't you come with me and I can show you where you can stay. Then I propose we meet up on the back patio, enjoy a cocktail, and watch the sunset."

Rick nodded and followed Scott up the stairs.

As planned, the three met back on the patio and enjoyed a spectacular sunset. They talked well into the evening, catching up on a decade's worth of life, and turned in just before midnight.

CHAPTER FOURTEEN

The sun had been up for almost two hours before Rick opened his eyes. It took him a moment to realize where he was, and then it hit him that he was still in Nantucket and in a guest bed in the Posts' house. He swung his feet out and grabbed his clothes off the chair next to the bed. Despite Fel's suggestions to use some of her dad's clothes, the thought of that did not sit well with Rick. This was a man he idolized growing up, and he should not be able to slip into the man's wardrobe so easily.

After taking a few minutes to enjoy the amazing view of the harbor and confirm that it was yet another gorgeous day, he made his way down the stairs. He followed the smell of coffee and frying bacon into the kitchen, where he found Felicity hard at work at the stove.

"Good morning," Rick said, rubbing his eyes.

"Good morning. Did you sleep okay?" she asked, deftly flipping an egg in the skillet.

"Great, actually. Between the amazingly comfortable mattress and the salt air, I slept like a baby."

"I'm so glad. Can I make you some breakfast? Maybe scrambled eggs and bacon, okay?"

Rick filled a mug with coffee and settled at the table. "That would be terrific. Is there anything I can do?"

"No, I got this. Breakfast is my favorite meal, and I tend to make it for myself every day, so I have the drill down pretty solid." She walked over to the refrigerator and grabbed the necessary ingredients.

"Scott still sleeping?" Rick sipped his coffee.

"Yeah. I don't think we are going to see him for a while. He's still on Taiwan time, which is, I think, twelve hours ahead of us. So, for him, it's after eight in the evening."

"I've never traveled like that. I bet it's a tough adjustment to make."

Felicity nodded. "It'll take him a few days to get back to normal. My bet is he'll sleep until noon. Maybe even later." She deftly slid the eggs onto a plate, added a couple of pieces of bacon and two slices of buttered toast, and placed it on the table.

"This smells delicious."

"Hope so." She loaded another plate and placed it across from Rick. "More coffee?"

"No, thanks. This is perfect. Thank you."

Felicity sat down and immediately tucked into her food. She paused and looked at Rick. "After breakfast, I'd really like to go through the journal like we talked about yesterday."

Rick nodded. "Of course. But are you sure Scott will be okay with that? He seemed a bit upset last night when you mentioned it to him."

She finished her bite before saying, "I think he'll be fine. As I said, he never had the same interest in Dad's journals as I did. And if we can find something that might explain his behavior?" She looked down, eyes filling with tears.

Rick reached over and placed his hand on hers. "I know you want answers. You want to understand how this could have happened. But it was an accident. Or…"

"Or what?" she sniffed.

Rick paused, weighing what he was about to say. "This will be hard to hear, but could your dad have committed suicide?"

Felicity snatched her hand back and looked at him in anger. "What? That's outrageous. My dad would never have taken his own life!"

"Are you sure about that? I've had a number of cases where someone, outwardly happy and content to all those around them, took their own life."

She nodded. "I'm sure. But not my dad."

"All I'm saying, based on what I know of your dad and the circumstances around his death, is that that might be a possibility."

Felicity stopped eating and crossed her arms. "I'm sorry. I cannot believe that. I cannot believe he would leave Mom alone. He would not do that willingly."

Rick nodded, took a final bite of the bacon, and sipped his coffee. "Okay. I'm ready when you are. Let's go look at those journals." He got up from the table and walked his plate over to the sink, where he washed it and put it in the dishwasher. He did the same for Fel. "Thanks so much for breakfast. That really hit the spot."

"You're welcome. More coffee?"

He looked down at his empty mug, the Wharf Rat mascot staring up at him. "Yes, please."

Felicity filled both cups and then led them across the hallway into her father's study. The journal and legal pad were still on the desk from the night before. She motioned for Rick to take a seat and pulled up an extra chair next to him.

"Okay. We didn't get into details last night, but this is his most recent journal. The first entry is dated this past April; the last is from this past Thursday, the day before he went out on the boat with his partners." She flipped through the pages. "It's pretty much his standard fare. Most of the entries are about the weather, things he and mom did, observations about the news, that sort of thing. But there were a couple of entries that got my attention." She flipped to a page and turned it to face Rick.

Rick looked at the lines and then smiled up at her. "Um, despite your excellent lesson yesterday on codes, I'm afraid I haven't magically become fluent overnight in the Pigpen cipher."

Felicity laughed softly. "Sorry. Hang on, let me grab something." She stood up and left the study. Rick heard noises in the kitchen, and then she returned carrying an Apple MacBook. "Here, let's do this. There are a number of Pigpen sites on the net. Let's use those to make sure I'm reading these entries correctly."

"Good idea. Where do you want to start?"

"Let's start with this one," she said, pointing down at a line in the journal. Rick looked down and saw:

LⒺⓄLⒶⒻⒺⒶⓄⒿ ⒶⒶⱽ ⒿLⁿ ⱽ>ⒻⒿ>Ⓐⁿ< ⱀⱽ ⒶⒺ> ⱁⒺⱽⁿⒶⒻ

Fel followed the shapes with her finger as she keyed them into the website. "It's a bit cumbersome to point and click on each of the geometric shapes," she said as she used the mousepad to move from shape to shape, clicking as she went. 'But I want to make sure my translation is correct." She finished clicking and turned the screen to face Rick.

"Concerned new MCP strategy is not kosher," said Rick, reading off the screen. He looked at Felicity. "What do you think he meant by that?"

"Well, MCP is his firm, Miacomet Capital Partners. And I remember Dad telling me that he met with the partners late last year, and they decided to try a new investment strategy in the hopes of boosting returns."

"Do you know what that new strategy was?" Rick looked back down at the journal.

Felicity shook her head. "Dad didn't get into specifics, but I know that some of their investors were upset."

"Upset how?"

"MCP followed what many firms would call an old-fashioned approach. They pooled money from investors and then looked to take positions in companies with strong growth prospects. Their latest five-year performance was an annual return of six point three percent."

"Six point three? That sounds pretty good to me."

Felicity scoffed. "For you, maybe. But some of these investors expect more. Much more. Like ten to fifteen percent."

"Yeah, who wouldn't? But is that reasonable?"

"With this approach? No. Dad always said they were in it for the long game. He used to say, 'slow and steady wins the race,'" she said and smiled sadly. "I mean, to the point that Dad made sure they never had the financial news on in the office during the day. Said it made them think in the short term and could potentially cause them to have a knee-jerk reaction to the trends of the day."

"But investors didn't like this long-game approach?"

"Some did, for sure. I mean, MCP has been in business for over thirty years. This was the strategy they were founded on and what they followed up until late last year."

"So why the change?"

Felicity let out a sigh. "There were a handful of investors who threatened to pull their money out after the lock-up period, which for MCP was only six months."

"Six months for the lock-up? Why so short? Aren't typical lock-ups a year or more?"

"Yes. But Dad and the partners, Sean and Cormac, thought a short lock-up period would be attractive to potential investors. So if they aren't happy with MCP's performance, they can pull their money fairly soon and take it elsewhere."

"I think that would have been stressful for the partners, always hanging over their heads."

"Yeah, they talked about changing it to something more typical, like two years, but then were concerned that might send a negative message to investors. So in the end, they decided on this new strategy."

"But you don't know what that strategy was?"

"No. But I think cryptocurrency was a part of it. And green energy as well."

"And how did they do?"

She stared intently at the journal, looking for answers. "Well. From what I heard from Mom, their most recent results were low double digits. So, yeah, it looked like the new strategy was working."

"So then, why this? " Rick said, pointing at the screen. What does he mean by 'not kosher'?"

"I don't know," she said, clearly frustrated.

"Hmm," said Rick. "Any other entries of interest?"

"Yes, there's this one. From two weeks ago." She flipped through the pages and found the one she was looking for.

⌐Lᒷ⌐ᒥ⊏□⅃ ⊏⌐ᒐⵒⅤ >ᒷ >∩<ᒫ⨆ ⅃⌐⌐∧□. ⊏□ᒷ ∨⌐ᒷᒐ ⵑᗺ⊏∀ >∩□ ⅂∀. >∩⌐ᗺ⨆ ⌐⅃⨆⨆⌐>∨.

After a minute of clicking, the translation appeared on the screen:

Copied files to thumb drive. Fel will know the PW. Think rabbits.

"Copied what files? And what rabbits?" asked Rick. "Do you know what he's talking about?"

Felicity shook her head. "I don't. I also haven't found a thumb drive, although I've looked. I checked the safe, his closet, and of course, the desk. So far, nothing."

"And Fel will know the PW? I assume he means password?"

"That's what I thought as well. Although, to be honest, I have no clue as to what the password might be. Think rabbits?" She frowned in confusion.

"I have one more entry to show you." She flipped the journal open to the last entry. "Here," she said, pointing to the last line.

⊏Γ∨∩Γ⊡⊓ ⊏ΓΓ⊐⨆< ∀Γ>∩ ∟ ⊐⊡⊐ ∨. ∩⊏⊓Γ⊡⊓ ⊏⊏Γ ⊐⊡∨∀⊐ΓV.

This time, Rick entered the shapes into the website. He double-checked before each click and was taking a long time. It was all Fel could do not to grab the laptop out of his hand and do it herself. Finally, after what seemed like an eternity, he showed it to her.

Fishing Friday with C and S. Hoping for answers.

"C and S?" asked Rick.

"Cormac and Sean. His partners. I think my dad was planning on asking them about this new strategy. About the results they were getting."

"Hoping for answers. That could mean anything", said Rick. "I mean, was he planning on talking about business? Or was it a fantasy football league? Or something else totally irrelevant?"

Felicity sighed. "I know. He doesn't spell it out, but knowing my dad, I think he was planning on asking them something about the new strategy."

"Okay," said Rick. "So are you suggesting that your dad raised some questions about the new strategy and then his partners threw him off the boat?"

"Oh, my god, no!" said Felicity. "They were like brothers. But I don't know, maybe something they discussed upset my dad."

"Upset him enough to commit suicide?" asked Rick.

Felicity's eyes started to well up. "No, of course not. I don't know. I'm just trying to understand."

Rick took her hand. "I get it, I really do. I can't imagine how hard this is on you. And I appreciate you showing me his journal. But I have to be honest. I have spent the last eight years of my career with the FBI. Based on what you've shared with me, I don't see anything that would lead to your dad's death. I'll say it again: it was just a very unfortunate accident. We will never know why he did what he did."

Fel gripped his hand hard. "Maybe if we could find that thumb drive?"

Rick shook his head slowly. "I don't think there's anything there. I'm not sure what he was referencing, but I don't think it will explain anything." Rick paused and pointed at the journals on the shelf. "Have you been through all of them? Is there anything else?"

"I have. And no, all of his entries are pretty mundane. He doesn't even mention the firm much. Mostly, it's about sailing, events in his life, and that sort of thing. These were really the only ones to me that sounded suspicious."

Rick released her hand and stood up. He walked behind Felicity and put his hands on her shoulders. "I'm sorry. I am really sorry for your loss. But I need to get back to Boston."

She leaned her head onto his hand and squeezed. "Thanks. I appreciate your time. At least I got to see you. And I know Scott was happy to catch up with his former babysitter." She stood, and they hugged.

Rick pulled away. "Please pass along my regrets to Scott at not being able to say goodbye."

"I will."

"And you take care of yourself. The offer still stands. Call me if you guys need anything."

Felicity nodded. Rick turned and left.

CHAPTER FIFTEEN

For the third time in twenty-four hours, Rick Caton was trying to leave Nantucket. The taxi, driven by the same young Jamaican man who had picked him up the day before, dropped him off at the end of Straight Wharf. Rick handed him a fare with a nice tip. The driver smiled broadly and said in a melodic tenor, "Thanks for the tip, man. Hope to see you again soon." Rick returned the smile and made his way down to the wharf. A line of passengers had already started forming, waiting to board the boat.

He was busy petting a cute short-hair dachshund when his phone vibrated. He pulled it out of his pocket and looked at the screen. It was Felicity.

"Fel?" he said, somewhat cautiously.

"I found it!"

"Found what?" asked Rick. perplexed.

"The thumb drive! I found it!"

"What," asked Rick. "Where?"

She spoke so quickly it was almost hard to understand her. "It was on his boat. I went through the office, the desk, and the safe again, and of course, there was nothing. Then I happened to look out and see the sailboat. It reminded me he had a cubby in the galley where he occasionally would hide presents for my mom."

"Presents for your mom?" Rick asked, staring as the crew began to load the baggage carts onto the ferry.

Felicity laughed at the memory. "Yeah. My dad loved to buy my mom jewelry - especially watches. She didn't go out on the boat much, so he used this little cubby to hide presents until it was time to give them to her."

"And that's where you looked?" He noticed that the front of the line had started to move. The ferry was boarding.

"Yes. It was buried under some navigational maps and other papers. But it is a thumb drive, and it looks brand new."

"Have you tried to open it?" Rick asked, smiling as the dachshund he had been petting eagerly brushed past him to board.

"No. I was hoping you could help me with that," Felicity implored.

"Fel," said Rick firmly, "I need to get back to Boston. I've got to get back to the office."

"Please? Just humor me for another hour. I'll even come pick you up."

Rick thought for a while and smiled. *At worst, at least I'll get to see Fel again.* "Okay. Pick me up at the end of Straight Wharf."

"I'll be there in 20."

Rick disconnected the call and walked quickly over to the Hy-Line ticket office. There were a few people in line waiting for an agent. As he stood, he reflected on his evening with Scott and Felicity and felt a pang of sadness for his inability to bring any answers or comfort to them. They were struggling and, Fel especially, looking for answers as to why this could have happened. More and more, he suspected a medical event that triggered the behavior, probably a micro-stroke or a brain aneurysm. He made a mental note to follow up on that. And maybe there was something on that thumb drive.

"Next," a voice called.

Rick stepped forward and was happy to see that the same agent who had changed his ticket twice already, a kindly looking lady approaching retirement, was behind the counter. She looked at him and smiled. "Back again?"

He chuckled. "I know, I know. I can't seem to quit this place."

"What time should I put you down for now?" she asked charmingly.

"Let's just say the nine o'clock boat tonight for now. Although I reserve the right to change it again," he said and grinned.

She handed him the ticket. "Anything you want, love."

Rick took the ticket and winked at her. "I'll see you tonight, hon."

He left the ticket office and walked to the end of the wharf, where he found Felicity waiting for him in a classic old Ford Bronco, dark blue with chrome Crager rims. The hard top roof was off and replaced by a tan convertible top stacked over the tailgate. The doors had been removed as well, creating a very open-air machine. He could see she was wearing light yellow shorts, displaying her shapely, tan legs.

"Your dad still has this? God, I remember this from my high school days. I'd always see your dad driving around town, top down. He never failed to wave when he saw me." He jumped into the passenger seat. "And it is still in such great shape."

"It is!" said Felicity. "But it's had some work. About ten years ago, he found a bunch of rust on the frame. So he shipped it off-island to a restoration shop. They replaced the frame, fixed some bodywork rot, and rebuilt the engine and transmission. Dad didn't care about the cost; he just wanted to keep it looking original. The only major mechanical change was to move the shifter from the steering column to the transmission tunnel."

"The three-on-the-tree became four-on-the-floor?" asked Rick.

"Actually, no, it's still just a three-speed. But it's a lot easier to shift now." She put it in gear and navigated down Main Street, passing some of the tourists who had just gotten off the ferry, many of them pulling their luggage over the uneven sidewalk.

"I bet. Well, it's gorgeous. Looks just like it did twenty years ago."

"He'd be happy to hear that." She smiled wistfully.

"And you found the thumb drive? I think he might be happy about that, too."

Felicity grinned like a detective who had just solved a major case. "I hope so. I'm praying there's something on it that will make sense of it all."

"Then let's go find out what's on it."

She hit the gas. The old truck bounced over the cobblestones. Rick leaned back in the seat and watched Felicity as she drove, shifting effortlessly, the thrum of the big V8 providing the backdrop. Her hair floated in the wind, her long tan legs expertly working the three pedals. For the second time in as many days, Rick was entranced.

They were at the house in no time. Felicity drove quickly over the gravel drive and skidded to a stop a few feet from the front door. "I'll put it back in the garage later. Let's go!"

Rick jumped out of the car and followed her into the house. "Is Scott still sleeping?

"No, he's up. But he's a bit groggy and out of it. He was in the kitchen when I left to come get you."

Rick poked his head in the kitchen. "Not here."

"Probably on a walk. Enough about him." She was already disappearing down the hallway.

He followed her into the study. The laptop was still sitting on the desk along with the journal they had reviewed just an hour or two before.

"Here it is," said Fel, handing Rick the thumb drive. It was blue, shaped like a torpedo, and looked brand new. The only markings on it showed that it had a sixty-four megabyte capacity.

Rick turned the laptop to face him and inserted the thumb drive into the USB slot. He had done this dozens of times in his work to catch financial mischief but wasn't sure what to expect today.

The laptop buzzed and clicked, and an icon appeared on the desktop. *MCP Files*

He double-clicked on the drive, and a small, rectangular screen appeared.

This drive is protected. Please enter the password.

Glancing at Felicity, he asked, "Any ideas?"

"Maybe my birthday? He did say I would know the password; maybe that's what he meant?"

"Remind me"

"March twenty-third, nineteen ninety-two."

Rick keyed in the numbers. The screen jiggled.

Incorrect Password.

"Maybe my middle name?"

Rick entered Patricia.

"You remember my middle name but not my birthday?" Felicity said, with a teasing glint in her green eyes.

"Yeah," said Rick shyly. "It was my grandmother's name."

Felicity smiled while the computer screen jiggled again.

Incorrect Password.

"Hmm, Maybe my mom's birthday?"

"No, I don't think so. He said you would know, so I have to think he was referencing something the two of you shared."

Felicity thought for a few minutes, and then her face lit up. "Try Hazel Fiver Bigwig."

"What?"

"It's the three main characters from the novel *Watership Down*. My dad read that to me growing up. He gave it to me on my seventh birthday. That's what he meant by think rabbits! It was his favorite book as a kid, and he wanted to read it to me. So every night, after my bath, we would cuddle on the bed, and he would read for thirty minutes or so. It took months - I think the book was something like four hundred pages. But it was sweet, and we both cried at the end."

"At the end? What happened?"

She looked at him in surprise. "You haven't read it?"

He shook his head.

"It is such a sweet story. And I am going to encourage you to read it when we are done with this. So I'll let you discover the end on your own."

"Okay," said Rick curiously, and turned back to the screen. "What was that again?"

"Hazel Fiver Bigwig"

He typed in the box, and again, the screen jiggled.

Incorrect Password.

"Hmph," said Felicity. "I thought for sure that was right." She thought for a minute. "Okay, try this. Hazel, the number five, and then Bigwig."

Rick looked at her quizzically and then turned to the screen and typed.

Hazel5Bigwig

Incorrect Password.

"Damn," she said. "I thought for sure that was it. Is there some computer program or software that could crack this for us?"

Rick laughed knowingly. "Um, remember you telling me about the codebreakers in World War Two? This is about a gazillion times harder."

"Seriously?"

"This thumb drive is protected with a 16-digit alphanumeric key. So, there are over a quintillion possible combinations. Or even more depending on the characters allowed."

"A quintillion?"

"Yeah. Think of the number one followed by eighteen zeros. In other words, not breakable."

"It's got to be something."

A seagull squawked outside, and her eyes lit up.

"Kehaar!"

"Key what?" said Rick, confused.

"Kehaar. He is a character in the book. Helps the rabbits at the end. That's it, I know it is!"

She grabbed the laptop from Rick and spun it to face her. She typed:

Hazel5BigwigKeha

"That can't be it. Too many characters. Damn!"

"When did you read the book?"

She thought for a minute and smiled. She looked down at the screen, leaned over Rick and typed:

Hazel5Kehaar1999

The computer clicked, and the screen changed to show the thumb drive's directory. Felicity squealed in excitement. A single file and a folder were listed. Rick pointed at the file. "Click on that."

Felicity clicked on the file, and a new screen appeared revealing a one-page Word document. The top half of the page contained the Pigpen cipher, while the other half was blank.

"Bingo!" exclaimed Felicity.

"Hang on there; we are not sure if it says anything serious. He could just be sending you a special message, like how he wants you to manage his estate. Or just to say goodbye."

"No, Dad already left us those letters in his safe. I think this is something important."

Rick looked down on the geometric gibberish. "Is there any way to translate this faster than pecking away on that website?"

"Dad's writing is pretty precise. Let's see if we can cut and paste it into the online decoder." Her fingers slid over the mouse pad as she highlighted and then copied the text in the document. She then pulled up the online tool, clicked into the decipher box, and pasted the text. A spinning clock appeared briefly before the translation appeared.

Rick and Felicity read it in amazement.

My dearest Fel

If you are reading this, then I know you found the entries in my journal. And I'm probably not around, as I know the first thing you would do is ask me what's up. Here's what's up. I have concerns that MCP might be engaged in illegal activities. Something is just not right with our books and our recent financial performance. And you know me, I would never want anything illegal or untoward associated with our family name. I think the recent returns for Q3 were much better than they should have been because of this activity. In this drive, you'll find a number of files that I found on the office network that look suspicious to me, in particular one called Eel Point Amusements. Please share these with someone you trust. You know I always want to do the right thing.

I love you, Felicity. You, Mom, and Scott were the best things that ever happened to me. Please be happy and enjoy life. Read Watership Down and think of me. It is one of my fondest memories of your childhood and my life.

/d

Felicity was crying. Rick reached out and pulled her into a hug. Sniffling, she pulled back, looked up at him through teary green eyes, and said, "I told you something was wrong."

Rick nodded and rubbed her back. "You were right. Your dad had suspicions. I just wonder why he didn't do anything himself to address them."

"Maybe he had just discovered them? Or maybe he had suspicions for a while but was hoping he was wrong. Kind of putting his head in the sand," she said, sniffling.

"Do you think he would do that?" asked Rick.

"In some ways, yeah. Knowing him, he always wants to think the best in people. Sean and Cormac are like brothers; they've known each other since college. So, believing that something is wrong means one or both of them is knowingly deceiving my dad. That would be really hard for him to accept."

Rick nodded. "Let's take a look at these files. Maybe they'll shed some light on things." He slid his fingers over the mousepad to highlight the folder and double-clicked. A list of six files, all spreadsheets, appeared on the screen.

SWLTDQ3.xls

TOLSINDQ3.xls

SABLEOKLLCQ3.xls

EELPTAQ3.xls

SNKTYLLCQ3.xls

TIELNFLDLLCQ3.xls

"Do you think those are different companies?" asked Felicity.

"Yes. If I had to guess, I'd say these are the Q3 financial reports from each of them."

"Why don't we start at the top?" said Fel, pointing to the first file.

"Why not?" said Rick and double-clicked on the file.

The computer whirred, and then a new screen appeared, showing a spreadsheet with cells laden with numbers.

"This looks like the financials for one of their investments," he said, pointing at the different worksheets along the bottom. They were named IS, BS, CF, EQ, and Schds.

"What are those?" asked Felicity, pointing at the tabs. "Sorry, I never took accounting in college."

"Those are the four financial statements that make up the typical financial report and include the income statement, balance sheet, cash flow statements, and changes in owners' equity.

Essentially, everything that describes the financial performance of a firm. Schds would be schedules. Those are the supporting details behind the numbers."

"So if things are 'not kosher,' as my dad said in the journal, how would we tell?"

"Well, it's clearly not something obvious, or he would have addressed it. You know, like money disappearing from a corporate bank account or unusual expenses being charged to the firm. I'm thinking your dad must have suspected something much more sophisticated, something that wasn't immediately obvious."

"Like what?"

"Since his suspicions were focused on the unusually high returns, I would say there are two areas we need to look at. The first is essentially a Ponzi scheme, you know, think Bernie Madoff. You rob Peter to pay Paul and create a false set of books to hide the transactions. You can then claim impressive returns that satisfy current investors and attract new ones. But you are building a house of cards that will eventually fall."

"How so?"

"Well, in the case of Madoff, the triggering event was the 2008 financial crisis. Investors started requesting redemptions of their money from Madoff. More money was requested than he had access to, and the whole scheme collapsed. Many investors lost everything."

"How awful!"

"Yeah. But sadly, it isn't the only time it has ever happened. Ponzi schemes have been going on for nearly a hundred years. In fact, it's named after Charles Ponzi, who promised extremely high returns to investors in the early twentieth century. But like Madoff, it was just a scam."

"You mentioned two possibilities. What's the other?"

"Money laundering."

"I've heard the term but not really sure what it means," said Felicity.

"It's actually quite simple. Let's say you are running a criminal enterprise, like drugs, that generates huge amounts of cash. You can't just take suitcases of money down to the bank and deposit them. Banks are required to report every transaction over ten thousand dollars to the government so your operation would be discovered in a heartbeat. Likewise, cash is difficult to use in any type of large, legal transaction, like buying a car. So, it needs to be cleaned and deposited into a bank account without any traces of its illegal history. "

"So what do they do?" She said, looking at him intently.

He paused, feeling adrift in her gaze. Shaking it off, he responded, "They clean the money by running it through an outwardly appearing legitimate business. Usually, they will establish or purchase cash-intensive businesses such as bars, liquor stores, grocery stores, or casinos and then funnel the cash through those businesses. During the process, the cash is washed free of its criminal origins and eventually emerges as a regular deposit in a bank or brokerage account. Then the money can be sent anywhere via check or wire transfer."

"Okay," said Felicity. "Can you tell by looking at this file if either of these activities is going on?"

"I wish! My job would be so much easier at the FBI. In reality, even if you suspect it's happening, financial fraud can be very hard to detect. At a minimum, you need an intense forensic accounting to really see if anything illegal is going on."

"So, my dad suspects something is going on at his firm, enough to store some files on a thumb drive that he hides on his boat, and then he dies in an accidental death while fishing with his partners who may or may not be involved in some sort of financial fraud."

Rick looked at her and nodded. "I think that pretty much sums up what we know so far."

"And do you still believe that his death was accidental?" She said, already knowing his answer.

"Um, I think I would have to admit that there might be another possibility, however unlikely."

Felicity smiled victoriously. "Alright then! What do we do now?"

"Let me make a call. Maybe we can access some of the resources at the FBI. Although, honestly, there is still very little to go on. All we have is your dad's suspicions and the latest financial reports of half a dozen companies. But it's worth a try."

"Thank you!" said Fel and hugged Rick intensely. "You know my dad thought so highly of you. Always knew you'd do well. I think he'd be very pleased that you're the one looking into things."

Rick blushed, thrilled that he had made her happy. "Well, let's not get too far ahead of our skis, Fel."

CHAPTER SIXTEEN

Rick left Felicity in her dad's office and walked outside. He needed some fresh air and some alone time to think. What they had discovered was certainly interesting, but did it mean that anything really had changed? He still suspected some sort of medical event had probably been the reason behind Mr. Posts' drowning. Couldn't that same medical event have made him paranoid? Or delusional?

He pulled out his phone and typed out a quick text to his boss.

Do you have 5 for a quick chat?

Bubbles appeared, and then his phone dinged.

Wrapping up meeting. I'll call you in 10

He tapbacked a thumbs up and then started walking down the gravel drive. The old Bronco stood by the door and, looking at it, brought back many memories of Mr. Charles Post. Yes, it had been over ten years since Rick had had any interactions with the man, but at the time, he had been sharp as a tack, the same impressive man from Rick's childhood. And no one in his immediate circle suspected any behavior changes from the man leading up to the day of his death. But they could have been unaware or intentionally not seeing it. He paced up and down the shell driveway turning the case over in his mind. The evidence to date suggests four possibilities for Mr. Posts' death.

One. He decided, for reasons unknown, to commit suicide. As he is preparing to jump off the boat, he loses his balance, hits his head, and falls into the water. Possibly unconscious and with damaged or malfunctioning PFD, drowns within minutes.

Two. He needs to pee badly and, for reasons known only to him, decides to go off the side of the boat. Might have underestimated the wave state. Loses his balance, hits his head, and falls into the water. Possibly unconscious and with damaged or malfunctioning PFD, drowns within minutes.

Three. At some point in the days leading up to the fishing trip - or even during the trip itself - he suffers a stroke, aneurism, or another medical event that impacts his impulse control or encourages suicidal thoughts, explaining the first two options.

Four. He confronts the partners about his suspicions. One or both of them react violently and perhaps hit him over the head, then throw him overboard. But that doesn't explain the malfunctioning PFD unless...

Rick mentally scratched off the first option and was leaning heavily on the second possibility. It really did explain the death in a way that fit the evidence as well as his knowledge of the man's behavior. But now, with the discovery of the thumb drive and Mr. Posts' suspicions, the fourth option was a possibility, if a longshot.

His phone vibrated. He looked down to see it was Hanna.

"Hanna, thanks so much for calling me back so quickly."

"Sure. Although I must admit, I'm a bit surprised. First you extend your trip by a day and now you want to talk. I'm guessing maybe you want to stay a week or so and cancel the workshop at Quantico?" she said, a hint of reproach in her tone.

Rick huffed a laugh. "Well, I wouldn't mind canceling the workshop at Quantico if I'm honest, but that's not the reason for my call."

He felt her energy shift as she focused. "What's up?"

"The reason I came over to Nantucket, that favor I mentioned to you on Tuesday, was to share what I had learned about the accidental drowning of an old family friend, Charles Post.

Apparently, he fell off the transom of a boat while fishing with his two business partners."

She was silent for a few breaths. "Okay. What did you learn?"

He paced, feeling the crunch of shells beneath his feet. "Not much. It did look like an accidental death. Unfortunately, the wife of the man who drowned, who had asked me for the favor, was killed in a car accident two nights ago."

"Oh, Rick, I'm sorry." She took a pause, then asked the obvious follow-up for someone who had been in the Bureau for years. "Do you think the two are at all possibly connected?"

"It certainly feels odd to me. She, er, her name was Ann Post, died in a single-vehicle accident. The report states she swerved to avoid a deer and hit a tree. Likely killed her instantly."

"Then, what's on your mind? The accidental drowning? That would have been her husband?"

"Yes. Charles Post. I've known them both since I was young. Both salt of the earth types. And very successful. Charles ran a firm here on Nantucket called Miacomet Capital Partners. Founded over thirty years ago with two of his college buddies. By all accounts, he did well financially."

"Then what's the concern?" asked Hanna, curious.

"Charles left a few entries in his journal that suggested he was concerned that the firm might have been doing some, let's say, extra-legal activities."

"Did he mention specifics?" she said, sounding doubtful.

"No, but he did mention a thumb drive with files that he had downloaded from the company servers."

"Have you seen the files?"

"I have. The daughter, Felicity, was able to locate the thumb drive. When we opened the drive, we found a letter from her dad along with financial reports from six companies. I don't know for sure, but I suspect that the firm, Miacomet Capital, either owned or had significant investments in each of them."

"Okay. So what's the problem? What do you need from me?"

Rick continued pacing. "In the letter, Charles claims that he believes there is indeed illegal activity going on at Miacomet Capital. It's possible that he confronted the partners on the fishing trip, and one or both reacted violently, throwing him off the boat to silence him."

"Hmm. Possible, I suppose. So what do you want to do?"

He could tell that Hanna was waiting for him to come out and say it. Taking a leap of faith, Rick confessed, "I'd really like to formalize this as a suspected case of criminal fraud. That way, I can access the forensic accountants to review the books and determine what, if anything, was happening."

The phone was quiet.

"Hanna?"

"Sorry, I was just thinking. I have concerns. One is that your personal involvement might make you more susceptible to thinking a crime had occurred."

Rick replied, frustrated, "But, Hanna."

She cut him off. "Let me finish. The evidence you've presented is pretty light; I mean, a couple of journal entries and a letter? We would need more. And finally, do we even know if this case warrants an FBI investigation? As you know, this case, if there is one, would fall either on the Nantucket Police Department or the Massachusetts State Police."

"I hear you, I do. But I just have a feeling," he said, practically begging.

She shut him down. "I get it, I do. And I know you are damn good at your job. Your closure rate over the past five years confirms it. But what you know so far is not enough for us to devote valuable resources. I'm sorry."

Rick sighed. "I know you're right." He thought for a minute. "Can I ask another favor then?"

"Shoot," she said dryly.

"Let me take one more day. That will give me a chance to talk to the locals, the NPD, and maybe the sheriff's office. Share with them what I've found and see if they would be willing to take this on."

"I think that's a great idea. But you need to promise me that come Sunday afternoon, you are done with this and that your butt is in a plane seat heading down to D.C."

Rick smiled. "I wouldn't miss that workshop for the world," he said, heavy on the sarcasm.

"Thanks. I look forward to your report."

Rick ended the call and considered the next steps. He was disappointed that he couldn't access the FBI, but what did he really expect? His evidence was light to nonexistent, and even if something was going on, it really was the purview of the local authorities. And if warranted, they would need to be the ones to request resources from the State Police or, if the case was big enough, the FBI.

He sighed and walked back into the house. He found Felicity and Scott in the kitchen talking.

"Hi, Scott, I didn't realize you were back," said Rick.

"I got back ten minutes ago. Saw you were on the phone. Didn't want to interrupt."

Felicity piped in, "I've been telling Scott about what we found —Dad's letter, the files. He thinks I'm crazy."

"I didn't say you were crazy," said Scott. "Just that it seems so preposterous to me. I can't believe that anything illegal would be happening at MCP." He looked a bit uncomfortable.

She turned to Rick. "What did you find out?" she asked eagerly.

"As I feared, my boss turned me down. Said that the evidence was light and even if something were going on, it would be the responsibility of the NPD or the sheriff's department to investigate."

"Damn!" said Fel. "I was really hoping."

"Well, don't give up yet. I was able to extend my PTO a couple more days. I have until Sunday afternoon to move things forward. Then I'm on a plane to DC."

"I'm so glad you will keep looking into this, Rick; I really am."

"Is it alright to stay here?"

"Of course."

"I think it is a total waste of time," said Scott defensively. "There is no way Sean or Cormac were doing anything wrong or illegal. I've known them forever, and I just can't see it."

"And I really hope you are right," said Rick.

"So what's next?" asked Felicity.

"First, I'm going to talk with a detective friend from the NPD. Get her thoughts on what we have and hopefully rope her into the investigation. Then I think I might visit Miacomet Capital. Talk to the partners and get a feel for things."

"Anything I can do?"

"No, not at the moment. Oh, and I guess I need to change my ferry reservation. Again."

CHAPTER SEVENTEEN

Tuna sat at her desk and stared down at the neat stack of paper in front of her. She had just printed out her final report on the accidental death of Charles Post. Her report was thorough and contained the ME's findings, condensed statements from the wife and business partners, as well as her timeline of events that led to the discovery of Charles Posts' body in the breaking waves at Great Point.

The problem was she couldn't bring herself to sign it.

Instinctively, the bundle in front of her contained the explanation that makes the most sense. A man fishing with his business partners falls overboard while attempting to urinate. But then there's the personal flotation device. Why did it not inflate? Was it defective? Did it malfunction? Or was there something more there? That report was still a day or two away.

Growing up, her mother always told her to listen to that little voice inside her, that a woman's intuition was one of her strongest assets. She followed that advice throughout her life, and it saved her more than she could count. That little voice is speaking to her again today.

Tuna had a niggling feeling that this was not as cut and dry as it appeared to be. Something was not settling well, and she couldn't put her finger on it. Was it that every person she talked to who knew Charles Post couldn't accept the behavior of the man that led to his death? Was it that there was no clear indication medically of anything unusual that would lead to his death? Or was her gut trying to tell her that something suspicious was going on, that maybe that death wasn't accidental at all?

Her pen was wavering over the signature line of the report when her phone buzzed. Relieved, she picked it up, noted the number, and clicked on accept. "Officer Downs. How are you?"

"I'm good, Tuna. You?"

"Doing alright."

"That's good to hear. Hey, did you hear about that case in Newport last week?" Officer John Downs, ambitious to become a detective, often scoured the news for interesting murder cases, always anxious to understand how the guilty parties were caught and prosecuted. He then shared those findings with usually reluctant ears above his pay grade, hoping to impress and facilitate his odds of promotion.

"I haven't," Tuna admitted, her voice low and cautious as she leaned back, her office chair creaking. "Anything interesting?"

On the other end of the line, Downs let out a soft chuckle, the kind that suggested he was enjoying the buildup to something. "Husband and wife on the Cliff Walk. Have you ever done it?"

"What, the Cliff Walk?" She squinted out the narrow window beside her desk, as if she could picture the place better that way. "Sure. Ellen and I spent a long weekend down there last fall. We took a nice stroll. It's lovely."

"Did you do the whole thing?"

She frowned slightly. "What do you mean?"

"The majority of people just complete the easy portion, the first half," he said, his tone suddenly professorial. "They think it ends at The Breakers mansion."

"And doesn't it?"

"Nope," Downs replied, the word drawn out. "It actually continues for another two miles. And the path itself gets really hairy. In some sections, you have to carefully step through rock fields - some quite literally boulders - just feet from crashing waves."

Tuna straightened, curiosity getting the better of her. "Okay. So what happened with this husband and wife?"

Tuna could almost hear him smiling as he recounted the case file to her. "They got to a section known as Lands End, where the man claims his wife slipped on a seaweed-covered rock and fell about ten feet, hitting her head on the edge of a large, ragged stone. The fall fractured her skull. She was dead when the EMTs arrived about a half hour later. Brain bleed."

Tuna winced. "Jesus. A half-hour to respond?"

"The section they were on is incredibly difficult to get to. As it was, they had to cross private property, find access to the trail, and then make their way to the victim."

She drummed her fingers against her desk, eyes narrowing. "Wow. Okay. So you think it wasn't accidental?"

"The investigating officers put it down to accidental death. Apparently, the woman's hiking shoes were worn, and the rocks were very slippery from the seaweed and a recent rain shower. Not to mention that people slip and fall every year. It's a very challenging section of the trail."

"So?" she asked, sensing something more.

"So," he said in a sing-song voice, "technology saves the day."

"I'm sorry," said Tuna, "how exactly did technology help?"

The silence on the line was filled with the hum of amusement. She didn't need to see his face to know that Officer Downs was smiling.

"One of the investigators went door to door - or maybe mansion to mansion would be a better descriptor," Downs said, his voice light with irony. "Luckily, she found that one of the privately owned homes had extensive surveillance cameras on the back of its property. Apparently, the owners had had some people jump the fence thinking their house was open to the public."

Tuna yawned and tried to think of polite ways to end this conversation. She admired his enthusiasm but, given her job, didn't really like to hear stories of true crime.

"And get this," Downs continued, undeterred. "They keep the footage for six months - thanks to the cloud - so she was able to review the video on the day of the accident. And wouldn't you know, one of the cameras had a perfect shot of the husband pushing the wife. Boom!"

There was a pause. Tuna couldn't help the small smile that tugged at the corner of her mouth, though it didn't quite reach her eyes. Once upon a time, she might have gotten excited about a case like this, too, but she had seen far too much pain and death firsthand, especially between spouses. "That's interesting, John. But I really gotta go and finalize the report on the Charles Post case."

"Oh wait," Downs interjected quickly. "That's why I was calling."

She blinked, caught off guard. "Really? Not just to share that case from Newport," said Tuna a bit caustically.

"No. Sorry. I get a bit excited about those things."

Tuna could hear the shuffling of paper.

Downs continued. "I got a call today from the recycling yard where they sent Mrs. Posts' car. Apparently, they found some anomalies in the vehicle's software."

"Anomalies in the software?" asked Tuna, confused.

"Yeah." Downs said, his tone slipping back into lecture mode. "All modern cars have extensive software to control everything from the steering to the radio to the air conditioning."

Tuna sighed, her patience already thinning. "John, I drive a thirty-year-old Ford Explorer. Can you cut to the chase, please?"

"Sure," said Downs' laughing. "Mrs. Post's car was a one-year-old high-end German luxury brand. They are incredibly complex and expensive."

"Okay," said Tuna, shifting in her chair. "So?"

"When a car like this is totaled, the recyclers go through it with a fine toothed comb to pull parts that can be reused to repair other vehicles. They are especially interested in the computers - the control modules - because they are rarely damaged and generate good profits for them."

Tuna was running short on patience. First, a murder in Newport and now a lecture on modern automotive recycling. "John, I really got to go."

"Mrs. Post's car appears to have been tampered with," said Officer Downs firmly.

"What?" exclaimed Tuna, sitting up in her chair and suddenly interested. "How can you say that?"

"As I mentioned, modern cars use computers to run just about everything in the car. One of those computers is called the DCM, or Driver's Control Module. It manages all the inputs from the driver and converts them into actions for the car."

"Alright, John, you are losing me again."

"Look. In your Explorer, the throttle, the brake, and the steering wheel are all physically connected either by a cable or a shaft. So, for example, when you press down on the accelerator, a physical cable pushes on the fuel injection to allow more gas into the engine, which increases your speed. But that's not the case with modern cars. The only connection is through wires and software."

"Seriously?" Tuna blinked, surprised. "There's no physical connection?"

"None. It's called drive-by-wire. Instead of a physical connection, there are sensors that determine the inputs from the driver and then process those inputs through a computer, which then tells the systems - throttle, brakes, steering, etc. - what to do."

"Sounds scary."

"Actually, it's all perfectly safe. Unless someone messes with it."

A chill crept up her spine. "What are you saying, John?"

"As part of the recycling process, all modules are scanned to ensure they have the latest version of software from the manufacturer. You see, the software is constantly being optimized to address bugs as well as identified improvements."

"And?"

"And in the case of the DCM from Mrs. Post's car, the software had been updated but with an unauthorized version."

Tuna's mouth went dry. "Would that be difficult to do?"

"No, not really. Automotive software is just like any other software. It can be hacked, changed, deleted."

"So why mess with the DCM?" Tuna asked.

"That's just it," Downs said, voice tightening. "No one messes with the DCM. It's too risky. It controls the essential stuff like steering, throttle, braking. You screw with that, you're talking serious danger. Lawsuits. Jail time."

Tuna's voice was steady now, all business. "So why would someone change that software? Do we know what was altered?"

"Unfortunately, no. The recycling yard just scans the software to be sure it's the current version. They don't have the ability to look at the code and determine what's been changed. That's way above their pay grade."

"So it's nothing?" she asked, though her gut told her otherwise.

"That's not what I said," said Downs defensively. "What I'm saying is that further investigation is needed to understand what was changed and why."

"Are you saying that the crash that killed Mrs. Post was not accidental?"

There was a long pause on the other end of the phone. Downs blew out a breath and then said, "Look. It's just really suspicious. The fact that it was the software in the Driver's Control Module tells me that someone was trying to cause damage. Or..."

"Or?" she prompted.

"Or causing a bad accident that could severely injure or even kill someone."

"And they could do that by just changing the software?" asked Tuna incredulously.

"Absolutely. Just tweaking a few lines of code could cause the car to accelerate when you hit the brake pedal. Or steer left when you want to go right. Or cause the input controls to not work at all. If you wanted, you could even program it so the car accelerated and then turned all on its own without any driver involvement."

"Holy shit," said Tuna. "Murder by car?"

"Exactly," said Downs. "But for now, it's just a suspicion. What we really need is someone who can look at the code and tell us exactly what changes were made and the impact they would have on the vehicle's controls. It might be nothing, but given the circumstances, I would recommend it."

She nodded slowly, her mind already racing. "I think you are spot on. Who can do that for us?"

"Do you, by chance, know anyone at the FBI?"

"Um, maybe. Why?" said Tuna with a wry smile.

"This type of software hack is no different than other hacks they investigate, like ransomware and remote exploits like this. They have the tools and resources to quickly examine the code and tell us what has been changed. And if they can't determine it, they have relationships with all of the major automotive manufacturers."

"That's excellent. Can you have them send this module thingy to us?"

"One step ahead of you," he said, a grin in his voice. "I should have it tomorrow."

"Nice work, John."

"Thanks. I'll bring it over to you as soon as I receive it."

"Perfect."

Tuna ended the call and placed the phone on her desk. She thought for a minute and then picked up the final report on Mr. Post's death, tore it in half, and disposed of it in the shred bin under her desk. Officer John Downs had just confirmed that her little voice was right. This was most certainly not an accidental death, and she had a lot more work to do.

CHAPTER EIGHTEEN

Tuna picked up her phone and dialed.

Rick answered on the first ring. "Tuna, to what do I owe the pleasure?"

She smiled. "Are you, by chance, still on the island?"

"I am. I've taken a few days more leave to allow me to look into this in a little more detail. Fel, the daughter, has uncovered some interesting information about her dad and his firm."

"Who is that?" asked Felicity. She was standing next to Rick and resisting the urge to tug at his sleeve.

Rick pulled the phone and covered the mic. "It's Tuna. Let me see what she needs."

Felicity nodded quickly.

"Sorry, Tuna. I just had to answer a question for Fel here," said Rick.

"It's okay. I was just asking about what information she found."

"There was a coded letter from Mr. Post in the safe addressed to her. It was a simple code - actually a pigeon cipher - that mentioned a thumb drive. She had to search for it a bit but eventually found it hidden in a cabinet on her dad's sailboat."

"Interesting. Was there anything on it? Or was it just his backup for family photos?"

"Actually, quite a bit, especially as it relates to the case. Fortunately, Fel was able to guess the password - something about a childhood book. The drive contained another letter to her where he - Mr. Post - stated that he suspects that there was something illegal going on at his firm."

"Wow. Okay, that's interesting. Was there anything else on the drive?"

"Yes. There were a number of spreadsheets, which we suspect were the quarterly financials for some of the companies that the firm invests in."

"Did you have a chance to look at those files?" asked Tuna.

"We scanned a few of them, but there were no obvious smoking guns. Given my years in financial crimes, we really need to have a forensic accountant look at them to determine if anything illegal or improper is going on. I tried to gain some resources at the FBI but was shot down. My boss said I should leave the whole thing up to you, that is, local law enforcement."

"I like that sound of that," said Tuna. "Let's do this. Do you have any plans today?"

Rick pulled his phone from his ear and glanced at the time. It was already well after five. He returned it and said, "How about we meet for a drink and compare notes? And maybe craft an investigative plan?"

"Works for me. Where shall we meet?"

"Let's keep it simple. Faregrounds?"

"You won't mind being so close to your old office?" The restaurant and bar were across the street from the headquarters of the Nantucket Police. It was also mildly famous for providing the annual Thanksgiving meal for the 46th President.

"I think it's time I stood up to my fears," said Rick, laughingly. "Shall we say six?"

"Six it is. I'll see you there," said Tuna and disconnected the line.

Rick slipped his phone into his pocket and looked at Felicity. "You finding that thumb drive has definitely piqued Tuna's interest. She wants to meet and talk through our investigative approach."

"That's great. When do we meet her?"

"*I'm* meeting her in an hour."

Felicity's shoulders slumped.

"Look," said Rick, "I know you want to be involved, and I promise you will be. But let me keep this professional for now - agent to detective. Once we have a plan, I assure you that you'll be a part of it. Okay?"

"Okay," said Felicity reluctantly. "Promise?"

Rick smiled. "I promise. Now, would you mind if I borrowed the Bronco?" he asked sheepishly.

* * *

Rick jumped into the driver's seat and started the old Bronco. As soon as it fired up, he was thrust back into time to the days when Charles Post would give him rides home from the Yacht Club. The sights, sounds, and smells of the classic vehicle made him feel like a teenager again. He smiled sadly and then pushed in the clutch, selected first gear, tipped into the throttle, and then smoothly let out the clutch. He turned quickly and let a little spray of gravel behind him as he exited the Post residence.

He had some time—the restaurant was barely a couple of miles away—so coming to the end of Monomoy Pond Road, he took a left onto Polpis and accelerated quickly. This had always been one of his favorite drives on the island. He noticed a few new houses along the way, but the majority of the land was just the way he remembered: scrub brush, cranberry bogs, and saltwater marshes. It was beautiful.

The Bronco purred along, its exhaust note a deep throaty bass, while the wind tousled Rick's hair. It was a perfect September evening, and for a few minutes he forgot why he was on Nantucket. The old Ford was like a time machine taking him back to simpler, happier times. Rounding a curve, he came across Quidnet Pond, its waters a deep blue with small waves reflecting the sun's rays like a million diamonds. He spied a small turnout and quickly pulled in. He pushed in the parking brake with his left foot, slid the transmission into neutral, and turned off the car. The sudden silence was almost deafening.

He leaned back and let the setting sun warm his face. Somewhat reluctantly, he realized how much he had missed Nantucket. For the last decade, he had tried to convince himself that this part of his life was dead and gone and that the magic of the island no longer had that pull on him. But now he realized just how wrong he had been. Looking over the blue waters of the pond brought an ache to his heart. He had come to the island reluctantly. Now, he wasn't too sure he'd be able or want to leave.

And then there was Felicity. The gap-toothed, gawky ten-year-old he remembered from babysitting Scott had turned into an impressive and beautiful woman. Her passion and energy excited him, and he hoped desperately he could help her achieve some level of closure with the deaths of her parents. As he thought of her, his phone buzzed. It was Tuna.

Where r u?

He quickly typed back.

Sorry. Be there in 10.

He started the car, pulled out, and headed back toward town. Nine minutes later, he was swinging into the Faregrounds parking lot. He hustled inside quickly and found Tuna sitting at the corner of the bar, talking to a small group of locals. Seeing Rick, they bade their goodbyes and let them have their privacy.

"Sorry I'm late," Rick said, sliding onto the barstool beside her. His jacket was dusted with salt from the sea air. "Lost track of time."

"That's fine," Tuna replied, smiling as she shifted on her seat to face him. "Just wanted to make sure you weren't going to stand me up."

The bartender approached. "Can I get you anything, sir?"

He looked at Tuna. "What are you having?"

"Just a Cisco Whale's Tale."

He turned to the bartender. "I'll have a Whale's Tale, too, please." She nodded, grabbed a bottle from the cooler, popped the cap, and slid it in front of him.

Rick picked up the bottle and held it out to Tuna. "Thanks for calling me."

She clinked her bottle to his. "Absolutely. I just want to get to the bottom of this."

Rick took a deep pull on his beer and then looked at Tuna. "Have you changed your mind on whether or not this was an accidental death?"

"Honestly," she said and leaned her elbows onto the bar. "I was about to close the file on this case earlier today."

His brows lifted. "And? Why didn't you?"

"I got a call from the investigating officer for Mrs. Post's accident."

"Okay," said Rick warily. "New information?"

"I'll say. The recycling yard that was processing her car believes one of the control modules was tampered with. "

Rick's eyes went wide. "Seriously?"

"Yeah. I don't really understand the technical details, but Officer Downs was pretty adamant that it was very suspicious. The yard is sending us the module for further evaluation." She paused, studying Rick. "Do you know anyone in the FBI that would be able to help us with that?"

He leaned back on his barstool, the gears in his mind turning. "Actually, I do. During my training at Quantico, I got close to several of the other candidates. A few of them I still stay in touch with. One of them, Margot North, was a computer wiz. She's now the district Chip for the New York field office."

"The district what?"

"Sorry. You know we love our acronyms. Her official title is Computer Hacking and Intellectual Property Coordinator. We call them Chips for short."

Tuna shook her head slowly. "I'm so glad we keep things simple here on the island. A chip here is something you eat. Anyway, do you think she could help us?"

Rick nodded. "I think so, at least unofficially. Normally, a request would need to be submitted through the local field office - for us that's Boston - to secure the resources for a formal investigation. But I'm sure she wouldn't mind taking a quick look and give us some idea on what we are dealing with."

'That would be great. I should have the device tomorrow. Just let me know where to send it."

"I'm happy to take care of it. Just let me know when you get it."

"Thanks. Now, what about you? What more can you tell me about this mysterious thumb drive?" asked Tuna.

Rick took another sip of his beer. "It's pretty clear that Post thought something fishy was going on at his firm. As I mentioned, there were a number of files on the drive which looked like the quarterly financials for six companies. I'm assuming these companies are ones that the firm, Miacomet Capital, invested in."

"And you didn't see anything in those files that made you suspicious?"

Rick gave a knowing smile. "Although I'm in the financial crimes division, my expertise is not in accounting. What we really need is someone that can take a look at those files and determine if anything was going on that we need to be concerned about."

"I think I have just the guy," said Tuna.

Rick tilted his head. "Really? Who?"

"His name is Peter Bois. I've met him but really only know him through his reputation."

"And he's a forensic accountant?"

Tuna laughed. "No, actually, he's a retired rich guy that runs a foundation here on the island. But he got rich by building a plastics company in Connecticut. I've heard he is super smart and knows his way around the world of finance. We need to have him take a look at those files and get his POV."

"Okay. Do you have his contact info?"

"I don't. But I'll get it and give him a call and see when he might be able to meet with us."

"Done. So what's next?" asked Rick.

"First, I need to get you the device from Mrs. Post's car so you can send it to your contact in New York. Second, I need to connect with Mr. Bois and see when he can see us."

"What about the partners in the firm? Worth another talk?"

"Let's hold off on that," said Tuna. "I'd like to know a bit more of what we are dealing with before we approach them again."

"Okay. And now the most important question of all."

"What's that," asked Tuna cautiously.

"Do you want another beer?"

Tuna laughed in relief. "Abso-effing-lutley!"

CHAPTER NINETEEN

It was just past nine when Rick finally pulled into the gravel drive of the Post residence. The sky outside had gone deep navy, the last hints of light swallowed by the horizon. The beach house stood quiet except for the muted murmur of voices drifting through the open window.

Felicity and Scott were seated on the wide linen couch, a small table between them cluttered with empty glasses and the remains of a light dinner. Scott nursed a tumbler of whiskey, his gaze distant. Felicity sat cross-legged, a bottle of sparkling water sweating on the coffee table in front of her.

"Get you anything?" asked Scott, rising up from the sofa.

"No, I'm good, thanks."

"How did it go with Tuna?" asked Felicity eagerly.

Rick settled into the armchair across from them, exhaling as he ran a hand through his hair. "Overall, I think it went well," he answered. "I think she's starting to smell something with your parents' deaths. I mean, both could still be accidental, but she thinks what we know so far warrants looking at both cases in more detail. With that, she wants to open two lines of inquiry."

"Our parents' deaths?" asked Scott suspiciously.

Rick nodded. "Yes. In addition to the files that Fel found on the thumb drive, it appears that one of the modules in your mom's car was tampered with."

Both Felicity and Scott looked shocked.

"Tampered with?" Scott said, his tone rising. "What are you saying?"

Rick held up a calming hand. "Well, we don't know much of anything yet, just suspicions. But the recycling yard that was processing your mom's car found some unauthorized software on one of the control modules."

Felicity leaned forward, brow furrowed. "Unauthorized software? What does that mean?"

Rick sighed. "Honestly, it could mean anything. Maybe your parents were having a problem with the car, and the local repair shop attempted to fix it. Or maybe?"

"Or?" Scott pressed.

Rick hesitated. "Or someone intentionally modified the software with the intention of causing an accident."

Felicity stood abruptly, her water forgotten. "Are you saying my mom was murdered!"

Rick motioned for her to sit and said calmingly, "We don't know that yet. The recycling yard is sending us the device they suspect has been tampered with. I'm going to forward it to a colleague at the FBI who can give us an assessment of the changes involved and what, if any, impact they would have on your mom's car."

"But it wasn't hers," said Scott.

"Wasn't hers?" asked Rick.

Scott glanced over at his sister, then back to Rick. "No. That evening, she drove my dad's car. He's the one who likes those high-end German SUVs. Mom preferred things much simpler. She had a little Mini convertible that she loved."

"Hmm," muttered Rick, thinking aloud. "Then, if the car was tampered with malignant intentions, maybe your dad was the intended target?"

"I knew it!" said Felicity. "Somebody wanted Dad dead. There is no way his falling off the boat is an accident."

Rick lifted his hand. "Wait. We don't know that. All we know is we have a control module from his car that was tampered with - maybe innocently - and a thumb drive with a few files and a note saying he was suspicious of activities at the firm."

Felicity crossed her arms. "And what about the files we found on the thumb drive? What did Tuna say about those?"

"She suggested we have a gentleman on the island take a look at them. Some guy named Paul Bois."

Felicity perked up. "You mean Peter Bois?"

"Yes, sorry. Peter Bois," he corrected.

Felicity smiled. "Mr. Bois? Of course, why didn't I think of that?"

"You know him?"

Felicity nodded eagerly. "Yes! I'm the director of a non-profit in Providence. My dad sent me an article on the work that Mr. Bois and his foundation were doing on the island. It was impressive, let me tell you. They had some really interesting ideas around affordable housing. Ideas that I thought we could learn from in Providence. So I emailed him hoping he might have time to meet with me."

"And did you?"

"I did! I emailed him right away but figured he was way too busy and important to talk to me. I thought maybe I'd hear back from an assistant if I was lucky. But he literally responded to my note in a matter of hours. Said he would be delighted to meet and asked when I'd be on the island. He even offered to come to Providence; can you believe that?"

"Sounds like a good guy," Rick said, clearly impressed. "Did you catch a chance to meet with him?"

"Yes. He spent an entire afternoon with me. Gave me a tour of their offices on Main Street. Introduced me to his entire team and the work each of them does. He also went into great detail about what has worked and what hasn't for them. It was a huge learning opportunity for us."

"Would you be comfortable reaching out to him and asking him for some of his time?"

"Of course!" said Felicity. "I'll text him first thing in the morning."

Rick smiled already reaching for his phone. "Perfect, thank you." He quickly sent a text to Tuna.

Fel knows Bois. She is setting up meeting. Will advise details

He had barely pocketed his phone when it dinged. He looked at the screen and smiled.

"You know I'm going with you," Felicity said, her voice low but firm, her green eyes locked on Rick's with clear determination.

Rick smiled. "I expected as much and wouldn't want it any other way."

Felicity returned his smile, something softer behind her expression now. "Thanks," she said softly. "I promise I won't be too much trouble."

She looked radiant in the warm glow of the living room lamp, her auburn hair catching flecks of gold from the light. Rick found himself wondering, not for the first time, what exactly he'd walked into here.

He cleared his throat. "Now, I don't know about you guys, but I'm exhausted. And to be honest, I'm feeling in dire need of a shower and fresh clothes."

"I'd offer you some of my wardrobe, but I don't think they would fit," said Scott, standing and stretching. "I'm probably a couple of inches taller and at least thirty pounds heavier than you."

"Please help yourself to my dad's closet. I know if he were here, he'd be offering them to you directly," said Felicity.

"I know you're right; he was always a generous man. It just feels somehow wrong to me. And what about you two? Do you want to see me wearing some of your dad's things?"

"I'm fine with it," said Scott.

"Fel?"

"Yes," she said. "Especially if it helps us figure out once and for all what happened to him. And my mom," she added, her voice catching slightly.

Rick offered a grateful smile. "Okay. Thank you."

"Of course. And if you look under the cabinet in the guest bath, you'll see an assortment of shampoos, bath gels, deodorant, even some cologne," said Felicity. "My mom always wanted to make sure our guests would feel comfortable."

"Thanks," said Rick, touched by the simple gesture. He nodded to them both and turned toward the stairs, his footsteps soft against the hardwood as he disappeared down the hall.

"Do you want something stronger?" asked Scott, looking at her water.

She gave him a faint smile. "You know, maybe I will. What are you having?"

"Just the local Nor'Easter bourbon."

"Sure, I'll do that. But you can water it down a bit?"

Scott smiled. "That's my sis."

He stood and walked into the kitchen. He grabbed a heavy highball glass from the antique hutch and added a few ice cubes from the freezer. Pouring a generous serving of the bourbon, he filled the remaining space with water. He walked back into the family room and handed it to his sister. He sat down across from her in a navy upholstered armchair.

She cautiously took a sip. "Wow, that's strong!"

Scott smiled. "Give it a minute," he said, swirling the amber liquid in his own glass. "Let your taste buds adjust. It's a little trick I learned when I did the Bourbon Trail in Kentucky a few years ago."

Felicity took another tentative sip. This time, she smiled. "Wow, that really is delicious."

Scott nodded knowingly. "Yes, it is."

They sat quietly for a few minutes, enjoying their drinks. Outside the large glass windows, they could make out a gathering of fog in the distance.

Felicity stared through the large glass windows, her voice soft when she finally spoke. "I can't believe they are gone."

"I know. I can't either." Scott's voice was quiet. "It just seems like a bad dream, you know?"

She nodded. "And to die just a couple of days apart?"

Scott coughed. "I hope you are not buying into all of this. That somehow they were both murdered."

Felicity turned to him, brow furrowed. "What are you saying?"

He raised his hand. "They were both accidents, nothing more. A tragic coincidence, for sure. And damn if I wish neither had ever happened," he said and took a long sip of his bourbon. "I would love to say there was more to it than that, but logic would say otherwise."

She scoffed. "Even though Dad thought something funny was going on at the firm?"

Scott exhaled hard. "Yes. You know Dad was a smart guy, but he's also not familiar with some of the aspects of modern finance."

"What? Are you saying that Dad didn't know what he was doing?"

"That's not what I said," said Scott forcefully. "But Dad was the sales guy, the face of the firm. He didn't get too involved in the day-to-day. And as I've seen in our own firm, modern finance can get pretty complex for those who don't fully understand it."

Felicity's expression tightened. "I don't think I like what you're implying"

Scott smiled sadly and took a sip of his bourbon. "You know I love, er loved, Dad. But his knowledge and experience in the financial world were from a different time. Hell, he didn't even use a smartphone. He was an analog man living in a digital world."

Felicity nodded. "I know what you're saying Scott and I know dad wasn't the most progressive as it relates to technology. But he thought something was going on at the firm. It doesn't take knowledge of high technology to know that people might be doing something they shouldn't."

"True," admitted Scott. "But he could just as well be confusing it with some of the modern tools the firm uses, like algorithmic driven trades."

Felicity leaned forward. "So what about mom?"

"What about her?"

"That she was driving Dad's car, which now appears to have been tampered with. And then she has an accident that kills her? Seems far too coincidental to me."

"Fel..." Scott's voice was weary now. "I think you are tilting at windmills. I feel sick that we have lost Mom and Dad, but I refuse to believe it was anything more than two tragic accidents. I think you want to believe that to keep your mind busy and not think about the fact that you and I are now orphans."

She stared at him for a long moment. Then, without a word, she set her bourbon down on the coffee table. "Believe what you want. I'm just glad that Rick is here. And he seems to have gotten that detective interested as well. Hopefully, between the two of them, they can get to the bottom of what really happened." She stood abruptly. "Good night!" she said forcefully and walked out of the room.

Scott sighed and turned out the lights. He sat in the chair, sipped his bourbon, and watched the fog roll in to embrace the island.

CHAPTER TWENTY

Rick awoke to a beautiful Nantucket morning. All traces of the prior night's fog had vanished, leaving only a cloudless, deep blue sky. Standing, he stretched and took an assessment of the clothes he had found in Mr. Post's closet the night before. He had selected thick khaki pants and a navy and pale yellow flannel shirt. Certainly, not a combination he would normally wear, but thought that beggars couldn't be choosers. He slid on the pants, buttoned the shirt, and headed down the stairs.

He found Felicity in the kitchen, pouring a cup of coffee. "Morning," he said, his voice still rough with sleep.

She turned and smiled brightly. "Morning!" She then noticed his clothing choices and giggled. "Is that the best you could do? You look like you are going out to chop some firewood."

Rick glanced down at himself—plaid flannel shirt tucked loosely into worn jeans, the cuffs rolled up awkwardly. He blushed and scratched at the back of his neck."I'm sorry. I just grabbed the first thing I could find. I still feel funny about wearing your dad's clothes, and I really didn't want to go digging through all his stuff."

"It's ok," said Felicity, laughing gently. "I don't ever remember seeing my dad wear that, so that's a good thing. Can I pour you some coffee?"

"Please," he replied. "Is Scott still sleeping?"

"No. He was up early and out for a run. He should be back soon." She handed him a steaming mug. Their fingers touched as he took it. She didn't pull away quickly.

"Is it that late?" asked Rick, taking a tentative sip.

"It's almost nine. I guess you really must have needed that rest."

Rick gave a soft chuckle. "Wow. I haven't slept this late in years."

She smiled knowingly. "Must be all that salt air."

Rick returned the smile. "That must be it." He took another sip letting the warmth of the coffee settle him. "When do you think you'll reach out to this Bois guy?"

"Already did."

"Really?"

She nodded. "One of the things he mentioned to me was that he was an early riser and always did his best work in the morning when he was fresh. So I figured, why not?"

"And?"

"And we are on for eleven this morning."

"Wow! That was fast."

She shrugged. "Yeah, but not surprising. I gave him a brief overview of what we wanted to talk about and said it was pretty time-sensitive. He also knew my dad. Said he was really sorry for what had happened and would be happy to do whatever he could to help our situation."

Rick let out a low whistle. "Okay, then. That leaves us barely two hours to prepare. I better let Tuna know." He pulled out his phone and keyed a quick text to her.

"Did you want Scott to join us as well?" asked Rick.

"No," she said quickly, a sharp edge to her voice. "He believes this whole thing is a wild goose chase. He really does think that both were accidents."

Rick nodded slowly. "That's fine. Honestly, I'm still leaning that way myself until we find something definitive to support foul play with either case."

Felicity frowned, her mood shifting. "You really think they were accidents?"

Rick hesitated, choosing his words carefully. "I need to go where the evidence tells me. I'll admit there are some inconsistencies that we are trying to resolve, but despite that, they still look accidental to me if weirdly coincidental."

She set her mug down a little too hard on the counter. "Fine," said Felicity testily. "Help yourself to whatever you want." She left the room quickly and ran up the stairs.

Rick could hear her moving around above him. She did not sound happy. He sighed and went over to the 'fridge, pulling out a couple of eggs and some cheese. He toasted some of the local bread while he fried up the eggs. He then put the bundle together into a sandwich, plated it, refreshed his coffee, and sat at the table.

He ate mindlessly, his thoughts swirling between the deaths of the Posts, his feelings for the island, his attraction to Fel, and the time - or lack of it - that he had remaining to get to the bottom of these two deaths. He picked up his phone and did some mental calculations. With the impending workshop, he realistically only had a couple more days to spare. He had to leave enough time to get back to his apartment, pack a suitcase, gather his other work gear, and get to the airport. The last nonstop flight to DC from Logan was at eight on Sunday evening, which meant he had to be on the noon ferry at the latest to make it work.

He heard the front door close and footsteps in the hall. Scott walked into the kitchen, sweaty from his run.

"Morning," said Rick. "Good run?"

"Morning. Yeah," said Scott, filling a glass with water. He took a long drink and then placed it on the counter. "I like your outfit," he said sarcastically.

Rick looked down at his shirt. "Fel said it looked like I was going to chop wood."

Scott laughed. "She's right about that."

"Sorry."

"Stop. Anyway, glad you found something." He refilled his glass and took another long drink.

There was a pause, the quiet hum of the refrigerator filling the space between them.

"So," Scott said, turning to face him. "You really don't believe my parents were murdered, do you?"

Rick set his coffee mug down and met his gaze evenly. "As I was telling Fel just a few minutes ago, we need to go where the evidence leads us. Right now, that evidence, what little we have, suggests two separate and unrelated accidents. So, to answer you directly, I'd have to say no."

"Good," Scott nodded slowly, as if he'd needed to hear it out loud. "I wish you could convince Fel of that. I fear she's using these suspicions to avoid feeling the pain of our loss."

Rick nodded. "It wouldn't be the first time I've seen that. It's also human nature. We want to understand how things happen and why. When something like this happens - especially to both your parents independently - it makes it that much harder to accept."

Scott exhaled and rubbed a hand over his face. "Well, I appreciate you taking the time to look into it if only to convince Fel that they were both accidents."

"You're welcome. You know your parents meant a lot to me, so I'm happy to do at least something to help you guys deal with this."

"Thanks. Now I need to shower up. I've got a conference call with my team in Denver shortly and need to finish my report on that Taiwanese start-up." He placed his empty glass in the sink and left the kitchen.

Rick's phone dinged. It was Tuna.

Thx for the advance notice. Meet you there.

He smiled. He could feel the sarcasm flowing from her text.

*   *   *

Rick and Felicity took the Bronco. Felicity was driving and expertly working the clutch, shifter and throttle. She was driving a bit aggressively, but Rick put that down to her frustration with what he had said to her earlier. She had barely spoken a word to him since. He watched her green eyes survey the road ahead and her auburn hair trailing behind her in the wind. She turned her head and caught him looking. She smiled subtly and turned her attention back to the road.

"Mr. Bois's foundation has an office on Main Street. Downtown," she said, her voice clear over the roar of the wind.

"Oh, you're talking to me again, are you?" asked Rick teasingly.

"I'm sorry," she murmured, her hands tight on the wheel. "I'm just struggling to accept things."

"It's okay, I get that." He reached over and touched her arm. "I promise you we will get to the bottom of this, accident or not."

She smiled wanly. "Thanks. I am glad you are here and appreciate all you are doing."

They made it to Main Street, and she turned the Bronco onto the cobblestones. The nearly fifty-year-old vehicle swayed heavily from side to side. Rick had to grab the header of the windshield to keep him from being tossed into Felicity's lap.

"Sorry," she said, grinning now. "The one thing Dad didn't update was the suspension in this thing."

Rick laughed. "No worries. But I think I'll get a kidney belt if we're to do this again."

She pulled the Bronco into one of the few available parking spots and killed the engine. "His office is right up there," she said, pointing at a brick building a few steps away.

Rick got out and slammed the door. He looked toward the building and saw Tuna sitting on one of the green benches lining Main Street. Seeing him, she stood up and walked over to greet them.

"Morning, Rick." She turned. "And you must be Felicity."

"Yes, Detective. Very nice to meet you," she extended her hand. "And please, call me Fel."

"Nice to meet you, Fel," Tuna said, shaking it warmly.

Rick put his hands on his hips. "Ready? Fel, why don't you lead the way?"

They followed her through an old black door and up a steep, ancient staircase. They walked up the narrow stairs, the well-worn treads creaking and groaning with each step. At the top was a small foyer with a glass-paneled door to the left. On the wall to the right of the door was a small, shiny brass plaque that read *The Jack Tate & Tristam Coffin Foundation.*

Felicity turned. "This is it." She put her hand on the brass knob and turned. They walked into an airy, well-lit room with walls of exposed brick and large white paned windows that looked out over the cobblestones. There were twelve desks spread out across the wooden floor, each occupied.

A woman at the front desk looked up and smiled. "Good morning, you must be Felicity."

"I am. This is Rick Caton and Detective Tuna…"

"Fisch," said Tuna, finishing her sentence.

"Welcome. I'm Jen. Peter is expecting you. Please follow me."

They made their way through the room, navigating between the desks. At each, they were met with warm smiles. Jen led them into a conference room in the back where an attractive middle-aged man sat in a black office chair, his head buried in a three-ring binder. He looked up as they entered.

"Peter. This is…"

"Felicity!" said Peter, standing. "So great to see you again." He walked quickly over to them. "Thanks, Jen."

Jen nodded and left the room.

Felicity embraced him warmly. "Thanks so much for seeing us so quickly."

"Of course. And I am so sorry for your loss. I didn't know your parents well, but I know they were kind, curious, and passionate stewards of this island."

"Thank you. Let me introduce Detective Tuna Fisch and Rick Caton."

"*Agent* Caton of the Federal Bureau of Investigation," added Tuna, smoothly.

Peter's eyes went wide. "FBI?" He looked back at Felicity. "You didn't mention it was this serious."

Felicity smiled. "Rick is an old family friend. He's taken a few days off from the FBI to help us understand what happened."

Peter turned to Rick. "Nice to meet you."

"And you, sir," said Rick.

"Please have a seat," said Peter and motioned to the chairs surrounding a large oak and glass conference table.

Rick slid his chair in. "So tell me, Mr. Bois, what is it you do here?"

"Please, call me Peter. The Jack Tate and Tristam Coffin Foundation was established five years ago to help address some of the critical needs my wife and I identified here on Nantucket."

Felicity jumped in. "I know affordable housing is one of your areas of focus."

"It is," said Peter. "Our other areas of concentration include food insecurity, education, and conservation."

"Impressive," said Rick. "And what did you do before this?"

"I was in business. A company called Shimmo Plastics. I bought it and built it up. During that time, our R&D group invented a new type of plastic resin that effectively melted harmlessly in seawater, addressing a significant issue with single-use plastics ending up in our oceans."

"Wow. And how did you end up here?"

"This was really my wife's idea. We had made enough money to be comfortable, so we sold the manufacturing part of the company, licensed the resin technology, and established this foundation."

Tuna chipped in. "Who were Jack Tate and Tristam Coffin?"

Peter's expression sobered. "Jack Tate was a childhood friend. Probably my best friend growing up. We worked together here on the island - he was a native Nantucketer. Unfortunately, he drowned while the two of us were swimming one day after work. He drowned, saving my life - I had gotten caught in a rip tide. He was just eighteen."

"I'm so sorry," said Felicity. "I didn't know."

"It's okay. Jen, who you met, is Jack's sister," Peter added. "So I like to think I still have part of him in my life every day."

"And Tristam Coffin?" asked Rick.

"Tristam is actually an ancestor of mine," Peter said, his tone lightening. "He lived on Nantucket in the 1800s. He was a whaler."

"Fascinating," said Tuna. "And why did you name the foundation after him?"

Peter blushed. "It's a very long story. And maybe one day we'll have the time. But in short, he was a remarkable man who influenced me in ways that I still struggle to believe."

There was an awkward pause. Rick stepped in. "Thanks again for seeing us."

Peter looked curious. "I'm happy to. Just not sure what help I can provide."

"We were hoping you might take a look at a few files we discovered in Charles Post's office. They appear to be the quarterly financials of several companies that his firm had invested in."

"Miacomet Capital?" asked Peter.

"Yes," said Rick.

"And you are suspecting something in these files?" Peter sat forward, interest piqued.

"My dad left me a note," said Felicity. "Along with these files. He suspected that there was something unusual going on at his firm. He didn't get into any details; he just thought that the firm might be doing something illegal."

"Illegal? Really?" exclaimed Peter. "Your dad had the reputation of being an incredibly honest and upfront man."

"He was," agreed Felicity. "Which is why I think he was so concerned. He didn't want anyone to think that he or anyone in our family would do something wrong."

Peter leaned back in his chair and folded his hands in his lap. "Okay, then. How can I help?"

Rick leaned forward and handed him a thumb drive. "On this thumb drive, we copied the six files we found on the original thumb drive that Mr. Post left for Felicity. We were hoping you might take a look at the files and let us know if you find anything unusual or suspicious."

Peter turned the small device over in his hand. "What am I looking for?"

"Some sort of financial irregularities," said Rick. "If I had to guess, I'd say that Mr. Post was worried about incorrect financial reporting. Mrs. Post had told me that he thought their returns were too good."

"So a little cooking the books to make things look good for the investors?" asked Peter.

"Something like that. I did a quick review, but I couldn't find anything obvious. I was hoping that someone like you with a long history in business might have a better chance."

"I'd be happy to. Do you mind if I share these with someone else?"

"I think that would be fine," said Rick. "Who did you have in mind?"

"Charles Thompson. He's the CEO of Greenhand Plastics. They're the firm we set up to manage the licensing of the resin technology. He's a financial wizard, and I've known him since prep school. I'm sure he'd be happy to take a look as well."

"That would be fine," said Tuna. "But I have to ask that if you do find anything unusual, er, or illegal, that you would keep it confidential."

"Of course. I'm assuming the other partners, I believe there are two, are not aware of this, um, effort?"

"For now, no," said Tuna. "And until we find anything of concern, I think it's best we leave it that way."

"Understood. Well, if you can let me have a few days…" said Peter.

Rick coughed, interrupting him. "I hate to be demanding, but is there any way you could look through them today, maybe this afternoon? I've got to be on a ferry Sunday, and I'd really like to have some answers for Felicity and her family by then."

Peter nodded. "Of course. Not demanding at all. In fact, I already have a call scheduled with Chuck this afternoon to talk about licensing expansion. We will just have to change the subject matter." He smiled broadly.

Felicity was the first to stand. "Thank you so much, Mr. Bois. "I can't tell you how much we appreciate this."

"Peter, please. And I'm happy to do it. Again, I'm just sorry for your loss. Please let me know if there's anything we can do to help. Let me walk you out."

The three followed Peter back through the maze of desks, smiling faces tracking their progress. At the door, he turned. "I will get back to you on this tomorrow morning. Who should I work with?"

Felicity started to raise her hand, but Rick was quick to grab it and hold it down. "That would be me. Maybe just text me after you've had a chance to review the files? Let me know if it's worth talking again?"

"That would work."

Rick handed Peter his card. "Here's my cell."

"Thanks," said Peter, taking the card. He opened the door, and Rick, Felicity, and Tuna filed through.

They made their way down the narrow stairs and out onto the brick sidewalk.

"So what now?" asked Felicity.

Tuna spoke up. "I need to check on that module. It was due here first thing."

"And I need to call my colleague at the FBI, brief her on what we know, and make sure she'll be able to help with the evaluation of that module." He turned to Tuna. "Call me when you get it."

Tuna nodded.

"And Fel, give me a few minutes, and then maybe it's time you introduce me to your dad's business partners?"

CHAPTER TWENTY-ONE

Rick left Felicity at the Hub to grab a coffee and wait for him while he called his contact at the FBI. He meandered his way down Federal Street to the library, the Atheneum. Aside from housing an incredible collection of books, the Atheneum had a lovely outdoor space with well-tended gardens, gorgeous trees, and a number of seating areas.

It was the kind of place where one could reflect, read, or, in his case, make contact with the Federal Bureau of Investigation without drawing too much attention. He found a bench near a hydrangea bush in full bloom, sat down, and scrolled through his contacts until he landed on one: Margot North.

He hit call. The line rang twice before her unmistakable voice came through—thick with the Jersey roots she could never quite shake, despite years of trying.

"Cola? Good to hear from you. How are things up in Boston?"

Rick chuckled. When they first met at Quantico, Margot had pointed out that his initials—RC—matched her favorite soda. From then on, she'd called him "Cola," and the nickname had stuck. In return, he'd mercilessly teased her for her accent, saying her "Joisey" was showing.

"All good, Margot. Still doing my part to protect innocent retirees and clueless startups from fraud. You?"

"Drowning in cases. Criminals are getting smarter—more digital. Honestly? Some days I feel like we're sprinting to keep up, and they're already at the finish line."

"I bet. Is AI part of the problem?"

She sighed. "Honestly, I think we are just seeing the tip of the iceberg as it relates to AI-driven crime. I lay awake at night worried about what things are going to look like in just a few years and whether or not we will be able to do anything to stop them."

"That's a scary thought," said Rick.

"It is. And I wish I was exaggerating. Even now, criminals are using publicly available AI tools to create tightly targeted phishing campaigns and bundle them with hyper-realistic video and voice impersonations of trusted individuals. As the power of AI grows, so will the criminals' ability."

Rick winced. "Maybe we should just pull the plug?"

"Too late for that. The horse has already left the barn. Anyway, enough about the dystopian future of cybercrime. What can I do for you?"

Rick leaned back, eyes following the sway of a tree branch above him. "You saw my texts. I'm on Nantucket looking into a suspicious death—Ann Post. Family friend. Official report says she swerved to avoid a deer and hit a tree. Died on impact."

"Okay," said Margot. "Sorry to hear that about your friend, but sounds cut and dry to me."

"That's what the authorities thought as well and closed the case. The remains of the car were shipped off island to an automotive recycling yard for processing. During that operation, they discovered that the driver control module contained unauthorized software." Rick explained the process, how recycling yards had evolved, how parts—especially electronic ones—were scanned and verified before resale. He walked her through the diagnostic equipment, the flag on the software version, and the suspicion that the code had been tampered with.

"So that's where I come in?" Margot asked.

"That's right. I need to know if the changes made to the DCM could've impacted the vehicle's performance. Could someone have caused that crash—intentionally?"

"Funny timing."

"What do you mean?"

"I just finished a week-long course on hacking cars."

"Hacking cars?"

"Yeah, believe it or not, it's a whole new area where criminals can do bad things."

"To a car?"

Margot laughed knowingly. "Yes, to a car. Vehicles today are nothing more than rolling interconnected computers. Manufacturers thought it would be a great idea to connect cars to the internet. That way, they felt they could offer new services, make updates remotely, even turn on additional features."

"Seriously?"

"Yeah. One German brand decided to make their heated seats available only with a monthly subscription fee. So when you bought the car, you received a six-month free trial, but if you didn't sign up for the monthly fee, they would turn that feature off remotely."

Rick groaned. "That is ridiculous! After you've spent all that money?"

"I know. But it didn't take. Customers were furious when they found out, and overall sales for the brand started to go down. So management stopped that program and promised they wouldn't change features in the future."

"Serves 'em right."

"But that interconnectivity is still used for updates, additional features, and even remote control of the vehicle."

"Remote control?"

"A lot of cars today come with apps you load onto your phone. Then, from the app, you can do things like close the windows, lock the doors, remotely start the engine, and check on things like fuel level, tire pressures, and when your next round of maintenance is due."

"Wow. I had no idea. I drive a government-issued piece of crap."

Margot smiled. "And as reliable as the sun coming up, criminals have figured out how to do bad things to cars using that interconnectivity."

"Like what?"

"You name it. I mean, it depends on the level of interconnectivity built into the vehicle, but on most cars built in the last year or two, criminals can pretty much do almost anything they want."

"But how?"

"Good old computer hacking. For example, one Japanese manufacturer had their consumer website hacked. All the bad guys needed was the car's license plate number which you can find on all sorts of publicly available sites. Then, knowing the plate, they were able to access the vehicle identification number - the VIN - and from that, connect to the car through the hacked website. They were able to turn on the cameras, mess with the entertainment system, and even turn off the engine. All remotely by sitting in front of their computers."

Rick blinked. "Really?"

"Yeah. Frightening. I mean, think about it: you could be cruising down the highway, and some hacker a thousand miles away hits a key, and your car quits, stopping smack dab in the middle of eighty-mile-an-hour traffic."

"Holy shit," exclaimed Rick.

"Yeah, it's not good. And you thought ransomware was only for companies and hospitals. Hackers can brick a car, making it completely unusable until you pay up."

"I love human creativity," said Rick sarcastically. "Why can't people just be nice?"

"Well, then we would be out of a job."

"I'm fine with that. I'd be happy to do something else. Anyway, it sounds like, in the case of Mrs. Post's car, these unauthorized changes to the DCM could have been done remotely?"

"Yes. It depends on the brand. But like I said, if they know the license plate, they can get the VIN. That's public info. From the VIN, they pretty much know everything about the car, including the year, make, model, engine type, etc. And if they can access the car, then they can make changes they want, like the software in the DCM."

Rick rubbed his temples. "Silly me. I had visions of some thug dressed in black crawling under the car and screwing with things."

Margot laughed. "It was probably some geeky-looking guy sitting at his computer somewhere, making changes with a few taps of his keyboard."

"I had no idea."

"I know. Fortunately, the manufacturers are catching up with their overall security, but there are still bugs and flaws that can be leveraged."

"Okay. Good to know. Now, do I need to send this thing to you, or do I just connect it to the internet?" asked Rick.

"Well, if you had the appropriate equipment, then yes, you could just connect it, and our team could access it remotely. But I doubt you have that equipment."

"Um, no."

"Then you do need to send the module to me. Let me text you the best address." The phone went silent for a few moments, and then Rick heard his phone ding. He looked and saw a new text from Margot.

"Got it. I'll send it next day priority. You should have it first thing."

"Perfect. I'll just need a couple of hours with it so let's plan on talking late morning. I'll text you as soon as I'm ready."

"Thanks so much. You don't know how much I appreciate this."

"My pleasure. Any chance you're going to that workshop next week at Quantico?"

"Um, maybe," said Rick cautiously.

"Well, payback is a bitch. You can take me to dinner."

Rick smiled. "Deal."

"Later, Cola," said Margot and ended the call.

Rick pocketed his phone and ambled a couple of blocks to the Hub. He found Felicity where he had left her, although she was no longer alone. She was talking animatedly to a good-looking young man who seemed to be hanging on her every word. Rick slowed his pace.

"You ready, Fel?" said Rick as he approached her bench.

"Sure thing," she said brightly. "Rick, let me introduce you to an old friend of mine, Cooper Werks."

Rick extended his hand. Cooper took it and pumped it furiously. "Nice to meet you, Rick," said Cooper.

"And you."

Cooper turned to Felicity. "Great to see you. Maybe we could grab a drink or dinner sometime?"

"I'd like that."

"Terrific. I'll text you," said Cooper. He leaned in and gave her a kiss on the cheek, nodded at Rick, and then walked briskly down Main Street.

"Um, who was that?" asked Rick, a bit jealous.

"Oh, Cooper? He's an old boyfriend. We dated the summer after my sophomore year in college."

Rick raised an eyebrow. "Really?"

"Are you jealous, Agent Caton?" said Felicity teasingly.

Rick cleared his throat. "No, not at all. It's just an old habit of wanting to know. Anyway, let's go see your dad's partners."

Felicity smiled as they made their way over to the Bronco. "Hop in," she said, tossing her hair over her shoulder.

CHAPTER TWENTY-TWO

Felicity and Rick hopped in the Bronco and made their way slowly up Main Street, the old car swaying heavily from side to side. They made their way the few hundred feet to Orange and turned onto the paved street. The relief from the cobblestones was immediate.

She turned to Rick. "Shouldn't we call them first?"

"No," Rick said, casually resting an arm on the windowsill. "You have every right to be there; it is your dad's firm, after all. And I want to assess how they react when they see you."

She nodded slowly. "Makes sense. And are you going as Rick Caton? Or as FBI agent Rick Caton? I saw the effect that had on Mr. Bois. Might make things interesting."

Rick smirked. "Let's improv with that. Let me see how they react to you first."

"Okay," said Felicity, looking ahead and biting her bottom lip. "So why are we going there? We don't want to say we are there to interview them, do we?"

"No, not at all." Rick thought for a minute. "Maybe we tell them you're looking for your dad's will."

Felicity shook her head. "They won't buy that. They know how detail-oriented my dad was. They'll know he had all his ducks in a row for my mom."

"Can you think of something?"

Her forehead wrinkled in concentration, and then her face lit up. "My parents' wedding picture! He has the original on his desk. We can say we're just stopping by to grab it for a memorial service. They'll know my dad wouldn't have a digital copy." She paused for a minute, her face clouding in remembrance. "My parents' memorial service? Oh my god, I can't believe they are both gone."

Rick leaned over and rubbed her shoulder. "I know. It is absolutely awful. It's going to take some time, a lot of time, until things feel a little less empty."

She turned and looked at him, the glint in her eyes softening. "Working with you on this is certainly helping me keep my mind off things."

He gave her a small smile. "I'm glad for that."

They drove in silence for a beat before she asked, "Have you thought about what you are going to ask them?"

"Not really. I think I'm just going to feel them out. See which way the conversation moves. I'm really just trying to get a feel for what they might know and if they're hiding anything."

"So, no mention of my dad's note or the files he left?" she asked.

"Absolutely not. If they are involved, we don't want to tip our hands just yet. Let them think all is roses right now."

"Well, not really roses," said Felicity, looking sad again.

Rick winced. "Oh, I'm sorry. You know that's not what I meant. I just don't want them to think they are under any suspicions whatsoever.

Felicity swung the Bronco into a narrow lane and pulled into a small parking lot. There were a few other cars there. She slid into a parking spot and killed the engine.

"Is that the office?" said Rick, pointing at a small, gray-shingled building.

"It is. This is the back entrance, though, but the front is no more impressive."

"Not what I was expecting for a multi-million dollar investment fund."

"You can say what you really think," said Felicity. "It's a dump. The inside's better but certainly not fancy."

Rick nodded, taking in the weathered siding and the cracked trim on the doorframe. "Did they not have money to take care of it? I would think your dad and his partners were loaded."

"They are. They just didn't want to spend the money on the building. They thought keeping a low profile would benefit them with the clients. You know, they weren't spending their profits on a fancy headquarters."

"I guess it makes sense. But you also want your clients to think you're at least moderately successful and can afford basic maintenance on your offices."

"I know," agreed Felicity. "It actually drove my dad crazy. But the partners each had a vote on the matter, and my dad usually lost."

"Interesting," Rick murmured, filing that detail away.

"Ready?" asked Felicity, unbuckling her seatbelt.

"As I'll ever be," said Rick.

They got out of the Bronco and walked through the back door and into the offices of Miacomet Capital Partners. The interior was certainly nicer than the exterior but still not as high-end as Rick was expecting. Felicity led them down the hall and into a spacious office. Tongue-in groove wainscoting, painted white, lined the walls to a chair rail. Above the rail, a pale yellow wall sported numerous personal pictures of the family, his sailboat, and what

Rick suspected were the partners in various situations: fishing, golfing, celebrating. In each, everyone looked happy.

They heard footsteps approaching down the hall. In walked a tall, thin, and bald man. He was wearing tan slacks and a navy pinstripe button-down. His expression brightened when he saw Felicity.

"Felicity?"

She turned. "Hi, Sean. How are you?"

Sean walked briskly over to her and embraced her. "I am so, so sorry for your loss, Fel. I can't believe they are both gone."

"I can't either," she said softly. "I keep expecting to wake up from this awful dream."

He pulled back and turned to Rick. "Oh, hello. I'm Sean Axmacher. I'm one of the partners here," and extended his hand.

Rick shook it. "Nice to meet you, Sean. I'm Rick Caton."

Sean nodded, his gaze flicking back to Felicity. "So what brings you in? Certainly, you could have called. I would have brought you anything you need."

"Thanks. But actually, I wanted to see my dad's office again. I have many fond memories of this place, playing on the carpet when I was a kid, doing homework at his desk in high school, those sorts of things."

Sean nodded solemnly. "I understand."

"And," continued Felicity, scanning the room, "I wasn't one hundred percent sure it would be here."

"That what would be here?" asked Sean, a flicker of concern passing across his face.

Felicity scanned the room, her eyes landing on her dad's desk. In the middle of a group of framed pictures, she spotted the one she was looking for. She grabbed it and showed it to Sean and Rick.

"My mom and dad's wedding picture, taken almost forty years ago." Her eyes began to well up. Rick walked over and put his arm around her.

"I remember that day," said Sean fondly. "Your parents were so happy."

"I don't remember them being anything but happy. I don't think they ever fought," said Felicity. "At least not in front of us."

"I miss them," said Sean. "I think about them constantly. It's just so sad to lose them both just days apart."

Rick watched Sean carefully. There was genuine emotion there, but something about the way his hands fidgeted, the way his eyes flitted to the desk and back—it wasn't quite sitting right.

Felicity nodded. "Yes, it is. It's been awful. Fortunately, Rick came down from Boston to help Scott and me."

Sean turned to Rick. "How do you know the family?"

"I grew up on the island and often babysat for the Posts," said Rick casually.

"He babysat you?" said Sean, looking at Felicity and smiling.

"Me and Scott," Felicity corrected. "But now he's a big shot FBI agent."

Sean's expression froze. "FBI?"

Rick smiled. "Yes, I'm an agent with the Boston field office. I've been with them for eight years. I focus on financial crimes."

Sean's face went white. There was a beat of awkward silence and then he swayed slightly on his feet.

"Are you okay?" asked Felicity, her voice laced with concern.

Sean gathered himself. "Yes, sorry. I've been having episodes of low blood pressure recently. My doctor has tried a number of different medications, but nothing has eliminated them completely."

"I'm sorry to hear that," said Felicity.

"I'm sure we will get it worked out," said Sean. "Is there anything we can do for you or the family?"

Footsteps clomped down the hallway, and a short, broad man with a reddish complexion burst into the room. "Fel!" he boomed. "My dear. I thought I heard your voice." He walked up to her and embraced her. "I am so sorry for what has happened. How are you holding up?"

"I'm okay, given the circumstances."

"And Scott?"

"He's alright. Just got into town. I'm sure you'll be hearing from him once he recovers from his jet lag."

"Asia, wasn't it?"

She nodded.

Cormac turned. "And who might this be?"

"Hi, Rick Caton. I'm a long-time friend of the Posts."

"And an FBI agent," Sean added with forced lightness. "Financial crimes."

Cormac kept a straight face. "Nice to meet you, Rick. I'm sure you have some interesting stories to tell. We should grab a beer sometime."

"I'd like that," Rick lied. He had taken an immediate dislike to the Irishman. Something was not sitting right with his internal radar.

The four stood in Charles Post office, the air thick with unspoken tension.

Finally, Rick spoke. "Fel, I think we need to get going. We promised Scott we'd meet him to go through the details of the memorial service."

"The memorial service? " asked Sean. "When are you planning that?"

"Er, we are still not sure we will have one," said Felicity. "Dad left instructions that he absolutely did not want any type of service. Just wanted to slip off without a fuss."

"Sounds like Charles," laughed Cormac.

"But with my mom, she was not as clear cut. So Scott and I need to figure out what we want to do. And when."

Cormac nodded. "Please let us know if there is anything we can do to help. If you do decide to proceed, we could always use my club if that would be convenient."

"Thanks, I appreciate the offer. I'll let you know what we decide."

He nodded.

Felicity turned to Rick. "Ready?"

"Yes."

They said their goodbyes, polite but perfunctory. Rick kept his expression neutral, his body language loose. But as they stepped out of the room, down the hallway, and back into the sunlight, his mind was racing.

They climbed into the Bronco. Felicity pulled the door shut with a satisfying thunk and turned to Rick. "What do you think?"

"Something's not right here. Sean seemed fine, except for that low blood pressure thing when you told him I was with the FBI. But Cormac? I'm getting major vibes from him. My gut tells me he's hiding something."

Felicity nodded. "Yes, he seemed off to me too. I've known both of them since I was a baby, and Sean hasn't changed much - except for getting older, of course. But Cormac is definitely a different man than I remember."

"Different how?"

"Hard to put my finger on it. But he seems more curt, more aggressive, guarded. He's not the 'hail fellow well met' guy I remember from my earlier years."

"Is he married? Kids?"

"No, never married. Lifelong bachelor. And it's not that he didn't have ample opportunity. I just think he prefers being on his own. Not having to tend to or answer to anyone. Happy being alone and in total control."

Rick scoffed. "That fits him. Let's see what surfaces with those files and the control module. But I'm thinking we'll be talking to Cormac again soon."

She turned onto the main road.

"Where to?"

"Police station, please."

"Are you sure?"

"Yes. Tuna texted me saying she had the module, and I'd like to get that to my colleague as soon as possible."

"Okay," said Felicity.

"And Fel?"

"Yes."

"Don't spare the horsepower," said Rick, grinning broadly.

She backed out of the parking lot, revved up the engine, dropped the clutch, and left a twenty-foot black stripe outside the office of Miacomet Capital Partners. Rick leaned back in his seat, a crooked smile tugging at his lips. If he didn't know better, he'd say he was falling for her.

And that… might just complicate everything.

*   *   *

Inside Miacomet Capital, Sean and Cormac were still in Post's office. Sean was pacing nervously.

"What was that about?" asked Sean, his face twisted in anxiety.

"Sean, it's nothing. She's grieving."

"Not her. Him! He's a bloody FBI agent, for chrissakes, Cormac. Financial crimes!"

"Yes," said Cormac, talking slowly. "But he's not here as an FBI agent. He's here as a family friend, helping Fel and Scott through some difficult times. He's not on the job."

Sean stopped pacing and stared at Cormac. "I hope you're right, I really do."

"In his eyes, we've done nothing wrong, Sean boy. Relax."

"Are you sure? Charles asked us about Eel Point. He knew! Do you think maybe he left a note for Felicity, or god help us, Scott? You know how organized the man was. He was a detail freak."

A flash of worry briefly lit Cormac's eyes. "It's possible. But if he had left anything remotely suspicious, I'm sure we would have already had some questions from that damn detective."

"I hope you're right, Cormac. I really do. I wouldn't want to be the one that had to explain that screw-up to our friends."

Cormac nodded and put his arm on Sean's shoulder. We're okay, Sean boy. I promise."

CHAPTER TWENTY-THREE

Is that really it?" asked Rick, pointing at a small plastic box. They were in the parking lot of the Nantucket Police Department. Tuna had brought out the suspected module. Felicity waited in the Bronco, watching the two of them.

"You know, you can really come in," said Tuna, motioning at the building. "We don't need to meet in the parking lot like a couple of people doing a Craigslist deal."

Rick chuckled yet eyed the building suspiciously. "I'm good, thanks." He picked up the module and turned it over, examining it from several angles. It was black, not much bigger than a pack of cards, and had a row of recessed gray connectors on each of the narrow ends. "This is really it?"

"Yep, I know. I was expecting something much bigger and more impressive," Tuna replied, crossing her arms.

"Me too. Hard to believe all the steering, braking, and throttle inputs go through this little thing. Doesn't instill much confidence, does it?" He gave it a little shake, as if expecting it to rattle.

"The more I learn about technology and the things it controls in our lives, the more I'm happy that I'm a Luddite," said Tuna, laughing.

"Honestly, I'm starting to lean myself that way as well," said Rick, continuing to eye the small plastic box.

"Getting serious, I need you to sign the chain of custody if you still intend to send it to your colleague at the FBI."

"Understand. And yes, Margot should be able to give us a top-line of what might have been done."

"Excellent. Sign here," said Tuna, handing Rick a paper form. It noted the date, time, the evidence in question, general condition, who was in possession of the evidence, and a signature. He completed the form and handed it back to Tuna.

"Let me make a copy for the file. We'll send the original with the module to your contact."

"Thanks." Rick walked over to the Bronco and leaned against the windshield frame. He showed the module to Felicity. "Can you take me by the FedEx office? I need to send this out."

"Of course. It's just over by the airport. " She glanced at her watch. "But it closes in twenty minutes. We better hustle."

"Shouldn't be much longer. Getting hungry?"

"I am. Seems like it's been a long day."

"Yeah. But we've gotten a lot done. I think we've made some good progress."

Felicity smiled softly. "But are we getting closer to knowing what really happened to mom and dad?"

Rick hesitated, then shook his head. "No, not yet. But we've got some irons in the fire, and I think we will know a lot more in the next day or two. So hang in there."

"I will," she said softly.

Tuna arrived and handed Rick the chain of custody paperwork. "Here you go."

"Thanks. Want to join us for some dinner?"

She shook her head. "I haven't seen Ellen all week. Between this and her caseload, we've been like two ships passing in the night. I need to recharge and spend some time with her. Sorry."

"No apologies, Tuna. I totally understand. Thanks for this," he said, holding up the paperwork. "I'll give you a call in the morning?"

"That works." Tuna waved to Felicity and got in her car.

Rick walked back to the Bronco and jumped into the passenger seat. "Let's do it."

Felicity made quick work of the two miles to the FedEx office, and Rick handed over the shipment with minutes to spare. He walked out of the building to where Felicity sat, the Bronco idling menacingly.

"Man, this thing sounds good," Rick added, admiring the tone of the exhaust.

"It does sound sweet, doesn't it? That's what a 351 Windsor with headers and a lumpy cam will do for you," she said, smiling. "Dad could be pretty straight-laced, but he did like his cars."

"Where to?" asked Rick.

"How about the Tap Room? We could sit outside on the patio."

"Perfect. Should we invite Scott to join us?"

She shook her head. "He's having dinner with an old friend tonight. Something about business. So it's just the two of us, if that's okay."

Rick glanced at her, watching the way the last light of day played against her auburn hair. "Of course, it's okay. Let's go."

* * *

The hostess sat them at the high top under the awning. A space heater above the table was on low to take the damp chill off the air.

Rick looked around. "I've never sat outside. I always went down to the basement bar. This is really nice."

Felicity smiled, brushing a lock of auburn hair behind her ear. "It was a favorite of my mom and dad. They'd like to sit and watch Nantucket go by. It's a perfect place for people-watching."

"I bet. So what's good here?" said Rick, picking up the menu.

"Pretty much everything. But if you are in the mood for a burger, I would recommend the Big M-ACK. "

Rick scanned the menu and then looked up at Felicity. "But it's not on here."

Felicity smiled. "It's an off-the-menu item. You need to be in the know."

Rick chuckled. "Guess I'm lucky I came with a local. What are you thinking?"

"The chowder. I'm a simple girl." She put her menu down as their server approached.

The server arrived, and they placed their orders—Felicity choosing the chowder and a glass of sauvignon blanc, Rick going for the off-menu burger and an IPA called the Maine Lunch. After the server left, they sat in a comfortable quiet for a moment, listening to the sounds of clinking glasses and soft laughter from other tables.

"So," Felicity said, watching a couple stroll past on the sidewalk. "Does it feel good to be back?"

Rick followed her gaze. The couple walked slowly, arm in arm, their steps perfectly in sync. There was something about them— easy, quiet, content—that hit him square in the chest. He turned back to Felicity. "In some ways, yes, but I wish for different circumstances."

Felicity nodded. "Have you really not been back since you left?"

He shook his head. "Nope. I left a few weeks after I was fired from the NPD. Stayed long enough to pack up my things and say some goodbyes. My parents tried to convince me to stay, but I needed to get out."

The server returned and set the drinks on the table.

Felicity picked up her glass and looked at Rick. "Thanks for all your help."

Rick held out his glass, and they clinked. "You're welcome. Just glad to be able to help." He took a drink of his beer. "Man, that is good."

Felicity took a sip of her wine and then her eyes searched his. "What really happened to you? Seeing you work the last couple of days, I can't imagine why you'd be let go. I would think you'd be an asset for them."

"Yeah, well, maybe. But not when you're married to the police chief's daughter."

"Is that what happened? My mom told me when you left, but she didn't let on too many of the details."

Rick was quiet for a moment, not sure how much he wanted to share with Felicity. That painful chapter of his life had been closed for years, replaced by a satisfying, if not exactly happy, time living in Cambridge and working at the FBI. He looked at Felicity. She had her elbows on the table, her chin cupped in her hands, and was staring intently at him. A lock of her auburn hair fell over her left eye, which she smoothly hooked over her ear. She looked like he could tell her anything. Maybe it was time.

"I met her senior year in high school," he said finally.

"Your ex-wife?"

"Yes. Allison. Her family had just moved to the island. Her dad had started as the new police chief. She didn't know anyone and was a bit shy. One day at lunch in the cafeteria I saw her sitting by herself and kind of felt bad for her. So I sat down with her, and well, one thing led to another."

Felicity listened without interrupting, her green eyes never leaving his.

Rick continued. "I'd always wanted to be in law enforcement. You know I spent my summers as a CRO, er, Community Resource Officer, so when I graduated from Nantucket High I went straight to UMass to get my degree in criminal justice. Allison and I dated long distance - we had the bus and ferry schedules memorized - until I came back to the island and started with the NPD."

"Was that weird for you?"

"Not really. My first few months on the force were spent in training, and then once I joined full-time, I had several layers of management between me and the chief. But it did get a little weird at family functions sometimes. But we were both diligent at making sure to keep those things separate."

He paused to take a sip of his beer. "We were engaged that fall. I took her for dinner, and then we went on a sunset sail on the Endeavor. As we rounded Brant Point on the return to port, I asked her to marry me. Her saying yes was one of the happiest times of my life. Little did I know."

Their food arrived. Felicity opened a pack of oyster crackers and added them to her chowder. Rick squeezed some ketchup on his burger and put some on the side of his plate for the fries.

"This looks delicious," he said and took a big bite. His facial expression confirmed his initial prediction. "Wow, so good. How's yours?"

"Really, really, good."

They ate for a moment in silence before she asked gently, "So then what?"

Rick set down his burger, thinking. "Oh, yeah. Where was I?"

"You had just gotten engaged."

"Right. We planned to marry the following spring and things were good preparing for the wedding. Allison was busy with her mom taking care of all the details; I was busy learning the ropes of being a cop. The time flew by, and before I knew it, we were married. Went to Disney World for the honeymoon and then settled in a small, rented cottage out past Bartlett's Farm. I thought it was going to be happily ever after."

"And it wasn't?"

Rick snorted. "Lasted about a week."

"A week?" exclaimed Felicity. "What happened?"

"Turns out, dating long-distance isn't the same as living together. We barely knew each other beyond the physical stuff. For five years, our relationship was based on the occasional weekend, during which most of our time was, um, being intimate." Rick blushed.

Felicity smiled. "It's okay. I'm a big girl."

He nodded. "Well, that didn't leave much time to get to know her. I mean, really get to know her and what she wanted from life. And once real life started, so did the pressure."

"So it wasn't what you had expected?"

"Not at all. I'm not sure if it was living on this island and all the wealthy summer residents or if it was something else. But soon after our wedding, the demands started."

"The demands?"

"Yes. She wanted things. Clothing, jewelry, purses. She said she needed them to fit in. Talked about buying a house and a new car. All of a sudden, I felt this intense pressure on me, but she didn't want to hear it. Said it was my responsibility."

"Wow," said Felicity. "That must have been really hard on you."

"It was," admitted Rick. "Honestly, she kind of made me feel like a total loser. Like I wasn't good enough to be her husband. And then those feelings started to affect my work. I had always gotten great performance reviews, but the week after our first anniversary, I got my first crappy performance review."

"That bad?"

"It wasn't awful, but it was worse than any review I had gotten before. And then she just turned up the pressure. She was reluctantly working at one of the clothing stores on Main Street. She'd come home and complain, saying that she should be the one doing the buying, not the selling. She just had this sense of entitlement, like she deserved everything and was angry with me because I couldn't provide it."

"Oh, Rick," said Felicity, "I'm so sorry."

"Thanks. And then I found out she was having an affair."

"Oh my god. Seriously?"

"Yeah. We'd been married a few years at this point. Some wealthy guy was on the island for a few weeks and had come into the store where she was working. Apparently, to get something for his mom or girlfriend, I don't remember which. But I guess he and Allison hit it off and had a brief but intense fling."

"That must have hurt."

Rick nodded. "It did, especially on top of all the demands she had been making on me financially. But I hung in there. We made up and had a heart-to-heart talk. She apologized for the affair and the demands and said she would turn over a new leaf."

"And did she?"

"For a year or so. I thought perhaps we were going to be okay. But then it started again, the demands. But this time, she didn't ask; she just went and bought the things she wanted. She maxed out three credit cards, and I found myself owing thousands at ridiculously high interest rates. I confronted her, and she just said she deserved these things and that I should be taking better care of her."

"Wow."

"I tried talking to her parents, but that wasn't easy, given he was technically my boss. And by this point, I could tell where she had gotten the behavior from. Her mom was just the same, wanting the latest and greatest fashion, new cars, vacations. Her dad was certainly making a lot more than me but I think he was struggling to keep up as well, financially."

He paused to take another drink of beer. He looked out at the street, gathering his thoughts, and then turned his attention back to Felicity.

"The end came quickly. That is, for my career at the NPD. I found out that she was having another affair.

"Another affair? No!" Felicity reached across the table and gently touched his hand.

Rick nodded. "It was a Saturday night in July, and Town was packed. I was working the four to twelve shift and had just finished a call at the Hy-Line. A bunch of college kids had gotten hammered on the boat and were being a little too rowdy when they got here. I wrapped that up and was heading back when I walked by the Straight Wharf restaurant and saw her through the window.

She was smiling and laughing, hanging out with this guy who looked like he just stepped off a yacht. Then he leaned over and gave her a big kiss. On the lips. With some tongue. Honestly, I just snapped." He looked down at her hand resting on his.

"What did you do?"

"I lost it. I barged my way through the bar, pulled the guy out of his chair, and went to hit him. Allison screamed, got between us, and started yelling at me, like I'm the one to blame? Then, all the frustrations, the disappointments, the financial pressure just came out. I pushed her away. It wasn't that forceful, but she got caught up in her chair, and fell hard on the floor. She wasn't hurt - just terribly embarrassed. I was in uniform, of course, and one of the patrons at the bar had filmed the whole thing and posted it on social media. Before long, I was trending, and the scene at the bar went viral. And Allison was apoplectic about her newfound fame."

"I had no idea." She shook her head sadly.

"Well, as you can imagine, the NPD, the Town Manager, and the Tourism Board were none too happy. And being the chief's daughter, whose side were they going to take? I was relieved of duty immediately. They had a hearing for me, but I didn't stand a chance. I was formally dismissed the following week, citing gross negligence, breach of conduct, and any other sham charge they could think of. I'm pretty sure my wife had convinced her dad to throw the book at me."

"That doesn't sound fair," said Felicity.

"No, it was absolutely not fair. But it didn't matter; at this point, I was done. The divorce came quickly, although it cost me an arm and a leg. And, of course, I got stuck with all of her credit card debt. Within a month, I was gone, off the island."

"And then?"

"And then? Just floated around. I found a relatively affordable apartment on the Cape and bounced around odd jobs, sold cars, did some private security. Tried my hand at a few things, but nothing seemed right. But I made enough money to pay off the debt and get myself back on firm footing, financially."

"Good for you," said Felicity.

"Thanks. It was a tough time for me. Really tough. And then a friend suggested the FBI. At first, I didn't think I stood a chance with the whole NPD affair, but I aced my exams and did really well in the interviews. Fortunately, I think they understood the underlying causes that led to my dismissal, that it wasn't a character flaw or cause for concern. So they extended an offer, and I happily accepted. Since then, life's been pretty good for me. I have a great boss, work with a super team, and really enjoy catching the bad guys. And gals."

"I'm so happy to hear that. Whatever happened to your ex-wife?"

"Fate can really be a bitch sometimes, can't it?" said Rick mischiefly.

Felicity smiled, unsure. "What do you mean?"

"To start, her dad, the chief, apparently had been taking, um, let's call it unapproved donations, to look the other way for certain illicit and illegal behaviors."

"You mean he was taking bribes?" exclaimed Felicity.

"Yes. The NPD managed to keep it quiet so as not to bring more embarrassment to the department. But he resigned," Rick held up his hands in air quotes, "to pursue another opportunity."

"That is crazy. And your ex-wife?"

"She left the island as well, following her dad as he pursued that other opportunity. Last I heard, she was in Maine and on marriage number three. Keeps trying to find someone who can satisfy her financial desires. The latest might be able to do it - he's a senior manager at a bank - but who knows? Anyway, I haven't talked with her since the divorce. And really have no plans to if I can help it."

"Thanks so much for sharing all that."

He sighed. "Actually feels good to finally get it out. Thank you for listening."

She smiled. "You seem… grounded. Like you came through the fire."

"Still a little scorched," he admitted.

There was a beat of silence.

"What about now?" she asked softly. "Are you seeing anyone?"

"No. I think I'm a bit gun-shy, to be honest. I've had a few dates but really have had no interest in a commitment. Just haven't met the right person, I guess. What about you?"

"About the same. I've had a few relationships, but nothing serious. I fear there aren't any decent men left. The guys I meet don't seem to be able to hold down jobs or have much ambition. Some still live with their parents. One guy who took me to dinner even admitted he was married. Really? I mean, where the hell are all the decent men out there? You know, the ones that hold the door for a woman, say please and thank you, are honest, respectful, and kind? It's just been so frustrating."

Rick laughed, the sound low and warm. "Sounds like a solid dating pool."

"Do you now," Felicity teased. "So you've been looking for a decent man?"

He laughed, his eyes twinkling. "You know what I mean." He paused, considering. "I think there's at least one still out there," he said, meeting her gaze.

She looked down at her wine glass and smiled. "I'm just giving you crap. So what's next when you are done here?"

"As I mentioned, I have a workshop at Quantico next week. Then it'll be back to Boston. I have a couple of cases pending that I'm anxious to close. Are you going back to Providence?"

Felicity looked down at her hands. "To be honest, I'm not sure. I have some work to do here to settle things with my parents. And figure out what to do with the house, the boat, the cars."

"The Bronco? You'd never let that go, would you?"

"Never," she said with mock seriousness. "My dad would haunt me."

They shared a quiet laugh.

Rick leaned forward. "Can I tempt you with dessert? Maybe an ice cream at the Juice Bar?"

She tilted her head, considering. "I think I could be persuaded."

He waved down the server, paid the bill, and together they stepped into the cool night air. The sidewalks were quieter now, the island beginning to wind down. They walked side by side, close but not quite touching, their footsteps in easy rhythm as they headed toward the warm, sugary glow of the Juice Bar.

CHAPTER TWENTY-FOUR

Saturday morning broke gray, cool, and rainy. A soft rain drizzled over the island, misting the windows and pattering against the roof in a steady rhythm. The wind had picked up slightly, swaying the trees outside the Post house and sending occasional creaks through the old wood frame. Felicity was at the kitchen table drinking her coffee and scanning her phone while the wind rustled the trees outside. Her auburn hair was pulled back in a loose braid, and she wore one of her dad's old Nantucket Whalers sweatshirts which hung loosely on her. Scott walked in, dressed in black running tights and a light, water-resistant jacket already dotted with rain.

She looked up from her phone, arching a brow. "Are you really going to go run in this? You'll get soaked."

Scott nodded. "I've been through worse. And I really need to burn off some of this nervous energy.

She set her phone down. "Nervous energy?" asked Felicity.

Scott sighed. "It hasn't been just the past few days that have been awful. Life for me has been really tough the last few months. The firm isn't doing particularly well, and that EV start-up I was visiting shared some really crappy numbers. They are nowhere near their projections."

"I'm sorry, Scott," she said, her voice softening. "I thought things were going well business-wise."

He scoffed. "Thanks. We'll manage. I have some other sources that are performing well, so it will all balance out. But it's really stressful nonetheless." He poured himself some coffee, looked out at the rain, and then turned back to Felicity. "I'm assuming Rick is still here?"

Felicity took a slow sip of her coffee. "Yes. We got in a bit late last night."

"Oh really?" Scott asked a hint of accusation in his voice.

Felicity smiled forcefully. "It's not what you think. We just had a nice dinner and then grabbed an ice cream." She paused and took another sip of her coffee. "You know, he was really treated unfairly by the NPD. I feel bad for him."

"It sounds like things have worked out for him now, being with the FBI and all."

"Fortunately, yes. But it was certainly hard on him."

"I'm sure. Is he heading back today?" Scott asked hopefully.

Felicity shook her head. "No. We've got a few more things to look into. The more of this onion we peel away, the more Mom and Dad's deaths seem suspicious."

Scott sighed. "I know you want someone or something to blame for Mom and Dad. So do I. But they were just accidents, nothing more. My advice would be to just accept that and not torture yourself anymore with this."

She stared at him, eyes suddenly flashing. "Maybe if you had been around for the last year or so, you'd know how wrong this is. I believe, and I think Rick's getting there too, that someone killed our parents! I want to know who and why, and I want to see them brought to justice."

Scott shook his head slowly. "You're tilting at windmills. I'm sorry. I'm angry, too. And you know the firm and the pregnancy have kept me incredibly busy. Plus, being in Denver? It's not like I can just drop in for the weekend like you do."

She scoffed. "I'm not buying it, Scott. It's almost like you didn't want to be here. Has Lizzie convinced you to not be part of this family anymore? I knew marrying a girl from the West Coast would pull you away from here."

"You leave her out of it!" Scott snapped. "And you know I'll always love Nantucket."

A silence fell between them, heavy and sharp.

"You guys okay?" said a new voice. Rick stood at the doorway to the kitchen, unsure of whether or not he wanted to enter what looked like a family war zone. His eyes moved from Scott to Felicity and back again.

Scott turned to him. "Yeah, we're good. Fel and I are just getting our frustrations out about this whole thing."

Rick walked up and put his hands on Scott's shoulder. "I know how hard this must be for you, Scott. I promise we will get to the bottom of it and find out what really happened to your mom and dad."

Scott looked anxiously back at Rick and then at Felicity. "Thanks," he said meekly. "I'm going for a run." He put his coffee down on the island and walked quickly out of the room. The front door slammed a few moments later.

"Is he okay?" asked Rick, pouring himself a coffee and pointing his thumb in the direction of the front door.

"I'm not sure," said Felicity. "I think he's really struggling with things right now, both personally and professionally."

He nodded and sat down across from her. "Maybe we can bring him some closure if we can figure out what the hell really happened."

She leaned back in her chair, clutching her mug. "That's my hope. Speaking of which, where do we stand?"

Rick took a sip and smiled. "Bois texted me earlier and said he found some things of interest. Wants to meet with us again this morning."

Felicity's face brightened. "Did he say what he found?"

Rick shook his head. "No. Just that he wanted to meet."

"Will Tuna be joining us?"

"No. She has a conflict but asked for me to call her when we are done to share the gist of what Bois has to say."

Felicity nodded and checked her phone. "Okay. What time?"

"Peter suggested ten o'clock at his offices on Main Street."

She stood, stretching slightly, and looked out at the rain. "That gives us a little time. What do you think about Downy Flake for breakfast?"

Rick glanced at her, then grinned. "That sounds like a lovely idea. Let me run upstairs and freshen up. Be ready in ten?"

Felicity smiled and nodded. "I'll be right here."

She turned back to the window, watching the rain slide down the glass in slow, meandering lines. Despite the tension, despite the grief, there was something else now.

Movement.

Momentum.

* * *

After breakfast, Rick and Felicity walked into the offices of the Bois foundation, dripping water on the old oak flooring. The weather had deteriorated further, and they had just made it into the offices when a fresh squall line moved through. Through the large windows looking out on Main Street, they could see the rain coming down in sheets as people walked at an angle, battling the wind.

"Good morning!" said Peter heartily as he approached them, navigating between the desks in the large open room. He reached them, gave Felicity a quick hug, and extended his hand to Rick.

He shook his hand and then said, "Mr. Bois. Thanks so much for seeing us again."

"Peter, please. And it's my pleasure. As I said yesterday, I'm happy to help. Is the detective joining us?"

"No," said Rick. "She had a conflict."

"Sorry to hear that. I'm sure she'd want to hear what we found."

Rick's eyebrows arched. "You found something?"

Peter nodded. "We did. Let's go back to the conference room, where we'll have some privacy."

He led them back to the meeting room, and they settled into their chairs. Peter had a laptop set up on the glass tabletop and connected to the overhead projector. A large flatscreen hanging on the wall displayed a spreadsheet from one of the suspected companies.

"Would you like a coffee? Water?" asked Peter.

Rick and Felicity both shook their heads. Their faces were expectant.

Peter settled into his seat and turned back to the screen. "Right then. Let me show you what we found." He moved the mouse next to the laptop and clicked on a tab within the worksheet. The screen changed. "This file includes the quarterly financials for Eel Point Amusements. This is the income statement, and as you can see, the firm had excellent revenues. What's interesting though, is despite very high mortgage costs, they still managed a very healthy profit margin."

"Wow," exclaimed Rick, looking at the numbers. "A sixty percent operating margin?"

"Exactly," said Peter. "I mean, it's not unheard of; some software companies have been known to earn up to seventy percent. But Eel Point Amusements is not software."

"What do they do exactly?" asked Felicity.

"That was the first mystery we had to solve. Not much showed up in our online searches, and there wasn't anything on the thumb drive that would explain things. So we had to piece that together based on the financials."

"What did you find?" asked Rick.

"Their income statement had revenues from a chain of liquor stores throughout the Atlantic coastline, from Maryland extending down into Georgia."

"My dad would not want to be in the liquor business," said Felicity strongly.

Peter nodded. "Hold that thought." He turned to the screen and used a laser pointer to circle a few further down on the spreadsheet. "Here, we also have income derived from a few strip clubs, a small chain of laundromats, and a sports betting operation in New Jersey."

Felicity recoiled. "No way! My dad would never have invested in those types of businesses!"

Peter held up his hand. "I know," he said gently. "I know this wouldn't be your dad's intention."

Rick looked at Peter knowingly. "Cash-heavy businesses."

Peter gave a confirming nod.

"What?" Felicity asked, confused.

Rick turned to her gently. "With these types of businesses, people frequently pay in cash."

Felicity looked at Rick and then back to Peter. "Money laundering?" she asked tentatively.

"Not always," said Peter. "There are a lot of legitimate companies out there that run these types of businesses. But it does beg the question, so we dug a little deeper." He clicked on another tab marked BS. "This is the balance sheet for Eel Point. As you can see, they have a substantial amount shown in hard assets, which we suspected was the value of the real estate for all of the locations."

"Makes sense," said Rick.

"It does. But if you look at liabilities, those properties were heavily mortgaged. As in over one hundred percent."

"Over one hundred percent?"

Peter nodded. "Yes. It is actually just shy of two hundred percent."

Rick let out a low whistle. "How do they stay in business? Their mortgage payments must bleed them dry."

"For a normal business, yes. But if your mortgage is held by someone you know, say another one of your firms..." Peter minimized the file and clicked on another file on his desktop. "These are the financial statements for Sankaty Beach, LLC." He clicked on a tab at the bottom and brought up their balance sheet. "The Sankaty Beach business owns the paper for all the locations for Eel Point Amusements."

"All of them?" asked Rick.

"Yes. And look at this." Peter clicked another tab and brought up the income statement.

Rick whistled. "That is some serious revenue. Is that all from the real estate holdings? What do they have besides the Eel Point properties?"

"Nothing," said Peter. "Eel Point is their only customer." He navigated to the bottom of the spreadsheet. "We did some quick calculations, and Sankaty Beach was charging Eel Point through the nose for those mortgages. The interest rates were fifteen points over prime."

"Fifteen points!" exclaimed Rick.

"Is that significant?" asked Felicity.

Peter turned to her. "A lot of mortgages and business loans are based on the prime interest rate. If you are a really good customer with excellent credit, you might get a loan at prime plus one or two percentage points. A credit card might be ten to twelve points over. But fifteen points over prime? That's very high."

"But just below what might be considered usury," added Rick.

"Exactly," agreed Peter. "It's extremely high but still within state limits, so it would not draw any unwanted attention if discovered."

Felicity looked at Rick, confused. "What does this all mean?"

"Let me show you one more thing." Peter navigated back to the spreadsheet for Eel Point amusements and clicked on the tab marked *Schds*. "This is the underlying detail behind the numbers." He moved the mouse and scrolled down. "This is the schedule supporting the real estate assets." On the screen, they saw a list of dozens and dozens of addresses. "These are the addresses for each of their liquor store locations."

"Okay," said Felicity, looking over the list. "As you said, it looks like they go from Maryland south down to Georgia."

"That's what you are meant to think," said Peter. He minimized the spreadsheet and clicked on another program at the bottom of the screen. Up popped a street image of an empty lot cluttered with weeds and surrounded by chain-link fencing.

"What are we looking at?" asked Rick.

"This," said Peter, pointing at the screen, "is the number one producing liquor store in the Eel Point portfolio."

Felicity's eyes went wide. "What? I don't get it. It's an empty lot. How can that be the best location? Do they have a pop-up or something?"

Peter clicked back to the schedule and copied an address at random. He navigated back to the mapping app and pasted the address in the search bar. Up popped an image of a cornfield and a country road. There was no building in sight.

"Oh my god," said Rick, amazed. "Ghost locations."

"Exactly," agreed Peter.

"I'm sorry," said Felicity. "I'm not sure what I'm seeing."

Peter turned to her. "Ghost locations are just that. A location that doesn't exist."

"But then, how can it make money?"

"It doesn't," said Rick. "At least not in reality. But on paper, it does. So anyone looking through the financials for Eel Point amusements would see what appears to be a successful operation complete with physical locations up and down the Eastern seaboard."

"But why would anyone do that?" Felicity asked again, her voice catching. In her gut, she knew what he was going to say.

"To launder money," said Peter quietly.

"My dad's firm was laundering money?" exclaimed Felicity. "Oh my god!" She put her head in her hands and started to cry.

Rick reached over and rubbed her shoulder.

She sniffled and looked up through wet eyes. "I can't believe this."

Peter gave her a moment before continuing. "I'm sorry. We also looked at the other files you gave me, and it appears those firms, too, were involved in laundering. They used different fronts - one of them was a real estate flipping business - but the end goal was still the same."

"But why would they do that?" asked Felicity, wiping her eyes.

"That's what we need to find out," said Rick. "Based on your dad's note and suspicions, it was clear that he was unaware of what was happening at the firm. So that would mean his partners, Sean or Cormac, or both, were actively involved in this scheme."

"But don't you need cash to launder? Where would they have gotten that if they didn't have real locations?" Felicity asked.

"Crypto," said Peter.

"Crypto?"

"Yes. Cryptocurrency. It appears Eel Point was set up not just to launder physical cash but also to convert crypto into legitimate deposits at a bank."

"But I thought crypto was supposed to be secure, no?"

Rick answered. "That was the original intent of the concept, yes, but some criminal elements have figured out ways to hide the origins of ill-gotten crypto through things called tumblers. These mix the tainted crypto with legitimate crypto. Then those conjoined assets are moved through a business like Eel Point to fully cleanse them and allow them to be distributed as cash."

"But why?" asked Felicity.

"Most likely that crypto was either stolen or secured through criminal activity," said Peter. "And let me just say that these are just my suspicions based on the files you shared with me. We really need to have a forensic accountant confirm my findings."

"Agreed," said Rick. "With these findings, I'm sure the NPD can secure some resources from the FBI to investigate."

"But wouldn't that be you," asked Felicity hopefully.

"Maybe," said Rick. "But given my relationship with your family, it will likely be another member of our team. That is if we can get the FBI to approve."

"Okay. But what does this mean about my dad's firm?"

Rick looked at Peter.

"What?" asked Felicity.

Peter answered. His voice was calm and gentle. "Fel. This is evidence of a criminal enterprise. And what appears to be a significant one based on the amounts involved. I'm sorry."

"A criminal enterprise? Rick?"

Rick nodded. "I hate to say it, but Peter's right. Somehow, Miacomet Capital has gotten involved in some serious money laundering."

"Oh my god! Why would they be doing that?"

"Probably two reasons," said Peter. "One would be to inflate the returns at Miacomet Capital and show their performance is better than it really is. That would satisfy current investors and attract new ones. It would also satisfy your dad so he wouldn't get curious and start digging into things. And two, to make some serious money. I'm sure they are taking a cut of whoever's money they are working with."

"What do you mean whoever they are working with?" asked Felicity.

"Someone is funneling a large amount of money through Miacomet Capital. Money that I can almost guarantee was earned illegally."

"Illegally? From what?"

"If I had to guess, I'd say drugs or illegal gambling."

"Are you out of your mind? My dad's firm. Involved in drugs?" Her tears returned, her face twisted with fresh disbelief.

Rick rubbed her heaving shoulders and looked at Peter. "We need to brief Tuna on this. It really does cast a new light on the Post's deaths."

Silence fell across the room, broken only by the faint hum of the projector fan.

"I need to tell Scott," said Felicity suddenly and pulled out her phone.

"Let's hold off on that," said Rick calmly. "I think this is something that needs to be done in person."

She lowered her phone. "You're right. But he is going to be stunned."

"Yes. And he'll need you there for support. This will be a lot to take in for him." Rick gently placed a hand on hers.

Felicity nodded and dabbed at her eyes.

"But first. Tuna," said Rick, pulling out his phone and typing quickly.

Bois found smoking gun. Can u meet now?

He turned to Peter. "Thanks so much for your help with this. Despite the outcome, I really appreciate it."

"Glad I could help. I only wish we had better news."

Rick nodded. His phone dinged.

Wrapping up now. Meet at NPD in twenty?

Rick hesitated, then replied with a thumbs-up. He turned to Felicity. "Tuna's available in twenty minutes. Did you want me to run you home first so you can talk with Scott?"

She shook her head adamantly. "No. I want to go with you to meet Tuna."

"Okay," said Rick, and he stood. "Thank you again, Peter."

He nodded. "Let me know if there is anything else I can do." He turned to Felicity and gave her a long embrace. "I'm so sorry for what we found. Please let me know if there is anything I can do for you or Scott."

"Thanks so much, Mr. Bois."

"And Rick?" said Peter.

"Yes?"

"Please keep me in the loop. I'd like to know what happens with this information."

Rick nodded. "Absolutely."

As they stepped back into the rain, Felicity reached for Rick's hand without saying a word.

And this time, he didn't let go.

CHAPTER TWENTY-FIVE

Rick and Felicity drove through the rain and wind to the Nantucket Government Center on Fairgrounds Road. Fortunately, Felicity had anticipated the ugly weather and had put the top up and the doors back on the night before. They pulled into a visitor's parking spot and hurried their way inside. Tuna was waiting for them in the front lobby.

"Good morning," said Tuna.

"Morning," said Rick. He looked around nervously. "Place doesn't seem to have changed much since I was last here."

Tuna nodded. "A few things have, mainly technology-related. But it's pretty much the same place you know and love."

"Wonderful," said Rick, his voice dripping with sarcasm. "Do you have somewhere we can go?"

"Yes. I booked a conference room upstairs. I think you know the way," she said jokingly.

"We'll follow you," said Rick. He was not smiling.

They trailed Tuna up the stairs and down a long hallway to a small conference room. It was windowless and wasn't much bigger than the typical office cubicle. Posters from the Nantucket Chamber of Commerce lined the walls reflecting various scenic images from around the island: Brant Point Lighthouse, a view of downtown and the twin steeples of the Unitarian and Congregational churches, Sankaty Head Lighthouse and the Miacomet golf course. The latter certainly fitting, given the subject of their upcoming discussion.

The three settled into chairs, the room quiet save for a buzzing from the overhead fluorescents. Tuna looked at Felicity. "How are you holding up through all of this?"

Felicity gave a small, tired smile. "I'm doing okay. Thanks for asking. It really helps that we seem to be making progress."

Tuna nodded and turned to Rick. "So what did Peter Bois have to say?" She opened her notebook and began to write.

Rick leaned forward. "In big picture terms, he believes that Miacomet Capital Partners was operating a large criminal enterprise."

"Really?" exclaimed Tuna. "Those were his words?"

"Yes. From the files he was able to review, he believes that the firm was laundering money - both cash and crypto - for an unidentified outside source. But he was careful to point out that this is only his opinion and that we really need a forensic accountant to review the files and confirm his findings."

"Did he find any detail on how it was being done?"

Rick nodded. "He walked us through how two of the companies, Eel Point Amusements and Sankaty Beach, LLC and how they were structured to essentially conceal transactions he believes were crypto-related."

"Crypto?" Tuna repeated with frown.

"Yeah. Laundering is no longer just a cash-based enterprise. Criminals have discovered the many benefits of crypto-currency."

"Lovely," said Tuna sarcastically. "Well, if the laundering is true, that certainly brings a new perspective to our inquiries on the Posts."

"Yes," said Rick. "But first, we need to confirm the validity of the thumb drive and the information it contained."

Felicity jumped in. "Are you saying that these files might not belong to my dad's firm?" she said anxiously. "Who else's could they be?"

He looked at her intently. "All we have right now is a bunch of spreadsheets that outline a fairly complex business. For all we know, maybe Cormac or Sean were writing a novel or preparing to teach a class on finance. Or maybe they were just thinking about money laundering and practicing their creative accounting. To be a hundred percent sure, we need to find a physical connection between these listed firms and Miacomet Capital."

"A physical connection?" asked Felicity.

"Yes. We need to find the money. We need to show that the numbers shown in the spreadsheet really do flow into Miacomet Capital. And if they do flow in, where are they going? And to whom?"

Tuna nodded. "Agreed. We also need to confirm that these organizations and their files truly are part of the Miacomet Capital structure. And if we can confirm that, then we will need to reevaluate our initial determination of the accidental death of Mr. Post."

Rick nodded. "Based on what we found with Fel's help - the letter and the files - I think we can assume that he was unaware of the laundering scheme underway at the firm, and perhaps surfacing that concern with his partners led to their taking actions against him."

"You mean murder," said Tuna flatly.

Rick nodded. "Yes."

Tuna leaned back in her chair, locked her fingers behind her head, and stared up at the ceiling. "Okay. And I agree with your position, by the way." She paused to gather her thoughts and then leaned forward. "We need to brief the chief."

"Now?" asked Rick nervously.

Tuna smiled. "Yes. If she's available. And I don't know why you are hesitant. The leadership team that led to your dismissal are long gone. We have a new sheriff in town, so to speak," said Tuna, chuckling. "And I really think you'll not only like her but be very impressed with her as well. She has had an amazing career in law enforcement."

Felicity leaned over and placed her hand on Rick's arm. "This is a chance for them to see the real you, not that man they ran out of town on sham charges."

He nodded. "Sorry, I don't mean to be a baby about this."

Tuna nodded. "I get it, Rick. I really do. But trust me on this."

Rick nodded slowly. "Okay. Fine."

"Good. Give me a minute. I'll be right back." Tuna stood, grabbed her notebook, and walked quickly from the room.

Rick stood up and paced the room nervously. He stopped and looked at Felicity. "If what we have found proves to be accurate, that there is indeed a large sum of money being laundered through Miacomet, and knowing your dad, my guess is that he somehow found out what was going on and wanted it to stop. Hell, maybe he was going to confess the firm's activities to authorities."

Felicity nodded, eyes dark. "That certainly sounds like what my dad would do. If he was anything, he was honest to the core."

Rick stopped pacing. "Which means that maybe his death was intended to keep that from happening."

Her eyes went wide and her breath caught. "You mean Sean or Cormac..." her voice trailed off.

"Not necessarily. It could also have been someone from whatever organization is the source of the funds to be laundered. If it is indeed drugs, then you have to think of a cartel. Gambling could be organized crime. Either way, these are not nice people to deal with, and they wouldn't think twice about preventing the discovery of their operations."

"Oh my god," said Felicity. "Do you think I'm safe? And Scott?"

Rick walked to her chair and placed his hands on her shoulders. "I do. I see no reason why they would hurt either of you."

"But my mom!"

"Which was probably an accident," he said reassuringly. "I'm sure you and Scott are okay."

She turned her head and looked up at him. "I hope you're right. I would hate to feel like I'm in danger."

Tuna popped her head in. "You kids okay? Chief Calpers is ready for us."

"You ready?" asked Felicity, her eyes locked intently on Rick's.

"Let's do it."

They followed Tuna out of the conference room and down the hall. They came to a corner office, and Tuna rapped on the wall outside the door.

"Come in."

The three filed into a spacious office. A large oak desk sat perpendicular to the corner where two sets of windows looked out on a rainy, gray day. A trim, fit, sandy-haired woman was sitting behind a computer monitor, the keys clacking as she typed. She peered over the screen and, seeing Rick and Felicity, stood and made her way around the desk.

"You must be Rick Caton. I'm Chief Jodi Calpers." She extended her hand.

"Chief," said Rick, nodding. He shook her hand and released it.

"And you must be Felicity Post," said the chief. "I am so sorry for your loss. Rest assured that Detective Fisch is active in the investigation and is keeping me informed on a daily basis. We will determine exactly what happened to your mom and dad."

"Thank you," said Felicity.

The chief turned back to Rick. "And to you, Agent Caton, I know all about your history here at the NPD and how it was, shall I say, mismanaged. I'd like to offer you the department's official apology for how your case was treated and for what I see as a highly questionable rationale for your dismissal. Your records indicate you were an exceptional policeman, and I'm very sorry that we lost you."

Rick blinked. "Thank you, Chief. That means a lot. It really does."

"Well overdue in my eyes," said the chief. "I hope that we can make up for it in some way."

"Solving this case would help," said Rick. "Ann and Charles Post were like family to me growing up on the island. We," he motioned to Felicity, "would really like to know what happened and, if foul play is involved, would like to see those involved brought to justice."

"I couldn't agree more. Detective Fisch has briefed me on the latest developments regarding the suspected money laundering at Miacomet Capital. She also mentioned some suspicions about a control module for the Posts' car?"

"Yes," said Rick. "I've just sent the driver's control module recovered from the car to a colleague at the FBI. She should have received it this morning. She'll run it through their lab and determine if the module was tampered with and, if so, what implications that might have had on the vehicle. She's doing it as a favor, so it will be an unofficial conclusion, but I should know something by later today or first thing tomorrow."

"Excellent," said the chief. "Given the situation at Miacomet and your experience, how would you recommend I proceed?"

"Simply put, we need the resources of the FBI in play here. They have an experienced forensic accounting team that can more accurately understand exactly what, if anything, is going on at Miacomet Capital. They can also secure the necessary evidence to support a search warrant if their analysis reflects criminal activity."

"And do you suspect that the remaining partners are involved?"

Rick nodded. "One or both have to be at least aware of the laundering scheme. More likely, they are actively managing it. One possibility is that Mr. Post uncovered the illegal activity and confronted the partners. Perhaps he was silenced because of that."

"And Mrs. Post?"

"My thinking remains that that is accidental as originally thought, but that might change based on what we hear about the module."

The chief thought for a moment. "Nice work, especially for someone here on their own time," she said, smiling. "I will call the Boston field office right now and make a formal request. Anyone in particular I should call?"

"Um, yes. My supervisor, Hanna Fines, would be the right contact." He pulled one of his business cards, wrote a number on the back, and handed it to the chief. "That's her direct line. We've briefly discussed the case, and she knows I'm here to help the Post family."

"Thank you," said the chief and took the card. "Please keep me apprised of any developments. And nice to meet you both." She returned to her desk.

Being dismissed, Rick, Felicity, and Tuna left the chief's office and headed down the hall.

"Man, she is sharp," said Rick. "And I certainly didn't expect that apology from her."

"She knows you were treated very poorly, and she wants her department to be on the right side of things. She's had to clean up a bunch of loose ends from that administration, but I think you were high on her list."

"So what next?" asked Felicity expectantly.

"I think we should head home and brief Scott on what we've found," said Rick. "Especially since you two were arguing this morning."

"You're right. I just dread it - he's not going to believe us."

"Whether he believes us or not, he needs to know what we've found. And maybe that might jog something in his memory that could be helpful."

Rick's phone rang. He pulled it out and looked at the screen. "I've got to take this. It's my boss." He walked a few feet away and clicked accept. "Hanna, I thought you might be calling. Just not this quickly."

Hanna laughed. "After talking with Chief Calpers, I get the impression that she is a woman who likes to get things done right now."

Rick chuckled. "She is definitely a pro and a go-getter. Very impressive."

"Well, she was very impressed by you and quite complimentary."

"Thanks for sharing that. Our meeting went well."

"Speaking of which, she brought me up to speed on the latest developments in the Post case and made a formal request for assistance to investigate a firm called Miacomet Capital Partners. That's the one you mentioned when you called?"

"Yes. That is Mr. Post's firm. We had a local businessman look at the files we discovered, and in his expert opinion, there is definitely some illegal activity going on."

"So you are aligned with this request?"

"Absolutely. The NPD doesn't have the expertise, but we do. I can have the files in question in your inbox as soon as I can connect my laptop. Put Nia on it, and she'll probably have it figured out in half a day."

"Okay. Send them. I'll review with her and see if she has the capacity for it."

"Thanks, Hanna."

"You're welcome. I'm assuming that this won't have an impact on your upcoming travel plans?"

Rick smiled. "I'm going, Hanna. I promise."

"Excellent. Talk soon."

Rick hit the end button and thought for a minute. He scrolled through his contacts, found the one he was looking for, and hit send. She picked up a few moments later.

"RC! What are you up to?"

"Hey, Nia. Still working this case on Nantucket. You good?"

"Never better. What can I do for you?"

"Hanna will be in your office in a few minutes. The NPD here has requested assistance with this case. Based on what we have uncovered, we suspect that a local firm may have been laundering money. I was hoping you could take a look at the files and give us your expert opinion."

"Hmm," said Nia. "Is this expert opinion to secure a search warrant? Or is it an expert opinion to confirm your suspicions?"

"More the latter. I need confirmation so that I can approach the partners and confront them with our evidence. I've met them, and I think I can get one of them to talk."

"Okay. Well, I don't have plans tonight. Or tomorrow, for that matter. Jon's regiment is running field exercises this month."

"Any news on deployment orders?"

"Not yet. So for now, we are managing as best we can and stealing whatever time we can get together."

"That must be rough. Please tell him hi for me."

"Will do. And I'll take a look at those files as soon as Hanna gives me the green light. Does she have them yet?"

"No, but they'll be in her inbox within the hour."

"Okay. Give me a few hours, and I'll get back to you. Any plans tonight for you? Any hot dates?" she said teasingly.

Rick laughed. "My job is my date. Thanks for the help. Ping me when you are ready to chat."

"Will do RC. Better jet; I hear Hanna coming down the hall."

Rick ended the call and walked back to Felicity and Tuna. They were deep in discussion about the best lobster roll on the island. It was a highly subjective argument, with the only quantitative data being the price recorded by a local magazine. Known as the lobster roll index or LRI, it reflected the menu price of the delicacy at every establishment on the island. They stopped talking as he approached and turned with hopeful faces.

"I just briefed my colleague at the FBI. She's going to jump on the files as soon as they receive them. Tuna, is there a guest wifi I can jump on so I can get these to her?"

"Actually, we don't due to security issues. We got hacked last year. Why don't you give me the thumb drive and her email address? I'll send them from my laptop immediately."

"Perfect." He wrote Hanna's email on the back of his card and handed it along with the thumb drive to Tuna.

"Thanks. Be right back."

Rick turned to Felicity. "Should we go see Scott?"

"He's not home. I just texted him. Said he'll be back late this afternoon."

"Okay. Hungry?"

"Starving. What did you have in mind?"

"Let's keep it simple. How about the lunch counter at the pharmacy?"

"Hmmm. Egg salad sandwich and a chocolate frappe sounds delicious - especially on such a crappy day."

Tuna returned and handed Rick the thumb drive. "Files sent."

"Thanks so much, Tuna. Feel like joining us for lunch?"

She shook her head. "Too much to do here, now. Securing the FBI assistance does ramp things up for me. Chief Calpers has made this an official investigation, which means I have some catch-up to do on my paperwork."

"Understand. I'll follow up with you later. I hope to hear something on those files by the end of the day."

"That would be terrific. Let me know when you hear."

"Will do."

CHAPTER TWENTY-SIX

Felicity and Rick had just finished lunch when Rick's phone dinged. He pulled it out of his pocket and looked at the screen.

Prelim results of DCM are in. Call me.

"What is it?" asked Felicity, concerned.

"It's my colleague at the FBI who was evaluating the module from your parents' car. She says the initial analysis is complete and wants to talk."

Her eyes widened. "That's great. I hope she has something."

"Me too." Rick paid the tab and escorted Felicity out the door and into a chilly and damp afternoon. He zipped up his jacket. "I need somewhere warm and dry to call her back."

Felicity looked across the street. "I'm sure Mr. Bois wouldn't mind if we used his conference room. If it's available, of course."

"Excellent idea."

They walked quickly across the street, slipping a few times on the wet cobblestones, and made their way up the narrow staircase and into the offices of *The Jack Tate & Tristam Coffin Foundation.*

"Hi, Jen," said Felicity.

Jen looked up from her desk. "Hey, you two! Staying dry?"

"Trying to," said Rick, dripping onto the old wooden floor. "Do you think it would be okay to use the conference room for an hour or so?"

"Of course! Peter and most of the team are at an off-site today with the Affordable Housing Trust. You can have it all afternoon if you need it."

"Thank you," said Felicity.

"Of course. Can I get you two anything?"

"No. Just having a warm and dry place to work is enough for me," Rick replied with a grateful smile.

"Well, if you change your mind, please let me know," Jen said, already turning back to her screen.

They made their way past the desks and down the hall into the conference room.

Felicity sat down across from Rick. "Do you mind if I listen in?"

"I think that'd be okay. It's just the preliminary. But please let me ask the questions, okay?"

Felicity nodded. Rick pulled out his phone and texted Margo.

Now good?

Rick's phone started ringing seconds later. He hit accept and tapped the speaker button before placing the phone on the table.

"Rick?" came Margot's voice.

"Hi Margot. I've got Felicity Post here with me."

"Hi, Felicity. Nice to meet you."

"And you," replied Felicity.

"So, Margot. What did you find?"

Her voice turned professional. "What we found is that the software in the driver's control module was not an authorized version from the manufacturer. In fact, it showed that likely hundreds of lines of code had been modified."

Rick's expression darkened. "Okay. Do we know what the impact of those changes might be?"

"We couldn't ascertain that specifically as we just don't have that expertise," Margot admitted. "We usually deal with hacks to the car's interface, bus system, and main control modules. This is actually the first time my team has ever even looked at a driver's control module."

"So how can we find out?"

"One step ahead of you, Cola."

Felicity looked questioningly at Rick and mouthed, "Cola?"

Rick smiled and held up a finger. "I'll tell you in a minute," he whispered. And more loudly to the phone, "You were always one step ahead of me."

Laughter came over the phone's small speaker. "You are too kind, Cola. But we got lucky this time."

"How so?"

"Well, a friend of a friend of a friend of mine is married to a software engineer who works for a Tier One supplier to the automotive industry."

"A friend of a friend of a friend of yours?"

Margot laughed. "Yeah. Well, actually, we play in the same pickleball league, and to be honest, I really only know her from her play on court. Which is actually pretty good."

"Okay. So how can she help?"

"Like I said, Lisa - that's her name - is married to a software engineer. He writes code to manage the antilock braking systems, among other things. He doesn't work for this manufacturer, but he is well-versed in the typical code and actions you would find in any DCM module. I downloaded the code and emailed it to him. His name is Carlos, by the way."

"What did he, um, Carlos, find?"

"Keep in mind that this is very preliminary, Rick. And really should be considered directional, not absolute. But I've also emailed the code to the vehicle's manufacturer with a formal request for analysis. I should have that next week."

"Understood. So what did he find? Preliminarily, at least."

Felicity leaned forward.

"He found three things of interest. The first is that the code controlling the throttle, brakes, and steering was definitely affected. He found lines of code embedded in a subroutine that commanded the steering hard right, the throttle to increase, and to disable the brake pedal sensor."

Rick sat back. "Wait. What?"

"Yes, you heard me right. This subroutine, if triggered, would cause the car to veer hard right, accelerate, and prevent the brakes from being applied even if the driver put all possible force on the brake pedal."

"Holy shit," said Rick. He glanced at Felicity, and her face was white. "That pretty much perfectly describes the accident scene. The investigating officer had suspected the driver, Mrs. Post, had swerved to miss a deer, lost control, and rammed into a tree."

"I think any investigator would likely have come to that same conclusion. Why would they think otherwise?" replied Margot.

"Why would they want to kill my mom?" asked Felicity. Her eyes welled up as she processed what she heard.

Rick reached across the table and squeezed her hand gently. "Okay, you said she found three things?"

"Yes. There was a line of code that contained an RCE."

"You've lost me. I don't know coding at all. What's an RCE?"

"Sorry. An RCE is a Remote Code Execution. Think of it as a remote triggering mechanism."

"Really?"

"Yeah. In this case, the code was written to look for a command on a web server every few seconds. And if it found that command, then it would activate the affected software."

"Meaning they could control if and when the malicious software was activated," said Rick.

"Exactly. We put a trace on the web server, but it has long since been removed. So that's a dead end."

"And the third thing?"

"Ah, yes. The third area of interest in the coding changes was the inclusion of a geofence."

"A geofence? What's that?" asked Felicity. Rick looked at her, and she smiled wanly. "Sorry," she mouthed.

Margot replied. "A geofence uses GPS, the global satellite positioning system, to create a virtual fence or barrier around a specified location. So for example, you could have a tracking device for a senior citizen that is geofenced to their home. If the person with that device leaves the geofenced area, then an alarm could be triggered."

"Makes sense," said Rick. "But why would it be used here?"

"It looks like they wanted it to be activated within a very limited area on Nantucket."

"What do you mean? That they planned where they wanted the crash to occur?"

"Exactly. If their goal was to have the car hit a tree at high speed, then you would want to trigger that in an area with a lot of large trees, right?"

Rick looked at Felicity. She was crying. He reached out and squeezed her hand.

"So, do you have the location from the code?"

"I do. It's forty-one degrees, eighteen point three minutes north by seventy degrees, zero point three minutes west."

"Do you have your phone?" he asked Felicity.

"I do," she replied, sniffling, relieved to have something to do. She wiped her eyes with the back of her hand and pulled out her phone.

"Please open it and pull up the Maps app. Hang on a minute, Margot. We are going to plot that here."

"No worries. I'll hang on."

Felicity swiped several times back and forth before she found the requested app. She tapped on it and then looked at Rick. "Okay."

"Now, click on the three dots in the corner."

She did as instructed, and a menu appeared. She showed it to Rick.

"Perfect. Now tap on the GPS location option."

Felicity did, and up popped two white boxes. One was labeled latitude. The other longitude. A button below them was labeled *Map It*.

"In the latitude box, please type forty-one point one eight three."

Felicity tapped on her phone. "Okay."

"Now, in longitude, please enter seventy point zero three one. Then tap the map it button."

Felicity completed the entries and tapped the button. The screen churned for a minute before an image of Nantucket popped up. A single red pin appeared in the upper right part of the map.

"Zoom in on that," said Rick, pointing at the dot.

Felicity tapped on the plus sign several times. Her face went white. She showed the screen to Rick.

"What is it?" asked Margot.

Rick looked at the screen. "Those coordinates align with the exact location of the accident that killed Ann Post."

There was a long silence.

Finally, Margot broke the quiet. "I think then we can confirm then that the change to the code was intended to cause an accident," she said in a professional voice.

"Oh my god," said Felicity, crying hard. "They murdered my mom!"

Rick reached out and held her hand, trying to steady the tremble in his own fingers, as sobs wracked her body.

"You guys okay?" asked Margot.

"Yeah. Just a lot to take in, especially for Felicity."

"I'm sure."

"So, Margot," said Rick, his voice tightening, "Based on your experience with a cyber crime like this, is it a safe assumption that some external person loaded malicious software into the Posts' vehicle's DCM with the intent to kill or cause severe bodily harm?"

"That's exactly what it looks like. Now, please keep in mind that the original determination for this accident could be correct. That indeed, the driver swerved to miss a deer, lost control, and hit a tree. We have no evidence within this module or the code to determine if this malicious software was ever activated. It could quite literally be a coincidence."

"Is there a way we could find out positively?"

"Yes. We would need to secure the EDR, the vehicle's event data recorder. That would tell us exactly what was happening at the time of the accident: throttle position, steering angle, braking, roll angle, and much more. Do you think it could be accessed?"

"I'd have to check with the recycling yard and see what has happened to it. Hopefully, they still have it, and we can get that data. Let me see what I can find out, and I'll get back to you."

"Sounds good. Do you guys have any questions for me?"

"No. But thank you so much for this analysis. It explains a lot of things. Can you send me the formal analysis as soon as it's complete?"

"Sure thing. And do let me know when you get that EDR. That is the final piece of this puzzle to understand what happened."

"Will do. Thanks."

"And looking forward to that dinner next week, Cola."

Felicity looked at him curiously. Rick smiled and said, "Me too. See you then."

"Later, Cola," said Margot and ended the call.

Felicity looked at Rick with eyes damp from crying. His heart ached to see her hurting so badly, and he desperately wanted to find out who had caused her all this pain.

"So what is this Cola business," she asked, sniffling. "And you two are going to dinner?"

He smiled. "I've known Margot since basic field training at Quantico. She grew up drinking Royal Crown soda, or RC, which are also my initials. She called me Cola one day during a break in a seminar, and it stuck, at least for her."

The story seemed to brighten her spirits. "Can I call you Cola?" she teased.

"Um, no. Please. I kind of like Rick."

"Okay. So where are you two going to dinner?"

"Our group, during training, always went to Sam's Inn. It's an old-school kind of place. So I'm sure we'll go there. What, are you jealous?"

Felicity smiled softly. "Should I be?"

Rick laughed heartily. "I love Margot as a friend and a colleague, but it could never go past that."

"Why not?"

"I'm simply not her type."

"Not her type!" said Felicity, a little defensively.

"She's gay," said Rick. "And very happy in a long-term relationship with her partner, Amber."

"Oh. Sorry," said Felicity, a little embarrassed.

"It's okay. I'm touched, though. Thanks. Now, I need to get a hold of Tuna and brief her on what Margot found. We also need to see if she can track down that event data recorder from your mom's car."

Rick picked up his phone and texted Tuna.

Code in module was def malicious. Have time to debrief?

"I can't believe someone would murder my mom," said Felicity, her eyes welling back up with tears. "Who would want to hurt her?"

Rick reached out to hold her hand. "I promise you we'll find out. Between the NPD and the FBI, we will track these people down and bring justice for your parents."

She squeezed his hand. "I'm just so thankful I have you here with me."

"Me too, me too."

His phone dinged.

Can u come back here?

Rick typed back.

Be there in 30.

He placed his phone down. "Tuna's expecting me in thirty minutes. Can I run you home?"

Felicity looked exhausted; her body slumped from the weight of what they learned about the control module. "That would be great. I really think I need to lie down. I feel so tired, physically, mentally, and emotionally."

Rick looked at her caringly. "I'm sure. You have been through the wringer this week, and I think things have just caught up with you. Do you know if Scott's back yet?"

She shook her head. "I think so. He mentioned he had a video call with his partners. He was going to use dad's office for the meeting."

"I think I should be there when you update him on things."

"Actually, would you mind telling him everything we've learned? He thinks I'm chasing phantoms. Maybe if he hears it from you, it will actually sink in. That our parents were likely murdered to cover up a crime at Dad's firm."

"I'd be happy to. Let's do this. I'll run you home, go meet with Tuna, and then will be back at the house. Maybe I can bring you some dinner?"

"That sounds great, Rick. Thank you." She smiled. "Or should I call you Cola?"

CHAPTER TWENTY-SEVEN

Are you sure you don't mind if I skip the meeting with Tuna?" asked Felicity. She was sitting in the passenger seat as he drove the old Bronco through the rotary and down Milestone Road. The old wipers were struggling to keep up with the rain, squeaking noisily with each pass.

"Absolutely not. Six days ago, your world was turned on its head with the death of your dad. Then you lose your mom in a car accident, which now looks suspiciously like a premeditated murder. And to top it all off, you learn that Miacomet Capital Partners, a firm your dad co-founded nearly forty years ago, is possibly a criminal enterprise. I think anyone would be totally spent dealing with all of that."

"Thanks for understanding," said Felicity. She looked at him through weary eyes.

He smiled caringly at her as he turned the Bronco onto Monomoy Road. He was amazed at how she was managing through all of this. She was a strong and impressive woman. Soon, they were pulling up in front of the Post house.

"Can I bring you anything when I come back later besides some dinner?" asked Rick.

"Thanks, but no. I think I just need to get some sleep."

She unbuckled her seat belt and climbed out of the car. She leaned on the window frame, her green eyes blurry with exhaustion. "Promise me you'll be back later. Let me know what happens with Tuna."

"Of course. Also happy to update Scott."

"That would be great, Rick. Thank you. I'll see you then."

"Rest well," said Rick. He watched as she slowly made it to the front door and opened it. She turned and waved faintly, then closed the door.

Rick pulled out of the driveway and headed back towards the NPD offices. It was Friday afternoon. He had arrived on the island Tuesday morning. What had been barely three days felt more like three weeks. And it scared him a bit how easily he had settled back into life on the island. Despite all his misgivings about returning to Nantucket, it had slipped onto him like a well-worn and loved bathrobe. Certainly, the Chief's apology had helped significantly, but it was much more than that. After he had been fired he turned his anger of the NPD against everything he loved about the island. He realized now how misdirected that frustration had been. And with his feelings about the NPD's treatment of him somewhat resolved, his fondness for the island and his previous life here had blossomed. But before he allowed himself to even think about what that meant in his life, he forced those thoughts out of his mind. He had work to do and a murder, or possibly murders, to solve.

He pulled into the parking lot of the Nantucket Police Department. The rain had stopped, but the blustery winds remained. Despite it still technically being summer, the dampness in the air and the strong breezes brought a chill. He had goosebumps on his arms, and it wasn't from being anxious about entering the NPD.

Rick made his way through the lobby and up the stairs to Tuna's office. He stuck his head in and saw she was staring intently at her computer screen. He tapped lightly on the door frame. "Tuna?"

She looked up. "Rick. Thanks for getting here so quickly. Please take a seat." She motioned to one of the two simple chairs in front of her desk. Unlike Nia back at the FBI Field Office in

Boston, Tuna hadn't tried to personalize hers with any pillows. Rick sat at the chair directly across from her.

"What's got you so interested?" asked Rick, pointing at her screen.

"This?" Tuna grunted. "This is the report on Charles Posts' life preserver."

Rick's body straightened. "Really? What does it say?"

"It was clearly altered in a way to prevent it from inflating."

"Seriously?" said Rick, intrigued. "What did they find?"

Tuna angled her screen toward Rick. "Two things. The first is that the arming mechanism, essentially a small CO_2 cartridge, had been removed."

"Removed? Is that easy to do?" asked Rick.

Tuna nodded. "If you know what you are doing. They are designed to be easily replaced during their annual servicing. If you have any experience doing that then it would be no problem to pull out the mechanism in a half a minute or so."

"But why was it missing?"

"I'm no expert on boats, as you know, but if I had to guess I'd say either someone screwed up badly when they were doing the annual service. You know, like forgot to rearm it. Or..."

"Or?"

"It was intentionally removed."

Rick let out a sigh. "Wow. So either incompetence or intent. Which do you think?"

Tuna shrugged. "Don't know. But it does explain why it didn't inflate."

Rick thought for a moment. "You mentioned two things. What was the second?"

"This particular life preserver model also featured a manual inflation tube. So worst case scenario, if your preserver doesn't inflate automatically, you can inflate it manually."

"Okay," said Rick, angling over and trying to read the screen. "But?"

"There was a slit at the base of the tube rendering it useless. Unfortunately, the examiner couldn't determine if it was intentionally cut or if it was a result of damage or normal wear and tear. This particular life preserver was several years old so it could have been age related. But regardless, we know that when Charles Post hit the water, he was on his own. There would be no way for him to inflate his life preserver."

Rick sighed sadly, imagining the struggle Mr. Post must have faced.

Tuna clicked the window closed on her screen with a sigh. "Okay. Your turn. What did you find out about the module?"

Rick leaned forward. "Definitely has unauthorized changes, and it appears to be malicious code."

Tuna blinked. "Okay. So what does that mean for our investigation?"

"It means that it is possible, even highly likely, that the accident that killed Ann Post was intentional."

"Really?" Tuna asked, surprised. "How would they have managed that?"

Rick shook his head. "Keep in mind this is preliminary, but it appears that changes to the code would have impacted the steering, throttle, and brakes and were intended to happen at a specific time and a specific place."

"Seriously?" exclaimed Tuna. "Holy crap."

"I know. We'll know more once we get the formal assessment. My colleague, Margot, has requested that from the manufacturer. We should have it in a few days. But in the meantime, I think we need to consider this highly suspicious."

Tuna leaned back and let out a long breath. "Agreed. Is there anything else we can do?"

"Yes. We need to find the event data recorder for Mrs. Post's vehicle."

"The event data recorder?"

Rick smiled. "Some people call it the black box. It just tracks a number of different parameters of a vehicle's operations. It can tell us exactly what was going on at the time of the accident."

"Hmm. Okay. Give me a sec." Tuna pulled out her phone and dialed. The line connected. "John, I'm going to put you on speaker. I have Agent Rick Caton here with me. He's assisting in the Post investigation." She tapped the speaker icon and placed the phone on her desk.

"John?" she asked.

"Yeah, I'm here."

"Rick, can you share with John what you just told me? About the DCN, or whatever you call it?"

"The DCM," said Rick, smiling. "Sure." Leaning into the phone, Rick spent several minutes giving Officer John Downs an overview of the suspected changes to the driver's control module. When he finished, there was silence on the line.

"John, you still there?"

"Yeah, sorry," he said, his voice tight. "Just can't believe this. I mean I knew there was some suspect software on there but had no idea it would be like this."

"I know," said Rick. "But we need your help to confirm it."

"Of course! What can I do?"

"Did you download the data from the event data recorder as part of the investigation into the Post crash?" Rick pressed.

"Normally, we do, especially if there is more than one vehicle involved or if the cause of the accident is unknown or suspicious, like DUI. But with the Post case, it seemed cut and dry, so we didn't look at those data."

Rick smiled at the officer's correct use of the plural form of the noun. "But did you download the data?"

"Oh, yes. Of course. The data file is on the server. Tuna, you should be able to access it. Just go to the open case files on the shared drive. A copy of the data will be within the Post accident folder."

"But does she have the software on her computer to open the file?" asked Rick.

"Oh. Um, no. Sorry."

Rick looked at Tuna with pleading eyes.

"Can you open the file for us?" asked Tuna. "And maybe print out the report for the minute or two leading up to the accident?"

"Yes! I can do that. Are you in your office?"

"I am."

"Give me ten minutes." And with that, the line went dead.

"Is it me? He seemed a bit flustered."

"Actually, it is you," said Tuna. "Officer Downs is a good cop, but he can be a bit star-struck sometimes by authority figures."

"Starstruck? By me?" asked Rick incredulously.

"Well, you are FBI, after all," said Tuna, smiling.

"You are too funny," said Rick. "Seriously, let's put this accident aside for the moment. What are your thoughts on the death of Charles Post?"

Tuna opened her notebook.

"Honestly, I don't think we are any closer to confirming foul play than we were when you landed here on Tuesday. Certainly, the suspected financial irregularities at Miacomet Capital point to a possible motive, but nothing confirms that Charles Post was murdered."

Rick nodded and leaned forward in his chair. "Agree. But what does your gut tell you?

She didn't hesitate. "I can't prove it, but I believe he was thrown off that boat. There are just too many weird coincidences in this case. It's the only logical outcome. Especially with the damn faulty life preserver."

"I think you are spot on. So how do we get there?"

Tuna tapped the pencil against her notepad. "Short of any magical video evidence finding its way to my desk, the only approach will be to secure a confession from one of the men on that boat."

"I've been thinking about that since I met with the partners yesterday. Of the two, I think we have the best chance with Sean. He struck me as the weaker of the two. Cormac? I think he's a fighter. We would be hard-pressed to get him to confess that he woke up this morning."

Tuna smiled. "Okay. So how and when do we make that happen?"

Rick sat back in his chair and stared at the ceiling. "I need Nia, the FBI agent in Boston, to confirm the laundering. Once we have that evidence, we sit Axmacher down and hit him hard. I think he'll fold like a cheap suit. Maybe even turn state's witness."

She nodded. "When do you think you'll hear back from Nia?"

"I asked her to give us her opinion by the end of the day. But knowing her, she will probably have a complete report with enough evidence to support a warrant."

"She's that good?"

Rick nodded and smiled. "She's the best. If a clerk from a convenience store was skimming pennies, she would find them."

Tuna laughed. "Okay, then. If we do get what we need tonight, then I think we need to hit Sean in the morning."

Rick held up his hand. "Let's wait and see what we get from Nia first. If she finds enough to support a warrant, I'd rather execute that first and see what we find. That would also really turn the temperature up on Axmacher and Walsh. Then they'll know for certain that they are in the crosshairs."

Tuna's phone rang. "Yes? Sure. Right. We are in my office." She put the phone down. "That was Officer Downs. He ran the report on the black box. He's heading down here to share the results."

"Excellent! Let's hope the report confirms our suspicions."

Tuna's expression darkened. "Yes. But if true, I still don't understand the motive. I mean, why kill Ann Post? She wasn't involved in the business."

"Unless they think that Charles may have told her something. Maybe with Charles' death, they were worried she might go to the authorities."

"I suppose," said Tuna. She tapped her pencil on her notebook, thinking. "Do you think maybe, and I'm just brainstorming here, that the intended target was Charles? That maybe Ann was just an innocent bystander?"

"I see where you are going. The changes to the module would require some planning. I don't know coding, but I think it would take at least a few days or more to put those plans in motion."

"Yes. And maybe the fishing trip gave them an opportunity to take out Charles early. Or maybe they had to? Like he confronted the partners about what was happening at Miacomet. Maybe he said he was going straight to the police. Then they would have to silence him then and there."

"Makes sense. But wouldn't they then cancel the planned accident?"

"You'd think," said Tuna.

"Unless?"

"Unless what?"

"Well, what if Sean and Cormac weren't involved in the car accident?"

Tuna raised an eyebrow. "What do you mean?"

"Think about it. This type of targeting requires some pretty extensive knowledge of automotive systems, not to mention computer expertise. Do you think those two have what it takes?"

"Hmm, probably not. But couldn't they hire it out?" asked Tuna.

"I suppose. But it's not like you can just post a request online for this. You'd need to know someone personally. Otherwise, you are opening yourself up criminally big time."

Tuna nodded. "Cartel?"

Rick sighed. "Yes. Whoever is behind the laundering, I think they are the ones who planned this attack. And my guess is the target was indeed Charles. They must have had some plan to lure him out on that section of road."

"Maybe they didn't know he was already dead? Or maybe they didn't have enough time to cancel the hit?"

"Either way, that makes more sense."

There was a knock at the door. Tuna looked up. "John. Please come in."

The policeman entered, clutching a handful of paper. He nodded to Tuna and extended his hand to Rick. "Officer John Downs. Nice to meet you in person."

Rick rose and shook hands. "Rick Caton. Nice to meet you, too, John. Is that the report from the black box?"

"It is."

"Please sit," said Tuna, motioning to the chair next to Rick. "What did you find?"

John handed each of them a copy of the report. "This is the output from the event data recorder in the Post vehicle. The data table shows the position of key inputs as well as vehicle data for the ten seconds leading up to the accident."

Rick nodded. "Okay." He glanced at the row upon row of numbers and looked back at John, confused. "Can you simplify this? I mean, what are we looking at?"

"Sorry, " said John, ruffled. "These data essentially confirm your suspicion of foul play."

"Seriously?" exclaimed Rick. "How did you determine that?"

"You told me earlier that the malicious code discovered on the DCM would control the steering, brakes, and throttle, correct?"

"Yes," said Rick. "That's what my colleague at the FBI suspected."

John put the report on Tuna's desk. "Well, look at these data," said John, pointing to the last few rows, highlighted in yellow. "The columns on the left show the position of key driver inputs: steering angle, throttle position, brake activation. The columns on the right show vehicle metrics such as speed, acceleration force, location."

"Okay," said Tuna. "But what does it mean?"

"It means, two seconds before impact, Mrs. Post was steering straight ahead with the throttle position at twenty percent. Essentially, she was cruising as expected on that type of road."

"And then?"

"And then the data show nothing changed input-wise except that brake pedal pressure went up to nearly eighty percent. And this," he said, pointing to a circled number in the table, "is when she hit the tree. Impact was just over forty G."

Rick shook his head. "Sorry, I'm just not getting this."

John nodded. "It's okay. Let me explain it this way. Ann Post was driving along normally and suddenly hit the brakes as hard as she could. And then hit the tree."

"Isn't that what we expected?" asked Tuna.

"The braking? Yes. But what we didn't expect to see is that the steering wheel angle and the throttle position didn't change. These data suggest she was still driving straight ahead at normal speeds when, in fact, we know this is incorrect."

"Meaning?"

"The vehicle had what they call in aviation an uncommanded control execution. Put simply, despite the inputs Mrs. Post was managing, the DCM likely executed a significant increase in throttle while veering the car hard to the right."

"But what about the braking force?" asked Rick.

"She was simply trying to stop the car. Think about it. Imagine you are driving along, and all of a sudden, the throttle gets floored, and your car veers off the road. Without you doing anything! You'd probably be pushing down as hard on the brake pedal as you could. Given Mrs. Post's size and the vehicle type, eighty percent pedal application is probably as much as she could manage."

Rick looked at the data and noted the increased vehicle speed. "But the car was accelerating. Why didn't the brakes slow her?"

"Because the pedal application sensor had been bypassed in the DCM."

"Bypassed?" asked Tuna.

John looked at her and nodded. "Probably easier to think of it as disconnected. Any inputs from the brake pedal sensor to the DCM were being ignored."

"Holy shit," said Rick. "So this was an intentional act?"

John nodded grimly. "Yes. Based on what you shared about the code changes and these data? The accident was absolutely the intended outcome."

Rick looked at Tuna and said softly, "So, Ann Post was murdered."

Tuna nodded. "Yes." She turned to John. "Thank you, Officer Downs. This is great work."

John blushed at the compliment. "Thanks, Detective." He stood. "Do you need anything else from me?"

Tuna shook her head. "I think we are good for now. But we'll reach out if we need anything."

Officer Downs acknowledged her, stood and left the room.

Tuna watched him leave and then turned to Rick. "Well, we know the how. Now, we need to find out the why. And the who."

Rick nodded. "Absolutely. And I think we'll add that to our planned discussion with Sean tomorrow. If we can get him to talk, then hopefully, he can explain. If he even knows."

"What's next for you?"

Rick glanced at his phone. "I promised Felicity I'd come by with dinner. I need to update her on this. And bring Scott up to speed. He's been tied up in meetings, so there is a lot he doesn't know about the investigation."

"Is there anything I can do tonight?"

Rick thought for a moment. "Honestly, no. Right now, everything hinges on what Nia can find in those financials. Until we have that we are in a holding pattern. But maybe?"

"Maybe what?"

"Let's dial up the heat a bit. Do you have Axmacher's phone number?"

She nodded and pulled up her battered notebook. He dialed as she read him the number.

"Um, yes, Mr. Axmacher. This is Agent Rick Caton. I just wanted to touch base and follow up on a couple of things with you and Mr. Walsh. Just taking care of a couple of loose ends, so if you get a chance, please give me a call and let me know when you two might have ten minutes. Cheers."

He disconnected the call and looked at Tuna. "Voicemail. But maybe that will stir the pot a little bit. Let them know they aren't in the clear yet."

Tuna nodded. "Okay. Well, I need to brief the Chief on this and let her know we have a confirmed murder on our hands."

"Yes, but we really need to keep that news close to the vest. If the partners get wind of the murder, they might try and run."

"The Chief is not a talker, but I'll reiterate the sensitivity of this."

"Thanks."

Rick stood to leave.

"Call or text if you hear from Nia tonight," said Tuna.

"Will do. Thanks."

"Of course. Try and enjoy your evening."

He scoffed. "I don't think it will be a pleasant one, given the likely topics of conversation."

Tuna smiled sadly. "I'll see you tomorrow."

"Yeah. Night, Tuna," said Rick, and he left her office.

She turned her attention back to the screen on her desk. "Goddam paperwork," she muttered.

CHAPTER TWENTY-EIGHT

Scott Post had struggled his entire life living in his father's shadow.

He ended the video call with a hollow click of the trackpad. His screen went black, reflecting only the outline of his face in the glow of the rain-streaked window behind him. His report of the poor-performing EV start-up set the tone of the meeting. Anticipated returns for the quarter were looking dismal - something every fund manager dreads. The CFO was projecting, at best, a break-even and, at worst, a negative one point five percent. If it weren't for their cryptocurrency performance and their new investors, losses would have been far worse and potentially trigger a cascade of outflows from clients. That would likely mean the end of his company.

He closed the laptop and leaned back in the leather chair.

Taking the meeting in his dad's office didn't help. Everywhere he looked, he saw signs of his dad's success. Of a life well lived. Pictures of family and friends lined the walls. Sailing trophies were displayed casually on a shelf beside his desk, while framed pictures of Scott, Fel, and his mom were featured prominently on a corner of his desk, just behind his phone. Behind him, dozens of leather-bound books, chronologically organized, documented that life.

Felicity liked to read them. Said they were grounding.

Scott could barely look at them.

He stood and walked into the kitchen, looking for his sister. Apparently, she was still out playing detective with his old babysitter, trying to find answers to a question only she seemed to be asking. He put on his windbreaker, grabbed the keys to his mom's Mini, and walked out of the house.

Her car was parked halfway around the circular drive. He opened the door, and the scent of his mom's perfume hit him hard, bringing tears to his eyes. Reluctantly, he slid the driver's seat all the way back and slipped in. He placed his hands on the wheel and noticed all the little touches that made this car his mom's: the little seagull hanging from the rearview mirror, the cord emerging from the console where she plugged in her iPhone to listen to the jazz she enjoyed so much, the pair of sunglasses she kept in the door cubby. His dad had bought her this car as a surprise for her sixtieth birthday, and she absolutely loved it. Scott closed his eyes and exhaled slowly. Everything his father touched seemed to turn out right.

That wasn't how things had worked for Scott.

Charles Post had been born into a modest middle-class family in Hackensack, New Jersey, just a stone's throw from the City. He finished his senior year at Hackensack High School at the top of his class and received a full ride to a post-graduate year at Mount Herman. From there it was a stellar four years at Yale.

Scott's academic achievements were far less impressive. After a middling performance at Choate, he made his way to New Orleans to study business at Tulane. He had realized early on in his life that he simply did not have the drive and dedication of his father. Dad was a cum laude at Yale. He was in the bottom third of his class at Tulane. Dad spent his college years studying, running the debate club, and spinning albums of classical music as a DJ for Yale's radio station. Scott had spent his time partying in New Orleans, boasting to friends that he had witnessed thirteen sunrises from local bars in his first semester as a freshman.

Although he knew his father loved him and supported him in whatever choices he made, Scott felt he would never be as successful as his dad in both business and life. Charles Post was known throughout the community as a kind, caring, and generous man. He may have been financially successful, but one would not know that by either his appearance or his behavior. He treated everyone he met as an equal regardless of their position or social standing.

Over the past forty years, Charles Post, along with his partners, had built an impressive investment management firm. Scott had tried to follow in his dad's footsteps with the creation of his own investment firm with three fraternity brothers from Tulane. In reality, they had intended to carve out a good living while maintaining easy access to the slopes of Vail and Aspen. Yet despite all their hard work and considerable connections, the firm had done little more than tread water in its early years of existence. They were fairly smart guys but just didn't have the depth of financial skill needed to win.

He would never be as successful as his dad nor as happy. And he knew, deep down, that his father knew it too.

Even if he never said so.

The one bright spot of his life, where he thought he had matched his dad, was Lizzie. He had met her at a friend's Super Bowl party and found her to be very much like his mom. She was bright, beautiful, and ambitious, and she graduated near the top of her class in Berkeley Law. Now a rising star in the legal world of Denver, she had contributed significantly to the couple's financial success. And while she had visited Nantucket several times during their engagement and had enjoyed the charm, she saw no reason to spend any more time there than necessary to satisfy family obligations. She was much more comfortable in the mountains outside of Denver, where the couple had bought a lovely cabin on several acres.

He had also found delight in seeing his parents' excitement and joy about becoming grandparents. He felt like he had finally done something right. Something that would make his family proud of him. But that had been taken swiftly away in the space of a weekend, their deaths a punch in the gut.

His life's happiness had taken a major downturn at a financial advisor conference in Las Vegas. His goals had been simple: network with advisors to secure additional investments in their funds and explore potential investments for the firm. After the third day of shaking hands and coming up empty, he realized he had failed on both counts. He had retired to the bar to drown his sorrows before heading back to Denver the next morning.

That's where he met her.

She said she worked at a major East Coast fund. She was smart, engaged, flirty in a way that wasn't overtly suggestive.

They had mostly talked business, and it appeared his trip might just be turning around. That is, until he woke up alone in a strange bed the next morning, just hours before his flight home. What the hell had happened to him? He hadn't had that much to drink.

Reality hit him hard between the eyes the following week at the office. An overnight package had arrived to his attention marked Personal & Confidential. Curious, he had opened it only to find a thumb drive. Cautiously, he put it in the USB port of his laptop. The computer churned and whirred before a window appeared on the screen listing the file contents. There were only two:

Playme.mov

Readme.txt

A knot grew in his stomach. He slowly moved his mouse to highlight the Playme file and double-clicked it. The screen went black and was filled with a grainy image from what looked like a hotel room. Scott put his reading glasses on and squinted at the image. Then he recoiled in shock. The video was of him and the woman he had met in the bar. She was on top and clearly enjoying her position. Scott lay below her and was not quite as active a participant as she was.

The video was short, not more than a few minutes. Then, the live motion cut to some stills, which clearly showed Scott and the woman together in various stages of compromise.

The screen went black, and Scott clicked to close the window. He moved his cursor over the Readme file. His hand shook, and he could not bring himself to open the file. Minutes passed. The long pull of a truck's horn from the highway traffic twenty stories below him roused him from his trance. He closed his eyes and double-clicked. The file opened, and its contents would change his life forever.

It was a note - anonymous, of course - that outlined what Scott must do to keep the video and still images from arriving on the doorsteps of all those he considered dear in his life, namely his wife, business partners, and parents. Whoever had done this had done their homework and intentionally targeted him with this honey trap. The note closed with an innocent-looking email address where he was to send his acknowledgment of receipt and agreement to discuss the next steps.

Scott knew he had two choices. The first and most difficult option would have been to come clean with Lizzie. Explain to her what had happened and that it had been a trap. Convince her that he must have been drugged as he had no memory of anything beyond meeting the woman in the bar. Unfortunately, Scott had a similar incident occur when they had been dating. Lizzie had been out of town visiting her family when he had attended a sorority party invited by a female friend from his accounting class. One thing led to another, and the two spent the evening together. Being in the same sorority, it hadn't taken too long for Lizzie to find out about his indiscretion, and it nearly caused a permanent split between them.

He had apologized profusely, blamed it on excessive alcohol, and persuaded her to forgive him. Thankfully, she had, and their relationship grew stronger as a result. They were engaged a year later.

She would not forgive him a second time and would never believe he was a victim in this staged affair.

The only viable option he felt was to prevent this from ever getting out, regardless of the cost.

An hour after opening the envelope, he had sent an email stating he was open to the next steps. An automated out-of-office reply came back to him, thanking him for his email and stating he would be contacted shortly with more details.

That had been just over three years ago. At first, it was just a few thousand dollars. Then more. They trained him—whoever they were—in the art of cloaking transactions. Crypto. Tumblers. Paper trails that looped into oblivion.

To his own horror, Scott had a knack for it.

And his partners were willing.

And the firm thrived.

No one suspected a thing.

Not Lizzie. Not the authorities. Not even his dad.

Life returned to something resembling normal.

It wasn't until months into the operation that Scott began to understand who he was truly working for. At first, everything had been transactional, clean, clinical, with instructions arriving via encrypted emails and payments routed through a web of shell entities. But eventually, questions led to clues, and clues led to truths he couldn't ignore. The aliases used in correspondence began to appear in federal sanction lists. Wire instructions referenced banks in jurisdictions known for laundering cartel money. Then came the meeting, a request for a face-to-face with a man introduced only as "Jefe," under the guise of discussing "expansion strategy." The setting was too careful, the bodyguards too conspicuous, the message too clear. Scott left that meeting pale and shaken, realizing with grim certainty that the people he'd been laundering for were not rogue investors or corrupt financiers, they were part of a cartel. A very real, very dangerous one. And he was in deep.

While laundering money for the cartel sometimes made it difficult for him to sleep at night, it did have its rewards. The operation significantly improved the performance of his firm, Willow Street Investors, and with it their personal finances. Of course, Lizzie knew none of this and just believed that Scott and his partners were making strong investments and doing well for their clients. Despite the stresses of being caught or upsetting the cartel, Scott's life had more or less achieved a balance.

Looking back at it now, he desperately wished he had just left it there. Or even had gotten caught. He would be happy going to prison if it would mean his parents would still be here. But he didn't.

Nearly two years into his new financial relationship with the cartel, Scott and Lizzie had visited Nantucket for the Thanksgiving holiday. His father's partners, Cormac and Sean, had been like uncles to Felicity and him growing up. Scott had interned at his dad's firm the summer before his senior year at Tulane and had worked closely with Cormac. The internship created a bond between the two, and they talked regularly and frankly about their firms.

It was on one such call that Cormac confessed that Miacomet was not performing as well as they expected and were looking into new avenues to explore. After discussing a number of options, Scott cautiously mentioned an option he doubted Cormac had even considered. Maybe Miacomet would like to work with the cartel?

At first, Cormac was shocked. Shocked that Scott would be involved in such an illegal enterprise and shocked that he would even suggest it for his father's firm. But once he got that out of his system, Scott thought that maybe Cormac was seriously considering it. With that, he dived into why it made sense for Miacomet and the benefits they could expect. The chances of getting caught were there but very, very slim, especially since Miacomet had a forty-plus-year history of honesty and integrity behind them. No one would ever believe it was even a possibility. It was the perfect cover.

Slowly, Cormac came around, and when it was time, Scott made the necessary introductions. His only caveat to Cormac was that his father could never, ever know that the firm would be working with the cartel or that the idea for that came from Scott. That would probably be the end of their relationship.

And making that connection had worked. Cormac and Sean had leveraged this new opportunity to significantly improve performance at Miacomet Capital. The partners, including Charles, as well as their clients, were happy. The firm had turned the corner, a grandbaby was due within weeks, and everyone in the Post family was happy and healthy. Life was good.

That had been eighteen months ago, and now both his parents were dead. The weight of it crushed his chest. He leaned forward in the driver's seat, his forehead resting on the steering wheel, the scent of his mother's perfume all around him.

Something had gone off the rails. He needed to talk to Cormac and find out what.

CHAPTER TWENTY-NINE

The two remaining partners of Miacomet Capital sat in Cormac's office. Like Charles', it featured waist-high wainscotting painted a glossy white and abutted a chair rail of a similar color. However, whereas Charles maintained a cheerful pale yellow wall color, Cormac's was a more vibrant and aggressive blue. And where Charles had framed images of family and friends, Cormac sported pictures of himself in moments of victory. Holding up the trophy from the local soccer club, various hunting pictures with his latest kill, and a wide assortment of images of Cormac with politicians, celebrities, and local VIPs.

A bulky dark oak desk sat parallel to a large plaid sofa. A sizable window let in lots of natural light. A shaft of sunlight pierced the blinds and lit a patch on the beige carpeting. Sean was pacing the room while Cormac sat at his desk.

"What the hell is going on Cormac? I just got a call from that FBI agent. He wants to meet with us!" He was clearly agitated, his face flushed and sweating.

"Calm down, Sean. He is just doing this for Felicity. Probably just wants to make her happy so he can get in her pants. He knows that we had nothing to do with Charles' death. You and I both know it was an accident."

"Yeah? Well, what about Ann?" asked Sean.

"Sean, please relax. Sit down. Let me grab you a water. The police investigated that accident. She swerved to miss a deer and lost control of the car. I talked to the investigating officer myself. It was tragic, yes, but still an accident."

Sean started to calm down, Cormac's assurances of their innocence having the desired effect. He sat down on the couch.

Cormac opened the mini fridge beside his desk and grabbed a water, which he handed to Sean. He opened the bottle and took a long drink.

"Thanks."

"Of course."

"So what do we do now?"

"Nothing. We do nothing. It is simply tragic that we lost both Charles and Ann within days of each other. They were great people and our close friends for the last forty years. We need to mourn them. We need to support Felicity and Scott with whatever they need. But then we need to move on."

"Move on?" exclaimed Sean. "How the hell are we going to move on? Charles was the face of this firm." He stood up from the couch and started pacing, breathing heavily. He was getting upset again.

"Yes, we move on. Please calm down. It will be alright." Cormac was starting to lose his patience.

"Who the hell is going to replace him? Let's face it: I'm not good with clients. And honestly, I'm not sure you are much better. I think you intimidate the hell out of half of them."

Cormac appreciated the reference. He liked being the bulldog, the one that struck anxiety in the hearts of others. If he intimidated half of them when he was trying to be nice, imagine what he could do if he was actually trying to intimidate. He smiled at the thought.

"What the hell are you smiling about? Do you not care about our future? The future of this firm? I don't know about you, but I need this job. I have eight grandchildren to put through college and a wife who has gotten quite used to a high standard of living. And you know goddamn well how expensive living on this island can be!"

"Relax, relax, relax," said Cormac, forcefully. He stood and walked around his desk, intercepting Sean. He placed his arms on his shoulders and looked up at his flushed face. "We are going to be okay. I promise."

Sean nodded. "Okay. You're right, of course. I'm sorry to get upset."

Cormac squeezed his arm and smiled. "Hang in there. It's all going to be okay."

They both turned to the sound of heavy footsteps coming down the hall. Sean suddenly looked worried again.

Scott came into the room, panting heavily. He, too, looked distressed. "We need to talk."

Cormac was feeling like he had to take care of a couple of toddlers. *Did these guys get born without spines?*

"Of course, Scott," said Cormac. "Please sit down. Can I get you anything? Maybe some coffee? A water?"

"No, I'm fine," said Scott. "And I'd prefer to stand."

"Very well. What's on your mind?" asked Cormac.

"What really happened to my parents?"

Cormac looked at Sean and then back to Scott. His face showed concern.

"I know how you must be feeling losing both your parents but they were both accidents."

"Do you know how I feel? Do you know what it's like to lose your parents like this?" said Scott angrily.

Cormac's face tightened. "Yes, I do, you little shit!" he said and glared at Scott. "I lost both my parents to a car bomb back in nineteen seventy-four. My parents were on a date at a pub in Monaghan town. It was during the Troubles. My dad had met my mum for a drink early on a Friday evening. It was their date night. My younger brother and I were at home with a sitter."

He paused and walked over to the window. Looking out, he continued, his voice softening. "They were at one of their favorite pubs, a place they would go several times a month. It's where my dad had proposed twenty years before. But this time, it was different. This time, there was a bomb in a car parked in front."

Sean and Scott looked at each other, shocked.

He continued. "That bomb exploded. The blast blew out the front window and peppered my father with metal shrapnel. He died instantly. My mother, who was likely protected from the worst of the blast by my dad, was severely injured. She hung on for a week but never regained consciousness." Cormac paused. "Five other people in that pub perished that day."

Cormac turned and stared at Scott. "I was ten, you bastard. I was ten and suddenly an orphan. My family had no close relatives, so my brother and I became wards of the state."

"Cormac, I'm sorry, I didn't know."

"Thanks," he said acidly. "It's not something I have ever shared. I never told Sean or your father. As far as they were concerned, I had a pretty normal upbringing in Ireland until I landed here. And not a day goes by that I'm not thankful for this country. I came here at eighteen to go to University and never looked back."

Scott nodded. "And you really think my parents' deaths were accidents?"

"I know they were. But I have to be honest. I really do think something happened with your dad. Not sure if he had a stroke or an episode of some sort, but he acted out of character very suddenly. He did things I had never seen him do before. Like the drinking. Or peeing off the stern. That wasn't like him."

"My sister thinks it was something more nefarious."

Cormac looked surprised. "Felicity? She's just grieving and trying to make sense of things. It is hard to accept. It is for both Sean and I. Your dad was like a brother to us. And we've fished together for years. This wasn't our first rodeo, as they say. But something snapped inside him on that boat. I wish I knew what it was."

"Can you tell me again what happened?"

Cormac looked at Sean. "Of course. As I told you before, the day started out like any other. We met at the boat at six and motored out to Georges Bank. It was a beautiful day. Warm with light winds, the seas were calm. Spent the better part of the day trolling for tuna and swordfish but didn't have much luck."

"And my dad seemed okay?"

"He did! Charles was his same old self. He seemed as happy and content as I can remember. I think he was really looking forward to being a grandparent."

Scott nodded and looked at his feet.

"It was on the return trip that something happened."

Scott looked up. "And you didn't see it coming?"

"Neither of us did, unfortunately. Sean was on the bridge, getting us home. We hit a little bit of weather on the return, which kept him busy. Plus, we were entering the Great Point rip, so the currents were a bit wild. You've been there. You've seen how crazy the water can get. I think it was all Sean could do to keep our course steady and minimize the impacts of some of the bigger waves."

"And that's when my dad decided to take a pee off the stern?" asked Scott incredulously.

Cormac glanced at Sean. "I don't know Scott. I was down below in the head, going to the bathroom. When I came out a few minutes later, I saw your dad going off the back of the boat."

"Like he jumped? That doesn't make any sense!"

"He didn't jump," said Cormac, trying to sound reassuring. "He fell. What he was doing on the stern of the boat, I'll never know, but he most certainly didn't jump. We had just hit a rather big wave; he lost his balance and fell."

Scott shook his head. "No. I can't believe that." He turned to Sean. "So you didn't see him fall either?"

Sean looked nervous and shook his head. "I didn't. I was focused on driving the boat. As Cormac mentioned, we ran into some weather, and we were in the rip, so we had some tricky currents and large swells to manage."

Scott glared at Cormac. "So what did you do next?"

"What did we do? Sean damn near flipped the boat, turning around. But we were going close to twenty knots, so it took a minute to get back to where we thought he had fallen in, but there was no sight of him. The waves were a solid six to eight feet, and the currents were swirling. I'm not sure if it was the rip that grabbed him or he just went under."

"So you just let him go?"

"Absolutely not!" said Sean. "Cormac threw a life ring to mark the spot and be there just in case he did surface. I called the Coast Guard immediately on channel sixteen. We searched the area until it was dark. We wanted to continue, but we were advancing toward low tide, and I was worried about grounding the boat."

"So what the hell happened to him? How the hell could he fall off the boat?"

Cormac shook his head. "I don't know. I honestly don't know."

Scott paced the room, agitated. He wasn't satisfied with the answers he was hearing from the partners. "And my mom? Was that an accident, too?"

"Scott. Son. Yes," Cormac drew Scott into a hug. He then pulled back and looked up into Scott's eyes."She was coming back from Sean's house and swerved to miss a deer. I don't think she was that familiar with your dad's car. It was certainly much bigger and heavier than her Mini, and she lost control. It was a tragic accident."

He pushed Cormac away and turned to Sean. "And why the hell was she even at your house?" he asked angrily.

Sean looked back to Scott with tears in his eyes. "For comfort," he said. "She was really hurting. And she was angry, just like you. She wanted to know how this could have happened to your dad. Missy and I comforted her, listened to her, and, I hope, made her feel better. At least she said she felt better when she left our house that evening."

"Was she drunk?" asked Scott. "I know she did like her wine."

"No, Scott. She was not drunk. She had a few sips of wine with us but didn't even finish half her glass."

Scott walked over to the window and looked out at the busy street. Cars came and went, their drivers running errands, going to appointments, the everyday routines of daily life. But the world Scott knew was in shambles. He turned and looked at Cormac. "So, can you assure me our friends had nothing to do with this? With either of them?"

Cormac nodded slowly. "I can assure you. There was no involvement from them."

"And what about Rick? Our family friend. My babysitter, for chrissakes. And an FBI agent. He's staying at my house. What if he starts asking questions? What should I tell him?"

"You tell him the truth," said Cormac. "Your parents, God rest their souls, died in a pair of tragic but unrelated accidents. There was nothing anyone could have done to prevent that. Or to save them, for that matter."

Scott nodded and crossed his arms. "I'm not sure he's buying that. My sister has been whispering in his ear about a conspiracy claiming that my parents were murdered. What if he believes her and starts to dig a little deeper?"

"He's not going to find anything, I promise. We have been extremely careful. There is nothing to find."

"Do you think Charles might have mentioned Eel Point Amusements to anyone?" asked Sean, who had been quietly watching the conversation from the corner.

"What?" asked Scott, turning to Sean. "What are you talking about?"

Cormac looked angrily at Sean. He quickly composed himself and turned back to Scott. "It's nothing. It was a simulation we were running."

"A simulation?"

"Yes," said Cormac. "Sean here is preparing to teach a class on money laundering at Boston University and was putting together some proforma spreadsheets to document how it could be done and to use as examples with the students. Your dad found a copy on the server and was curious what it was all about."

"Just curious?"

"Just curious, Scott. In fact, once he reviewed it, he had some ideas on how to tweak the methods that Sean had developed."

"And that spreadsheet, what did you call it, Sean? Eel Point Amusements? That wasn't anything with our business with our new friends down south?"

"Oh my god, no!" said Sean, defiantly. "Do you really think I'd be that stupid? To leave a file like that where Charles would have access?"

"So you are sure my dad had absolutely no idea of what we were doing? The 'new strategy,'" said Scott, using air quotes.

"None!" said Cormac. "Sean was extremely careful. We swore to you that your dad would never know. And he didn't, I promise."

Scott's shoulders slumped. He was emotionally drained, the conversation taking its toll on him. He walked over to the sofa and collapsed. He put his head into his hands and started to cry. His body was racked with sobs. "I'm such a failure. Such a loser."

Cormac sat down next to him and put his arm around his shoulders, trying to comfort him. "You are not a failure."

"Bullshit," said Scott. "This is all my fault."

"Look at me!" said Cormac. Scott quieted and turned to face Cormac, his eyes red and cheeks wet. "This was not your fault! The deaths of your mom and dad were accidents. Nothing more."

Scott eyed him warily. "I hope you are right, Cormac. I don't think I could live with myself otherwise."

"I am right. Trust me. Now, you need to pull yourself together. In case that FBI agent wants to talk to you about this we need you to be strong and confident. No blaming yourself. They were accidents. Tragic accidents of two beautiful people." He pulled Scott into a long hug. "And you know you can always rely on Sean and me if you need anything."

"Thanks, Cormac. And you too, Sean." He stood and started walking toward the door. "I think I need to rest. I feel exhausted."

"I'm sure. You're probably still on Asia time. Go get some rest. And then maybe we can grab some dinner. I'd love to hear about your trip."

Scott nodded and walked slowly from the room. A moment later, they heard the back door close. Sean let out a long breath. Cormac looked at him curiously. "Are you okay, Sean boy?"

"Do you think that went alright?"

"Of course it did. The poor guy just lost both his parents. He just wants answers like we all do."

"And you don't think he suspects anything, do you?"

Cormac smiled softly. "It's okay. For the tenth damn time, it's all going to be okay. I promise."

CHAPTER THIRTY

Rick glanced at his watch and saw it was well past dinner time. He made a quick call to a number he had hoped was still in business. Smiling when his prayers were answered, he ordered from memory and was told it would be ready in thirty minutes. He made good use of that time. As he sat in the old Bronco in the parking lot outside of his favorite pizza place, Sophie T's, he called his colleague Nia to get a sense of what, if anything, she was finding with the files he had sent earlier in the day.

"RC"

"Nia, my darling. How goes the battle?"

"It's still going," she said, laughing. "Safe to assume you're calling about the files the NPD shared with me earlier?"

"I am. Any progress to report?"

"Honestly, I've barely had a minute to even open the files. Can you give me an hour or two? At least to get a feel for what might be happening?"

"Of course. And sorry to push. I've just got this damn interagency training thing staring me in the face on Sunday, and feeling like the clock is ticking."

"I get it. I really do. I just grabbed a bite to eat and am going to dig into these spreadsheets. I'll ping you when I'm ready to chat."

"Perfect. Thanks."

"You bet, RC." The phone went dead.

Rick checked the time and saw he still had a few minutes to kill. He tapped his screen and waited.

"Hi Rick," said Tuna. "What's up? Did you hear back from your colleague yet on those spreadsheets?"

"Sorry to bother you. And no, not yet. She is hoping to have something for us in a couple of hours."

"Okay. Something on your mind?"

He paused, unsure if he wanted to vocalize his thoughts.

"You there?" asked Tuna.

"Sorry. Just not sure I want to ask this question."

"Which is?" she asked, leading.

Rick let out a sigh. "Do you really think the NPD would take me back?"

Now, it was Tuna's turn to be quiet.

"Tuna?"

"Oh my god, Rick, yes! I think they would take you back in a heartbeat. Are you seriously considering it?"

"Let's just say I'm evaluating my options."

"Are you ready to leave the FBI?"

"You know, I have absolutely loved my time with the Agency. They really saved me during a time of some pretty dark thoughts. And it's been very rewarding. But being back here? It reminded me how much I miss community policing."

"I so understand that, I really do. That's why I'm here. And why I'm not going anywhere. I'll retire here."

"Cool, cool," said Rick. "But do me a favor and keep this to yourself for now."

"It's safe with me. But let me say on a personal level that I think you'd be very happy here. And you'd be very appreciated, not just from the department but also from the community. They remember you, and I think they'd be thrilled to have you back."

"Thanks."

A screen door opened, and a voice yelled out. "Caton?"

"Gotta' go, Tuna. Dinner's ready."

"You bet. Don't forget to let me know if you hear anything tonight."

"Will do. Thanks, T," he said and ended the call.

He went inside, collected his two large pizzas and a Greek salad, paid his bill with a substantial tip, and headed back to the Bronco. Within minutes, he pulled into the gravel drive of the Post residence.

"You brought me Sophie T's?" said Felicity, excitedly. "This has always been my favorite pizza on the island!"

Rick grinned. "I knew you loved it. I remember getting it when I was babysitting you guys. You were always wanting another slice."

She smiled and took a big bite. "Delicious as always. Thank you."

Rick looked at her softly. "Happy to."

"So what did Tuna say?" asked Felicity through a mouthful of pizza.

Rick was concerned that maybe somehow she knew of his recent discussion but quickly realized she was referring to his meeting earlier in the afternoon. "Let's not worry about that now. Please just enjoy dinner. Did you get some rest?"

"I did, wow," she said, yawning. "I think I must have slept for two hours. I still feel a little groggy, though, but this is helping."

Rick nodded. "Good. Is Scott back?"

She shook her head. "No. He texted me and said he was going to meet with Sean and Cormac." She took another bite. "You know he interned with Cormac when he was a senior at Tulane?"

Rick raised an eyebrow. "Really? I didn't know that. Were they close?"

She nodded. "Yes. I think Cormac became a bit of a father figure to him."

Rick eyed her questioningly.

She shook her head quickly. "It's not like Scott and my dad weren't close. They were. But I think Scott could relate to Cormac better than with my dad. Especially on the professional front."

Rick nodded thoughtfully. "Makes sense. So they stayed in touch?"

She nodded. "Yes. When Scott started his own firm, I think he leaned heavily on Cormac for advice and direction."

"When did Scott start his firm?"

She thought as she chewed. "Let me see. That would have been five years ago. No, wait, six years. I remember because Scott was so young. He had just turned thirty. I remember my dad acting surprised at the news. But also a little proud."

"Well, clearly, Scott has been successful, no?"

She nodded. "Absolutely. I know his firm had a few rough spots, especially during Covid, but I think he has done pretty well. I think he does well financially, and he and Lizzie have made a great life for themselves in Boulder."

Rick nodded. "I'm so glad. And I'm sure that will help him through his grief, keeping his mind off things."

"So tell me, Cola, what about you?" She asked him, her green eyes radiating with energy. "What are your plans now? Any chance you'll come back to Nantucket and take over the police force?"

Rick laughed hard, almost spitting out the water he had sipped a moment before. "Um, no. I don't think I'll be taking over the police force."

"But what about coming back home? To Nantucket." she asked seriously.

Rick thought for a moment and considered telling her of his conversation with Tuna. He dabbed the corner of his mouth with the napkin and then looked at her. "If you had asked me that question a week ago, I would have said never. But today? I have to be honest. There is some appeal to that idea."

"Really?" asked Felicity, excited.

"Maybe," said Rick. His phone dinged. He pulled it from his pocket and glanced at the screen.

Call me. Now.

"What is it?"

"It's from my colleague, Nia. I'm thinking she might have found something in the files."

Felicity tensed. "What do you think it is?"

"I don't know." He stood, and his chair scraped the floor. "I need to call her." He looked at his phone. "Signal strength is terrible in here. I'm going outside."

"Okay," she said.

He walked out the front door, saw two bars, and tapped his phone. Nia picked up on the second ring.

"RC. Long time."

Rick chuckled. "You found something?"

"I did indeed," she said, her tone suddenly all business. "I think your friends' family firm was knee-deep in laundering money."

Rick's stomach dropped. "So you suspect the spreadsheets are real, then?"

"Absolutely. Classic case of laundering, although I will admit whoever developed their process was pretty sharp. Unless you had access to these files and knew exactly what they were doing, from the outside it would look completely normal."

"Any idea on who's money they are laundering?"

"If I had to guess, I'd say it's drug-related. Most likely a cartel."

Rick winced. "Why do you say that?"

"Put simply, only the cartels have the ability to generate such large volumes of cash. I'm not even halfway through those spreadsheets and have already estimated close to twenty million in the last few months alone."

"Twenty? Seriously?" Rick echoed, stunned.

"Yes. So, I'm going to update Hanna on this and start the paperwork for the warrants. We need to know more about where the dirty cash is coming from and where it's going."

"Excellent! Anything you need me to do?"

"Yes. Can you type up a quick overview of your investigation? Just need to make sure I have the players and the details correct. Certainly, with these files, we have more than enough to support probable cause."

"Of course. I'll have it to you later tonight."

"Thanks."

"No, thank you. I appreciate all your help with this. Although it makes me sick to know our suspicions were correct, now we need to get to the bottom of things."

"You are welcome. Thanks for sending the background. I'll call with any questions. But we should be able to serve that warrant by end of day tomorrow."

"Great. Enjoy your evening."

Nia laughed. "Oh yeah, it'll be a blast." The line went dead.

Rick looked across the expansive green lawn and out to the harbor. Up until now, this had all been a simple exercise of what if. But now, Nia had found the proverbial smoking gun and confirmed his worst fears. The firm of his childhood idol, a man who he respected and knew to be incredibly honest, was, in fact, an ongoing criminal enterprise. The only remaining question was to find out who was involved.

"Rick?" Felicity had come out to check on him. "Are you still on the phone?"

Rick shook his head slowly. He started toward the door but was interrupted by the sound of tires on gravel. He turned to see the Mini pull in and park. Scott got out of the car and walked over to him, his expression unreadable.

"What are you two doing? Everything okay?" Scott asked cautiously.

Rick met his eyes. "Hi, yes. But we need to talk."

CHAPTER THIRTY ONE

"Sure. Of course," said Scott wearily, "Let's go inside."

The three of them made their way to the family room, the silence between them charged with something unspoken. Rick took the wingback chair, its overstuffed arms worn smooth by decades of quiet conversation. Scott and Felicity sat side by side on the couch, a few feet apart but oceans away from each other emotionally.

"Can I get anyone anything?" asked Felicity. Both men shook their heads.

"What's up?" asked Scott cautiously.

Rick exhaled slowly and looked directly at Scott. "I need to brief both of you on the investigation so far."

"The investigation?" asked Scott. "What are you referring to?" His tone was cautious, his jaw tense.

Rick nodded. "I'm sorry we haven't really had a chance to talk. I know you've been busy with work and overcoming your jet lag, but we've learned a lot in the last two days about the deaths of your parents. And the activities at Miacomet Capital."

"The activities?" said Scott, his eyes wide. "What are you talking about?"

Rick took a moment and then blew out a breath. "This is going to be tough to hear, but we now know that your dad's firm was laundering money."

Scott blinked, visibly stunned. "What? Are you crazy? There is no way that my dad's firm would be engaged in something like that!"

Rick held up his hand to calm Scott. "I know this is difficult to hear, Scott. But I just got off the phone with one of my colleagues at the FBI. She examined a number of files that your dad left on a thumb drive. The thumb drive that Fel found on the boat."

Scott turned toward his sister, eyes narrowed. "What, you're in on this?"

"I just wanted to know what happened to Mom and Dad."

"Mom and Dad both died in accidents, Fel. You know that!" Scott snapped.

Rick stepped in. "Actually, no, they didn't. We have evidence that your mom was indeed murdered."

Felicity looked at Rick, "So you..."

Rick nodded slowly. "Yes. We have confirmed that the control module in your dad's car had been tampered with. The accident that killed your mom was premeditated and carefully thought out."

Felicity's hand shot to her mouth. "Oh my god, she really was murdered?"

"I'm sorry, Fel. The data from your dad's car confirmed it. Your mom had no control that evening. It had been designed to intentionally drive that vehicle into a tree. Unfortunately, she was just a passenger at that point."

Scott sat staring into space, his face pale.

"Scott?" asked Rick.

He shook his head. "No way. Not possible."

Felicity leaned over to hug her brother. He pushed her away, stood up, and started pacing the room.

"This isn't happening," said Scott, agitated. He wasn't listening. He acted like a man unraveling.

Rick tried again. "Scott, I know how you're feeling. And I'm sorry. But we've worked hard the last couple of days to really understand what was happening at the firm. And with your parents."

"Are you saying my dad was killed as well?"

"We don't know that with any degree of certainty, but given what happened to your mom, then that would be my guess, yes."

"So you are saying Sean and Cormac are money launderers and murderers?" asked Scott, his voice cracking.

Rick stared intently at Scott. "We don't know that yet. We're not sure who has been involved in the laundering and if one or both had anything to do with your parents' deaths. But the evidence we have compiled so far suggests that."

"The hell with your evidence!" Scott roared. "I've known those guys my entire life. They would never do anything that you are suggesting. You have to be wrong!"

"Scott, we are not wrong. I've had some of the smartest people I know at the FBI looking at this, and they all agree."

"Bullshit!"

Felicity stood. "Scott, please. Calm down. You're going to have a heart attack."

"No, no, no," Scott mumbled, eyes darting, his breath coming fast. "This isn't right. This isn't—"

"It's true. All of it," said Felicity calmly.

Scott shook his head violently. "No. No way!"

"I tried to talk to you. You didn't want to hear it. Dad knew something was wrong at the firm. He said so in his journal. That's why he copied the files onto that thumb drive and left me the message. He suspected something illegal was happening at the firm. And as it turns out, he was right."

"No. Can't be. There is nothing illegal happening at the firm," said Scott, again, adamantly.

"I'm sorry, but you are wrong," said Rick. "This isn't just a suspicion of the two of us," said Rick, pointing to Felicity and himself. "We have had several experts, including the FBI, look at the files your dad left us, and they all agree. Miacomet Capital Partners was laundering money. The only thing left to really discover is who was involved and whose money they were laundering. And that will be answered shortly. I was just talking with a colleague at the FBI, and she is drafting the warrants as we speak. We should be able to serve them tomorrow which will give us access to the offices, corporate systems as well as all financial records. By this time tomorrow, we should know where the money is coming from and where it's going."

"I just can't, I can't handle this," said Scott. He continued to pace the room and looked as if he was about to have a breakdown. "There must be some mistake."

Felicity looked at Rick, her eyes wet with tears and pleading for him to take action.

"Scott," said Rick. "Please. Talk to us."

"Those bastards," said Scott in a whisper.

"What? What are you saying?" asked Rick.

Scott's voice came low and ragged. "Those bastards. They said my parent's deaths were accidents. They said they had nothing to do with it. I'm going to kill them!"

"Kill who?" asked Rick, confused.

Scott let out a scream. "Those sons of bitches!"

Rick put his arm on Scott's shoulder, trying to calm him down. "What are you saying, Scott?"

"Get out of my way," said Scott, pushing him forcefully. Rick stumbled back, caught his foot on a chair leg, and fell hard.

Felicity jumped up and rushed to him. She knelt beside him and helped him up.

Rick stood and dusted off his pants. "I'm okay."

"Where's Scott?" asked Felicity, looking around.

Rick scanned the room frantically. He heard the Mini's engine fire up and ran to the front door. He opened it in time to see Scott peeling out of the driveway, spraying gravel all over the lawn.

"We should go after him!" said Felicity as she joined him at the door.

Rick turned and said, "We won't be able to catch him. Any idea on where he's going?"

"Probably to whoever he was calling 'those bastards.'"

Rick snapped his fingers. "Sean and Cormac. Has to be."

Felicity's face blanched. "You don't think he's going to do something rash, do you?"

"He's pretty upset. And if he thinks one or both of them had something to do with your parent's deaths, who knows what he might do? Do you know where they live?"

Felicity thought for a moment. "I think Sean lives near Quidnet. Cormac? I'm not too sure."

"Quick, think. Do you have their addresses? Maybe in your dad's office?"

Felicity nodded and ran to her dad's desk. She scrounged quickly through the drawers until she found what she was looking for: his address book. She flipped through the pages quickly.

"Here!" she said, pointing to an entry. "Sean lives on Quidnet Road. That's not too far from here."

"And Cormac?"

She flipped through the small book. "He's on the other side of the island. Out by Madaket."

"So, who do you think he would go to first?"

"I'm thinking Cormac. Especially with the relationship they have."

"Right. Let's go."

They ran out and jumped in the Bronco. Felicity took the driver's seat, and Rick climbed into the passenger seat. The top was off, and the air was a bit chilly. She started the engine and flicked the headlights on; two dim shafts of light extended in front of the old truck.

"Do you know where you are going?" asked Rick.

"Roughly. I'm going to need you to direct me the last mile or so. Not sure which driveway is his." She accelerated quickly out of the driveway and squealed the tires as she turned onto Monomoy Road.

Rick pulled out his phone and loaded the mapping app. He keyed in Cormac's address. "Got it. Says we should be there in ten minutes."

"God, I hope we are not too late. I don't think I have ever seen Scott this upset."

"Hopefully, the drive will calm him down."

Felicity stole a glance at him, her eyes revealing she wasn't so sure that would happen. She approached the Milestone Rotary and downshifted the Bronco into second. She eyed oncoming traffic and blasted through, nearly colliding with a pickup truck. She waved in response to the horn and put her foot farther down. They sped quickly through the next rotary, thankfully empty of traffic and hitting nearly fifty down Sparks Avenue. She barely slowed down at Four Corners and squealed the tires again as they made their way past Cottage Hospital. Rick briefly wondered if maybe Felicity's driving would land them there.

Passing the old windmill, Felicity urged the Bronco faster and blasted down Prospect. She skidded to a stop at the intersection with Milk Street, looked both ways and then floored it. They quickly arrived at the next stop sign and rolled through to make the left onto Madaket Road. Nearly doubling the thirty-five-mile-an-hour speed limit, she was intent on beating the anticipated time that the mapping app had estimated. She knocked out three miles in just over two and a half minutes. Her aggression did little to calm Rick's nerves.

"Are we getting close?" asked Felicity anxiously.

Rick looked at his phone. "1.2 miles. Driveway will be on the left."

Felicity pushed further down on the throttle, the old Bronco responding to her commands.

"Easy," said Rick. "We have some curves coming up. I'm not sure this old truck will handle them well."

"I got this, Rick," said Felicity. She braked smoothly and deftly steered the old truck through the bends. As she apexed the last corner, she eased back down on the gas, the Bronco accelerating, the exhaust booming into the topless cabin.

"Okay, two thousand feet. One thousand. Five hundred."

Felicity lifted off the gas and applied the brakes. The truck slowed quickly, swaying side to side.

Rick peered through the windshield, trying to make out the turn in the dim light thrown by the headlights. "There!" he exclaimed, pointing to a black mailbox on the side of the road.

She turned the Bronco into the driveway and saw it was long and lined with hedges. The road was sandy and bumpy, and both of them were tossed about as the old suspension hit bump after bump. Rick could hear the branches screeching down the flanks of the Bronco and thought of the damage being done to the paint. But that was probably the least of their worries right now.

A few hundred feet down the driveway, they emerged into an opening. The road ended into a shell driveway, and Rick could see the dark outline of a monster house in front of them. A separate building, probably a garage, was a shadow off to their left. Felicity brought the Bronco to a stop next to the Mini. The house stood dark, the only lights coming from the truck. Rick could hear Scott pounding on the door and shouting.

He jumped out of the Bronco and ran up to the door. "Scott?"

Scott turned. In the dim light from the headlights, he could see that Scott's face was twisted in pain and plastered with tears. "He's not here. That bastard is not here." He slumped down on his knees.

Felicity ran up and hugged Scott.

"Where is he? Could he be at the office?" asked Rick standing above him.

Scott looked up, the anger burning in his eyes. "He's running, the bastard. That fat, little Irish shit is running."

CHAPTER THIRTY TWO

Friday Afternoon

Off Georges Bank, 70 miles east of Nantucket

"That's the beauty of Eel Point," said Cormac. He rose from the fighting chair, unclipped his belt from the reel, and placed the rod in a holder at the stern.

"The beauty? What are you doing, laundering money for a cartel?" said Charles sarcastically.

Cormac looked across the boat at Sean and then back to Charles. "Well, put simply. Yes."

Charles' mouth dropped. He walked slowly to the edge of the boat and sat on the gunwale. He looked quietly out over the water, unsure of how to process what he had just heard. His two best friends, his business partners, his brothers in his professional life had just dropped a bombshell on him. He looked back and forth between the pair, unable to process the flurry of thoughts that were running through his head.

"We are laundering money?" he asked hesitantly and looked back over the water, incredulous at the words he had just spoken.

The boat swayed gently as the three men slowly entered a new reality together. A gull cried out in the distance while waves lapped softly on the hull.

Sean was the first to speak. "I know this is hard to hear, Charles, but we didn't have a choice. It was our only option. That or declare bankruptcy."

It was just too much for Charles to take in. When they had left the harbor this morning all had been right with his world. The business was doing well; he and Ann were the happiest they had ever been, and they were expecting their first grandchild in a month. Life had been perfect. And now, a dark cloud had passed overhead, and he felt the first weight of guilt press down. He was a partner in a criminal enterprise. An unknowing partner, yes, but a partner nonetheless. The bright future that had lain ahead of him this morning was replaced by an approaching squall line. He would have none of it.

He stood and stared intently at Sean and then Cormac. "No."

"No?" asked Cormac.

"No," Charles repeated. "I will not be part of this. Reel in the bait, stow the gear. Let's head home now."

"And then what?" asked Sean.

"Then we go to the authorities. We come clean. Explain what has happened. Try to minimize the damage."

"Minimize the damage? Do you know who the hell we are dealing with?" said Cormac angrily.

"No, I don't. I haven't been privy to those discussions. But I will say it again. I will not be part of this."

Sean stood and glared at Charles. "Whether you like it or not, you are part of this. And if you go to the authorities, the one thing I can guarantee you is that we will all be dead."

"What?" asked Charles emphatically. "How can you say that?"

Cormac spoke. "Because that is who we are dealing with. Do you think we are talking about some two-bit crime operation? Really? No! We are talking about a large criminal enterprise headquartered south of the border; if you get my drift, who will not idly stand by while you 'confess' our activities to the authorities! They will take action, and that action will most certainly not be pleasant."

Charles was quiet, this newly discovered threat sinking in. Finally, he spoke. "I'm sorry, really, but I will not be part of this."

"Charles, I beg you. No. Please don't do this," pleaded Sean. "They will kill us all. And our families."

"I'm sure you are overreacting. We will be fine. They can find someone else to do their dirty work."

"So that's it?" shouted Cormac. "You are going to turn us in and let us take the fall with the cartel?"

"I'm sorry. I really am. But you made this bed, and now you are going to have to sleep in it." He turned to Sean. "Get us home. Now!"

Sean walked slowly to the transom and grabbed one of the rods. Charles grabbed the other, and together, they reeled in the bait. The lines secured, Sean stowed the poles under the gunwale. He moved quickly across the deck and climbed the ladder to the flybridge. He turned the boat and advanced the throttles. Soon, *Hedged* was moving at close to twenty knots. The boat was capable of much more speed but consumed large quantities of marine-grade fuel. Sean saw himself as a bit of a conservationist.

The wind started picking up, and as the waves gradually increased, the ride got rougher. Sean slid the throttles back, and the boat slowed quickly. Soon, they were sitting still in the water and rocking heavily in the worsening seas. Sean had climbed down the ladder into the cockpit.

Comac looked at Sean. "What's wrong?"

"Life preservers. We need to put them on. They're predicting thirty to forty knot winds by the time we hit the rip, so the ride is going to get rough. Don't want to take any chances."

"Okay," said Cormac. "I'll get them." He disappeared into the galley and emerged a few minutes later with three preservers.

"What took you so long?" asked Sean.

"Sorry. Had a hard time finding the third. It was buried under some coats." He handed a preserver to Sean, who slipped it over his head.

"Here, Charles," said Cormac and extended a preserver.

Charles took it without saying a word and quickly slipped it on, taking care to cinch the buckle at his waist.

"Happy?" said Cormac to Sean.

"Yes. Thanks." Sean turned and climbed back up to the flybridge. He advanced the throttles, and soon, the boat was back at cruising speed.

Little was said for the next few hours. Sean was busy steering a course for home, and Cormac thought it best to give his friend a chance to think things through and maybe accept the new reality they had dropped on him.

Looking ahead, Cormac could just make out the Great Point lighthouse and knew he didn't have much time left to convince Charles to change his mind. The gentle swell they had enjoyed for much of the day started to turn. The boat was hitting larger and larger waves as they entered the rip. Cormac could see white caps ahead of them. He turned his attention to Charles.

Charles had spent the last few hours pacing the deck, doing his best to manage the swaying of the boat below him. He was running scenarios through his head, trying to figure out how he was going to manage this. What would he tell Ann? And Scott? Hadn't he been a role model to Scott and gotten him into this business? And Felicity? He thought of friends across the island and the various charities where he volunteered. He even wondered if he would be able to weather the storm he knew they would face. Maybe they would have to leave Nantucket. That would crush Ann. Maybe she would even do the unthinkable and leave him.

He almost couldn't face it.

"Charles?" said Cormac. "I promise you it is really going to be okay." It was the first words he had said to him in several hours.

Brought out of his thoughts, Charles looked at the Irishman with such anger that Cormac was briefly scared of what he might do to him.

"You have ruined my life, you sonofabitch. Both of you. I'll be lucky if my family will still talk to me."

"It doesn't have to be that way. We don't need to tell anyone. Maybe we can figure out a way to ease out of this and get back to what we did before. And no one ever needs to know."

Charles shook his head. "But I'll know. And I'll never be able to live with myself."

The boat crashed against a particularly big wave and showered the men with salt water. On the flybridge, Sean was concentrating fiercely on steering the boat through the chop.

"You don't want to do this," said Cormac. "Please. We can keep this quiet."

"I'm sorry. I'll never be able to look at myself in the mirror. I can't do it. I can't live a lie."

"God help us," said Cormac. He looked up at Sean, whose focus was on the sea state in front of them.

"I'm sorry it has to be this way," said Charles. "I am. But it's the only answer." Charles turned and looked out at the water, pondering his future.

"Not as sorry as I am," said Cormac. He grabbed the steel gaff from the gunwale and swung it hard at the back of his friend's head. The shaft, glinting in the sun, made a sickening thud as it connected with the back of Charles' skull. He collapsed onto the deck of the boat.

Looking up to confirm Sean was oblivious to what was happening below, Cormac quickly turned Charles over and pushed him toward the transom. Groaning, Charles tried to resist but was too weak. Cormac jumped over him to open the transom door, usually reserved for landing prized trophy fish, and dragged Charles into the opening. He stepped back and then put both hands on Charles' waist and pushed him off the back of the boat. He slipped easily into the frothy wake. Cormac quickly closed the transom door.

The shock of the cold water revived Charles. He flayed in the water, quickly falling behind the wake of the boat. He was waving his arms. Cormac watched him struggle with mild interest. He looked up to confirm that Sean's attention was still focused on driving the boat and then, when he felt they had traveled far enough, yelled up at him.

"Man overboard!" Cormac yelled loudly, almost screeching. "Stop the boat!"

Sean looked down and saw Cormac frantically waving his arms. He pulled the throttles all the way to stop. "What's going on?" he yelled down. The boat slowed in the water and soon began swaying heavily from side to side in the rough surf.

"Charles just jumped off the boat! We must go back!"

"What?" asked Sean, confused.

"Turn around, Sean. Now! We need to get back there!" Cormac pointed wildly to a spot a few hundred feet behind them.

Sean carefully swung the boat around and advanced the throttles. The boat was crashing from one wave into the next. He scanned the water furiously, looking for any sign of his friend and business partner. He grabbed the mic and turned the VHF to channel sixteen. "Mayday, mayday. This is Hedged. We have a man overboard. We are approximately one mile northeast of Great Point. Over."

The speaker crackled. "Hedged, this is Coast Guard Station Brant Point. Repeat."

"Mayday, Mayday. We have a man overboard. We are approximately one mile northeast of Great Point lighthouse."

"Roger, Hedged. Do you have a visual?"

"Negative Coast Guard. We have thrown a life ring to mark where we believe he entered the water and dropped a pin on the GPS."

"Roger. We are dispatching assistance. Stay onsite until arrival."

"Confirmed." Sean hung the mic on its bracket and turned to Cormac. "We are never going to find him in this," said Sean, clearly upset. "What the hell happened?"

"I don't know, Sean. He'd been sitting on the transom since we left Georges. When we entered the rip, he stood up and then stood on the transom. I thought maybe he was just going to pee, but then he let himself fall into the water."

"Why the hell would he do that?"

Cormac did his best to look pained at the loss of his friend. "It was us, Sean. The news about the cartel. I don't think he could take it." He paused. "I think he killed himself."

"What? Ridiculous. I can't believe Charles would do that."

"Why else would he jump off the boat? Maybe he thought it would save the family from a lot of pain."

"Oh my god, we've killed our friend," said Sean. "We never should have gotten involved with the cartel."

Cormac put his hand on Sean's shoulder. "It was that or declare bankruptcy, Sean. Now, that would have been painful. Honestly, I think Charles took the only way out that spared his family the embarrassment. He certainly wasn't going to allow us to continue."

Sean hung his head. "Yes, but he died because of our actions. I'm not sure I can forgive myself for that."

A blare of an airhorn caused them both to look back over the stern. The Coast Guard cutter had arrived. In the distance, they could hear a chopper pounding its way in their direction. The Coasties were intent on finding Charles Post.

The radio crackled. "Motor vessel, Hedged, motor vessel, Hedged. This is Master Chief Jim Stanley of the Coast Guard vessel Dionis. Any update on the MOB?"

Sean grabbed the mic. "This is Captain Sean Axmacher of Hedged. Negative Coast Guard."

"Where did the individual enter the water?"

"Coast Guard, I have those coordinates at forty-one point two four latitude and seventy point zero two longitude."

"Thank you, Captain. Assuming he was wearing a PFD?"

"Confirmed, Master Chief. The victim, Charles Post, was wearing an offshore automatic life preserver. We believe he may have jumped off the boat intentionally."

"He jumped?" asked the Master Chief, surprised.

Sean looked at Cormac, who shrugged. "Yes. We believe the victim was intending to commit suicide," said Sean sadly.

"Roger, Captain. We will assume responsibility for the scene. You are released."

"Thank you, Coast Guard."

Sean turned the boat and reluctantly aimed her to the southwest. Hours earlier, the three of them had left the slip in the Boat Basin, excited for a fun day fishing together. Now, at the end of the day, they were returning home a man down. His friend and partner of over forty years was missing in the waters off Great Point, and there was not a thing he could do to resolve the situation. Sadly, he advanced the throttles, and soon *Hedged* was cruising at just over thirty knots, heading for the lights of Nantucket Harbor.

CHAPTER THIRTY THREE

"What's going on, Scott? Why do you think Cormac would be running? Has he done something?" asked Rick.

Scott was on the ground, his body curled in a ball and his face buried in his hands. He was rocking back and forth and mumbling incoherently. Felicity was trying to comfort him to no avail.

Rick pulled out his phone and dialed Tuna. She picked up immediately.

"Rick?"

"Tuna, yeah, it's me. Look, we have something going down here. I honestly am not sure what it is, but we have Scott Post curled in a ball in front of Cormac Walsh's door, stating that he believes Cormac is on the run."

"Wait? What?"

"Yeah, you heard me right. He thinks Walsh is on the run. If true, then clearly Cormac was involved in some or all of the illegal activity we have identified. He may have even been involved in the deaths of the Posts."

"Where's he running to?"

"No idea. Scott is extremely upset and incoherent." He looked down. Felicity was gripping her brother tightly, trying to keep him from falling apart.

"And what about the other partner, Axmacher?"

"We need to get in front of him now and see if he can shed any light on what the hell Scott is saying. For all we know, Cormac might just be out for a late dinner. Not sure why Scott would think he's on the lam."

"He must know something. Hate to say it, but maybe he's involved in this?"

He turned his attention back to Tuna. "Let's do this. Can you send an officer to Axmacher's house and have him picked up for questioning? Not sure how you position it to him, but just let him think he's not in any trouble."

"We can manage that."

"Good. I'll see what I can do to calm Scott down and will bring him with me. Let's meet at the NPD and sort this all out."

"Okay. But what about Walsh?"

"If he really is running, I'm not sure he could have gotten far. Let's see what we are dealing with first, and then, if needed, we can put a plan together to track him down."

"Got it. I'll meet you in thirty."

"Thanks." He ended the call and looked down at Felicity. "Do you think we can get through to him?"

"I don't know," said Felicity. "He keeps mumbling about my parents and how it's his fault. I've never seen him like this. It's almost like he has had a total breakdown."

Rick knelt down to get eye to eye.

"Scott? Scott?" he said gently. "Look at me."

Scott stopped rocking and slowly turned his head to face Rick. His eyes were swollen and tear-filled. He looked to be in incredible emotional pain.

"Talk to me. Tell me why you think Cormac is on the run."

Scott opened his mouth to speak but quickly shut it and started rocking again.

"Scott? Please. Help us. We can find Cormac if you can tell us what's happening."

The rocking stopped. "I killed them."

"What? You killed who, Scott?"

"My parents."

Rick reached out and rubbed Scott's shoulder. His voice was quiet and gentle. "You did no such thing."

Scott nodded his head vigorously. "Yes, I did. It was all my fault!"

Rick looked at Felicity, whose face was twisted in confusion and concern. Catching his eye, she shrugged her shoulders, unsure of how to handle this confession.

"I need you to come with us."

He looked up, his eyes questioning. He mumbled. "Where?"

"Let's just go talk a bit. Get you somewhere warm. You can explain why you think it's your fault. Maybe have some coffee?"

Scott nodded. Rick stood and helped him stand. With Felicity on one arm, he helped him to the passenger side of the Bronco and eased him into the seat. He reached around him to grab the seatbelt and clicked it in place. He stepped back and looked at Felicity. "Can you bring the Mini?"

She shook her head. "I think I should drive him. I know how to keep him calm."

Rick nodded warily. "Okay, I'll follow in the Mini. But let me know if he starts to act up."

She scoffed. "He's my brother. He's not going to do anything. The poor guy looks crushed. Defeated. I just hope we can help him."

"Okay. Just please be careful. I'll be right behind you. Just head to Fairgrounds Road. Tuna's going to meet us there."

Felicity nodded.

They made their way slowly back down Madaket Road and through town. They arrived at the offices of the Nantucket Police to find Tuna waiting for them by the front door. She made her way over to the cars as they pulled in and parked.

Rick got out of the Mini to meet Tuna. "Axmacher?"

"He'll be here shortly. Officer Downs just radioed that Axmacher was cooperating."

"Good."

"How's he doing?" asked Tuna, nodding her head toward Scott. Felicity was unlatching the seatbelt and helping Scott get out of the car. He looked as if he'd aged forty years in the space of an afternoon.

"Not good. He keeps claiming that he killed his parents. It's almost as if he has had a breakdown."

She nodded. "Maybe he's more involved than we know."

Rick looked surprised. "Scott? What makes you think that?"

"Just a hunch."

"He's a good kid, Tuna. And really struggling right now. I think we are just going to go to the break room and grab a coffee. See if we can settle him down."

"Okay. I'll text you when Axmacher arrives."

"Thanks, Tuna." Rick turned and walked over to Felicity and Scott. He had stopped crying but still had a dazed, wary look in his eyes. He barely looked at Rick when he approached.

"You two want some coffee? It's not very good, but our options are kind of limited right now," he said, forcing a smile.

"Sure," said Felicity. She turned. "Scott?"

He nodded and started walking slowly. Felicity linked her arm in his and led them inside.

They walked into the break room on the first floor and settled into yellow molded vinyl chairs around a circular laminate table. Scott slumped in the chair and placed his head on the table. Felicity looked at him and back to Rick with worry in her eyes. He did his best to look reassuring.

"Cream or sugar?" Rick asked Felicity.

"Just cream, please."

"Scott?"

"He prefers black," she added softly, glancing at her brother.

Rick made the drinks and brought them to the table. He took a sip. "Sorry, this isn't very good. Cop coffee on government budgets. Not always the best." He forced a smile.

"Thanks," said Felicity. "What's next?"

"They are bringing Sean in for questioning."

"Do you think he had anything to do with my parent's death?" she asked excitedly.

"Honestly, I'm not sure. My gut says no, but I've been wrong before. I'm hoping he has some info on Cormac and whether or not he's on the run."

Scott mumbled.

"What is it, Scott?"

He raised his head from the table and looked at Rick intently. "Cormac is on the run. I guarantee it. I know that man and what he'll do to protect his ass."

"Do you know where he could be going?"

He shook his head. "Sorry, that I don't know. But I'm sure he has planned for it. This isn't a spontaneous escape."

Rick absorbed the comment. From his few interactions with Cormac, he realized he was a smart and ambitious man. He had no doubt that Cormac could escape with the proper planning and lead time. He needed to get in front of Axmacher to get an idea of where he could have gone. His phone buzzed. He looked down to see a text from Tuna.

Axmacher is here. Heading to interview 2

Rick quickly tapped a reply that he was on his way. He stood as he turned to Felicity. "I've got to go. Sean's here, and I need to go get some answers."

Felicity nodded. "I understand."

Rick looked at her with concern. "Are you two going to be okay?"

She nodded her head slowly. "Yeah, I think so. It's just a lot to get our heads around, you know. And at least I've had an inkling about it over the last few days. But poor Scott. He's just learning about this. It has to be a huge shock to his system."

"Look. I'm going to probably be a while. Why don't you take Scott home? Give him some leftover pizza. Maybe see if he can rest?"

"Sounds like a plan. Let me know if you hear anything?"

"Of course."

"Thanks, Rick." Felicity stood and embraced Rick. "I don't think I could have handled this without you."

He returned the hug. "Just glad I could help. You know how much your parents meant to me."

She pulled away and nodded. "See you later?"

"Yes." He walked over and rubbed Scott's shoulder. "It's going to be okay. I'll be back to the house as soon as I can. Go with Fel and get some rest."

Scott nodded but was quiet.

Rick took one last look at Felicity, smiled, and headed to interview room number two.

CHAPTER THIRTY FOUR

Rick entered the small interview room and took a seat next to Tuna across from Sean Axmacher. The room was cool, the HVAC system humming noisily above them. The bluish fluorescent light did nothing for his complexion. His face was pallid, and he was clearly upset and confused.

"Am I under arrest?" he asked shakily, his voice strained.

Rick smiled and tried to look kind. "Not at all. We just wanted to chat and ask you a few questions. I apologize that it's after nine o'clock on a Saturday night, but in cases like this, time can be of the essence."

Sean blinked, confused. "Cases like this?"

Rick ignored the question. "Can you remind me of what your position was at Miacomet Capital?"

"I was the CIO or Chief Investment Officer."

"And what do you do in that role?"

Sean straightened a little, the familiarity of the topic grounding him. "My primary focus was on the investment strategy. We manage millions of dollars of wealth for our clients, and it's my responsibility to pick investments, and in some cases acquisitions, that can grow that wealth for them."

Rick nodded slowly. "And that's always been your role?"

The tension in Sean's shoulders loosened ever so slightly as he allowed himself to sink into the rhythm of the conversation. "Yes. That's what really made the three of us so successful together. We each had very different but highly complementary skills."

"How so?" Rick prompted.

"Think of an investment firm as a three-legged stool. Each leg has to support the others, or the whole piece will collapse. I was the strategy leg, determining where and how we invested the money. Cormac was the financial and accounting leg. He tracked the investments, managed the internal systems, developed the reporting. Essentially handling anything that had a number associated with it," Sean said. He gestured absently with his hands, as though drawing it in the air.

"And Charles?"

Sean smiled at the thought of his deceased partner. "Charles? He was the face of this firm. He managed all of the relationships with the clients. He would prospect for new investors, communicate the firm's performance in quarterly messages, assuage concerns, and be our primary cheerleader."

"Was he good at that?"

"The best," said Sean sadly. "I never met anyone as comfortable in a room full of strangers than Charles. He could connect with people in so many ways. He was amazing."

Tuna was taking notes. Rick paused a few minutes, long enough so that Sean began to get uncomfortable. He squirmed in his chair and blinked at the light. A slight bead of perspiration appeared on his forehead despite the room's chill.

Rick leaned forward, voice still gentle. "What happened on the boat, Sean?"

Sean shook his head. "Oh my god, I don't know. One minute, everything was fine and we were making our way through the rip. The next thing I know, Cormac is yelling that we had a man overboard. I killed the throttles and turned the boat as fast as I could, but we never saw him. It was getting dark, and the waves were pretty big. Awful conditions to try and find a man overboard."

"And you saw him with his life preserver on?"

Sean exhaled, his breath shaky. "Yes, absolutely. I had stopped the boat on the way in and made everyone put theirs on. Usually, I don't worry about it too much; I leave it to personal choice. But with the forecasted winds and going through the rip, I felt it best to be cautious."

"So, how did the man end up in the water?"

"I don't know. I didn't see anything. All I heard was Cormac yelling for me to stop. He made it sound like Charles had jumped. Intentionally."

"You mean kill himself?" asked Rick, anger in his voice. "Why would he do such a thing?"

Sean quickly backtracked. "No, no, I'm sorry. It's just one thought that Cormac had. But you are right. It doesn't make sense. Charles wouldn't do that." He hung his head and looked in his lap. "I wish I knew. I really did."

Rick again paused for a few minutes to build the tension. He looked at Tuna, and she nodded.

"What can you tell me about an investment at your firm called Eel Point Amusements?"

Sean's body went rigid, and he looked up with panic on his face. The bead of perspiration had turned into a nervous sweat, dampening his armpits. "What? Eel, what?"

"Eel Point Amusements," said Rick, talking slowly and forcefully.

"Um, I'm not sure. I'd have to check my files. We have investments in nearly a hundred different assets and businesses. I don't recall specifically about Eel Point."

"Are you sure?"

"I am. Why?"

"Because we know that your firm, Miacomet Capital Partners, has been laundering money through Eel Point for at least the last year. Maybe two."

Sean's mouth opened slightly. "What. That can't be!"

Rick narrowed his eyes. "Do I look like an idiot to you, Sean? Do you think I'm just making this all up?"

Sean sat quietly, fidgeting in his chair. "Could I get some water, please?"

"Sure," said Tuna. She got up and left the room.

"You've made a big mistake."

"What? What are you talking about," he asked nervously. His hands trembled as he fidgeted with a loose thread on his sleeve.

Tuna returned and put a small cup of water on the table. Sean grabbed it and took a long swallow.

"You left a file on the shared drive that Charles found. He went through it and suspected you and Cormac were up to something. Something quite illegal."

Sean tried to put a calm face on. "Oh, that? That was for a class I was teaching trying to educate the students on AML."

"AML?"

"Anti-money laundering. It's a system designed to help ferret out and prevent money laundering."

"That's rich, coming from you," said Rick acidly.

Sean, confused, said, "What?"

"Drop the act, Sean. We turned those files over to my colleagues at the FBI. They've been through it and have identified at least twenty million in illegal laundering in the last few months alone. As we sit here, they are preparing formal search warrants that will allow us to look into every aspect of your life, including Cormac's and Miacomet Capital."

Sean looked like the proverbial deer in the headlights.

"It's over. By this time tomorrow night, we will have everything we need to put you, and I suspect Cormac, away for a very long time."

Sean started to cry. He pounded his fists on the table, showing the first real emotion since he had sat down. "I told him! Dammit. I told that fat little shit this was going to happen!"

Rick didn't move. "What are you saying?"

"I told him we were going to get caught. But he's such a cocky little bugger he refused to believe it. Said if we were careful, we could make it work. And make millions for the firm."

Rick's voice dropped. "I guess what I really want to know is why. Why risk everything you three built over the years?"

Sean looked at his hands and spoke quietly. "I fucked up. Badly."

"How so?"

He let out a long sigh. "Two years ago, we had a partner meeting about the firm's performance. We were doing okay generating returns in the mid-single digits. But we were being outpaced by the markets, and our clients were getting upset. So we decided to make some changes to our investment strategy, take on more risk, and hopefully increase our returns."

"And then what?"

"And then what? Our new strategy went to shit. Instead of improving returns, we made them worse. Far worse. We had to do something, or the firm would go under. So Cormac came up with this idea."

"To launder money?"

Sean swallowed, hard. Then he nodded. "He said a friend reached out to him about an opportunity. He looked into it and said we should do it. That it would solve all our problems."

"Who was this friend?"

"I've no idea. And I didn't want to know, honestly. I didn't even want to know who we were doing this for."

"But you do know, don't you? Cartel?"

He sat silently and looked up at the ceiling. His face a bluish-white. "Yes. I don't know which one, as we have a single point of contact, and he has made sure to keep us very much in the dark. But the money started flowing, and I have to say, it saved us. Suddenly, we were outperforming the markets and our peer groups. To Charles, the new strategy was delivering those results. But Cormac and I knew the truth."

Rick let that hang for a moment. "So, I'm to ask you again. What happened on that boat? Did Charles ask you about the Eel Point file?"

Sean went quiet again. New perspiration appeared on his forehead. He leaned forward and put his face in his hands. "Yes," he said softly.

"Yes? Charles confronted you two about it?"

Sean lifted his head and nodded. "He did. Cormac tried to assure him that it was okay, but Charles wouldn't hear about it. Said he couldn't be involved in an illegal enterprise."

"So what next?"

"He said he wanted to head to port immediately and turn ourselves in. Said that we could minimize the damage if we confessed."

"And I'm guessing that Cormac didn't think that was the best idea."

Sean shook his head adamantly. "No. He was pretty sure that the cartel might react violently. Maybe kill us or our families."

"And then Charles just jumped off the boat?"

Recognition flared in Sean's eyes. "Oh my god, no!" He looked at Tuna and then Rick. "He wouldn't do that."

"Are you sure? You said Cormac was a cocky little shit. Couldn't he kill Charles to save his own ass?"

Sean's whole body slumped in despair. "No, no, no."

"Did you see him jump?"

"No. All I heard was Cormac yelling man overboard."

"So don't you think Cormac could have attacked Charles? Pushed him into the water?'

Sean's hands were shaking violently now. "Oh my god. That little Irish bastard. He probably waited a minute or two, so we were far enough away before yelling to me. Knowing that extra distance would make it just about impossible to find Charles in the water."

Rick's tone was flat. "So where is he now? Cormac?"

"What do you mean?"

"Cormac is gone. We suspect running to get away from all this. Where do you think he might have gone?"

"I have no idea. I really don't. He's been here for decades. No idea where he would go," he mumbled, his head collapsing slowly into his hands. Soon, he began to sob.

"What about Ann?"

Sean lifted his head, his face wet with tears. "Ann? What about her?"

"Who wanted her dead?"

"What? What are you talking about? That was an accident."

Rick looked at him intently and then cocked his head.

"What?" exclaimed Sean. "She was killed?"

"Yes, Sean. She was murdered. She was driving Charles' car, and it had been tampered with - effectively making it a weapon. Ann didn't stand a chance."

Sean's eyes filled with tears again. "Oh. No. No. Who would want her dead?"

"That's what we are asking you."

Sean held up his hands defensively. "On my word, I have no idea why anyone would want to hurt her. She was a wonderful woman. Are you sure about all this? That she just didn't swerve to miss a deer?"

"It wasn't an accident. The car had been hacked, the software compromised to cause the accident that killed her."

Sean started to cry again.

Rick turned to Tuna. "I'm not sure we are going to get any more out of him. Let's close this out and get him processed."

Sean's head jerked up. "Processed? What's going to happen to me?"

Rick's voice was even. "I think that depends on you and your level of cooperation. Help us find Cormac, confess all you know, and you just might just get out of jail while you can still eat solid food."

CHAPTER THIRTY FIVE

The interview with Sean had lasted until nearly midnight. Rick and Tuna were convinced now that Cormac was on the run. And with Sean's confession, they knew why.

He had called his boss and briefed her on the situation. Hanna had pledged the resources of the FBI to help find and arrest Cormac Walsh. But where to look?

"What are you thinking?" asked Tuna. They had stepped outside to get some fresh air. There was a light fog in the air. Above them, the waning moon showed brightly.

"I'm wondering if he has already managed to get off the island. According to Sean, the last anyone had seen of Walsh was early this afternoon. About one o'clock. That means he has a nearly twelve-hour head start on us."

"We need to check the passenger manifests for the ferries, both the Steamship and the Hy-Line. We'll also need to check the airlines. There were at least a dozen or so flights today that theoretically he could have been on."

Rick nodded. "What about that other ferry? The one that goes to New Bedford and New York."

"Sea Streak?"

"That's the one."

"We can check, but unlikely. They only have one trip a day, and it leaves at one. Unless he had planned on running today, I doubt he was on that boat."

"Agree. This doesn't strike me as a well-planned getaway. More like he started to feel the heat and decided to get the hell out of town."

"So, if you're Cormac Walsh, and you need to get off the island quickly, how would you do it?" And more importantly, not leave any tracks to follow."

"Not that easy to do. You need either a private plane or your own boat."

"But a plane needs to file a flight plan, right?" asked Tuna.

"Theoretically, no, especially if visual flight rules apply. But with the congestion around Nantucket this time of year, I'd be amazed if any private plane or charter would take off without a flight plan."

"And we know he's not a pilot, himself. Right?"

"Actually, I don't know if that's true. Damn!" exclaimed Rick. "Could we have missed that?"

"Let's go find out."

Sean Axmacher was still in booking. He was being printed and photographed for his role in the massive criminal fraud at Miacomet Capital Partners. The U.S. Marshal Service would likely be arriving tomorrow to escort him off the island, where he would face a litany of federal charges. Rick and Tuna caught him as he was being led to the holding cell.

"Sean?" asked Rick.

Sean Axmacher, already thin, looked ghostly in the fluorescent light. All spark of life had left him, and he stared back vacantly at the mention of his name.

"Does Cormac know how to fly a plane?"

Sean seemed to have difficulty processing this question. He stared blankly at the wall and then shook his head.

"Are you sure?"

Axmacher nodded slowly.

"Okay. Does he have access to a plane? Or know someone who does?"

He stared back at them, expressionless, and shook his head. "I don't think so," he mumbled quietly.

Rick looked at Tuna. "Okay, so that's off the table. How else could he have gotten off the island undetected?"

"Mmmboat," mumbled Sean.

"What?" asked Rick. "What did you say?"

Sean looked to need every ounce of energy to form two words. "My boat," he said.

Rick looked at him intently. "Does Cormac have keys to your boat?"

Axmacher nodded.

Rick turned to Tuna. "Get on the radio. See if we can get some officers to the Boat Basin and check and see if the boat is there."

Tuna nodded and pulled out her cell phone. She walked down the hall as she was talking.

"Anything else you can tell us?"

He mumbled a few words. Rick leaned in to try and make them out. "I'm sorry, I don't understand what you are saying."

"I'm sorry," said Sean.

"You're sorry?" said Rick angrily. He felt no sympathy for the shell of the man standing in front of him, a man who had indirectly led to the deaths of two innocent and kind people. "You're a piece of shit, and I hope you spend the rest of your life in a cell. Take a good look at this island when you leave tomorrow. It will probably be the last time you ever see it."

Rick turned and walked briskly down the hall to where Tuna was standing. "Are you okay?" asked Tuna. Rick was visibly upset.

"Yeah, I'm fine. I just wish I could punch that bastard. Make him feel some of the pain that he's caused."

Tuna nodded. "I get that. But his life is over. The charges they have on him? He'll never see the light of day ever again."

"I hope you are right. Anyway, anything on the boat?"

"Not yet. Officer Downs is making his way over there now. We should know in a few minutes."

Rick nodded but was quiet. He was thinking intently.

"Rick?"

He shook his head. "Sorry, was just wondering. Do you think Sean might have a remote monitoring system for his boat?"

"I don't know much about boating, but maybe. I suppose the technology exists."

"If you owned a boat like his. What is it, like forty-two feet?"

"Yeah, maybe a little bigger."

"Gotta be worth close to a mil, don't you think?"

"Easily."

"Then I have to think he's got a tracker and probably controls it from an app on his phone. I'll be right back." Rick turned and rushed back to the booking room and found the officer in charge. "Do you have his phone?"

"I do. Here."

"Thanks. Can you let me into his cell?"

"Sure."

Rick walked quickly down to the holding cell while the officer struggled to keep pace, his keys jangling. He pulled them from his belt and slipped one into the lock. He turned the key and then opened the door. Axmacher was sitting quietly on the edge of the steel bed. Rick walked up to him and held the phone in front of his face. He heard a click.

He turned the phone to confirm it had unlocked. He went quickly into settings to remove the facial identification and then added a simple passcode of one one one two two two. Now, he would have complete control of the man's phone.

He swiped through the screens and found a folder labeled *Boating*. He tapped that and was faced with a half dozen apps ranging from tides to weather to fishing forecasts. He swiped left and found an additional three apps, including one called *Roam*. He tapped on that, and his screen filled with an overview of the sport fishing boat *Hedged,* including temperature, humidity, fuel remaining, and most importantly, GPS coordinates. He tapped on that, and his screen changed to a small boat icon tracking over a dashed black line through a blue sea. He used two fingers to scroll out to show land. He looked closely and realized that the boat was already nearly three hundred miles south of the island.

"Tuna!" He ran back down the hall to where she was standing. "We've got him!"

"Where?"

Rick angled the phone so she could see. He noticed that the screen also showed the speed of the boat as well as the current helm direction. Another icon on the screen confirmed the boat was on autopilot. "He's doing a little over thirty-eight knots heading south-southwest."

Tuna's phone rang. She picked up. "Fisch." She nodded and then said, "Good work." She ended the call and slipped the phone back in her pocket. "That was Officer Downs. The boat is gone. He was able to get through to the Harbormaster, and she recalled seeing the boat at the fuel docks right after lunch. She doesn't remember seeing anyone on it, though."

"That's it! He's making a run on Sean's boat. But where the hell does he think he's going?"

"South America? Maybe he has a deal with the cartel to shield him?"

"Possibly, but he certainly doesn't have the fuel to go non-stop. A boat like that probably has a range of four hundred, maybe four hundred fifty miles max. That would mean several stops." Rick pulled out his phone. "For argument's sake, let's just say he is heading to Mexico. The Yucatan peninsula would be the closest destination from Nantucket." He tapped his phone several times. "Okay, that's about fifteen hundred nautical miles. That's a minimum of three stops for fuel. And assuming he can maintain nearly forty-knot cruising speed, that's just about thirty hours, not including fuel stops."

Tuna nodded. "Difficult for one man but doable. Don't you think?"

"I don't know. Walsh has got to know that we would be on to him pretty quickly."

"Does he honestly think he can make it?"

"He is a cocky bastard, I'll give him that," said Rick. "Probably thinks he's smarter than us." He pulled Sean's phone up, keyed the code, and looked at the app. "Okay, according to this, he has about one hundred and fifty gallons left. At current speed," he eyed the app closely, "looks like he will need fuel within the next three hours, if not sooner."

"Is there an East Coast port that he could be heading to?"

Rick zoomed out and looked along the coastline. "Virginia Beach?"

"You think so?"

"Well, it's close to his maximum range, and it would be an easy in and out." Rick did some quick mental math. "Based on his current speed, he'll be making port around three a.m."

Tuna pulled out her phone and did a quick search. "It doesn't look like there are any fuel docks open at that hour. The ones shown don't open until eight."

Rick nodded. "Maybe he has someone meeting him there? I very much doubt he'll want to wait five hours."

"Could he have some auxiliary fuel tanks on board?"

"Doubt it. There is just no easy way to manage that quantity of fuel. Even if he had a dozen five-gallon jugs, that would only give him enough range to make forty miles or so."

"Whoa. I wouldn't want that fuel bill!"

Rick chuckled. "Big boats like that are not for the faint of wallet. Anyway, I thought maybe we could take him when he stopped for fuel, but now? Let's just nail the bastard." He pulled out his phone and dialed his boss. She picked up on the third ring, and sounded tired.

"Rick?" she asked sleepily. "You okay?"

"Sorry to bother you again, Hanna. I know it's only been a couple of hours since we talked but we have had some major developments in the Miacomet Capital case. You know we have one of the partners in custody. But it appears, the other partner, Cormac Walsh, is making a run for it in Axmacher's sport fishing boat."

"Okay, what are the details?" she asked.

"The boat, Hedged, is heading south-southwest at nearly forty knots. It currently appears to be heading to Virginia Beach, Virginia, we suspect to refuel, and is approximately eighty nautical miles out."

"Okay. What's your thinking?"

"I recommend we connect with the Coast Guard to have them send a patrol boat to pick him up."

"Do you think he's dangerous?"

"My gut tells me no, but you never know with a man on the run. He's a bulldog of a man, and I wouldn't be surprised if he at least has a rifle or pistol on him."

"Understood. Let me connect to the Coast Guard Commander there and see how quickly they can respond. I'll text you the details."

"Thanks, Hanna. I really appreciate the help."

"You bet. Nice work, Rick. How's your Sunday looking?"

Rick let out a long sigh. "Well, given it's already early Sunday morning, I'd say it's looking like a long one." He paused. "But I'll be on that damned plane, Hanna. I promise."

"You made my night. Talk soon." Hanna ended the call.

He pocketed his phone and turned to Tuna. "Okay. My boss will connect with the Coast Guard in Virginia Beach to scramble a patrol boat to intercept Cormac." He looked at his watch. "We may know something in the next hour or two."

"Okay, now what?"

"I need to follow up with Felicity and see how Scott is doing. He was really struggling when they left for home. Just want to make sure he's okay."

313

Tuna nodded. "Just keep me in the loop? I want to know when they've caught Walsh."

"Absolutely." Rick walked over to the Mini. As he got in, his phone rang. It was Felicity.

"Rick!"

"Fel? What's wrong?"

"It's Scott. I think he is going to kill himself!"

"What? Why do you think that?"

He could barely understand her through her sobs. "He took Dad's old pistol out of his desk and then walked out to the back lawn. I tried stopping him, but he just barged past me. He kept repeating that he had killed them."

"Okay. I'm just a few minutes away. Try to talk to him, distract him, keep him calm until I get there."

She sniffled. "I will. But please get here."

CHAPTER THIRTY SIX

Rick slipped the Mini into first gear and floored it, the front tires spinning as they struggled to get a grip on the fog-dampened asphalt. He flew down Fairgrounds Road, barely slowing for the left onto Old South Road. Taking the hard right through the rotary, the rear end of the Mini stepped out. He easily corrected the slide with a little opposite lock and put the gas pedal to the floor. What he didn't see was the Nantucket Police cruiser sitting in the driveway at Creeks Preserve. As the Mini sped past, the officer turned on his headlights, hit the emergency lights, and peeled out in hot pursuit.

Rick glanced in the mirror and saw the flashing red and blues on his tail. He smiled. He made the quick left on Monomoy Road and soon was sliding to a stop in the gravel of the Post's driveway. The police car slid in right behind him. The door opened, and Rick heard him shout, "Police! Stop and put your hands up!"

He eased open the door to the Mini, extended his arms first through the opening, and then slowly stood.

"Rick? Is that you?" He had his hand on his gun.

"Hi, Noah. I bet you didn't expect to meet like this. Sorry, but we have an emergency here. Possible suicide attempt in progress."

"Oh my god. Go! I'll order back-up and the EMTs."

Rick shouted his approval over his shoulder as he sprinted into the Post's home. He ran through the kitchen and out the back door to the lawn. He could just make out two figures on the dock and ran as quickly as he could down the lawn. The grass was slippery with dew, and he nearly lost it several times. He slowed to a walk as he approached the dock, subtly easing himself into the situation.

Felicity had made her way to the edge of the dock, where it met the lawn and greeted Rick. "Thank god you're here," she said, turning to meet him. Her voice was breathless, panicked. "I've tried everything but can't seem to get through to him. Keeps saying he wants to kill himself."

He looked past Felicity to see Scott sitting cross-legged on the dock next to the Herreshoff. He had the gun in his lap, his right hand resting on the barrel. He was rhythmically rocking back and forth as if deciding what he really wanted to do.

He turned to Felicity and placed his hands on her arms. "It's okay. I've got this. Let me try and talk to him."

She nodded slowly, her expression helpless. "Let me know if I can do anything."

"Of course," Rick said softly.

He turned and walked down the dock slowly. The wood creaked underfoot. His hands remained visible, open at his sides. With measured steps, he walked toward Scott, stopping a few feet away. He lowered himself into a sitting position, cross-legged, matching Scott's posture.

Scott eyed him cautiously. "What do you want?" he asked warily.

"I just want to talk, Scott."

"I'm done talking. I just want to rid myself of this pain. I killed them."

Rick stayed calm, even. "I understand, Scott. This has been a terrible shock, but I don't understand how you think you were responsible."

Scott scoffed. "You don't know the half of it."

Rick nodded. "Okay. Why don't you tell me?"

"I don't think you'd understand."

"I've known you since you were a kid. You used to ride me piggyback style through the house. I know we haven't been in touch recently, but I know you are a good person."

"That's just it. I'm not."

"Not?"

"Not a good person."

Rick's voice softened. "I refuse to believe that. People don't change."

Scott stared ahead, his eyes glazed. "Maybe people don't change. But events change people."

Rick tilted his head. "I'm sure your parent's deaths have impacted you but changed you?"

"That's not what I'm talking about."

Rick leaned in slightly. "I'm sorry. Can you tell me what happened? What event changed you? Is it about becoming a parent? I know that would scare the crap out of me."

Scott looked at Rick defensively. "I'm excited about being a dad."

Rick wanted to reach out and put his arm around Scott to comfort him but didn't want to spook him. Instead, he softened his voice further and tried to sound as compassionate as possible. "Please, Scott. Please tell me what happened."

Scott continued rocking slowly, thinking about what, if anything, he wanted to share with his old babysitter. After a few minutes, he looked at Rick and said, "It all started at a financial conference in Vegas a few years ago."

Rick said nothing, waiting.

"I had gone hoping to secure some potential new clients for the firm but struck out with everyone I met. I was feeling frustrated and had retired to the bar to soothe my nerves and forget the day. I was heading back to Denver the next morning and was trying to think of ways I could share the news with my partners without looking like a complete loser."

He paused. "After a couple of bourbons, a beautiful young woman sat down next to me. She claimed to be an executive in a larger East Coast firm, and they were looking to establish a partnership to invest in some real estate. I think we talked for a bit, but then everything went black. The next thing I remember was waking up in a strange bed."

"Did you sleep with her?

"No, I don't think so. I know I hadn't had that much to drink. But I think she slipped a roofie in my drink." Scott said, his voice barely above a whisper.

Rick's jaw clenched. "A setup. A honey trap."

Scott nodded. "Yes."

Rick took a breath. His voice was firm but kind. "Scott... that was assault. What happened to you wasn't just a trap—it was a crime."

Scott blinked, the words hitting him harder than he expected. His shoulders shuddered. "You have no idea..."

"I do. I've seen this before," Rick said quietly. "They prey on vulnerability. They find the cracks and wedge them open. But what happened in that hotel room? That wasn't your doing. It was theirs."

Scott looked at him now, eyes brimming with tears. "A week later, I got a package in the mail. Thumb drive. It had a video. And photos. Me and her. I looked… I looked like I was participating. But I wasn't even conscious."

"They used it to blackmail you."

"Yeah." Scott nodded. "The note said if I didn't reply yes to a burner email, the videos would go to Lizzie, my partners, my parents. Everyone. They knew everything. Names. Addresses."

"And you replied?"

"I had no choice." He swallowed. "I cheated on Lizzie once. College. She forgave me, but barely. She'd never believe I was drugged. And I couldn't face my parents seeing me like that."

Rick smiled sadly and shook his head. "No. Of course not. So what did they want?"

Scott started crying. "It was a goddamn cartel! They wanted me, our firm, to launder money for them. They had researched us, knew that we were struggling, and targeted me as easy pickings."

"So you went along with them?"

He nodded slowly. "Honestly, I thought it would be a one or two-time deal. Do a little favor and be done."

"That's not how it usually works with them."

Scott started crying harder and began to toy with the gun in his lap. "No, it became much more intense as the amount of money to be laundered kept increasing."

"How did you keep it from your partners? Or did you?"

"At first, I tried but knew there was no way. I'm not a financial whiz. But my partners and I have known each other for a long time. I explained the situation, and to be honest, they were kind of excited about it."

"Really? Didn't they know who they were dealing with? And the dangers involved?"

"Oh, they watched *Ozark* and *Breaking Bad* and thought it was almost romantic. The thrill, the adventure, the money. And boy, there was a lot of money."

Rick nodded. "I can understand why that was so upsetting. But how does that relate to this?" he said, pointing at the gun in his lap. "Why do you want to kill yourself?"

A soft wail left Scott's lips. "Because I couldn't leave well enough alone!"

"What do you mean?"

"You know I interned for Cormac during my senior year of college, don't you?"

Rick nodded.

"Last year, I was on the island visiting Mom and Dad, and I met Cormac for dinner at Sea Grille. It was really just supposed to be a friendly catch-up, but as usual, things turned to business. Cormac confided in me that Miacomet Capital was not doing well. They had implemented a new investing strategy, and it had tanked. He even hinted at a possible bankruptcy."

"That certainly ties in with what Sean told us this evening." Suddenly, a wave of recognition crossed Rick's face. "You introduced them to the cartel, didn't you?"

Scott put his face in his hands and nodded slowly, sobbing.

Now, it made sense for Rick. Scott had fallen for a classic trap, gotten caught up in laundering, and then suggested the same for his dad's firm to steer them out of trouble. He eyed Scott with a mixture of disdain and sadness. He was a good kid that had been forced to make a very bad mistake. Life for him from here on out would be tough.

Rick sat very still. The wind off the harbor cut through his shirt. "Scott?"

Scott lifted his head and stared at him with tear-filled eyes.

"Give me the gun."

Scott shook his head.

"You don't want to do this. You just told me that you were excited to be a father. When is that, like a month away?"

Scott nodded.

"Do you really want to leave that baby without a father? And Lizzie a widow?"

"But I don't know what to do!" he blurted out.

"You have options. You can turn state's evidence. Help them track down and nail the cartel."

"But they will kill me and my family in a heartbeat."

"We can put you, Lizzie, and the baby in witness protection. It's not the easiest life, but honestly, it's a hell of a lot better than federal prison. And you get to stay with Lizzie, raise the baby. Have somewhat a normal life."

"And you can do this for me?" asked Scott. "And what about my partners?"

"We may be able to extend the same protection to them. It all just depends on their level of cooperation and what information they can give us."

Scott nodded and fumbled with the gun. Rick watched intently, waiting to see what he would do. After a few minutes of internal deliberation, Scott sighed, grabbed the gun by the barrel, and handed it to Rick.

Rick eagerly accepted the weapon. "You've made the right choice."

"I hope so. But I can't bring my parents back, can I?'

"No. But please remember, your only mistake was getting involved with the cartel in the first place. And it was certainly under duress. Based on what we heard from Sean tonight, I believe that the burden of responsibility falls on Cormac."

"That Irish piece of shit. I wish I could have killed him."

"Trust me, we will have him in custody within the hour, and then his life will be a living hell. You might enjoy watching it."

Scott stood awkwardly, almost falling. Rick grabbed his arm to steady him and then pulled him into a hug. Scott seemed to collapse into it and began to sob.

"It will be. There'll be some tough days ahead, but in the end, it will be okay. I promise."

Scott whispered through his tears, gratefully. "Thank you. You know my dad always thought very highly of you. Now I know why."

Rick smiled at the thought. Officer Noah Coffin walked down to the dock and took Scott by the arm. Their next stop would be Fairgrounds Road where he would be arrested and processed. Although his role in the Miacomet case was minimal, from a criminal perspective, he had his own crimes to answer for back in Denver.

His phone dinged. He looked down to see a text from Hanna.

Coast Guard en route. Gave them your contact info. Expect news shortly. Call me in the AM.

He tapbacked a thumbs up and made his way back to the house. Felicity was in the hearth room crying. She saw Rick and ran to him, hugging him forcefully. "Is it true? That's Scott's involved?"

"I'm sorry. But yes."

She held him tighter. He wrapped his arms around her and held her close, trying to take her pain away. Finally, she loosened her grip and pulled back. She sniffled. "So, what's going to happen to him now?"

"First, he needs to be processed. Then he'll be interviewed to really understand the extent of his involvement."

"That will be you?" she asked hopefully.

"No, that will be with my colleagues at the FBI. Denver Field Office."

She nodded. "Then what?"

"Then it's up to Scott. He has an opportunity to do some good here. He can turn evidence and help us get the cartel. The Feds look on things like that favorably."

"But won't that put him in danger?"

"Yes. He'll have to go into witness protection."

"Will I ever see him again?" she asked, frightened.

"Let's not get ahead of things. And I really need to go. Cormac is on the run, and I want to nail his ass."

She nodded, sniffled. "Of course. Sorry. Go! Go get that bastard!"

Rick kissed her cheek and ran to the Mini. The hunt was on.

CHAPTER THIRTY SEVEN

After the incident at the Post house, Rick wanted nothing more but to head up to the guest bedroom and collapse. He was exhausted. But his desire to catch Cormac far outweighed his need for sleep. He drove the Mini back to the police headquarters on Fairground Road and found Tuna in her office wrapping up her notes on the case. He knocked on her door.

"Burning the midnight oil, I see."

She looked up. "Yeah. Just wanted to capture my thoughts while they were still fresh. I love my job, but the paperwork? Not so much." She yawned and stretched. "Everything work out? You sure tore out of here earlier."

Rick dropped into the chair across from her. "Thankfully, yes. But you were right."

"What do you mean?"

"Scott. He was involved. In fact, he's the one that introduced the cartel to Miacomet."

Tuna's mouth opened slightly. "No shit?"

"No shit," Rick confirmed, eyes flat with exhaustion. "Scott had been the target of a honey trap run by the cartel. That got his firm involved in laundering. And when he heard that Miacomet Capital was floundering, he put a bug into Cormac's ear. Next thing you know, Miacomet is laundering, too."

"Wow." Her voice was hushed, the weight of the revelation landing in the quiet office.

"Wow is right. And the guilt was hitting him hard. He was giving serious thought to suicide."

Tuna sat up quickly. "Is he okay?"

Rick nodded. "He is. We managed to calm him down and convince him to surrender. The EMTs checked him out, and Noah Coffin brought him in. He's downstairs now getting booked."

"You've had quite the evening, haven't you?" she said with a tired smile.

"Yeah. And it doesn't look to be over any time soon." Rick yawned and rubbed at his eyes.

"Speaking of Cormac, any news yet?"

"Coast Guard is en route to intercept." Rick glanced at his watch. "I have to think they are close. I wish I could be there. See the look in his eyes when that patrol boat stops him. He thinks he's so damn smart."

"It would be fun to watch," Tuna agreed.

Rick's phone rang. It was a number he didn't recognize. He tapped accept and spoke. "This is Agent Caton."

Tuna watched as Rick's expression shifted rapidly—first anticipation, then confusion, and finally, anger. His jaw clenched.

"Thank you, Captain. I appreciate the update." He ended the call, looked up at the ceiling, and screamed. "Fuck!"

"Rick? What's wrong?" asked Tuna. "Didn't they get him?"

Rick shook his head in disbelief. "It was a goddamn decoy."

"A decoy?"

"Yeah. I mean, it was Sean's boat, but it was being piloted by a young kid. Apparently, he had instructions to drive it to Virginia Beach for an engine retrofit. He was told to leave the boat at a certain dockyard and fly back to Nantucket. He has tickets departing Norfolk International this evening."

"That was a crafty move," said Tuna. "What a son of a bitch."

"Yes. We were played." Rick ran a hand over his face. "So if not the boat, then how?"

"Well, I've been thinking about that. And now that you're telling me he's not on the boat, this makes more sense," she said, pointing at her screen.

"What makes more sense?" asked Rick.

"I think he's making a run for home."

Rick blinked. "Ireland?"

She nodded. "So often you hear about criminals trying to escape to somewhere different, like Belize or Eastern Europe. But in the end, they are usually miserable. Fish out of water. My guess is that he's going to go where he's comfortable and use his money and a new identity to hide."

Rick leaned in. "Okay. Did you find something that supports that?"

She tapped her keyboard. "Well, while you were at the Post's talking Scott off the ledge, I was looking through the ferry and flight manifests. My contacts at the airport, as well as the Hy-Line and Steamship, sent me the passenger lists for the last two days."

"And?"

"I dropped them into this spreadsheet and went through them. Since yesterday at noon, the last time anyone recalls seeing Cormac Walsh, we've had just over two thousand people depart the island."

"Two thousand?" Rick exclaimed. "Holy crap. How the hell did you get through all those names?"

Tuna smiled. "Easy peasy. The first thing I did was to eliminate all of the passengers who were completing the return trip on a round-trip ticket. I knew we were looking for someone who had a one-way ticket off island. Likely with no return. And that cut the list down significantly." She tapped her keyboard and brought up a list of two dozen names. "These are all the people leaving Nantucket yesterday on one-way outbound travel. And if we focus only on the males?" One more tap on the keyboard. "That leaves us nine potentials."

Rick scanned the list quickly. "No one jumps out at me. You?"

Tuna smiled. "Maybe." She tapped the screen with her pen. "This guy. Jack Murphy. He was booked on the five-thirty JetBlue yesterday afternoon to JFK."

"Okay. Who's Jack Murphy?"

"Well, at first, I thought he was just another Irishman. But now that we know he's not on the boat, I'm thinking this was his plan all along."

Rick stared. "What do you mean?"

"I think that's his alias. His new identity. Cormac Walsh is Jack Murphy."

"Why do you think that?"

"I did a quick search and discovered that is the most common name in Ireland. Kind of like being called John Smith here in the States. Don't you think if you are going to create a new identity, you'd want to stand out as little as possible?"

Rick smiled broadly. "Tuna, that's brilliant. I think I love you."

"Well, no, let's not go there," she said, chuckling. "But seriously, Jack Murphy is booked on the Aer Lingus flight one oh six, which, according to my flight tracker, is approximately thirty minutes from touchdown in Dublin."

"Holy crap. That is great work! Let's see if we can meet that bastard as he gets off the plane."

"He's booked in first class, so he'll be off the flight pretty quickly. And I'm sure he is traveling light, so don't expect any checked bags."

Rick pointed at her, looking triumphant as he pulled out his phone and dialed his boss. He was sure Hanna wouldn't mind being disturbed a second time.

The phone rang twice and connected. "Oh my god," Hanna groaned. "Caton, do you know what time it is?"

"I know. And I'm sorry. But we have another development in the Miacomet case."

"What. I thought you solved that. Boat. Coast Guard. Virginia Beach?"

"Yeah. That turned out to be a decoy."

"A decoy? He played you?"

"He did. But we found his true plan. He's on an Aer Lingus flight to Dublin. Lands in thirty minutes."

"Okay. Shit. That's not much time. Let me see what I can do. Can you send me the best picture you have of him, along with a general description?

"I'll have it to you in a minute. We think he's traveling under the name Jack Murphy."

"Got it. Send me that info ASAP."

"On it, boss. And thank you."

"You got it, Rick."

He ended the call and quickly tapped out a text. His phone whooshed as it was sent. He turned to Tuna. "Okay. That's about all we can do. Let's hope your intuition is correct. Certainly feels right to me."

"My fingers are crossed. Anything else we can do?"

"No. It's really just a wait-and-see. How close is he now?"

Tuna pulled out her phone and looked at the tracker app. "They just started the final approach. Showing touch down in twenty."

Rick leaned back, exhaustion finally catching up. "I hope Hanna is quick. They'll probably be deplaning in thirty minutes, thirty-five tops."

Tuna stood and stretched. "My god, it's almost four. I'm exhausted. Do you mind if I pack it up?"

"Not at all. Please, go home and get some rest. Call me when you get up, and hopefully, I'll have some good news for you."

"Thanks. I'll keep my fingers crossed." She grabbed her bag and slung it over her shoulder.

She looked at Rick. "I've really enjoyed working with you, Agent Caton. I hope our earlier discussion might prove worthwhile. That maybe you'll return to us here at the NPD?"

As tired as he was, Rick couldn't help but smile. "I've enjoyed it as well, I really have. And I'd say there might be a good chance for that."

She walked over and shook his hand. "I hope so. Now, go get some rest. There's nothing more you can do." She turned and headed to the door.

"Tuna?"

"Yeah," she said, looking back.

"Nice work."

She smiled, nodded, and walked out of the door.

Rick checked his phone to see if anything was happening. Nothing. He checked his watch. He had two hours to sunrise. He left Tuna's office and made his way down to the Mini. He got in, started it, and made his way out of the parking lot and down to the Milestone rotary. He went through slowly this time, and instead of taking the left on Monomoy, he proceeded straight, heading east toward the rising sun. He dropped the top and lowered the windows; the cool, damp air was bracing and energized his mood.

Now, with time and mental clarity to think, he admitted it felt strange driving Mrs. Post's car. Like he was trespassing. A week ago, she was probably scooting around the island, running errands, seeing friends, and getting ready for her new grandbaby. He could smell her perfume, and it made him sad. Such a wonderful woman. Killed for no reason. He shook his head and thought about his time on the island.

What a week it had been. Hell, it hadn't even been a week. Rick realized he had only been here five days. Seemed more like five weeks with everything that had happened. He drove slowly, the high beams on. A light fog hung in the air, and deer grazed by the side of the road.

He was still lost in thought ten minutes later when he arrived in the little village of Siasconset. He angled through the rotary and headed down Gully Road to the beach. He parked the Mini, got out, and stretched. The sky above him was crystal clear and carpeted with stars; the Milky Way splayed from east to west. The horizon was just showing the first hint of light as he made his way closer to the water. He could hear the waves crashing on the beach. He removed his shoes and socks and let his toes sink into the damp and chilly sand.

He walked clumsily across the beach to the white lifeguard stand. It would be removed in a few weeks, but this remnant from summer would provide the perfect spot to watch the sunrise. He climbed the side and sat down heavily on the bench. He looked out over the water and watched as the world came to life around him.

Gulls called out as they winged their way across the water looking for breakfast. Terns skittered along the shore, looking for the same. And every so often, the dark head of a seal would pop up and look at him curiously.

A few minutes after six, nearly an hour after Cormac was supposed to have landed in Dublin, the sun broke the surface of the water. It was a magical sight. Rick leaned back and let the emerging rays play over him. Their meager warmth helped to break the damp chill of the morning.

His phone dinged, disturbing the solitude of the dawn. He resisted the impulse to pull it out. Whatever was there could wait. He wanted to finish this. He thought of Felicity and the prospect, however slim, that maybe, just maybe she might be interested in him. He was certainly interested in her. In fact, he knew, that given time, he would probably fall in love with her. He smiled at the thought.

And what about the NPD? Was it time for him to come home? He knew Tuna was right. They would welcome him back with open arms. But was he ready for that? Community policing as opposed to working as an agent with the Federal Bureau of Investigations? In the end, it wasn't a difficult decision to make.

The sun fully up, he pulled out his phone. There was a single text from Hanna.

"Jack Murphy" surrendered. The Garda has Cormac Walsh in custody.

CHAPTER THIRTY EIGHT

Rick let out a shout with the news and pumped his fist in the air. He jumped down from the lifeguard stand and ran awkwardly through the cold, damp sand back to the Mini. He didn't bother with his shoes and threw them in the passenger footwell scattering sand all over the black carpets. He made a note to clean that later so as not to sully the memory of Mrs. Post.

He headed back to the Post home. The house was quiet, the morning mist still clinging to the lawn like breath holding tight in a chest. Inside, the air was heavy and still.

He found Felicity in the kitchen. She was sitting at the table nursing a large mug of coffee and looked as if she had been up all night. Her eyes were red and swollen, her hair a tangled mess, and her clothes wrinkled. But when she saw Rick, something in her shifted. Her shoulders lifted slightly. Her eyes, despite the exhaustion, brightened with fragile hope.

"We got him."

She blinked. "Cormac?"

Rick nodded. "Yes. Apprehended him deplaning in Dublin an hour or so ago."

She was on her feet in an instant, the chair scraping loudly across the hardwood."Oh my god, Rick. That is wonderful." She threw her arms around him, pressing her face into his shoulder. He held her tightly, feeling her chest hitch against him, her heart racing. And then, she broke. The tears came suddenly, violently. A week's worth of grief, shock, rage, and bone-deep sorrow tore through her as she sobbed into his shirt.

Rick just held on. He whispered softly, his voice close to her ear, his arms firm around her trembling frame. "It's okay. It's going to be okay. You're safe now. It's over."

After a few minutes, she calmed, eased out of his arms, and stared directly into his eyes, as if trying to measure the man who had carried her through all of this. "Thank you. Thank you for everything you have done."

"Of course, it's the least I could do," he said dismissively, glancing toward the counter for a distraction.

Her tone sharpened. "No, please, don't discount what you've done here."

He looked at her, surprised by the sudden edge in her voice.

She continued, "If not, for you I don't believe any of this would have been discovered. My parents' deaths would have been listed as accidents, and Miacomet would still be laundering cartel money. My mom knew you would make the difference. She trusted you. And she was right. God rest her soul."

Rick swallowed, guilt flashing through him. He wanted to believe that, wanted to accept her gratitude. But the image of Scott curled on the dock, sobbing, the pistol trembling in his lap haunted him. "I'm just sorry about Scott. That was certainly not expected."

"I know." Her voice wavered again, and she pulled the mug close to her chest. "I feel like I've lost my entire family this week. I just can't believe he would have been involved in this."

Rick leaned against the counter, folding his arms. "It will be okay. I promise. We will work things out. Hopefully, Scott will never see the inside of a jail cell."

A silence stretched between them. Rick shifted his weight, unsure if he should reach for her again or give her space.

She sniffled and nodded. "I hope you are right. Can I get you some coffee?"

"That would be lovely."

Rick's phone rang, its buzz cutting through the quiet clink of Felicity setting down his mug. He glanced at the screen, recognizing the number immediately. He tapped accept.

"Rick. Great work on this Miacomet case."

"Thanks, Hanna. But I couldn't have done it without you. Again, my apologies for waking you up in the middle of the night last night." There was humor in his voice.

"Well, you know, payback can be a bitch," Hanna said, laughing.

"What's the status with Walsh?" he asked as Felicity handed him a steaming mug. He blew on it and took a tentative sip.

Hanna chuckled. "He was the first person off the flight and walked straight into the arms of the Garda. The Inspector said he surrendered immediately and didn't even put up a fuss. Claims the whole thing is a misunderstanding."

"Money laundering and murder is a misunderstanding?" Rick scoffed.

"I know. They are holding him in a sterile environment at Dublin near the departure lounge. Since he never made it through Irish immigration, he technically hasn't left the States yet. Two U.S. Marshals are booked on the redeye from Logan tonight to escort him back to the States. He should be in custody in Chelsea by late tomorrow afternoon."

"Terrific. I'm hoping I can be part of the welcome party?"

"Damn straight, Rick. This is yours. I'm counting on you getting to the bottom of this."

"Excellent," said Rick. He was hesitant to ask the next question for fear of the answer. "But what about the workshop? DC? I'm supposed to be there tonight."

"You can be late, Rick." Hanna said, her voice light but firm. "I've already let them know this is priority. This is your case, after all. You should get the pleasure of getting this perp to talk."

"Thanks, Hanna. That means a lot."

"So they're expecting you on Wednesday."

Rick felt deflated. "Wednesday? Really?"

"Just think of all the good you can do with improved inter-agency communication and collaboration."

Rick swore he could hear her laughing softly.

"I'll be there," he said reluctantly.

"Thanks. I knew you wouldn't let me down. Safe travels. And let me know if you need anything," she said, pausing. "During normal business hours, please."

Rick ended the call and turned to Felicity.

"Thanks for the coffee."

She nodded but didn't meet his eyes. "What's up?"

"Cormac will be back in Boston tomorrow, and I need to be there to meet him. With everything we've learned from Scott and Sean, it shouldn't be too difficult to paint him into a corner."

Felicity's expression dropped slightly. Her fingers curled tighter around her mug. "Oh, I was hoping you might have time to help me sort through some things."

"Sorry." Rick shook his head slowly, guilt flickering in his chest. "I wish I could. But I need to get back to the mainland, pick up my car, get some fresh clothes. And get some damn rest. I'm exhausted."

She nodded knowingly. "I understand. What ferry are you shooting for?"

* * *

Rick walked into the Hy-Line ticket office and saw a friendly, familiar face behind the counter. There were four people in line ahead of him, and it was several minutes before it was his turn. He walked up the counter and gave the agent a smile.

"Hey, stranger. Have you decided to finally leave us?" she said teasingly.

Rick smiled. "My work here is done, and I need to get back to Boston."

"Sounds like it was important."

He nodded and said softly, "It was. Is the noon boat available?"

The agent tapped on her keys. "Plenty of space." A few more clicks, and then she handed him a ticket. "Hope to see you back on the island."

"Me too. Me too," he echoed, his voice quieter this time.

He exited the office. It was a stunning fall day, the air redolent of salt and a bright cloudless blue sky above them. A slight breeze tickled the leaves in the trees. In the distance, he could see the ferry rounding Brant Point as it made its way to the dock. They'd be boarding his boat in twenty minutes.

Felicity was waiting just beyond the door, leaning against a wooden post. Her arms were crossed against her chest, and the wind tugged softly at a strand of hair that had slipped from behind her ear. She looked tired, but resolved. And when she saw him emerge with a ticket in hand, her expression shifted—hopeful, but tinged with reluctance.

He walked over to Felicity. She looked at him anxiously. "Please tell me you'll be back when you are done with Cormac. I could really use your help with a few things."

Rick hated this part. The not-quite-saying. The moments before goodbye. He shook his head slowly. "I wish I could, but once that's wrapped up, I'm off to DC for a couple of weeks."

Felicity's shoulders drooped. She tried to keep her voice even, but it trembled just slightly. "I understand."

Rick stepped closer. He placed his hands gently on her shoulders and looked into her eyes. "I promise you I'll be back. Give me a few weeks to sort things out. Figure out what I want to do." He tilted his head. "Besides, aren't you heading back to Providence?"

She nodded. "I am. But only to clean out my office and pack up my apartment. I've decided to move back. Live here full time."

"Really," said Rick excitedly. "That's great. What are you going to do?"

"I've got some work to do with my parents' estate. It's mostly cut and dry. Dad was so thorough, you know, but there are still some documents to sign, that sort of thing. Then I start my new job."

"What? You have a new job? When the hell did that happen?"

Felicity laughed. "I know, such a crazy week. But Peter Bois called me late Friday after you dropped me off at the house. I thought it might have been something about the case, but instead, he offered me a job."

Rick shook his head in wonder. "Well, honestly, that doesn't surprise me. I think you impressed the hell out of him."

"I hope so. He asked me to head up their affordable housing initiative. Something that is near and dear to my heart and something this community needs desperately."

"I'm proud of you, Fel," Rick said, his voice warm. "This would make your mom and dad so happy."

"Yes, it would. I just wish they were here." A tear trickled down her cheeks.

Rick reached up gently and brushed the tear away with his thumb. Then, with his fingers still lightly on her chin, he leaned in and kissed her. It was soft and slow, the kind of kiss that said more than words ever could. She responded without hesitation, her hands gripping the front of his jacket like she didn't want to let go.

The line of passengers started to move, and Rick could hear the beeping of the handheld machines as the tickets were being scanned. The last thing he wanted to do was leave.

"I've got to go," he said breathlessly.

"No, please stay," she whispered, kissing him harder.

The beeping stopped, and Rick turned to see that the last of the passengers had boarded. He heard the engines start, and the shore crew began to disconnect the gangways.

"I really need to go." He pulled away. "I will see you soon. I promise."

She snuck in one last kiss and pulled away. She watched him walk up the serpentine gangway, through the doors, and up the stairs. He emerged on the top deck and waved down to her. The boat engines roared, and the ship began backing out of its dock quickly. Felicity followed the boat down to the end of the Straight Wharf dock, where it rotated, pointed the bow northeast, and accelerated. She watched as the ferry made its way around Brant Point. Her last glimpse of Rick was him standing at the stern rail, waving furiously.

Her phone dinged. She pulled it up.

I promise I will be back.

Felicity pressed the phone to her chest and stood at the edge of the dock, watching the foamy wake trail behind the ferry as it disappeared into the blue.

CHAPTER THIRTY NINE

Cormac Walsh landed at Logan International Airport early Monday afternoon and was quickly walked to a waiting FBI transport van. An accident on the Chelsea Street bridge had slowed them a bit, but by four o'clock, Cormac Walsh was sitting in interview room three at the FBI's Chelsea field office.

The room was barely big enough to house a brown Formica conference table surrounded by four faded yellow chairs. The chairs were free to move, but each table leg was bolted to the floor. Overhead, fluorescent lights buzzed harshly and threw a bluish hue even a supermodel would find unflattering. The beige walls were unbroken save for the door and a two-by-three-foot mirrored glass window on one end.

Rick had made it back to his apartment and had slept like the dead, catching up on several days of no sleep. He was feeling refreshed and chipper when he stepped into the room. The same couldn't be said of Cormac Walsh. He looked like death warmed over, no surprise given his recent travel schedule. He was resting his head in his crossed arms and didn't notice when Rick entered.

Rick sat down across from Cormac and waited for the Irishman to wake. He rapped on the table with his knuckles to stir the man. Slowly, Cormac raised his head and looked at Rick through bloodshot eyes.

"Oh good, I hope you can tell me why the hell I am here. I've spent the last twenty-four hours trying to understand what is going on. And why am I handcuffed to this table?" he said, eyeing the metal links that ended in a steel eye bolted to the table.

"Hello, Cormac. Good to see you too," said Rick, smiling. "Why don't you tell me why you think you are here."

Cormac's brows lifted. "I have no bloody clue, mate. I just said that."

Rick tilted his head. "Then why did you run?"

"Run? What the hell are you talking about? I was traveling to Ireland to attend a family reunion of sorts."

Rick folded his arms. "A family reunion? You expect me to believe that?"

"Of course I do. It's the truth."

Rick leaned back in his chair, crossing one leg over the other, feigning a calm he didn't possess. Rick watched him carefully, letting the silence gather weight. "If that's true, then why did you send Sean's boat toward South America?"

Cormac started to get agitated. "Sean's boat? South America? Not sure where you are going with that, but I was doing the man a favor," he lied.

"A favor?"

Cormac's mouth twitched with irritation. "Yeah. The engines were due for a full rebuild, and we had a client in Virginia Beach who had recommended a boatyard there that he thought could do a good job. So I had my landscaper take the boat down there late last week."

"What was the name of the boatyard?" asked Rick.

"How the bloody hell should I know?" replied Cormac angrily. "I was just doing the man a favor."

"And why didn't Sean take care of that? Couldn't he have arranged it?"

Cormac leaned forward, voice low and disdainful. "Because between you and me, the man's a pussy."

Rick sat stunned. Could he have totally misread this whole situation?

He paused to gather his thoughts and decided on a different tack.

"Can you tell me why you are traveling on a fake passport? Jack Walsh?"

"Because that's my bloody name!"

"What?" asked Rick, confused.

Cormac smiled menacingly. "That's my name, copper. I was born Jack Walsh. Son of Jack Senior and Siobhan Walsh."

"And you changed it?" asked Rick, stammering.

"I did when I arrived in the States. Nothing official, mind you; too much paperwork and too many questions. But when I settled on Nantucket, I used the name Cormac Walsh and never looked back. I figured people here would think it's quaint." Suddenly revived, he leaned back in his chair and crossed his arms defiantly. "Can I get some water?"

Rick looked back at the window and nodded. Minutes later, an agent entered, put a cup of water down on the table, and then left. The few minutes gave Rick a chance to regroup.

"C'mon. Please tell me why I'm here. It certainly can't be because of my name. Or an engine rebuild."

Rick leaned in, voice firm. "Do you really think I would waste the resources to drag your ass all the way back to Boston for a simple misunderstanding about Sean's boat and your legal name?"

"Okay, then."

"What would you like to tell me about Eel Point Amusements?"

Cormac's eyes briefly flared, but then he quickly gathered his composure. He sat up in his chair. "Eel Point? That was Sean's deal. He was teaching a finance class, trying to show his students what to look for with AML."

"Anti-money laundering?"

Cormac nodded. "He put together this bogus company, um, Eel Point, he called it. And then created some scenarios using imagined investments."

"Hmm," said Rick. He looked again at the window and subtly motioned. A moment later, Nia entered the room carrying a manila file folder stuffed with paper.

"Cormac. Or do you prefer Jack? This is my colleague Nia Parsons."

"Forgive me for not standing," said Cormac, nodding at the new guest and motioning to his wrist restraints.

Nia took a seat next to Rick and placed the folder on the table. She opened it, and Cormac strained to see what information it contained.

"Nia here has been digging into Eel Point Amusements, Cormac. You see, she's an expert on money laundering. I like to tell people she could nail a convenience clerk skimming pennies from the penny jar."

Cormac stayed silent, eyes darting between them, jaw tightening.

Rick turned to Nia. "Why don't you tell Cormac here what you found?"

"I'd be delighted, Rick." She turned her attention to Cormac. "I'll have to admit this is one impressive set of books. It honestly took me a while to trace the various cash flows from all of the different businesses you established. It was pretty clever."

Cormac sat there trying to look indifferent, but a hint of pride flashed across his face.

Nia continued. "It was good, sure, but not good enough." She pulled out a piece of paper and slid it over to Cormac who looked down, the blood draining from his face."There were a couple of clues as to the real intent of Eel Point. But it wasn't until we got access to Miacomet Capital's bank records that it all made sense."

Cormac got rigid. "You have no right!"

Rick interrupted him quickly. "Actually, we do. Thanks to Nia's work, we were able to document enough evidence to secure a search warrant. So while you've been galavanting to Ireland and back, we've been busy crawling up your ass. Our partners," said Rick, motioning to Nia, "executed those warrants this morning. They now have full access to your financial records, client lists, bank statements, you name it. Your life, and that of Miacomet Capital, is an open book. And let's just say it has been very interesting reading."

"What? You can't do that! It's private property!"

Rick shook his head. "Sorry Cormac. And by the way, Sean confessed to everything."

The Irishman's face went white. "What?"

"Yeah, you are right about him being a pussy. We had him turned in minutes. He was quick to give up on the whole enterprise. Said it was all your idea when his investment strategy went south."

"That bastard," said Cormac under his breath.

"He told us what happened on the boat, too. That you killed Charles," said Rick, lying, trying to bait him into the discussion.

"Wait? What? No! Charles fell off the boat. He was taking a piss."

"That's not what Sean says. He saw you take a swing on Charles."

"Bullshit. Charles lost it."

"You really expect me to believe that?" Rick was getting angry now. He stood up and walked around the table. He leaned into Cormac's face. "I think you killed him, you cocky little shit. I think he was on to your scam and confronted you with it. You panicked, hit him with something, and threw him overboard, didn't you?"

"I um, I," he replied, stuttering.

"Nia," said Rick, pausing and looking over the table at his colleague. "Do you think that section ten ruling would be applicable here?"

Nia looked thoughtful. "Actually, I do. This isn't the perfect demonstration for it, but I think a good lawyer would find enough compliance to compel a judge."

"What are you talking about?" asked Cormac, his eyes narrowing.

Rick stepped back. "A section ten ruling is relatively new guidance to secure an admission of guilt from a suspect during the act of a broader criminal enterprise."

He looked at them quizzically. "What does that mean?"

Rick walked to the other side of the table and stood next to Nia. He picked a piece of paper from the manila folder and waved it at Cormac. "It means if you confess to throwing Charles off the boat, then that act could be considered as part of the overall criminal enterprise. Put simply, it means no additional jail time."

"No additional jail time?"

"Actually, it might mean less. Judges look at section ten admissions as being cooperative, so in many cases, overall prison sentences are reduced."

"And why would you have this, this section two ruling?"

"Section ten," corrected Rick. "It's intended to close cases, especially those where the evidence is lacking or shaky. Let's be real. The FBI is a big bureaucracy, and we need to justify our existence. Posting high solve rates helps that."

"Hmm," said Cormac. "Interesting."

"So anything you want to add?"

The Irishman thought for a moment. "Okay. I'll bite. I hit Charles, but it was in self-defense."

Rick perked up. "What do you mean, self-defense?"

Cormac twisted in his seat. "He was upset. He had asked about Eel Point, and when he learned of the answer, he said we had to go to the police and confess everything."

"And you didn't like that answer?"

"That would have killed us all! Our Eel Point investors would not have been happy."

"You mean the cartel?"

Cormac nodded. "They don't fuck around. If they suspect any leaks, then you and maybe your family will disappear.

"You thought you could silence him?"

"I thought I could talk some sense into him, but he wouldn't listen. Said he wouldn't be able to look in the mirror. I gave him every chance, but he was adamant."

"So what did you do?"

Cormac looked down at his hand. He had picked one nail bloody during the interview and was working hard on a second. "I saw the lighthouse at Great Point and realized I was just about out of time. If we made port, then I knew he was going to go straight to the police. So I hit him."

"With what?"

"The back of the gaff."

"Did it knock him out?"

Cormac nodded slowly.

"How did he get in the water?"

"I opened the transom door. It was a struggle, but I was able to push him out into the wake."

"So you just dumped an unconscious man into the Great Point rip with a faulty life jacket?" asked Rick angrily.

"A faulty life jacket?"

"Don't pull that crap on me, Cormac. You are the one who sabotaged the life preserver. Removing the arming mechanism? Slicing a hole in the manual inflation tube? Do you know what they call that Cormac? That's called premeditation. And it means a lot in a murder case. It means a death sentence."

Cormac's face went white. He sat rigidly at the table, a vacant look in his eyes. The realization of what he had done began to sink in. He started to cry. "I didn't want to hurt him. He was one of my best friends. But I knew we would all be dead if he went to the police."

"You killed a good man. A much better man than you would ever be. You didn't deserve him as a friend."

Cormac was sobbing softly.

"You piece of shit," said Rick. He turned to face Nia. "Do you have any more questions?"

Nia replied. "No, I'm good. We have everything we need to put him away." She stood and made her way to the door. "Oh, and Rick?"

"Yeah?"

"Section ten? Brilliant."

He smiled as he watched Nia leave the room. Rick turned to face the window at the head of the room. "Please amend the charges to include…"

"Who are you talking to?" Cormac interrupted.

"Oh, them?" said Rick, thumbing his finger at the window. "A couple of people you might be interested in."

Cormac stopped crying and suddenly looked scared.

Rick continued. "We have the US Attorney for the District of Massachusetts. She will be leading the prosecution against you and Sean for the money laundering enterprise at Miacomet Capital Partners."

Cormac gulped.

"We also have representatives from the Suffolk County District Attorney. Based on your confession, they will likely be pressing charges for the premeditated first-degree murder of Charles Post."

"What? What about that section ten thing?" exclaimed Cormac, panicking.

"Oh, that," said Rick, smiling. "That was bullshit, Cormac. Made it up. But glad we were able to make it convincing enough."

"You bastard," whispered Cormac hatefully.

Rick's face went red with rage. "I'm the bastard? You killed a great man. And for what? To protect your own ass?" He calmed. "But see, that's the irony of it all. The cartel is still going down."

"What?"

"Yeah. Scott agreed to turn state's evidence."

Cormac looked up. "Wait? What about Scott?"

"He explained how he hooked you up with the cartel. He said that Miacomet was struggling and that he had a way out for you. With his help, we should be able to find and arrest those who were laundering money through Miacomet. So your attempt at shutting up Charles failed miserably."

The Irishman was silent.

"Quiet now, eh Cormac? Well, I do have one more question for you. Why kill Ann Post?"

"What? That was an accident. She swerved to miss a deer."

Rick shook his head. "It was no accident, Cormac. The software in the car she was driving - Charles' car - had been compromised. The damn car was booby-trapped. She didn't stand a chance."

"Oh my god," whispered Cormac.

"What?"

"It wasn't meant for her."

"What wasn't?"

Cormac took a deep breath. "I had expressed concern to my contact…"

"The contact being your connection to the cartel, yes?"

"Um, yes. I mentioned that we were worried that Charles suspected that something was happening. Sean thought maybe he had left a file on the server that Charles could find."

"How did they respond?"

"Just said that they would handle it. They would send a message so that Charles would back off."

"But they didn't say what they were going to do?"

Cormac shook his head. "No." He thought for a moment and looked at Rick intently. "Are you telling me Ann was murdered?"

Rick nodded. "She was just another one of your victims."

"My victims? I didn't want to hurt anyone! I was just trying to save our business, a business the three of us had built over nearly four decades together."

"Maybe you should have just come clean with Charles when the business ran into trouble. Maybe he would have had some ideas on how to fix it. Instead, you put the process in motion that led to the murders of Charles and Ann Post." Rick walked to the door. "I hope you rot in hell, Jack Murphy."

CHAPTER FORTY

Eight Years Later

"Dad! Come on!"

Rick hustled to his daughter's bed and laid down beside her. She was fresh from the tub and smelled of soap and lavender. Her auburn hair was damp. He held a well-worn copy of the novel *Watership Down* in his hands and was quickly thumbing through it.

"Where were we?" asked Annie, anxiously. "Do you remember?"

"Um, I do, right here," he pointed. "Chapter thirteen. Remember they had decided to join Cowslip in his warren? They were looking for shelter."

The young girl nodded passionately. She curled up in the crook of his arm as he opened the book and started to read.

Nearly twenty minutes went by when they heard a soft tap at the door. Rick looked to see Felicity standing there, smiling at them. "You two are so cute together. But it's bedtime, young lady. You have school tomorrow."

"Mom!" pleaded the little girl. "Please. Just one more chapter?"

Felicity tried to hide her smile and somehow sound stern. "Okay. But just one. You need your rest." She leaned over and kissed Annie on the forehead. "Just one, hon," she said to Rick, mockingly pointing her finger at him like a disobedient child. "And join me when you are done?" There was a conspiratorial tone to her voice.

Rick smiled and winked. He opened the book and resumed reading.

Felicity walked from the bed, paused at the door and looked at the two most important people in her life curled up together. They were both already totally absorbed in the book. Watching them brought a flood of memories rushing back—of another room, another bedtime, another father reading to his little girl. Her throat tightened, but she smiled, turned, and disappeared down the hall.

He managed to sneak in two more chapters, much to his daughter's delight, before putting her to bed. He tucked her in, kissed her forehead, and turned out the light. She rolled over on her side, cuddling her miniature stuffed horse, and fell asleep almost immediately with a contented smile on her face.

Rick walked quietly down the stairs and found Felicity in the hearth room. It was a chilly evening, and she had built a fire in the fireplace. It radiated a welcoming warmth. He joined her on the sofa and gave her a quick peck on the cheek.

"What am I, your sister?" she said teasingly.

"Um, sorry." He cupped her chin and gave her a long kiss. He pulled back, sensing something was not quite right. "You okay?" he asked tenderly.

She nodded slowly. "As much as I love to see you two enjoying your time together it does make me sad. I miss my dad. And my mom, of course," she added quickly. "I wish they were here."

Rick put his arm around her and pulled her tight. "I miss them too. They were good people."

She looked at him intently. "So, what do you think of Watership Down so far?"

"Overall, I think it is a great story, but I had no idea how powerful it would be. I mean, those rabbits do not have it easy. Lots of death and violence, but Annie is taking it in stride, surprisingly. I hope there's nothing else that will upset her."

Felicity nodded. "Well, I will say that the ending is sad, but I'm not going to spoil it for you. Just remember to have a few tissues handy. For the both of you."

Rick looked at her quizzically. "Okay. I will try and prepare myself."

Felicity laughed. "You'll be fine, lieutenant. Anyway, I heard from Paul today."

Rick straightened slightly. "How are they doing?"

As part of his witness protection program, Scott had assumed the name Paul Stevens and moved to an undisclosed location they suspected was in the southeast. He called every few months using a burner phone and rarely kept Felicity on the line longer than ten minutes.

"He sounds good." Her voice was soft, laced with longing. "Can you believe Charlie's going to be eight next week? I don't know where the time goes."

"Hah! Look at Annie. She'll be seven."

"I know. Crazy," Felicity said and tucked a strand of hair behind her ear. "Anyway, he really did sound good. Lizzie still seems to be struggling with the whole situation, though. She's had to give up her law practice and her career. Sometimes, I fear they aren't going to make it."

"They'll work it out, hon. They've been through a lot. But it must be hard on her, with her career and not being able to see family. And it must be hard on Charlie too. Not having grandparents, at least ones that can visit."

"Do you think they're still in danger?"

"I'd like to say no, but Scott's testimony brought down some very powerful people. People with lots of resources and long memories. Maybe one day he'll be able to leave protection but not anytime soon."

She leaned into him. "That makes me sad for him. And for me. I'd love to see him."

"I would too," said Rick, wistfully.

Felicity looked at her husband of seven years. "Are you okay? Something happen at work?"

He smiled. "No, work is great. Obviously, I'm thrilled with the promotion, and I love my new responsibilities."

"Even being Tuna's boss?"

Rick chuckled. "You know, they offered her the position first. Again. But just like last time she turned it down."

"Really? Why?"

"She just loves her job. Being a detective. And she's worried that being a supervisor will pull her away from that. Not to mention that she's just so damn good at what she does."

"So she's okay with you as her new boss?"

Rick laughed. "She's tickled actually. And you know, I don't see myself as her boss, really. More of a resource that can help her by making sure she has what she needs, breaking down the barriers, that sort of thing."

"So what is it? What's on your mind?"

Rick paused not wanting to further stir up old memories. "I got the news today that Cormac died in prison."

"Oh, okay," she said. "Were you worried that would upset me?" She reached for his hand.

"I just didn't want to bring up the past. That was a very tough time for you."

She hugged him tightly. "Thanks for always being on my side. But I'm okay. What happened?"

"Apparently, a heart attack. They found him during morning bed checks."

She thought of the pain that the man had brought to her family. He had killed her father, destroyed his business, and inadvertently caused the death of her mother. "That is just so sad," she said finally.

"What? I thought you might be pleased to have him out of our life for good."

She looked at him. "I'm just sad at what might have been. If Scott hadn't been caught in that damn trap. If he had never introduced the cartel to Cormac. And if Cormac would have had the inner strength to just say 'no'. If only he could have admitted to my dad that the firm was struggling, I'm sure they would've figured it out."

He hugged her tightly. "I know you're right. But Cormac thought he knew better."

She scoffed. "He was always arrogant. Thought he was the smartest guy in the room."

She paused and a quiet settled on the room. The only sound was the fire crackling and popping in the hearth.

"What about Sean?" she asked tentatively. "Have you heard anything there?"

Rick shook his head slowly. "No. I've asked to be notified of any changes in his status but don't think I'll hear anything anytime soon. Or if we do it won't be good"

"No?"

"If I remember correctly, he won't be eligible for parole until he's in his eighties. So, if we do hear anything, it will probably be bad news. Like Cormac."

She leaned into him and he hugged her tightly.

"I just can't help but wonder what might have been. How different decisions might have changed things," she said softly.

Rick nodded. "As difficult as those times were they did bring us together. If not for your mom's call I don't think I ever would have come back to the island. And I doubt we would have ever met."

"That's true. I hadn't thought of that," said Felicity, her face brightening. "You and Annie are the best things that have ever happened to me."

Rick looked at his wife and smiled, happy that phase of their life was finally over. "I love you," he said affectionately.

She looked deeply into Rick's eyes. This man who had once been her babysitter was now the most important person, along with Annie, in her world. She could not imagine life without him.

"I love you too, Lieutenant Rick Caton," she said laughingly and pulled him closer. "Now kiss me like you mean it."

And he did.

Author's Notes

Thank you for reading *A Drowning on Nantucket*. I hope you found the story fun and entertaining and that you will take a moment to leave a review wherever you purchased your book. Good reviews are the lifeblood of aspiring writers so I hope you'll let other readers know how much you (hopefully) enjoyed the book.

If you'd like to learn more about Peter Bois and his amazing backstory leading to the creation of the Jake Tate & Tristam Coffin Foundation, please enjoy *Starbuck, Nantucket Redemption*, my first novel.

If Tuna's ghost story about the disappearance of Jack Reiner's wife piqued your curiosity, then no doubt you would enjoy *Not All Bodies Stay Buried,* my second book.

For those that know Nantucket and Cambridge, you will notice that two of the restaurants I mention are sadly no longer in business. Those include The Downy Flake and Cambridge Brewing Company. Both were wonderful institutions and valuable assets to their communities. They will be missed.

I must also say that I have nothing but the utmost respect for the Nantucket Police Department. They have challenging jobs - especially in the summer months - and conduct themselves with honor and integrity. All of the questionable acts displayed in the book by the NPD are truly fiction.

Of course I must also mention my appreciation for the author Richard Adams and his 1972 masterpiece, *Watership Down*. That wonderful story had a huge impact on me and truly instilled in me a desire to write. I strongly encourage all those who haven't read it to give it a try. And if you have enjoyed it in the past, maybe it's time to read it again?

And as always, I always like to express my gratitude to the men and women in the military, the Coast Guard, our first responders, and all our healthcare providers. Thank you for all you do in keeping us safe, healthy and free.

Garth Jeffries
Gasconade County, Missouri
April 2025

Made in the USA
Monee, IL
02 July 2025

20405221R00225